Praise for Tasha Suri and the Burning Kingdoms

The Jasmine Throne

"Suri's writing always brings me to another world; one full of wonders and terrors, where every detail feels intricately and carefully imagined."　　　　—R. F. Kuang, author of *Babel*

"Raises the bar for what epic fantasy should be."
　　　　—Chloe Gong, author of *These Violent Delights*

"An intimate, complex, magical study of empire and the people caught in its bloody teeth. I loved it."
　　　　—Alix E. Harrow, author of *The Once and Future Witches*

"Suri's incandescent feminist masterpiece hits like a steel fist inside a velvet glove. Simply magnificent."
　　　　—Shelley Parker-Chan, author of *She Who Became the Sun*

The Oleander Sword

"A magnificently reimagined southern Asia where spirits walk the earth and fire has a will of its own."　　　　—*Wall Street Journal*

"A taut, emotional sequel that will leave series fans eager for the finale."　　　　—*Publishers Weekly* (starred review)

"This complex, sprawling story is filled with lush worldbuilding, politics versus personal feelings, and familial love and betrayal.... An epic tale of love: for family, for power, for country."
　　　　—*Library Journal* (starred review)

By Tasha Suri

THE BURNING KINGDOMS

The Jasmine Throne
The Oleander Sword
The Lotus Empire

THE BOOKS OF AMBHA

Empire of Sand
Realm of Ash

THE LOTUS EMPIRE

BOOK THREE OF
THE BURNING KINGDOMS

TASHA SURI

orbitbooks.net

Cover design by Lauren Panepinto
Cover illustration by Micah Epstein
Cover copyright © 2024 by Hachette Book Group, Inc.
Map by Tim Paul
Author photograph by Shekhar Bhatia

Orbit
Hachette Book Group
1290 Avenue of the Americas
New York, NY 10104
orbitbooks.net

First Edition: November 2024
Simultaneously published in Great Britain by Orbit

Orbit is an imprint of Hachette Book Group.
The Orbit name and logo are registered trademarks of Little, Brown Book Group Limited.

The publisher is not responsible for websites (or their content) that are not owned by the publisher.

The Hachette Speakers Bureau provides a wide range of authors for speaking events. To find out more, go to hachettespeakersbureau.com or email HachetteSpeakers@hbgusa.com.

Orbit books may be purchased in bulk for business, educational, or promotional use. For information, please contact your local bookseller or the Hachette Book Group Special Markets Department at special.markets@hbgusa.com.

Library of Congress Cataloging-in-Publication Data
Names: Suri, Tasha, author.
Title: The lotus empire / Tasha Suri.
Description: First edition. | New York, NY : Orbit, 2024. | Series: Burning kingdoms ; book 3
Identifiers: LCCN 2024012692 | ISBN 9780316538602 (trade paperback) |
    ISBN 9780316472913 (hardcover) | ISBN 9780316538572 (ebook)
Subjects: LCGFT: Fantasy fiction. | Novels.
Classification: LCC PR6119.U75 L68 2024 | DDC 823/.92—dc23/eng/20240325
LC record available at https://lccn.loc.gov/2024012692

ISBNs: 9780316538602 (trade paperback), 9780316472913 (hardcover, library edition), 9780316538572 (ebook)

Printed in the United States of America

LSC-C

Printing 2, 2024

For the Nastettes:
Paul, Sophie, Kate, Ellie & Carly.
Thank you for the adventures.

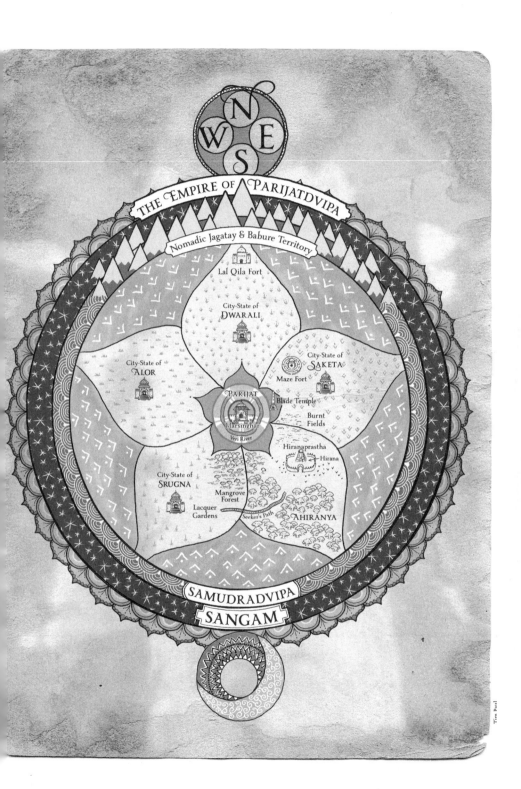

N W E S

THE EMPIRE OF PARIJATDVIPA

Nomadic Jagatay & Babure Territory

Lal Qila Fort

City-State of
DWARALI

City-State of
ALOR

City-State of
SAKETA

Maze Fort

PARIJAT
Blade Temple
Harsinghar
Burnt
Fields
Veri River

Hiranaprastha
Hirana

City-State of
SRUGNA

Mangrove
Forest

Lacquer
Gardens
Seeker's Path
AHIRANYA

SAMUDRADVIPA

SANGAM

Tim Paul

PROLOGUE

This was her last hope.

The monsoon rain was pouring. The woman rode through it on horseback, without the cover of a parasol, letting the water soak her through. The trees of the forest loomed around her, black in the fading light.

She missed, with a sudden and knife-sharp grief, the flower gardens of home. White jasmine and needle-flower, and her pink roses. There were no trees to loom over her there, and no parched battlefields underfoot, seeded with nothing but dead flesh to draw scavenging birds.

The only flowers she had seen in months had been on the skin of her enemies. The yaksa who had killed her father had been flower-haired—a glowing, smiling girl-like thing with pits for teeth and arms sharpened to fine points. She had skewered him through, and laughed as she did it.

The woman shuddered at the memory, and shuddered again from the cold. She should have traveled in a chariot instead, but she loathed to be contained.

The monastery loomed out of the darkness ahead of her. Its gray stone shone silver in the shafts of dull light that broke through the trees.

Her army halted as the priest emerged, and bowed, and offered to lead her to the lake. She dismounted and followed him, boots heavy on the wet soil.

She thought of her sons. Her eldest three boys, at war. Her youngest, still in the care of a wet nurse. She wondered if she would see them again. Sikander, her oldest, had promised to meet her on the road from Alor with news from home. She had carried sweets for him just in case. Dried mango. It was the fresh he loved the most, but that she couldn't easily provide. They'd burned all the orchards in Harsinghar to keep the yaksa at bay.

The lake was black. Although the rain fell fiercely, the lake was untouched, a disc of glossy stillness.

She knelt by its side. Her salwar kameez grew wetter at the knees.

"Look," the priest said. "Gaze into the water. Pray for the nameless to speak."

She looked. The darkness showed her nothing. Nothing for a long time, as she shivered and the night drew in.

She had been foolish to come here. What could she see that a priest of the nameless could not? There were no answers to this war. They would fight the yaksa until their last breaths, and they would be defeated. There was no hope anymore.

Something flickered in the darkness. She leaned closer.

It grew. First, an ember. Then a lamp. Then a blazing fire, swallowing up the water, swirling in screaming light.

Let me in, the fire said. And the woman said, without hesitation, *Yes.*

The fire was gone. The lake was black again.

"My lady," the priest said hesitantly. "Have you returned to yourself?"

He had seen nothing. She pressed her tongue to her teeth. Searched for her voice.

"Yes."

"Did the nameless speak?" the priest asked, eager and terrified.

She raised her head. Her vision swam, golden as fire. Despite the rain she felt suddenly warm—lit like a lantern from within.

Not the nameless, she thought. But it did not matter. They were saved.

"I know how to kill the yaksa," Divyanshi said.

1

PRIYA

On the first day, they made her kneel.

There, at the base of the Hirana, on soil laden with flowers, she lowered herself down. Her clothes were already filthy from her long journey. It didn't matter that the ground made her filthier. The yaksa with her brother's face had told her to kneel, so she had.

He bowed over her. Leaves surrounded her. It was like being beneath the boughs of a great tree.

"Priya," he said. "Wait here. Will you wait?"

What else could she do? She had come here, hadn't she? If a yaksa wanted her to kneel, she would. If they wanted her to walk again—walk and walk until her feet bled and she reached the edge of the world, and beyond—then she would. What else could she do but obey?

She was so impossibly tired.

"Yes," she said thinly. "I will."

The shadows of his leaves, points of cool darkness on her skin, rustled. They drifted away, leaving her in bare sunlight.

She was alone now, in silence, but the green was a cry in her ears: the susurration of growing things. The sharp, sap-bright crack of things rising from the soil, gasping for sunlight. All of Ahiranya, under her knees, inside her, around her.

Someone was approaching.

She raised her head again. But this figure did not tower over her. This ghost was small, slight—no more than a boy. Silvery, flat eyes. Soft petals flowering from his shoulders.

"Nandi?" Her mouth shaped his name without her say-so. Her little temple brother. A memory struck her like a clear bell: Nandi laughing, cheeks dimpled.

Nandi, lying dead on the ground in a burning room.

This Nandi smiled. Too many sharp teeth.

She touched the ground beneath him. Green things were growing beneath his bare feet. The world at this angle was all vibrant soil and falling leaves the color of moonlight. He curled his toes, and she heard the click of wood.

"You're not Nandi," she said. "I am sorry." She bowed, or tried to bow, in the way she'd always done before the effigies of the yaksa, with her forehead pressed to the ground and her hands beneath her. But her body had other ideas, and took that moment to collapse. Mouth full of dirt.

Hands on her upper arms. Lifting her back to her knees. The yaksa wearing Ashok's face was holding her up.

"You're tired," Nandi said. "Come with us."

"Where is Bhumika?"

"Come with us," he said again, and it was not a gentle urging any longer. It was an order. And because it was an order, her body obeyed. She rose, until she was standing. Walking.

She followed the two yaksa to the Hirana. There, in front of her, were familiar carvings. Familiar stone, weathered and ancient. She felt an ache: a pang like homesickness or homecoming.

Nandi touched a hand to the stone and it shifted, parting to open a way for them. The tunnel ahead was dark, but it called to her. She heard a song inside it.

My sapling.

Into the darkness she went. She walked, and walked, and the darkness opened—softened by blue light. And there before her were the deathless waters, and before it three more figures. Against the light behind them they were faceless, fleshless. No more than shadow.

A sudden fear gripped her heart like a fist. A yaksa would step forward wearing Bhumika's face. Bhumika, hollowed out, with flowering eyes and wooden smile, Bhumika gone—

Then one stepped forward, and it was Sanjana.

It was better. Terrible, but better, and when Sanjana told her to kneel again Priya did so without complaint, with something almost like thankfulness.

Elder Chandni and Elder Sendhil followed, and for a brief moment Priya wondered, wildly, whether she had died. How could she be meeting the dead if she were still alive?

"Priya," Sanjana said softly. She stepped behind Priya and took hold of her hair, her touch nearly tender. She gathered it up in her hands. "You're home."

She felt Sanjana's fingertips move up to her scalp—ten points of sharp touch, ten seeds ready to take root.

"Why am I here?" Priya asked. "Yaksa, ancient ones—why here, by the deathless waters? I'd do better resting in a bed."

There was something like laughter—rustling, rippling.

"Your soul needs rest," the yaksa who was not Sendhil said. "More than your body."

The one wearing Ashok's face knelt before her.

"You carry something precious within you," he told her, his voice hushed. He grasped her hands, turning them over. The bluish light of the deathless waters reflected on her skin, turning the brown of her palms soft gray. "We want to protect you."

She felt the sangam pour over her—cosmic and rippling, mingling with the light of the deathless waters before her. She breathed out, only half knowing her lungs, and felt Sanjana's nails press deeper against her scalp, points of grounding, points of pain.

Is this healing? Priya thought. *Is this rest?* It certainly didn't feel like it. But she had stabbed Malini and watched the terror and betrayal fill her eyes. She had left Sima behind. And Bhumika—wherever Bhumika was—could not help her.

"Rest," Nandi urged again. And Priya...

Priya closed her eyes.

*   *   *

On the second day, she dreamt.

She was in the sangam. Wholly, deeply, immersed in rivers of green and gold and blood red. And they were around her, the yaksa. All five of them, all utterly inhuman. Fish-scaled, flower-eyed, lichen-fleshed—river water oozing from their skin, and pearly sap adorning their finger bones. She loved them, a little, or perhaps entirely. She'd worshipped them all her life, after all. But she feared them too, and that was bitter, a sharp thorn under her tongue.

Are you hollow? the yaksa asked. *Are you ours, wholly and utterly?*

Are you hers?

Yes, she told them. Yes and yes. She had cut out her heart, after all. If they could see her soul, then surely they could see that. Her ribs of wood, and no human heart within them.

They picked at her. Picked her apart. They asked her again, and again.

Can you be trusted?

Will you stay? Will you serve?

Yes.

She isn't enough. She isn't ready. She isn't strong enough.

Words not meant for her that darted through her anyway; silvery arrows, piercing her.

Will you be what you need to be? Will you reach for her? Can you find her? Can you break your bones, your heart, your mind in her service? Can you yield?

Yield to it, Priya. Beloved. Yield.

Yes, and yes, and yes, and yes—

On the third day, she stopped counting.

Someone pressed water to her mouth. She drank.

She slept. She dreamt of the war: the churn of chariot wheels, and the Saketan warriors around her racing forward on their horses, and Sima holding up a shield to protect her.

More water. Pangs of hunger through her belly.

She was walking into the imperial court. She was sliding a knife between Malini's ribs. She was kissing Malini—kissing her even though she hadn't kissed Malini when she'd stabbed her. Kisses that tasted of blood, salt. *I'm sorry, I'm sorry. Hate me, you can hate me.*

Hate me and live.

She woke. Back in her own body, breathing and aching, sprawled in the dirt. There were flowers growing from her wrists, burrowing their heads into the soil. The yaksa were still there. She could feel them, even before she caught sight of them; kneeling as she had kneeled, as if they were tending to her, worshipping her.

She was dizzy with hunger. Her body hurt.

"Where is Bhumika?" Her voice cracked. "Where is my sister?"

Silence.

"Padma, then," Priya said, when no answer came. "Where is she?" She rose up on her elbows, dislodging growing things—feeling the soil under her thrum at her presence. "I came back for my family," Priya went on. "For my people. If you won't tell me about Bhumika, then at least tell me her child is safe."

"You think we would hurt a child?" Ashok—*not* Ashok—asked. But there was something assessing in the fathomless liquid of his eyes, in the leaf-rustle rasp of his voice.

"I think I know what nature does," Priya replied slowly. And what were the yaksa, if not nature? "And I know how I was raised. And I know...what was asked of me."

"Do you think," Sanjana asked, "that you have the right to ask?"

"I am an elder," Priya said. "I am thrice-born. Who else can ask, if not me?"

They said nothing, but the silence was weighty. There was a question inside it. It reminded her of her childhood—of her elders teaching her. They were waiting for her to fill the silence herself; to give a *proper* answer.

"That's what an elder should be," she went on, her throat sore.

"The one who can ask. Not just—a worshipper. If I am wrong, yaksa, then I am—sorry."

Elder Chandni—or the yaksa who mimicked her—leaned forward. Her dark hair was shining with water.

"Your sister ran," Elder Chandni said. "From her duties. From her purpose, in cowardice."

Lie. Bhumika would never have run. But as ground down as Priya was, she knew better than to say it.

"Did you kill her for it?" Priya asked. Her voice trembled. She couldn't help it.

"No," the yaksa wearing Ashok's face said. His eyes were fixed on the distance—on nothing, and everything. "We did not."

Was that a lie, too? She had not seen Bhumika in the sangam in so long.

She bowed to the earth again. Flowers against her face, the smell of petrichor seeping against her lips.

"Yaksa," she said. "I'm only mortal. Let me go. You've seen enough of my soul. My body needs to rest, too. To eat and to rest." *And I need to find my sister.*

"How long," the yaksa asked, "do you think you have been here?"

She turned her head, looking at him, then through him, at the rivulets of shining blue water, working their way down the stone wall. How long had the water run, bleeding like light in that same pattern, for the stone to scar as it had?

"I don't know," she said dully.

"If you were simply human," Sendhil murmured, "you would be dead."

She traced her lips with her tongue. It almost felt unnatural: tasting the salt of her skin, feeling the parched dryness of her mouth. *Simply human.* What was she meant to do with those words? She knew she wasn't simply human.

But she was human enough to be thirsty. Her knees hurt. And for all they'd been picking her apart from the soul upward, every shadowy root-and-spirit thread of her, she was more than her soul in the sangam. More than the sap under her skin. There was blood and flesh in her yet.

"You have my heart," said Priya. "Mani Ara has my heart. And you've seen everything of me that matters. Let me leave here. Let me serve you properly."

"And what service must you provide to us?" Elder Chandni prompted.

A flash of memory. Malini's betrayed eyes. A thorn blade. The feel of blood and flesh. She knew what Malini would do.

"There's going to be a war," Priya said. "The Parijatdvipans—they'll come. And you will need me. I'll serve. Just as the elders served in the Age of Flowers."

She raised her head, and saw as Chandni's mouth shaped a slow smile.

"Let me out, yaksa," Priya said. "So I can do the work you need from me."

She almost asked again. But she bit down on her tongue instead. Begging wouldn't get her anywhere. The yaksa would not respond to pleading. She'd learned a little more about them, in the time they had spent rummaging through her skin. She waited. Waited.

"Resting has fashioned something useful out of you," Chandni said indulgently. "Go, then, Elder Priya. Tend to your flesh. And then we will prepare for our war."

MALINI

Every night she returned to the court of the imperial mahal. She could not help it. Her dreams carried her there.

Every night was the same. Blue stone beneath her, the light of an unseen moon veiling the white marble, the pale sandstone, in water-deep shades. The gold of a fire ahead of her, blooming into flowers. Marigolds and ashoka and roses of bloody red, tumbling from the flames to her feet. And there, waiting for her, always: Priya.

Priya with leaves falling softly from her tangled hair. Priya, weeping—tracks of fire glittering on her cheeks.

Priya sliding a knife through Malini's ribs.

Malini woke, as she always did, with a sharp pain burrowing its way through her chest. She kept her eyes closed for a long moment, then rose to her feet. Removed her blouse with careful fingers. Pressed her fingertips to her own skin.

Smooth flesh first, and then the scars: the roughness of them, ugly beneath her fingers, a rope of hurt flesh knotted anew.

Touching the scars reminded her the knife was gone. Priya was gone. There was no reason at all for the pain.

She lay back down. Chest throbbing. A door open in her skull, a fire and a knife at the end of it.

The sun rose on the day of Aditya's funeral. She'd half expected that it would not.

The sky was still rose-pale when maids dragged buckets of fire-heated water into the marble bathing room, pouring them into the bath. Malini followed after them, slow-footed, heavy-hearted.

She lowered herself into the deep well of the bath, the water scalding around her, so hot it made her skin sting and ache. She closed her eyes, breathing the steam in as one maid poured oil into the water and another gathered up her hair, working through the tangles with an ivory comb and jasmine oil.

The maids moved silently. The smell of flower attar, even diluted, was nearly overpowering. But even so, when Malini rose out of the pool, she dipped her hand into the jug still held in a maid's waiting hands and pressed the fragrant oil behind her ear.

She knew how strong a pyre smelled. Better to smell flowers than fire, if she had the choice.

A drying cloth was wrapped around her body, her hair carefully daubed dry and then bound into a braid. No flowers in her hair today. No jewels at her wrists or her nose, her ears or throat. The sari that the maids wound around her body was pure mourning white.

Her chest ached as she moved at her maids' gentle urging. Pulled and tugged, the tight, scarred skin resisted her movements. The pain was all the greater because she refused to distract herself from it. Instead, she focused resolutely on her own body: the sweat already threatening to rise to her skin, the fading heat of the water, the scent of jasmine, and the ever-present ache within her ribs.

Funerals were meant to be performed as soon after a death as possible: the body burned, prayers made, mourning begun. But Aditya's funeral was no normal funeral. He had sacrificed himself for the empire. In the heart of a fort in Saketa, he had chosen to die.

Aditya had burned as the mothers burned. Aditya had smiled, or so people said—smiled and made the warriors around him vow to serve her, before the flames had consumed him whole.

Empress Malini, one of those warriors had said, head bowed. *In death, he gave you an everlasting crown.*

She let out a shuddering breath, tears threatening at her eyes. One of her maids made a high-pitched sound, resonant sympathy, her hands fluttering. She settled on adjusting Malini's pallu.

Strange to cry, when her heart felt so leaden inside her. Sometimes grief was pain, and sometimes it was simply absence—the wound in the shape of things that could not be felt or touched or comprehended.

A figure entered. Malini turned and saw Lata standing in the doorway, white-garbed and solemn.

"It's time," Lata said.

In the first hall stood Deepa and Raziya, and a whole throng of highborn dressed in uniform white. Some were already weeping. But Raziya was dry-eyed. She met Malini's eyes for a moment, then bowed—one sweeping movement mimicked in a ripple by the women around her.

Malini waited until they rose from their bows. The leaden feeling had spread from her heart to the rest of her body. She was not sure she could move her legs. But she had to. There was no alternative.

One step, then another. Another. And her court of women followed her, skirts whispering, a rustle like birds seeking flight.

She walked from her chambers, out, out.

And there, waiting for her, was a sea of highborn men. Her lords and kings. The rulers of her empire.

They bowed, too.

Through the throng of them, the High Priest emerged. Hemanth was the head of the priesthood that served the mothers of flame, and by extension served her. He was meant to be her spiritual advisor, by stature and standing.

But he was also the man who made Chandra into what Chandra had been. He was also the man who had burned women. The man who had almost burned her.

"Empress," Hemanth said. She could not read his expression. But she counted the new lines of grief and tension around his mouth. Noted the redness of his eyes. He was suffering, at least, and that pleased her. "Prince Aditya's soul awaits our prayers."

Distantly, through the high windows and from remote corridors, she could hear weeping and song. Prayer and music, and the beating of mourning drums. Would the mourning have been so ostentatious if the rot was not flowering across the empire, if rumors of the yaksa rising and walking once more had not begun to spread? People needed something to have faith in.

"High Priest," she said, loud enough for the waiting men to hear her. Her voice was clear as a bell. "Show us how to revere him."

Chandra's funeral had not been like this. It had been swift, and small. Ignoble. No one had been willing to burn his corpse during her sickness, and by the time she had recovered from her wound his body had rotted. Even the flowers and perfumes laid on his pyre, and the attar of roses dashed from small silver filigree jugs by the priests onto his remains, had not been enough to cover the smell. So there had been no public display of mourning for the people of Harsinghar to wail or cheer over. Instead, there had only been members of her council and the priests, and Malini herself. And the corpse, of course, swathed in white cloth to conceal its decay.

But for Aditya's funeral there was weeping and wailing. The people of Harsinghar had left sheaves of flowers outside the mahal's walls. And Aditya's funeral pyre—with no corpse to burn—was heaped with garlands. Pink, red; the rich, profuse gold of marigolds; the delicate white, too, of needle-flower.

She kneeled, prostrating herself before the bodiless pyre. All the people around her followed suit, and their prayers were a roar like waves, a billowing storm in her ears. Their grief was so ostentatious it was more akin to a celebration: of death, of sacrifice, of the faith of the mothers.

Of Aditya. Not as she had known him—not her brother, with all his infuriating flaws, his gentle eyes, his unbending morality—but as the immortal thing he'd become. Not a mother of flame, but a son of one—dying for Malini's empire, Malini's throne, Malini's fate.

She could not complain, could she? By the time she'd clawed her way from her sickbed, his tale had fused with her own, nourished her power even when sickness should have leached authority away from her. So empress she continued to be, crowned anew in the flames of his death.

She closed her eyes as Hemanth spoke his name.

Prince Aditya.

She couldn't remember the last thing she had said to him. She'd searched her memory, racked it. But the more she thought about it, the less she could recall: the more the memory writhed and twisted, evading her. Her mind, punishing her, or showing her compassion.

Malini opened her eyes, blinked as Aditya's face wavered before her swimming gaze.

Hemanth had fallen silent. He stepped forward and, with reverence, lit the pyre.

As the flames caught and rose, the sound of prayers rose with them.

The jasmine oil was a mistake. She realized that now. She could smell nothing but flowers: rotting flowers, burning flowers, flowers turning to smoke and flowers on her own skin, and the absence of burning flesh was almost more awful than the presence of it. Her stomach roiled. She almost wavered where she sat; almost slipped like all her bones had melted and she was nothing but wilting flesh. She felt the possibility of it like nausea, vertigo, and held it—somehow—at bay.

Maybe she was slipping. Losing her grasp on herself, on authority; maybe she was unraveling.

She hunched forward. A tear slipped free. That was fine. A little grief. A respectable amount of grief. A grief like worship. That could be allowed. That could—perhaps—be a necessity.

After the prayers ended she felt Lata's hand on one arm and Raziya's on the other. They raised her up. She found her feet and moved, the crowd moving with her.

She walked from the court to a veranda overlooking the city.

The sky was painfully blue above her, and her skirt began to billow, caught in a sweet breeze.

She looked out at the city. At its people, so many of them that she could not discern individual faces, only the movement and sway of bodies, all palely dressed, exultant and mourning and joyous in their grieving under the rise of the beating sun.

Empress Malini. Mother Malini. Empress, Empress, Empress.

She felt the tale settle around her, written in smoke and in death.

And her ribs still burned, and burned, and burned.

RAO

"There will be war, of course."

The snap of a flask. Liquor being poured. The scent of it was sharp—iron-rich, so close to blood that Rao could only turn his face from it and stare at one of the lamps along the wall. The flame inside it flickered orange and yellow.

A flame could burn blue, if it burned hot enough. Rao knew that now.

He kept silent as another voice muttered, and then another. War, yes. There would be war. The Ahiranyi had sent an assassin, after all, to murder Parijatdvipa's holy empress. There would have to be vengeance. No—*justice*. The Ahiranyi would learn Parijatdvipa's strength once more.

An assassin. The word rattled strangely in Rao's head.

Priya had saved them all at the Veri river. She'd fought for them, nearly *died* for them. He'd dragged her flower-riven body from the riverbed himself. Without her the empress would have no throne at all.

But there was no denying that she had stabbed Malini, in the end.

"…impassable borders," another man was murmuring. Rao turned his head, following the voice. One of the Srugani. Rao did not recognize him, and had no interest in recognizing him, but he noted the sweat on the man's forehead and the tension in his jaw with a disinterested eye, just for the sake of something to do apart from thinking of flame, and flame, and flame. "We sent warriors to Ahiranya, but the trees consumed them. Like teeth in the maw of a beast. You will not believe me, my brothers, but if I were asked to choose between the jaws of a tiger or Ahiranya's forest…" He shook his head. "I would choose the tiger," he said heavily.

I believe it, Rao thought. He'd seen what Ahiranya's forest was like firsthand. He'd seen what the rot could do to a body.

He said nothing. The highborn around him shifted uneasily on their bolster pillows. There was a clink, as more liquor was opened and shared.

Mourning meant no liquor, no gambling, no sex until the ritual of grieving was done. The empress and her court of loyal women prayed still by the smoking ashes of flowers. He hadn't gone to the funeral—he would rather have cut out his own eyes than watch an empty pyre burn in Aditya's name—but he'd heard florid descriptions of Malini's noble misery as she knelt by the flowers, and her gray face, and her white grief clothes, bleached like sun-touched bones. A perfect mourner. She had to be cajoled to even eat.

And yet here were her men in a dark room with the shutters closed and the curtains drawn and candles burning, drinking their way through the finest liquors in Parijat and eating their fill as they pondered the doom ahead of them.

"The priests claim the yaksa will return," a young Parijati noble said. His voice trembled a little.

A murmur of unease. One man laughed.

"Impossible," he said.

"If the priests say it, then it must be so," another man said. There was a ripple of disagreement.

The yaksa are returning, Rao thought. He'd seen a yaksa's severed arm, a relic of the Age of Flowers, blooming with new life. He'd seen a vision from the nameless god in a pool of water. *A coming. An inevitable coming.*

He'd seen Aditya's eyes when Rao had shown him the severed arm. He'd seen the moment when Aditya had made his choice:

when Aditya had decided the nameless had a purpose for him, that it was time to burn—

Rao stood abruptly, knocking over a cup of wine in the process. The man next to him swore as it pooled messily on his lap.

"Apologies," Rao said shortly. The man opened his mouth to say something—but when he met Rao's eyes, it abruptly snapped shut.

Rao turned and left the room. No one made any effort to stop him.

For days, Rao had been possessed by a vague but urgent desire to vanish into the anonymity of a pleasure house and drown himself in a vat of cheap wine surrounded by strangers, but the time he'd spent in the presence of his fellow highborn had made clear to him that he wasn't fit for company.

That was fine. He'd be alone instead. He bribed one of the guards for drink and kept on walking.

There were a few low-roofed chambers overlooking a garden of lotus ponds. He climbed up to the lowest of them, swinging up one-armed, his other arm cradling three flasks of arrack—his least favorite liquor. As soon as his legs were on firm roof-stone, he pried open a flask and set the rim to his lips. Bitter, fiery liquor burned against the roof of his mouth. He swallowed fast, letting the fire run right through him.

He wanted to drink until he couldn't feel his own skin; until he was a blank, buzzing, nauseated void of a man, all the grief scooped out of him.

Another swig. And two, and three. He leaned back on his elbows and stared out at Harsinghar.

From here, the city was a night sky laid out on the earth, dark and formless and flecked here and there with light. It looked almost peaceful. From here, he couldn't see the mourners still crying and praying outside the walls of the mahal. He couldn't hear them, either. It was a relief to hear nothing but the wind—to feel nothing but liquor and the sharp bite of the night's breeze against his face, turned up at the sky.

But, ah. If he could still feel his face, well—then he had more drinking to do.

So he drank more, until even the darkness had softened. When he heard a clatter—and felt a stone bash sharply against his leg—he swore with surprise, and the flask slipped from his drink-dulled grip. It rolled, spilling all the arrack left in it, which wasn't much.

"Rao?" a voice called. "It's me."

"Lata?" He sat up. "Why did you throw that? Come up."

"I can't climb to you," she replied, voice small in the dark—small and far away. "I've already tried. Didn't you hear me?"

"No," he said. *Slurred*, more like. "But I've had a great deal to drink. I'd climb down to you, but I'd probably break my neck."

He didn't have to hear her to know she was sighing and shaking her head, that her forehead had creased a little, the way it did when she was lost in thought or thoroughly vexed.

"I didn't see you at the funeral," she said.

A punch of grief through his chest. The funeral. The funeral.

"Did Malini notice?" Rao asked.

"No. The empress was... distracted."

He could hear the thread of worry in Lata's voice. Malini did not miss things. But Aditya's death, and the actions of Elder Priya, had changed her. *She's wounded*, Lata had said to him once. *Not just in the flesh. Somewhere deep within her, where no physician can heal her.*

Rao had understood. He knew how that felt.

"Good," he said. He thought about opening the next flask, but something like panic bubbled through him. His hands were shaking. "I should have come," he said. "But I... Lata. I didn't need to see Aditya burn. I already—"

"Rao," she said. Her voice was thick. "I know."

Suddenly he was tired of not seeing her face, of being alone on that roof with a vile drink he didn't even like. He slid to the edge and jumped down. He tumbled, his elbows catching the stone, face pressed to the ground. He watched Lata hurry toward him, her sari skirt a blue shadow against the grass. She grasped him by the shoulder.

"Get up," she said. "What did you drink?"

"Arrack," he said.

Another sigh. "Can you get up on your own, or do I need to find guards to help me?"

He insisted he could get up, and between them they managed to haul him to his feet. He leaned a little of his weight on her shoulder, and the two of them stumbled through the lotus garden into the corridors of the mahal.

"You're too heavy for this," she said after a few minutes. "Use the wall for support instead."

"Should have thrown me into the pond," he muttered, as he let her go and grasped a lantern sconce. "That would have woken me up."

"Or drowned you."

That wouldn't have been so bad, he thought. But thank the nameless, he had the sense not to say it.

Usually there were curtains covering the doors that led off the corridors of the mahal—expansive silk things in peacock green and lustrous blue, shot through with gemstones and silver thread. It took his dazed eyes a moment to register that all the curtains had been replaced with plain white cloth that hung heavy, too thick to billow with the soft night winds. He grasped one curtain in his hands. Felt its weight.

"Do you think," he heard himself say, as if from a distance, "that anyone really mourns him?"

"Of course they do," Lata said from somewhere behind him. "The empress does."

He swallowed, his throat unaccountably aching. Grasped the cloth tighter.

"Yes," he said. "She does."

He felt her hand on his upper arm. A light touch. Then a man's voice, from the gloom ahead of them.

"Prince Rao," the voice said. Heavy footsteps followed it. "I . . ."

The voice trailed off as the man emerged into the lamplight. Romesh was one of Low Prince Ashutosh's men—his high-collared, long-sleeved tunic, marked with Ashutosh's liegemarks, hid the leaves of rot at his arms and his throat. His eyes darted from Lata to Rao—from the empress's advisor to one of her generals—and then he bowed and said, "I'll take my leave."

"No," Lata said. "Please, take him. I'm afraid he's had too much to drink." She stepped away from Rao, walking swiftly toward Romesh—and then beyond him. "Take him to his chambers," she urged. "Prince Rao must rest. The empress will have need of him soon. There is much work to do."

Work. War, he supposed, was indeed work.

Romesh nodded his head in acknowledgment, then deferentially took Rao by the arm. They walked together in silence for a long moment.

Rao's head was not exactly beginning to clear, but the worst of his dizziness had shifted.

"You were looking for me," he said eventually.

"Perhaps when you're less in your cups, my lord," Romesh said gruffly.

"You want to speak to me? You'll find no better time. We're alone, after all." Silence—just their footsteps, the crackle and spit of the lanterns. "You're nervous," Rao said. "You sought me out. So speak. Tell me what you want."

He turned his head, lights blurring around him. Romesh's jaw was set, his expression conflicted. Then he said, "The Ahiranyi woman. The—good one. She's your prisoner?"

It took a long moment for Rao to understand what he meant. *The good one.* "Sima?"

Romesh nodded curtly.

"Me and the other men—we want to know how she is."

"She's caused no trouble." She really hadn't. All through the war, she'd been firm and determined. She'd waded into deep, corpse-infested water to save Priya. But ever since—ever since *everything*—she'd been gray and silent. When he'd arranged her safe chambers and promised her safety, she'd only nodded and murmured her thanks, and turned her face to the wall.

And Rao had . . . simply let her.

"She's proved herself trustworthy," Romesh muttered. "She was good in the war. She fought hard. My lord, if you'll let me speak plain—she's not responsible for the actions of the other one." A pause, and then he said, almost reluctantly, "I liked them both. But the other one . . . she made her choices."

Everyone knew what Priya had done. A thorn knife. A dead priest. Stone cracked through with flowers, and Malini clutching her own bloodied chest, weeping as the blood spilled through her own fingers.

"Sima is safe," Rao said. "Safe and well treated. I've vowed to protect her. That won't change. You can tell your men I've made a promise I won't break."

In his own chambers, he forced himself to drink some water. He could only take a few mouthfuls.

His tongue was dry and his mouth tasted foul. His eyes had started to burn. He rubbed them, the prickling heat only growing stronger.

He couldn't rest tonight. Not after Aditya's funeral. Not after an empty pyre had burned. Not when all he could remember was Aditya looking at him, tears bright and shining in his eyes.

What is a star?

Aditya, fire climbing over his skin. Aditya, in Rao's hands and then not.

Distant fire—

He was walking before he consciously chose to do so. He was steadier now. Steady enough, at least, to walk in a moderately straight line. Corridors, and flickering lights, and the faces of bowing maids—and then—

"Let me in," he said, and the soldiers protecting Sima's chambers stepped aside and opened the doors, and let him pass.

Sima jumped to her feet when he entered. She'd been sitting

on the floor cushions, but she straightened swiftly, brandishing something in her hands. There was a mirror behind her, great and silver, and in it he could see his own reflection—a wavering, insubstantial figure—and the tense lines of her back, ready for violence.

She met his eyes. Dropped whatever she'd been holding.

"I'm sorry," he said. "I don't know why I came here so—late. I should have known—not. Not to do so. Was that a knife?"

She wasn't supposed to have weapons. Even after Lata had asked him to look after her, he'd had to negotiate with Malini's other advisors for *custody* of her. *The Ahiranyi prisoner cannot have weapons. The Ahiranyi prisoner cannot leave her chambers. If the Ahiranyi prisoner seeks to break the rules of her imprisonment, then the price must be death.*

"No," she said, after a beat. Her voice was rough. "Just a clay bowl."

Rao looked down. The clay was a shard. Jagged enough to cut.

"Just a bowl," he agreed slowly.

Sima kept looking at him. She didn't ask him why he was here, but he could read the question in her face.

"I'm sorry," he said abruptly, "that I haven't made your imprisonment more bearable. And I am sorry…" He trailed off, unable to find words.

"It's not your fault," she said thinly. "Priya made her decision. And I made mine."

He still couldn't quite believe she'd chosen this: to part from Priya. To ally herself with Parijatdvipa, even if it meant imprisonment and suspicion. If it hadn't been for Lata, it could have meant Sima's death. And he'd seen Sima and Priya together. They'd fought for each other. Nearly died for each other. How could they have wrenched apart so swiftly, so completely?

He rubbed his aching, stinging eyes. "I'll do better," he promised. "There are people here in Harsinghar who care about you, Sima. You're not surrounded by enemies. Or—not only enemies. And if… if you want the company of friends… Or if…"

He was swaying. When had that begun?

"Rao!" Sima was shouting. He watched her mouth move, distantly aware, as his knees buckled.

He heard the doors bang open as the dark swallowed him.

A dream.

No. Not a dream. He knew this. He'd seen this before, in dark water. In Aditya's eyes.

A vision.

The void surrounded him. Dark, vast and liquid. And then it bloomed.

Mountains. White snow. A slash in the stone, a wound, bloodletting. Blood the color of deep waters.

A coming. An inevitable coming.

A man holding out his palm. Aditya, smiling even as he wept.

Rao. Rao—

He opened his eyes.

His vision swam for a moment, then steadied. The two soldiers were holding Sima tight by the arms.

"Let her go," he forced out. His words were rough and slurred, but the soldiers understood and set her free. He forced himself up onto his palms, his knees. His whole body was shaking, godstruck. "Didn't you think—a physician—might be more useful to me? Than...?" He gestured vaguely at Sima, who was rubbing her arms, her expression tight.

"Sorry, my lord," one soldier muttered, looking suitably ashamed. The other was already ducking out of the room—likely finally in search of some real help. Rao almost called out to summon him back. A vision was not an illness. No medicine could cure it.

But when he managed to get up to his knees, he heard Sima whisper his name.

He looked at Sima's gray face, her horrified eyes. And then he looked beyond her, unable to meet that gaze.

He met his own in the mirror.

His eyes, in the silvery glass, were a smear of fiery gold.

BHUMIKA

She felt as if she were being carried along by water. Her body swayed out of her control. She could not find her breath easily and when she did, she cried out, begging for something or someone she'd lost. The ache of grief yawned open in her like a chasm, and the voice that shushed her, growing steadily more frantic, was not the one she sought.

Her head ached, a storm in the cup of her skull.

"Breathe," the voice said. A man's voice. The man begged her, "Tell me what hurts."

I named her for a flower. I named her. I left her. I left her. I left her—

"Fever," the man's voice said. And then he made a noise that had no words but might have been a choked sob. "Shit," he said. Then he cursed again. The world tipped as he did so, and she felt breath on her hair. The water in her ears sounded suddenly like a heartbeat.

She wasn't being carried by water, she realized. It was flesh that guided her. Arms were cradling her. The wind roared, biting at her face. It hurt.

"Hold on," he said. "Hold on, my lady."

She held on. Even as the waters rose, as a storm tried to swallow her, she held on. Time passed and then she was still again, the whine of insects in her ears.

"Please." She heard the man's voice, ragged with exhaustion. "Auntie, I need help. My wife is sick."

With great effort, she managed to peel open her eyes. Her vision was a half-moon, a soft blur of dusk-gray sky fading into black earth. A stooped figure stood ahead of them, framed by a door. Silver hair, a sari.

"You're Ahiranyi," the figure said warily.

The man shifted her in his arms.

"By birth," he said. He sounded apologetic. Desperate. "But we moved to Srugna years ago, long before we wed. We were driven out from our village. Please, aunt. Don't drive us away too."

"What makes you think you'll be welcome here?"

"Hope," he said. "We've got no rot on us. I promise. Please."

The woman told him, eventually, that they could sleep behind the house. The man thanked her.

She felt a shawl being drawn over her. Water at her lips. Hard ground at her back; something soft tucked beneath her head by warm hands. Then nothing, for a long time.

She drifted in and out of consciousness. Every time she rose out of the waters of sleep, she caught snatches of conversation, strange in her ears, tangles of nonsense.

"It's a poor business." The old woman's anger was gone. Her voice held only pity. "Families split in two, parents separated from their children and their elderly by whatever evil has changed Ahiranya's borders. Did you lose anyone?"

"Her brother and sister." The familiar man's voice. "I had no other family."

A sigh. "Ahiranya is cursed. I am sorry for my caution, with you and your poor wife, but you understand—"

"I'm grateful." A hand on her forehead. A thumb brushing back her sweat-damp hair. "Thank you."

Sleep.

This time when she woke, the waters of her mind and her heart had settled around her. She'd been drowning, and now she was not. She could breathe. She wasn't burning. She opened her eyes, which were gritty with sleep and sickness. It was night.

The man was sitting against the wall of the house, upright,

legs crossed. He was asleep, a sword across his knees. She could hear his quiet breath. Inside the house a lamp was burning. In the grass and trees around them, she could hear a noise—a steady rhythmic dripping of water. She turned her head slowly.

There were people watching her. Water-drenched cloth was draped across their faces, tumbling in folds to the floor before them at their feet. They held bowls in their hands—bowls that streamed strange river water to the soil. Green water, gold, and red.

Their numbers shifted as she watched them—a dozen, then ten, then a blur of faces too vast for her to swiftly count. But she saw adults. Children.

"Who are you?" she whispered. Her voice came out a croak. She was thirsty, depleted.

Silence. Then, with a rustling sigh, one water-veiled girl stepped forward and kneeled. She held out her green bowl.

"Will you drink?"

She looked at that water. A strange sense came over her—a knowing. A part of her lay in the water swirling in that bowl: knowledge that her skull, already aching, storm-full, could not carry without help.

If she drank, she would know something huge and terrible.

She reached out a hand—and the man stirred behind her. The figures were gone.

"How do you feel?" he asked. "Do you need water? Food?"

She stared up at him. Dark hair, a sharp jaw beneath the shadow of stubble. He looked tired.

"Who are you?" she asked.

"I am Jeevan," he said, voice low.

That wasn't the name he had offered their helper.

"You are not my husband," she said, lowering her voice to match his. She did not want to be overheard.

"No, my lady," he said.

My lady. It jarred through her like a knock to the bone, so strange it barely resembled pain.

"If you have told these people you're my husband, you must not call me that again," she said. "What is my name?"

"Bhumika," he said.

Bhumika. The name felt like nothing. It did not slot neatly into her heart. She did not know who Bhumika was.

"Call me that, then," she said.

In the morning, the man swept their helper's steps and washed them clean. He brought the older woman firewood and uttered a terse but heartfelt thanks. The woman had clearly softened to him.

"You have a good husband, my dear," she said. "I hope you find a safe home together."

"As do I," said Bhumika.

Their helper clasped her hands. "I am sorry about your brother and sister," she said sympathetically. "I'll pray to the mothers that our empress will set them free from Ahiranya one day."

Her head was pounding. She thought of the watchers in their veils.

"Thank you," she replied. "I would not have survived without you."

The man named Jeevan walked with her away from the forest, through undergrowth under the palely rising sun. He turned to her.

"Where will you go?"

She had someone to find.

She was a vessel for knowledge. She needed someone else to carry it. Someone who could see far; someone with the power to be heard.

In the swirl of knowledge inside her lay an image: a lake. A holy place that trained its people to listen to the voices beyond the mortal world. That was where a seeker had learned how to end the Age of Flowers and kill the yaksa long ago. A seeker would return there again.

She turned to the watchers who stood in the distance. The dirt road to them was shining like a river: a twining, beckoning thing. She pointed a hand toward them. Her mouth tasted of silt, of water-smooth stone. The taste of stolen knowledge.

"To Alor," she said.

5

PRIYA

Priya walked slowly toward the mahal, trying to ignore the dread that was worming its way through her. She didn't know what she would find.

The yaksa had not come with her. They had simply let her leave, let her stumble back into the cold, bright air beyond the Hirana. But she could feel them as if they were with her. They were in her ears, her beating heart, her blood.

The green was within her, after all. And they were within the green.

Once, she'd felt Ahiranya like a limb—all its green a stretching, powerful part of her. Now she felt like she *was* Ahiranya: so enmeshed that when she breathed, the trees swayed, and the soil shifted, moving with her.

She could feel the mahal too, through the green that had consumed it. Its once beautiful sandstone was splintered. Lichen and creeping vines had crept through the stone; the flowers that grew from them were pulsing, bright, breathing alongside her. She could feel them all—like she could clench a fist and crumble the mahal in its entirety.

Could she? Surely not. Surely.

But Mani Ara had made something new of her. She didn't know the limits of her new strength.

She walked into the mahal, through once familiar corridors.

Pillars—once carved from sandstone, high and sweeping—were broken. The roof should have fallen in without their support, but the stone had been replaced by living trees, the trunks rising through the ruptured floor, branches clasping the roof, fronds of leaves falling like curtains.

I can hold the ceiling, she thought coolly, *or destroy it. With a twitch of my fingers.*

The voice in her head didn't sound like her own.

She forced herself to think normally: to think like a human, with the kind of practical, bone-deep compassion she knew was human too.

People can't live like this, Priya thought. And then the realization hit her, on its heels.

People can't live like this, but yaksa can.

I can.

Whether or not people could live here, they were certainly making their best efforts. The rooms that lined the corridors had been turned into makeshift bedchambers and prayer rooms, and there were more people around by far than there should have been. It took her a long moment to mark the beads of sacred woods at different wrists and throats. The vials of deathless water, broken from the source, strung at waists. Worshippers. So many of them, and many of them armed.

No one noticed her at first. She probably looked no different from the rot-riven. Then she saw an older woman striding along the corridor and felt a breathless shock of recognition.

Kritika, leader of the mask-keepers, saw her in return. Kritika's face went tight, as if shock and fear had both caught her unaware, neither gaining the advantage on her face, leaving her expression a rictus.

"Elder Priya," she said, her voice a rasp. "Are you... are you, *you?*"

Priya nodded, wordless. Her lungs felt empty, her mouth useless.

Kritika bowed low. When she raised herself up, her eyes were shining with tears, her expression determined.

"The yaksa have brought you back to us," she said, voice trembling. "I am so glad, Elder."

Funny. Priya had never thought Kritika particularly liked her. But Kritika was looking at her now, hopeful, eager, and Priya... Priya had to say something profound, didn't she? She racked her brain.

"I'm really hungry," Priya said, her voice cracking.

Billu fed her.

Kritika led her to the kitchen. Guiding her, like Priya wouldn't know where the kitchen was anymore, even though she'd once visited it multiple times a day. In the open courtyard, by the ovens and the ever-simmering vat of tea—that vat was likely to survive longer than any of them—Priya stood and ate, and drank nearly a whole jugful of water on her own. She ate like a feral thing, a starving animal, because her body was animal and hungry and she had no energy to conceal it.

The household gathered around her: Billu, who ruled the kitchens; Khalida and the maids, who had become the household's masters in the time since Ahiranya's independence; ex–imperial guards—but no Jeevan; and finally Ganam and the other mask-keepers, who were clustered around Kritika like children. She recognized them all. And recognized that they were all watching her, curious and wary-eyed, as if she were a hawk in a cage, or a serpent caught on the end of a stick, beautiful but liable to attack if provoked.

"Where have you been?" one mask-keeper finally blurted out. That broke the tension. Immediately, one of the laundresses added, "You look so thin, Priya. Were you with the empress's army this whole time? Did you come back here alone?"

"You haven't heard," Priya said numbly. She looked from face to face. "None of you have. Have you?"

"Heard what?"

"Our borders are shut," Ganam said flatly. "Anyone who tries to leave or enter dies. We know what's happened in Ahiranya. Nothing beyond that."

The food turned to nausea in her stomach. They didn't know.

The yaksa hadn't even spoken of it directly. It was Priya who'd said to them that she had cut out her own heart. She remembered it now, in sickening flashes: Malini, and the trust in her black eyes; the way they looked when that same trust snapped, a string brutally cut.

"I stabbed the empress," Priya said, more calmly than she'd thought she was capable of.

A beat of shocked silence.

"Does...does she still live, Elder?" Kritika finally asked.

"Yes," Priya said. But what followed was a fist of dread that gripped her straight round the heart, her lungs, making her air small.

How could she know if Malini had lived or died? She couldn't know. She knew how wounds could fester, even with the best care. She knew how fiercely, too, that Malini wanted to live. Was desire enough?

She breathed through her feelings and bullied the fear down. She took another mouthful of food. She chewed hard on her roti, the bread grinding down to soft pulp between her teeth, giving herself time to recover, to think. To be silent.

"Why did you do it?" a maid asked.

Priya swallowed and said simply, "The yaksa asked it of me."

"Then it was deserved," Kritika said determinedly. "And it was necessary. We must trust the yaksa," she stressed, as if the others had argued this point with her.

They didn't reply, and neither did Priya. She wasn't sure she needed to. She swallowed a mouthful of tea instead, blistering hot.

"I know Bhumika isn't here," she said instead. Her voice shook only a little.

"She vanished." Billu's face was impassive. "One day she was here, and then she wasn't."

So no one knew what had happened to Bhumika.

"Is Padma safe?" Priya asked. "And Rukh—"

"They're both here and safe," Billu said. "You don't need to worry about Rukh. Or the baby."

"Where are the soldiers who went with you to war? And where is Sima?" Ganam asked, eyes dark, expression grim. Like he already knew what her answer would be. "Are they safe elsewhere?"

Her throat closed up.

She did not, could not, know what had happened to Sima among the Parijatdvipans. But she'd left Sima there in the hope that whatever awaited Priya in Ahiranya, Sima would be safe from it.

"The war was risky," she said. An answer and no answer at all—she'd let them make their own assumptions.

"They've done something to you," Khalida blurted out. Then she covered her mouth with her hand, eyes frightened, darting. There was some uneasy shuffling of feet. Murmuring voices.

Priya thought of the vines and leaves around them—the way they were like an extension of her own eyes and ears. The way the yaksa lived in them, saw through them, felt through them, just as she did.

"Don't worry," Priya said. "Even if the yaksa can hear you, they know what they've done to me. It won't upset them to hear you've noticed—me."

"Lady Bhumika doesn't look like this," Khalida said, voice cracking a little, as she gestured one trembling hand at Priya. She swallowed, and when she next spoke there was a forced steadiness to her words. "She looks like herself."

"Looked," one of the mask-keepers corrected, their voice a mutter.

Priya resisted the urge to touch her own face—to feel the alienness of her skin. She clasped her own hands together.

"I am glad you are here to lead us," Kritika said, her voice pointedly pitched to drown them out. "We need a thrice-born elder to lead us. Just as the ones who came before us had in the Age of Flowers." She looked at Priya fiercely, as if she could reshape Priya into something worthy of all her hopes by just staring her down. "Everything will be better now."

I'm not Bhumika, Priya wanted to say immediately. *I'm not the one you should really be looking at for guidance. I did my work, trying to heal the rot and guarding our land from imperial soldiers, and it wasn't enough. I'm not... not a leader. Not what you're looking for.*

But she could not say it. She couldn't afford to hide in Bhumika's shadow. There was no Bhumika to hide behind anymore.

Where are you, sister? Are you even alive?

The household was quiet. Wide-eyed. Hanging on her silence, waiting for her words.

"We can start making things better," she said, trying to sound strong and practical. "I can tell the mahal is falling apart. I'll see to that."

"You've learned carpentry in the empire?" Ganam inquired, raising his eyebrows. Khalida gave a hiccupping cough, then covered her mouth hurriedly.

That was good. A little sharpness, a little humor, meant that they still recognized her as *her.*

"I can't make things worse," she said, trying for a grin. It felt strange on her face. She let it drop swiftly. "What else needs to be done? Whether you think I can do it or not—just tell me."

There was a long pause—and then suddenly everyone was talking at once.

"—food stores aren't enough for all the pilgrims, never mind the city, and the highborn are *hoarding*—"

"If we're going to talk about the pilgrims—"

"—impossible to get all the raw materials we need with the borders shut as they are—"

Now that she'd asked, she regretted doing so. The words pounded against her skull. She felt suddenly weak. She was with her own people, and she was almost—almost—safe. It was enough to make all the exhaustion she'd been holding back come over her in a wave.

"Tomorrow we'll make a start," she said. "Today and tonight, I rest. But tomorrow—we do the yaksa's work, and we do our own. And we survive."

* * *

She collapsed on the bed in her old chambers. She slept curled up on her side, her knees tucked to her chest. Even tangled in her own dirt-stained sari, she could see the shimmer of green life under her own skin, and feel the pulse of Ahiranya beating like blood in her veins. She forced her eyes shut and tried, oh tried, to dream human dreams. Her body was animal-tired, but the rest of her was vast, drifting—

"Priya," a voice said. It was young. Hesitant.

She opened her eyes. It was day, hot, light. She saw a figure, and knew it, knew him, even before he stepped from the shadows into the spill of light from the window.

"Rukh," she said. There was a bundle in his arms, a small face with dark curls turned against his shoulder. Priya straightened in her bed, suddenly awake. "Is that...?"

"You can't hold her," he said warily.

Was it because she wasn't quite human anymore? Did he fear she was a yaksa?

"I won't," she said. She sat up properly, tucking her feet under her.

For all her fears of being not quite human, her heart was racing. She felt shaky with the intensity of seeing him, of seeing Padma, safe and whole in his arms. Perhaps a little sleep had been enough to restore all the soft, terrified parts of her.

"Look at her," Priya said, voice a little choked. "She's so big now. How—how is she?"

Rukh was silent for a long moment, his eyes large, watchful. There was so much feeling in them that she couldn't read or understand.

"She...she's not loud like she used to be," Rukh said eventually, a telltale wobble to his voice as he looked at Priya and held Padma tight, so tight. "But I guess that's—normal. Considering. Everything."

How could Bhumika have left Padma behind? Priya couldn't fathom any of this. The question was an ache.

Bhumika had to be dead.

"I won't touch her," Priya said. "I promise. But you can come and sit beside me, if you like. She must be heavy."

Hesitation, again. She saw him swallow. He shifted on his feet, like he didn't know if he wanted to stay or flee.

"I don't know if you're...you," he said.

"That makes sense," Priya said, thinking of the teary horror in Khalida's eyes, and the determined, forceful hope in Kritika's. "But why did you come to me, Rukh? If you think I'm something the yaksa made, or if you think I'm one of them..." She exhaled and felt the rustle of flowers growing through the bedding beneath her. She forced them away. *Wither.* "I know you'd risk yourself out of curiosity," she went on. "That's your way. It doesn't surprise me. But her—ah, Rukh, that's not like you."

"I couldn't leave her," he burst out. "And I wanted to know if you—I hoped. I had to know if hoping was stupid. And if you're one of them, if you're a yaksa that looks like Priya, then nowhere's safe from you. And if you're Priya, then nowhere's safer than with you. So." He swallowed again, and she saw the tears streaking his face, miserable. "It's all hope. That's why."

"I'm me," she said softly, swallowing back her own tears. "You're going to have to decide for yourself if you can believe that or not, Rukh. But as far as I know, I'm still me. Priya, and a temple elder, and human enough. So come sit. Or don't. I'll understand."

"Will you?"

"Of course," she said. "There's always tomorrow. Maybe you'll trust me then. Or maybe the day after that. I'm not going anywhere again."

He stood still for a long, long moment. But Padma was heavy for him. She could tell. And he wanted to believe her.

He walked over to the bed and sat down. She didn't close the distance between them but felt herself relax—some unknowable tension unspooling from her shoulders, her spine.

"How are you, Rukh?" Priya asked gently.

"Oh, everything's awful here," he said, trying to sound casual.

"I'm asking about you. About how awful it's been for you,

specifically. Go on. You can tell me."

"I forgot you for a while," Rukh said, voice hushed. He was rocking Padma back and forth in his arms, resting her cheek against his knee. It didn't look like a comfortable position, but Padma was still half-asleep regardless, her face blotchy from crying, her eyes hooded. She was gnawing softly on her own fist. "I . . . the yaksa. The one that looks like Ashok. He did something to me, and it was like . . . like the memory of you was water, and *I* was taken away from the water, and so I didn't have the memory anymore."

He swallowed and lowered his head. Padma made a chuffing noise and tried to grab at the leaves in his hair, then settled again when he hushed her.

"But you remember me now," Priya said.

"I do," Rukh agreed. "It came back slowly. After he let me go. I just. I just wanted you to understand if I'm not the same . . ."

Priya huffed out a laugh. She waved her arm in front of herself, letting the light shine on her—on her green-dusted veins, the sap pearling at her fingertips.

"Yes," she said. "Because I'm not changed at all."

"That doesn't make me happy," Rukh said seriously. "Everyone says the yaksa . . . transformed you. Under the Hirana."

"They changed me before that," said Priya. "But it doesn't matter. I'd rather hear about you."

Rukh shrugged, careful not to jostle Padma too much. She had her eyes fully closed now. "You know everything that happened to me," Rukh said. "That one big thing—that was it."

She gave the child in his arms a pointed look.

"Oh yes. Nothing else has changed," she said dryly. "Where did you get Padma from?"

"She's mine now," said Rukh. "The yaksa gave her to me."

"What?" Priya sat up properly. "*Gave* her to you?"

"After Bhumika—left," he said haltingly. "One of them said to me—she's yours. Mine, I mean. So I can't give her to anyone else. Not even Khalida, though she's told me how to brush Padma's hair. And Billu makes her food properly for me, all soft so she can eat it."

"Why would the yaksa give her to you?"

"I don't know why they do anything," said Rukh. "Do you?"

She thought back to the Hirana. The things she'd seen there. *I might. I just might.*

"She's sad," Rukh was saying, looking at Priya with careful eyes. "She used to run around everywhere, but I think she's scared. She's all clingy."

"That's no surprise." Not after what Padma had lost. Spirits, she was so *small* still. Priya didn't think she'd ever been as small as Padma was. "Do you have a sling for carrying her?"

Rukh shook his head.

"I'll make you one," she told him. "But for now..." She patted the blanket. "Come lie down next to me. You can keep on holding her if you like. And I'll tell you what it was like, out there in Parijatdvipa. I won't touch her."

"Promise?"

"I promise."

He told her how Ahiranya had been in her absence. About the forest closing in, shutting them off from the world, and the way food and supplies had run ever lower. How pilgrims had come to rely entirely on the yaksa. They'd come at first out of faith, and later they had come for food and healing and hope, which was another kind of faith.

He told her, and then when he started to cry again—silent, tired tears—she told him a little about the war. Just the softest, safest things: about how Saketa looked, the blueness of the sky, the vastness of it. Of the Veri river, and the white horses of the Dwarali riders; of the imperial mahal, and its grand, strange beauty. Tale after carefully woven tale, until finally Rukh stopped asking her questions. His head was tilted forward. He'd fallen asleep.

She looked at his slack face, the lines of green through the skin of his throat, and Padma's closed eyes, their soft breaths mingling together—and felt her resolve solidify.

She couldn't go after Bhumika.

She couldn't have Malini again.

You are nothing, she said to her thoughts of Malini. *You have to be.*

She could protect the people here. She could protect Ahiranya. She could be their voice. Whatever the yaksa had done to Bhumika, Priya was Mani Ara's, and she was too valuable to destroy.

That had to count for something.

She touched one of the leaves that grew profusely from Rukh's head. The lightest touch.

You are nothing, she said again, to the ugly ghost of love still lingering in her own sap-rotten heart.

And this. This is everything.

6

MALINI

Lata had been visibly troubled for days. When she and Malini were crossing the mahal's grounds she finally spoke her mind.

"I think the path of war is unwise," Lata said. Her voice was a whisper, but it was firm.

Malini gestured a hand at the attendants around them. The maids carrying parasols whisked themselves away. The guards, gold-helmed and armed with sabers, bowed their heads and stepped back, leaving Lata and Malini in relative privacy.

Without the shade of parasols, the sun bloomed hot against Malini's shoulders. She met Lata's eyes, squinting against the light.

"Continue," Malini urged.

"Your allies have survived a terrible war. Your victory against Chandra came at a high cost. To you, and to them. To turn your strength on Ahiranya now—to draw your allies into another battle..." Lata shook her head. "You risk their loyalty," she went on. "And you risk the empire's survival."

"What would you have me do instead?"

"Wait," Lata said immediately. "Give them time. Give *yourself* time. We don't truly yet know what threat faces you from Ahiranya. Why not gather your strength and wait for more information?"

"*More* information? Every day I receive new messages telling me the rot is spreading. Every day *you* tell me that the empire will soon be at risk of a famine if the rot eats its way through our crops before harvest. You call war unwise, but how can I risk waiting to learn more?"

Lata lowered her eyes and said, quietly, "No matter what the priests may say, we've seen no yaksa. Will you take your followers to fight ghosts? Trees? What will they say when they reach Ahiranya and meet no enemies? The Ahiranyi have no army."

"No army that we've seen," Malini corrected, but she knew what Lata was saying was true. When Malini had summoned Priya to join her in the fight against Chandra, Priya had come with only the sparsest retinue. Herself. Her friend. A handful of men. Ahiranya was weak in manpower.

But the Ahiranyi—*Priya*—did not need an army to be a formidable foe. Priya had raised a whole river with her hands. She'd cracked and roiled the earth.

Malini had seen the power of a temple elder. She could not even imagine what a yaksa, with greater power still, would be able to do to her people.

"My followers will meet enemies," Malini said with certainty. "Whether we find the yaksa or not...we'll meet *something* at Ahiranya's borders. I am sure of that." An edge of humor touched her voice. "Besides, you would be wise not to underestimate Ahiranya's trees, Lata. They're more effective than many a soldier with a sword."

Lata didn't seem to find that funny. Her mouth was pursed into a worried line.

"If you're wrong..."

"I'm not," Malini said. "Lata, I do not discount your advice. I trust in your guidance. But I cannot avoid this path. I can only seek to prepare for it." She was fairly certain her maids and guards were not close enough to hear. But she still lowered her own voice further. "We have one weapon that may kill the yaksa. Only one." The memory of fire on the battlefield—strange, unnatural fire—lurched through her skull. "If we can raze Ahiranya with flame, there will be no need to prepare for a protracted war. Parijatdvipa will be safe."

Lata raised her head.

"And if the fire is not enough?" Lata asked. There was real fear in her face.

"Then at least we will know," said Malini. "And we will use what time we have to prepare and find another way to win." She filled her voice with steel. "We *will* win, Lata."

After a moment, Lata nodded.

Malini waited. When Lata remained silent, she began walking again. A heartbeat later, she was under the shade of parasols once more. Her guards were walking alongside her, a wall of steel and armor.

She entered the temple.

Her real grief had been folded away. She'd allowed herself tears and trembling weakness on the day of Aditya's funeral, but that was done now. She'd make sure of it.

Every day, she dressed in white: a sari the color of ivory, brocaded in silver-white thread. Her jewels were pale gold, moonstones, and pearls. And every morning, she worshipped as her mother had once taught her to worship, laying garlands at the feet of the statues of the mothers of flame. She prayed with her hands clasped, reciting their names over her prayer stones. Nanvishi, Suhana, Meenakshi, Ahamara. Divyanshi, her own ancestor.

And then—unlike her mother, or any woman who had come before her—she laid garlands at the feet of three new effigies. Two women wrought from silver: Alori and Narina, her heart sisters, the women who had burned at her brother Chandra's orders, burned when Malini had refused to. And finally, the statue of a man.

Aditya.

The first statue wrought of Aditya had been carved from gold. One of the finest artisans in Parijat had presented it to her, drawing back the cloth concealing it with a flourish. It had been hastily but skillfully cast, with her brother's particular strong nose and even, serious brows. Her brother's effigy had been garbed like an imperial crown prince, in a rich tunic that had billowed into flames at his knees. A symbol of his death and his immortality.

The statue had not possessed eyes. Until the eyes were carved in place, it would not become an idol for worship, complete and holy, to be garlanded and wreathed in incense. It was just molded gold.

Malini had looked at its empty, glorious face and hated it with all the spiteful breath within her.

"Melt it down," she'd said.

The man had bowed low to the floor, stammering apologies. He had not meant to offend the empress. The High Priest had asked him specifically to create a likeness of the prince. The High Priest had insisted—

"*Destroy it*," Malini had ordered again. There, before her entire court, trembling upon her throne.

Shaking. Her hands had been shaking. She had laid them on her lap, one over the other, forcing them into stillness. "Melt it down," she'd said again, with a calmness as hard as a blade, a calmness bitter with fury. "And I will select an artisan to remake his likeness."

"Empress," an advisor had begun tentatively. But she had not allowed him to continue.

"He was my brother. He died for the good of my empire. I will see him properly honored."

And mothers help her, she had tried. She truly had.

Instead of gold, the statue that stood before her now was wood, lacquered to a dark sheen. Wood from a monastery garden to the nameless, offered up by his fellow priests. The statues of Alori and Narina stood in a private alcove, veiled in white cloth. But the statue of Aditya stood at the side of the mothers—close in standing to his own ancestor Divyanshi.

The effigy was complete and holy, with her brother's gentle, piercing eyes. His soft, faintly curling hair, pinned back. His brows like her own, and his smiling mouth. She had not allowed this statue of him to be dressed as a crown prince. Instead he was a nameless priest—garbed in folds of cloth, chest bare, palms open.

She kneeled, laying her final garland before the effigy of her brother. She closed her eyes and thought of nothing, and consciously felt nothing—only the cold marble beneath her knees, and the weight of the jewels in her hair. She held her position for a long moment, and then, with a final bow of reverence, stood.

"Empress," Lata murmured behind her, and Malini turned.

Hemanth was waiting for her at the temple entrance. His jaw was tight, his mouth compressed. He bowed deeply to her.

"Empress," he said.

"High Priest," she said, inclining her head mildly in return. She walked toward him, skirts whispering against stone. "Are my advisors waiting?"

"Everything is ready," he said.

"I am honored," she said to him, in a voice that was low and warm, as if she liked him, "to have your guidance in this task."

"It is my honor."

I know how you hate me, she thought, and had to hold back the smile that threatened at her own mouth; that vicious thing, all teeth.

Instead she said, "You may walk with me."

Chandra had carried out his executions on pyres. He had burned women in the mahal's gardens. He had burned them in his own court.

But Malini would not do as he had done.

Her executions would be cleaner.

A training courtyard for the imperial guard had been commandeered, and men had been set at the entrances for privacy. Her generals stood waiting for her, beyond the shade of the veranda reserved for her throne: Lord Khalil of Dwarali, and Lord Prakash of Srugna; Lord Narayan of Saketa and Prince Rao of Alor, who refused to meet her eyes—who stared into the distance with golden sunlight a swathe and a mask across his face.

Hemanth moved to join them, standing in the last dregs of shade thrown by the veranda's columns. He had not asked if he could stand beside her in the shade, and she had not offered.

In the center of the courtyard kneeled ten men. They were all highborn and dressed in their finery: silk turbans pinned with jewels, sashed tunics. They had no weapons at their sides. They had lost that privilege, along with the privilege of a long life. Their hands were bound in chains, each chain looped to the next man's cuffs, to keep them all imprisoned in place.

In her father's day, executions had been a spectacle. There had been a grand execution ground and a mingled common and highborn audience gathered together to watch the parade of traitors and their just deaths: by dozens of arrows, or an elephant's foot to the skull, or the neat cut of a blade to the heart or the throat. Malini had never witnessed those executions. It had never been considered appropriate for a gently raised imperial woman to view such things. But she had asked Aditya once what it was like.

He'd looked pained, a little haunted, but she had pushed him until, reluctantly, he had spoken:

"It was terrible," he'd said. "Terrible, and I was not allowed to look away. I don't understand how people chose to look upon it for sport."

Today, she would not ask her allies to look upon sport, and she would not inflict it on the men who were fated to die.

For her traitors, Malini had ensured privacy and a sharp sword. For herself, Malini had ensured the shaded veranda and the presence of her closest advisors. Raziya and Deepa and Lata stood beside her.

Malini nodded her head.

One of her officials cleared his throat in response and in a clear voice announced the crimes of the kneeling traitors and their fate.

Loyalty to a false emperor. The murder of Parijati women. Refusal to serve the righteous empress, the chosen of the mothers. Treason. Treachery.

There could only be one punishment.

Malini stared, unblinking, as a warrior stepped forward and—without further ceremony—slit the first traitor's throat.

It was meant to be a clean death, but death was never clean, and certainly never bloodless. There was a rasping, wet sound as the saber was drawn across the man's neck. A splatter of blood, as it spurted in gouts from the wound of his throat. His body collapsed with a thud.

The two men kneeling beside him were drenched in his blood, their eyes closed and their faces gray. One leaned forward and heaved against the ground, retching dry. She had not ordered that he be denied food, but perhaps he had denied himself.

Her warrior moved to the next man. Another thud followed. Then the third.

The fourth along was the first to snap. He wrenched forward, heedless of his chains, dragging the other highborn traitors—dead and living—forward with him. "Empress," he called out, his voice wretched. "Empress, please, spare me. Spare us."

The warrior stepped toward him. Malini raised her hand.

The executioner paused.

"Lord Sushant," she said. Her voice was a void—not calm, but serenely empty. "Why do you believe you should be spared?"

"We acted as we thought was right," he stammered out, trembling, blood a slash of color beneath his sweat and tear-damp eyes. "We were trying to be good highborn men. Empress, please—"

"And yet you acted against the will of the mothers, Lord Sushant," Malini cut in. "I am their chosen. Do you deny it?"

"N-no, Empress. No, never."

"My generals and advisors and the warriors who fought on my behalf died because of the false emperor Chandra," Malini said, with that same terrible calm. "They paid with blood and with coin. Many of their kin paid with their lives. Should they suffer without justice?"

"Mercy," he whimpered. "E-Empress, you are not Emperor Chandra. Your brother w-was a monster. I admit I feared to gainsay him. But you, Empress, you must have some compassion—"

"Must I?"

Something in her voice finally quieted him. He gasped wetly, silent now, staring at her.

"I am not either of my brothers," Malini said. "I am what the mothers of flame require me to be. And they do not require the softness of mercy. They do not require compassion. They require a leader who can face the enemy that awaits us, and loyal men to follow her."

"I can be loyal," he said. "I—I—"

"You cannot be trusted, Lord Sushant. This, I assure you, is mercy enough."

She gestured—a twitch of her hand.

The executioner swung his blade, and Sushant was dead.

She left Hemanth to the task of tending to the bodies. She had insisted he do so personally. *Once, you knew these men, as you knew my brother Chandra*, she had told him. *They deserve the honor of your care.*

He had agreed. Face pinched. Knowing, no doubt, how much she wished he could be dead beside them.

But Hemanth had too much sway among the priests of the mothers for her to kill without consequences. He had been High Priest since long before her birth. And of course, he had proven useful to her. He had legitimized her claim, after all; he had kneeled before her and called her empress, condemning Chandra.

The brother he'd loved and served, and burned countless women alive for.

Hate and pragmatism warred in her heart. But pragmatism was stronger, in the end. Better to keep Hemanth alive and under watch where he could be useful to her. Better to make all her would-be enemies into weapons she could wield for her own gain.

Lata walked with her into the mahal's prison cells. They said nothing to each other as they entered dimly lit corridors, but Lata's expression showed visible relief at the welcome coolness and quiet of the prison, where nothing smelled of blood—only damp, and stone.

Prisons were not naturally quiet, but the men housed here had done nothing but pray from the moment they were locked away. They were men used to internal and external discipline. Their shadow-shrouded bodies through their cell bars were all arranged in meditation, spines straight and heads upraised, legs crossed beneath them.

She stopped before one cell. And in the dim shine of filtered sunlight, the soft glow of a single oil lamp, she saw the deep blackness of a warrior priest's eyes; they widened as they met her own.

"Empress," he rasped.

Around her—from the other cells—she heard a rustle of movement. Murmuring voices.

"Priest," she said. And Lata, with a voice sharp as a whip, said, "Bow to your empress."

The man rose from his crouch and bowed. She caught another glimpse of his face as he did so, and his eyes were burning with feeling. Not hatred, exactly—but a directionless fervor, a faith without a path or a leash.

Malini could give him that path, if he allowed it.

"Priest," she said. "Rise."

He did.

"I did not expect to be blessed with the presence of the empress," the man said. His expression was guarded. "I thought for a time you would die without passing judgment on my brothers and me."

Loose lips, made looser by darkness and loneliness and the isolation of four walls. She remained silent, letting him pour out words like blood from a wound.

"Even here, we heard how grievously the Ahiranyi bitch injured you, Empress," he said, his voice a vicious rumble. "The mahal has been under a pall, waiting for two imperial funerals, or three."

"A servant of the yaksa could not kill me," she said coolly. "The mothers intend a higher purpose for me. They always have."

He inclined his head.

"What is your judgment?" he asked. "When will my warrior brothers and I die?"

"You will not die today, or tomorrow," she said. "I have not deemed it your time. Not yet."

She'd spoken of prices that had to be paid, and of justice, when she had condemned Sushant and what remained of Chandra's council to death. As if she could afford to be even-handed. As if she could judge all her enemies equally and kill them with a swift and impersonal blade.

She could not. More than a simple knife to the heart had taught her that.

"Does the empress hope I will beg for my life? I will not. I regret nothing I did," he said, with exhausted defiance.

"I understand," Malini told him. "Certainly, you acted righteously. You believed my brother was meant to rule. You believed it was my fate and my duty to burn. You acted in the service of your faith. How could you do otherwise, when my brother wielded something that appeared to be mothers' fire? I understand, and I cannot fault you," Malini went on gently, even though she felt nothing for him but disgust—a coiling, oily feeling in her chest. "But still, you defied the will of the mothers. You acted in a way that could have condemned all of Parijatdvipa. The yaksa are here. I have heard reports from across the empire of rot worsening. And I, priest—I am the cure."

A dry, bitter sound escaped him. It might have been a laugh.

"Let me die with dignity, Empress," the man said. "I will not beg. But I ask."

"There is no dignity in death," she said bluntly. "Not for you, priest. Nor for your brothers. But there is dignity—and redemption—in using your strength to shape a Parijatdvipa worthy of the mothers of flame. A Parijatdvipa that will survive the yaksa and crush them beneath its great heel, its righteous fire.

"Live," she said. "Vow to serve me, and fight the yaksa on my behalf. Vow it on the death of Prince Aditya," she went on, her voice not even wavering over the candle-flicker of grief that refused to extinguish, that ever burned in her. "Vow it on your faith."

His stare was unwavering.

"We still believe you will burn, Empress," he said. "That you *must* burn. No vow I make upon my faith, no promise of service, will change that truth. If you will not accept it, then let me die. Let us all die, so we will not see Parijatdvipa's end."

"Is it for you to decide when I burn? Arrogance," she snapped. "I am Divyanshi's scion. I am her chosen. It is not for you—or any priest—to decide when I shall die. I will know just as my brother Aditya knew."

Her words were a knife. Now she took away the sharpness and left only the weight.

"I know my worth," she continued, in a low voice that carried across the prison like a deep undertow—a thing with impossible gravity. "I know my fate and the journey that lies ahead of me. You have listened to false men, priest. Now listen to me. Hear me, and serve."

She saw the words land—saw them like a hook in the mouth of a fish, catching him fast.

"Will you serve?" Malini asked again.

His breath shuddered from him.

"Will I be believed, Empress? Would you believe any of us?"

"Yes," she said simply. "I know your nature. I give you this chance not out of mercy but because of one truth: A priest died to save me from the yaksa. Priests of the mothers are my allies by nature, by duty, by fate. I believe in this. So. Will you fight for a glorious Parijatdvipa, where the yaksa lie dead, where we rise—or will you die here, forgotten?"

He said nothing. But the silence from the cells around her was weighty. Thoughtful.

She waited. Her hands ached with the promise of a weapon that was almost hers to use.

"I will allow you all time to consider," she said. "But when I return, I will seek your vow. A blade in your hands, or a blade to the throat." *A blade in my hands, or a blade I must break. That is what you are.* "Tomorrow I will be turning to Ahiranya. And a new war will begin. You may come, and fight. Or not."

She walked away as his mouth parted; walked away knowing what answer she would receive.

"Do you consider this unwise too, Lata?" Malini murmured as they emerged from the darkness.

"I think perhaps this isn't a time for wisdom," Lata said just as quietly. "Perhaps wisdom and war cannot go hand in hand."

Malini laughed, mirthless. "A sage's answer," she said. "I suppose we'll see soon enough."

7

PRIYA

Reshaping the mahal was a good place to begin.

She could break the earth with a casual breath, but carefully bowing trees to carry the weight of a domed ceiling, or closing the fractures in the columns that held up the roof with thick sap and root, was work that required absolute focus. When she wasn't working, her brain was full of Bhumika, and the hungers of the yaksa, and the heartache in her own chest, and all those feelings like rot-riddled roots knotted her up until she couldn't breathe through them. Focusing on the mahal pushed it all away.

Sometimes, after a day spent at work, she felt nothing at all. Just calm so vast it was like the deathless waters, shaping her into something hollow and new. It was bliss.

She soon moved on to the task of shoring up Hiranaprastha's defenses. New traps in the forest. New walls of thorn and root, and new pits of spear-sharp wood to keep enemies at bay. The defenses they would need against Parijatdvipa—against *Malini*—were vast. She knew Malini's stubbornness and cunning.

Her chest ached. She buried the thought of Malini.

She considered asking Ganam or one of the other mask-keepers to help her but soon decided against it. She'd known what once- and twice-born strength was like. It was nothing to her thrice-born power, and even less than nothing, somehow, to the strength Mani Ara had given her.

That strength still wasn't enough.

Mani Ara, she prayed, as she walked barefoot on sun-touched marble, as the leaves and flowers that rose and withered on her skin turned to the light. *Eldest yaksa, if I am your priestess, then speak to me. If I am your priestess, then give me the strength you offered me when I raised a river and murdered an army.*

Give me the strength to destroy my enemies once more. Let me keep Ahiranya safe.

But still, when she reached for Mani Ara, when she prayed, she found nothing. No matter what she did, the results were the same: Her hands and her magic reaching and reaching, straining for a power they couldn't touch.

Kritika wouldn't stop trailing after her.

Through corridors bursting with vines, down a narrow walkway with a living carpet of blue-green flowers that rippled like water, across a hall with columns of ancient trees. The older woman followed Priya through them all with all the bullish determination of a general going to battle against enemy forces.

"There are people who need to speak to you," she was saying. *Again.* "The harvest and grain supplies are things you must care about. You need to take up the burdens of leadership."

Priya wiped a hand across her forehead. It was midday, and the heat was relentless. She couldn't sink into her magic with Kritika prattling at her, and now Priya was sweaty and annoyed, and very ready to be left alone.

"Then help me deal with the harvest. Help me lead. How many times do I have to say it, Kritika? I'm not Bhumika. I need you to do what's needful."

"The yaksa have made you strong enough for the burdens of your position," Kritika said. There was a plaintive edge to her fervent voice, as if she wanted reassurance that Priya had, in fact, been shaped into a perfect leader.

Well. Tough.

That isn't what they've made me for. The thought was a voice flowering up inside Priya's skull. It was barely her own.

"Maybe they made me smart enough to delegate," Priya said dryly.

Kritika muttered something unsavory under her breath in response.

"What did you say?" Priya asked, because she clearly yearned for death.

Instead of replying, Kritika said slowly and firmly, "We mask-keepers can only act and serve Ahiranya if we know the will of the yaksa."

"Then ask the yaksa."

"You are the High Elder!" Kritika snapped. "Only you can speak for them. They are great spirits, Elder Priya—they only ask for worship, they only look through us, as if we are nothing. But you..." Her voice trailed off, choked with feeling.

"I what?" Priya asked.

"They look *at* you," Kritika said after a moment. "They speak to you. So you must lead us. Do you understand?" Her voice shook. "What if we anger them?"

Priya swallowed.

"Tell me what you think must be done, and how it must be done, and I'll...I'll make sure it's the will of the yaksa," she said finally. "And get the highborn here. I know they're hiding scared, but we can use them. They have gold, and food supplies. And soldiers. We'll need those soon enough."

Kritika sucked in a sharp breath. "The highborn are not," she said, "in any position to help Ahiranya."

Priya's own footsteps faltered, her stomach going cold, some instinctual part of her recognizing what that breath—and those words—meant.

"Are they all dead? Or just most of them?"

"No," Kritika said. "They're not dead, Elder. They await your guidance. As the yaksa bade them to."

Still, dread gnawed at her heart, like a canker of larvae in a ripe fruit.

She was silent—for too long, maybe, because Kritika huffed a sigh. "There is so much you're ignorant of," Kritika said.

How could she grow less ignorant if no one would tell her what she didn't know? How could she fix anything if Kritika spent all her time haranguing Priya, rather than helping? Rage swelled in her. It would be easy to make Kritika grovel and beg for forgiveness. She acted like she knew what Priya was, but she didn't, not at all. Priya was Mani Ara's chosen. There was more sap in her than blood, more cruelty than kindness.

It would take nothing to wrap a vine around Kritika's throat and snap her neck clean.

Saliva filled her mouth. The strength of rage left her all at once. She felt sickened by her own thoughts.

"I'm trying," Priya said tiredly. "Believe me, I am."

She couldn't look at Kritika now, but she heard the older woman's low sigh.

"You must rule, girl," said Kritika slowly, her voice finally softening into something real—something that recognized the Priya in front of her, all shattered and stitched-together parts, all bared teeth and grief. There was tiredness in her voice, too. "Whatever you once believed of yourself—there is no one else."

Priya found Ganam. He was leaning over a balcony's edge, staring down at the training grounds, where a handful of soldiers were practicing with hand sickles.

"I hear you're in charge of the guards now that Jeevan is gone," she said, leaning on the edge next to him.

"Hear?" Ganam repeated. "Who did you ask, the trees?"

"People still talk to me," Priya said defensively. "Some of them definitely think I'm a yaksa—"

"I did see Khalida run away from you yesterday," Ganam said agreeably.

"—but others are more sensible," Priya finished. She scowled at him and his mouth quirked up into a smile. "Are you more sensible?"

"You're still Priya," he said. "You're nothing like Elder

Bhumika, but you'll do."

A laugh leapt out of her, ragged at the edges.

"Yes," she said. "I'll have to do, won't I? I need to talk to you about the Parijatdvipan army. Their soldiers are coming for Ahiranya, and we need to be prepared."

He patiently answered her questions about their weaponry and their numbers of guards, the people who'd run from the mahal when Jeevan vanished, and the ones who'd stayed. But there was a faint tension around his mouth that didn't fade when she gave him suggestions on how to defend the city.

"Are my thoughts really that foolish?" Priya asked. "Come on. Be honest."

He shook his head.

"You're no expert, but you do well enough," he said. A pause. "Kritika trusts the yaksa. And most mask-keepers feel the same. But I... when I think of war..." He trailed off. Then, in a flat voice, he said, "I do what's needful. But it strikes me that the yaksa can defend Ahiranya without us. They've already turned our trees into a cage. What are we needed for? They're gods. We're just flesh."

"No," Priya said, shaking her head. "They need us."

They would not have tended to and tortured Priya beneath the Hirana if she weren't vital to them. But it was more than just her. They needed Ahiranya. They needed the rot-riven, the once-born, they *needed*...

She was on the edge of some kind of vast knowledge, a heavy thing she couldn't quite face or touch. Every time she reached for it, that truth eluded her.

She wished Bhumika were here. Bhumika would have been able to grasp it.

"It's the will of the yaksa that we be ready to fight," Priya said instead. "Will you help me?"

"Of course I will," he said. "You're the High Elder."

Below them, the guards were putting away their weapons. She could hear their voices rising and falling, though she couldn't make out the words. They vanished into one of the entrances to the mahal.

Ganam leaned back and cleared his throat.

"I have something for you," he said. "From Elder Bhumika. She left it for you."

He reached into his tunic and drew out a folded paper. Priya took it from him and unfolded it.

She recognized Bhumika's handwriting immediately.

The letter trembled in Priya's hand. It took her a moment to realize that it was her hand that was shaking, not the paper.

"Where did you find this?" Priya asked in a whisper.

"In her study," Ganam said. "I broke the door. I made a guess that if you came back, you'd want it. And if you didn't..." His hand flexed at his side; a spasm of feeling. "Maybe one day Padma would," he added, voice low. "That's what I thought."

"Have you read it?"

"Yes."

"That's—fine."

Priya couldn't read it. The words were swimming before her eyes.

"Maybe you should go somewhere quiet," he said, looking carefully away from her. Letting her rub a furious hand against her own cheeks, wiping unwanted tears away.

"Right," she said thinly. "Maybe I should."

She went to the only place she could think of going.

Bhumika's old chambers had once been called the rose palace. Now they looked more like a ruin than any other part of the mahal. An impressive feat. Cracks in the ceiling let the light pour through. She could hear birds trilling, rustling where they were nested in the hollows left by fallen and fissured stone.

There, in the song and hush and decay of Bhumika's chambers, Priya finally read the letter.

Priya—

—perhaps you're dead and gone—
  —I know that if you are alive—

The stone beneath Priya's feet began to splinter. Hairline fractures. Her vision was wet, wavering again.

I hope you can forgive me for leaving you behind.

The sister she'd known would never have run from Ahiranya. Never would have left her own child behind. And Priya wanted to believe Bhumika had done it with good reason. But all the faith in her had been twisted out of shape. Priya wasn't the same woman she'd once been—the woman who believed she could cure the rot, and help Ahiranya have a future, and maybe even have one herself.

Priya had set aside hope. Or thought she had.

But she must have kept hope alive somewhere deep within, because her body felt heavy and her heart ached. And she was swaying, leaning into the wall face-first, and pressing her face into the crook of her arm, and her own teeth into her skin, and she was screaming, screaming, muffling the sound as best she could.

She didn't know how long she cried. But the sun moved, the shadows shifting across the floor until she was in a pure spill of hot sunshine. She breathed in and out, and wiped her face again with her hand, for what good it would do. She was sore-headed from weeping, and tired, and angry with herself and the foolish softness of her own heart.

No more, she thought. And resolution settled, cold and steady in her bones. She had told herself she had to protect her people. Protect whatever Ahiranya was now, for the sake of those who lived inside it. That hadn't changed. She had to be pragmatic.

Had to think of Padma and Rukh, and hold that like a shining thread—a golden thing, stronger and braver than mere hope.

Maybe breaking and weeping should have felled her like a great tree. Stopped her from going on. But that was not the way Priya was. She'd never been able to stop. She straightened up instead, the vines haloing the walls of Bhumika's chambers uncoiling and knotting around her, like tangles of grief-rended hair. She sucked in a breath through gritted teeth, then turned on her heel and walked away from the chambers.

She went in search of a yaksa.

She went to the closest yaksa. She could feel them—deep in the orchard, a presence like a pulse, like a call.

The orchard was utterly changed. The old fruit trees were rich with rot. But there were new trees, too—glowing with life, blood running through their roots. And seated between the trees, legs folded, ankles buried in soil—

"Yaksa," she said. Bowed her head, and raised it. "I need to speak with you."

The yaksa who wore Sanjana's face looked up from where she'd been contemplating the ground—sleeping, or dreaming, or communing. Priya didn't know.

"I thought you would go to your brother," the yaksa said, and her voice was a lush thing, all susurrating leaves, damp from a storm.

Not my brother, Priya thought. And that was exactly why she had not gone to him. If she had to choose a wound to pick at, an old one was preferable. Her grief for Sanjana was as far off as her childhood. The loss of Ashok was still fresh and bloody, too painful to touch. She didn't want to face the yaksa wearing his skin. Not now.

"Yaksa," she said. "To face Parijatdvipa, I'm going to need to be stronger. You...beneath the Hirana. You all asked me to yield. You meant to Mani Ara. That is how I'll get power, isn't it? Power to fight Parijatdvipa. To save it."

The yaksa slowly inclined her head.

"But I can't reach Mani Ara," Priya said. "Yaksa, please. Help me."

"You're not really trying."

"I am."

"I have seen into your soul," the yaksa said, as dappled light reshaped the contours of her face—shifting it into softer and harsher edges as she rose and walked toward Priya, as she looked at Priya, her eyes all shadow. If she'd been human, Priya would have called the look on her face *disdain*. "I have seen your nature flayed open. I know all that you are." Her mouth widened. Not quite a smile. Something with too many teeth. "And still I don't know why Mani Ara chose you," she went on, viperously soft. "I do not know why I have to teach you this lesson, and why you ask me foolish questions when the answer is clear: *Try harder.*"

Sanjana began to glide past her.

"Mani Ara won't answer me," Priya said quietly. "I think...I think she's choosing not to."

The yaksa stopped, and with her the trees seemed to still; their leaves were frozen, alien to the breeze trying to draw them into movement. So Priya pressed on.

"I called to her when I walked across Parijatdvipa. When I walked—here. Home. And she didn't answer. I looked for her in the sangam, when you all tested me and asked me for my loyalty, and she wasn't there."

The yaksa's head turned with a click. Facing her.

If Priya hadn't known better, she would have thought that was fear flitting across the yaksa's face. But there was nothing fearful or animal in it, a heartbeat later. Only a smile, curving that mouth. Amused.

"Do you think the greatest of us obeys your whims?"

"No," Priya said. "I don't."

"Give her prayer. Give her offerings. Give her yourself, wholeheartedly. And then perhaps she will answer you. But for now..." A rustling sigh. "You can feel all of Ahiranya, can't you?"

Priya nodded silently.

"You are Mani Ara's creature," the yaksa continued. "More than a mere mortal. More even than a temple daughter. Wherever the rot spreads, our magic spreads. Where it goes, the soil and the trees change to welcome us. Where Mani Ara can go, *you* can go. Because you are more than any elder before you—not because you are deserving, but because you are chosen." The yaksa's breath, the fragrance of rainfall and loam, touched her cheek. Then the yaksa released her. "Reach. Look."

Priya squeezed her eyes shut. She stretched her senses, feeling all of Ahiranya laid out around her. Feeling beyond it. Reaching, reaching—

She winced. Pain shot through her skull.

The yaksa tutted.

"Perhaps this will help," she said. "Turn your head. Open your eyes."

Like an obedient puppet, Priya did.

Behind her, in a newly raised bed of vines, lay an offering.

She walked toward it and kneeled down, green crunching beneath her knees.

It was a mask. Beautifully wrought, its wood polished and dark, emanating heat.

The crown mask.

She touched her fingertips to it and felt a small shiver of power rush through her. Before she'd become thrice-born—before she'd traveled three times through the deathless waters and risked death with each immersion—touching the mask would have peeled the flesh from her bones.

She placed all her fingertips to it. Five points. Then she clasped it and raised it up. Beneath it, the vines that had held it were withered and strange.

This mask had belonged to Bhumika. Because Bhumika had been the High Elder.

But Bhumika was gone. And there was no one left but Priya. Kritika had been right about that.

"Keep your spirit open," the yaksa said. "Be watchful. And see what Mani Ara's strength can do."

"Thank you, yaksa," Priya said. "I'm grateful."

"It's meant for a High Elder," Sanjana said lightly. "You should have asked for it long ago."

As Priya looked at the mask—as she felt its power—she thought of what Ganam had said. That the yaksa should have been powerful enough to fight alone.

She thought of fire, and the fury in Malini's eyes, when Priya had stabbed her through.

"Yaksa," Priya said carefully. "I—"

"Speak."

"Even with Mani Ara's power..." She turned the mask over in her hands again. "The Parijatdvipans will have fire. Mothers' fire, or something akin to it."

She believed—hoped—Malini would not willingly burn. She was less sure Malini would not burn others as her brother had.

A laugh left Sanjana. A high, thin reed of noise.

"They have the promise of fire. But *we* already have the rot. We have already seeded ourselves in the worlds: in their flesh, their fields. Do you understand? Of course you do not." The trees seemed to laugh with her, seemed to creak and shudder. "To destroy us they must burn everything they need to live. They must burn their own kind. The world is almost ours. They simply do not know it yet."

Almost. The word rattled through her.

"I understand," Priya said. "Thank you, yaksa."

Another of those strange, sharp laughs. And Sanjana was gone.

Almost.

Somehow it rested on Priya. Well. There was no point waiting any longer.

Priya pressed the mask to her face and felt the power of it fill her to the brim.

8

SANVI

The priest wasn't the one who found her. There were fools who liked to think that holy priests of the mothers plucked girls from their beds and roped them to pyres, but Sanvi had been brought up better than that. The priest had not tricked her, nor had he sought her out; she had gone to him.

She found him at her neighborhood shrine, a small alcove that served multiple households. The statues of the mothers within it were modest—gold only at their eyes—but they were surrounded by candles and garlands. The people of Harsinghar, the city that Divyanshi's scions had built, loved the mothers.

Sanvi kneeled beside him. In the candlelight, her shadow eclipsed his. He was a small man—narrow-shouldered, slender— and she was a broad and tall woman who'd learned to wield a saber at age ten, when she had followed her mother into service in a high-born household with the wealth to properly protect its women.

"I have heard, priest, that you are from a holy temple far from the city," said Sanvi, watching him from under her lashes as he worshipped. "That you came here to serve under the High Priest. I hear you *choose* to pray in a small temple. That you seek out girls of faith who'd like a place in the empress's mahal."

A pause. "You hear a great deal," he said.

"Women talk, priest. You're lucky no spy of the empress has heard you seek out women who respect the pyre."

His shoulders were stiff, wary. But he remained where he kneeled, incense wreathing his face.

"Do you respect the pyre, little sister?"

She settled more comfortably on her knees.

"When Emperor Chandra burned holy women, the lady I serve and guard wept and hid in her manse," Sanvi said. "But I celebrated. I read the Book of Mothers, and I was glad for those girls. They're immortal now. With the mothers. What greater joy is there?

"I'm no highborn lady," she continued. "I'm not fit for burning, for that kind of purity. But I'm faithful. I believe."

"And what do you seek from me?" the priest asked.

"I am a guardswoman from Lady Gul's household," Sanvi said. "She is a widow, and loyal to the empress. My lady was approached by the head of the empress's personal guard. They're seeking women capable of protecting the empress. I volunteered myself."

"Is that so," he murmured. His gaze met her own. His eyes were pale, beautiful. "I do not believe the empress will allow herself to be guarded by a woman of true faith, I am afraid."

"Is that why you only seek maidservants? Women you think she won't notice? You need not fear, priest. I don't prattle about my faith. No one knows my heart but me. And now, you." She leaned forward, placing a coin on the shrine to the mothers. "If I can serve the mothers of flame," she said. "If I can serve the empire, I'd like to do so. I want my life to have purpose. I want to die for something that matters. I think I'm what you seek." She leaned back. "Maybe the mothers sent me to you. I hope so."

He said nothing, so Sanvi stood and choked back disappointment.

"I'll return tomorrow evening," she said. "If the mothers have a purpose for me, I hope you'll meet me here."

She returned the next eve, her heart in her throat. She walked up the small shrine's stairs, which were bluish in the fading light. Inside, the light of the candles glowed luminously on the shrine and shone in the eyes of the mothers.

And there, before the mothers, stood her priest. Waiting for her. Her heart soared.

"I am Mitul," he said. "Little sister, servant of the mothers: What must I call you?"

"Sanvi," she said. "What do the mothers need of me, priest?"

MALINI

On the day she left Harsinghar, Malini finally visited her sister-in-law.

The High Priest had blessed her that dawn for battle, garlanding her as priests sang prayers for her. *Victory for Parijatdvipa; the favor of the mothers for their empire; victory for the empress of flame.* She still wore the garland of fresh jasmine at her throat. She had to play at piety, so the garland would remain around her neck until dusk fell.

The corridor leading to Varsha's chambers was deathly silent. Malini could hear the rustle of the flowers at her throat. Even her own breath seemed as noisy as a drumbeat. She was not nervous, she reminded herself. There was nothing to be nervous of.

She had all the power here.

Guards opened the doors, announcing Malini's arrival. No voice greeted her from within. But she was empress, and this was her mahal. It was her right to enter, so she did.

Varsha's rooms were not a prison. They were the same chambers that had been granted to her when she had wed Chandra: wide, expansive rooms with warm ivory-tiled floors and silk-knot rugs, basins of water to cool the air, and curtains of gauze studded with embroidered flowers. They were comfortable chambers, well-suited to the wife of an emperor. But now that Chandra was dead and disgraced, the walls of her chambers had become a shroud.

Varsha had refused to attend both Chandra's ignoble funeral, and Aditya's grander one. Her maidservants—who reported directly to Deepa and Lata—claimed she did not even explore the garden that had been granted to her for her private use.

She's quiet, apparently, Lata had told her. *Deep in her grief. She barely speaks to anyone. They worry about her. She won't cause trouble.*

But she did not have to try to cause trouble. She carried trouble—and possibility—within her.

Varsha was dressed in clothes as blindingly white as Malini's, as was appropriate and expected for a recent widow. Even though Malini had been announced, Varsha had not risen to bow to her. She was seated, watching the birds outside the window. She had shredded a little of her roti and scattered it on the ledge, drawing the birds in, and was watching as their small bodies flitted back and forth, pecking through the lattice for bread, their shadows flickering against the stone like lamplight in a breeze. Her hair was in a long, loose braid, visible beneath her gauzy white dupatta.

"Sister," Malini said, and watched as Varsha turned her head and made a desultory effort to rise to her feet. "There's no need. Sit."

"Thank you, Empress," Varsha said thinly, settling back.

The swell of her belly was very visible, now.

Chandra's child. An heir, perhaps, for the empire.

An opportunity. Or a threat.

"You must forgive me for disturbing your mourning," Malini said, sweeping closer to her. She did not attempt to sit across from Varsha. She stood, instead. Hands clasped neatly behind her, her back straight. "I will be leaving for battle in Ahiranya."

A beat of silence.

Malini did not know how much Varsha knew of the political sea changes that had roiled over Parijatdvipa. She would have told Varsha, if Varsha had asked.

"I pray you will be well," Varsha said instead.

"The High Priest and I prayed this morning," said Malini. "He and I made offerings to the mothers of flame. We asked for them to guide me in the coming war. I feel them close to me. I know I will return safely."

How practiced she had become at telling lies about her own faith and the fervor in her own heart. She spoke the words without guilt—with utter conviction—and watched Varsha's face carefully as she did so.

"I am glad, Empress," Varsha said, her voice small but steady. Her eyes were lowered. She had her hands clasped over the swell of her belly—not exactly protectively, but as if she could create a circle with her hands and her body that was inviolate, a line that Malini could not cross.

Malini did not want Varsha to fear or hate her.

There were things she could do, perhaps, to win Varsha's trust and even her friendship. But the thought of doing them made bitterness coat her tongue. She knew what it was like to be imprisoned. She knew the dignity of anger.

And worse still, Varsha was right to fear her. Malini knew what she was capable of.

"I've arranged a female physician for you," she said. "Midwives, also. No matter how long this campaign may last, no matter how long I am away—you will be protected." She softened her voice. "There are women," she said, "who would counsel and comfort you if you allowed it. Many have joined my court in the last weeks. Not all of them will travel to war with me. Seek them out."

If you will not talk to me honestly, talk to them.

Perhaps Varsha understood.

"You are kind, Empress," she replied, bowing her head. "I am sorry to trouble you so."

"It's no trouble," Malini said softly. "We are kin. Your child will be my heir."

Varsha's gaze flickered. Perhaps she had not realized.

You're safe now, Malini thought of saying. In another time, another life, they would have been truly akin to sisters to one another—bound into family by marriage. But Malini stood beyond that now. Empresshood had made something new of her, and widowhood had done the same to Varsha. They were strangers to one another, at best.

But Varsha had spared Malini from the task of ensuring that Parijatdvipa would have an heir. The very thought of begetting a child made Malini's skin hot and cold all at once with horror. She could not, would not, say so. Not to a woman she did not trust, with the eyes and ears of maids and guards on them both. But she could give Varsha some small assurance of safety and power.

"This is not my brother Chandra's court any longer," said Malini. "This is mine. Things will not be as they were."

A heartbeat of time passed, and another, and Varsha exhaled a shaky breath that sounded like a sob.

"Thank you," Varsha said. "Thank you, Empress. Sister." She looked away, as if overwhelmed or abashed, turning back to the lattice.

Malini waited a long moment. But there were no more words from Varsha.

She nodded in farewell and departed, leaving nothing but Varsha's silence and the faint rustle of hungry songbirds behind her.

Her retinue was ready to depart.

The war against Chandra had been only recently won, and she could see the lingering scars in the absences in her army: the Saketan warriors lost at the Veri river. The Dwarali cavalry that died in fire at the walls of Harsinghar, before the imperial mahal fell finally into Malini's hands. Hundreds of men, dead or wounded. There should have been a respite from war, now that she had her throne.

Still, her army was a formidable force.

If only we were facing an army of men, instead of myths and ghosts and monsters, Malini thought, bitter amusement coursing through her.

She went to her chariot, surrounded by the wall of guards that accompanied her everywhere now, with Sahar at the lead. Sahar had been the head of Lady Raziya's guard, but Raziya had insisted on placing her in Malini's service when Malini had been recovering from her knife wound. "She will protect you as I would, if I had half her arm strength or skill with killing," Raziya had said, eyes gleaming with tears, a smile on her mouth as she'd sat at Malini's bedside and clutched Malini's hand in her own. "Please. Take her."

Malini was glad of Sahar's steady presence at her side. Sahar barked orders, forcing back the warriors and highborn thronged near her chariot, until Malini was nearly alone.

Nearly.

Hemanth waited by her chariot. He no longer wore the benevolent, calm-eyed look he'd worn at the dawn blessing. His face was hard, his chin raised. His hands were clasped around a black chest.

"Empress," he greeted her, bowing his head. His eyes never left her own. "A cart has been packed with all the fire that remains." He held the box forward, like an offering.

"Thank you, High Priest," Malini replied, offering him a smile. She took the box from his hands. The surface was warm under her palms.

His unsmiling face said, *This fire will not win your war. You fool.*

"You have released the imprisoned priests," he said. "You take them with you to war."

His words were not questions, but Malini nodded regardless.

"The priests erred, but I know the priesthood are my natural allies," Malini replied. "We all love the mothers, after all. I must trust in their wisdom."

If anything, his jaw grew tighter.

Malini climbed into her chariot. Sahar, acting as her temporary charioteer, took the reins of the horse and led them away from Hemanth and into the heart of Malini's army.

The beast of her army lumbered along, across the rot-scarred expanse of Parijat.

Lady Raziya and Lata both shared her chariot with her.

Her generals rode alongside on horseback or in chariots, at their own preference. Lord Prakash from Srugna and Lord Narayan of Saketa largely remained seated under the cover of canopies, jolting with the movement of their chariots' wheels as they sweated in the heat. Lord Khalil preferred to ride.

Rao was unpredictable. Uncharitably, Malini thought it depended on how much he'd drunk the night before, and *that* seemed as changeable as the wind.

On a horseback day, he drew his mount within shouting distance of her chariot, signaling at her and calling out over the clatter of horses' hooves and churning wheels, "If we need to travel faster—we can exchange horses at a coming estate of a lord—"

"No need," Malini interrupted, calling back. "We are not racing to Ahiranya."

There was a rustle of attention from her generals: a turning of heads, a hunching of shoulders.

She knew that her generals, like Lata, believed she was rushing headlong into combat without enough preparation. That this was reckless. But she had meant what she said to Lata: The fire was the only weapon she knew could work against the magic of Ahiranya.

The fire had burned Priya when she had stabbed Malini. Malini still remembered the smell of flesh viscerally—the sight of Priya's face, traitorous and loved. The pain in it.

"There are other warriors joining us for battle," she continued. "We must give them time to do so."

Rao's mouth had thinned. He nodded, and with a respectful murmur of her title, he rode away from her toward the blue horizon ahead of them.

His physical distance gave her an odd pang.

She had not allowed herself to see clearly how their shared grief had carved them into different shapes and cleaved them from one another. He had sat by her bedside as she'd healed, had wept with her, the scent of liquor on his skin and hair, his mouth an ugly twist of grief. But they'd exchanged no words that mattered, no words of real mourning or blame, and the liquor had stayed as the closeness vanished. Now it seemed they had no words of any worth left at all.

The dust was rising in a cloud around her army—churned from gray to gold as it ate sunlight on its rise toward the sky. Malini watched him vanish into it.

Four nights on the road, she dreamt of Priya. She dreamt of Priya standing in the court of the imperial mahal; dreamt firelight casting flowers on her face, her throat. Dreamt the fire dripping like gold, hollowing Priya's throat like a gourd as she wept and wept. *I had no choice, Malini. Malini, I'm sorry, I had no choice—*

Her chest ached as if the knife were burrowing into it all over again. As if the knife had left something there, seeded something.

Priya was in her head. In her wound. She could not seek help. She could not speak of it. But in Ahiranya, by the mothers—and by her own fucking fury—Malini would learn the truth.

On the fifth night she paced her tent until the entire camp was still, hushed with deep nighttime silence. She paced until she heard the noise of soldiers rising to swap shifts on watch, and the air was filled with low, muted voices and the thud of boots. When she slept, it was when pure exhaustion forcibly dragged her under, down to somewhere black and blessedly dreamless.

If Priya followed her there, she did not feel it.

The soldiers she was waiting for met her two weeks into the journey, on a sun-blasted road leading like an arrow to Ahiranya. One of her own warriors announced them—not by sounding his conch, which would have alerted her forces to danger, but by crying out, a high piercing cry that carried across the slow procession of cavalry.

"*Parijati ahead!*"

"Send a rider and archers," Khalil commanded. "Then report."

"My lord," one of the Dwarali soldiers replied. He bowed his head, then rode off swiftly.

Malini did not have to wait long in her chariot before the news arrived: The soldiers ahead of them were indeed Parijati. They were the men she had been waiting for. Gladness rushed through her.

"So Lord Mahesh finally joins us," she murmured. She turned to Rao. "Are we due to make camp?"

"Before nightfall," he said. "We could travel for a few hours more, if you order it."

She was tempted. Only reaching Ahiranya would put an end to the nightmares plaguing her. But there were shadows under Rao's eyes, and even Lord Khalil looked exhausted where he sat on his mount. "Send out the order," she said. "We rest until dawn. And have Lord Mahesh brought to me."

Her tent was swiftly erected but still in partial disarray when she entered. Her maid Swati hastily lit a set of lamps. Guardswomen arranged themselves discreetly around the edges of the room, half concealed in shadow.

And Malini stood, hands clasped before her, and waited as the tent flap was raised and Lord Mahesh's name was announced.

He entered and immediately bowed low to the floor. His armor was stained with dust from the road; his bared neck and his hands were dark from the sun and ruddy from exposure to wind and sand.

"Stand," she told him. And he did so, meeting her eyes briefly before lowering them again.

"Empress," he said. "You summoned me."

"I thought you would join us sooner," she remarked.

"There were—problems—upon the road here, Empress," he said. "I apologize."

"The High Prince's fort is safely in Saketan hands?"

"Yes," he said, his voice heavy. "My work in Saketa is done. But I will serve you however you require of me, Empress."

After the end of the war for Malini's throne, Mahesh had returned to Saketa to hold the deceased High Prince's fort on her behalf. She had sent him there, unwilling to keep a highborn who had betrayed her at her side. But he had gone willingly enough and had, she had heard, raised a shrine there to the memory of Aditya.

He'd been there when Aditya had burned. Had watched him die; had watched him, and made vows to him.

I intend to keep my vow, Empress, Mahesh had written to her. Lata had read the letter to Malini—her own eyes narrowed, critical and thoughtful, as she repeated, *I swear it, upon my faith.*

That was why—despite the low, thrumming dislike she felt for him—she could not end his life. He and the soldiers who had watched Aditya die had willingly and fervently spread the tale of her brother's death, and of the promise Aditya had exacted.

Prince Aditya died for Parijatdvipa. And as he died, we vowed to him we would serve Empress Malini, the true heir to Parijatdvipa.

So we vowed. And so all loyal Parijatdvipans should vow.

Malini did not discard useful things. She did not have to *like* him to make use of him again. The myth that had grown around her—this unbreakable myth, with its own breath and its own lungs—had begun with him. Better he lived to share it than die for her own petty satisfaction.

But still. Still.

"You vowed to serve me once, Lord Mahesh," Malini said. "You vowed it when Prince Rao kneeled down and named me— and revealed to me my destiny. And still, eventually you turned from me. You were not the general my army needed, and not the loyal general *I* needed. How can I be sure anything has truly changed?"

"Prince Aditya," he said simply. His eyes were clear, his gaze straightforward. "I may be honest now, Empress, as I could not have been in that time of war. I wished for Prince Aditya to take the throne. I wished to serve him."

"And now?" Malini prompted.

"Now I understand the truth. I see now what I did not then: that the mothers led my heart to Prince Aditya because they wished for me to witness his rise to immortality and carry his message with me. My betrayal was never true betrayal," he told her, fervent, earnest. "It led me to fight at his side. It led me to witness his death. It led me to a true and deep and unshakable vow. I love him, Empress, as I love the mothers. And for that son of flame, I will serve you to my death, and beyond it."

Son of flame. She had heard the term before, but it struck as it always did—a lash to the heart that made her want to *howl.* And perhaps she did not hide her feelings as well as she should have, because Mahesh reached for the saber at his waist—and as the guards in the shadows reared forward, he removed it and laid it on the ground before him. And kneeled once more.

The guards melted back at Malini's sharp look.

"Lord Mahesh," she said. "What are you doing?"

"Empress, if you wish me to die for my actions against you— my life is yours to take." He lowered his head, a conscious baring of his neck. He held his hands open at his sides, not touching the saber on the ground before him. It was a gesture of pure vulnerability. "Not all crimes are forgivable. I understand the weight of the duties upon your shoulders. Do as you must."

She stepped forward and leaned down to lift the saber. It was not like her narrow blade, honed to fit her hands and her strength. It was heavy and brutal, oiled to sharpness. With a sharp breath, she raised it—and offered it to him.

"I will not give you your family holdings or your old honor," she told him levelly, as he carefully took the blade from her hands. "Those your daughter Lady Deepa earned with her bravery and unfailing loyalty. But I can provide you another future: of war and of service. And if you serve me wholeheartedly, I can promise that you shall be remembered as one of the great men who severed the bloom of a new Age of Flowers in its infancy."

"Empress," he said, reverent and low. "Tell me what I must do."

"Lord Mahesh isn't wasting his time," Lata observed, when she joined Malini outdoors some hours later. The dusk was casting bloody gold light across the makeshift training ground between the tents. Malini stood without a parasol to cover her and watched the men train.

"He wants to demonstrate his eagerness," Malini said. She held a hand against her forehead, shading her eyes, as she watched Mahesh heft up his saber again, barking orders. In front of him the priestly warriors moved into formation as ordered—their faces carved into grim lines by the fading light, their eyes black and fervent.

"Lady Deepa..."

"Will not have to part with what she has rightly earned," Malini replied, when it became clear Lata would not say more, was hesitating over her words. "But it's sweet that you care about her well-being."

"We've been working closely together these past few months," Lata said. "Of course I care."

There was a thud as a man was shoved to the ground. He spat dirt, then rose back up, his gaze fixed on Mahesh.

"You've placed two sets of traitors together," Lata went on. But she didn't sound accusatory. She sounded thoughtful.

"Lord Mahesh's desires make him loyal."

"Do they?"

"What Lord Mahesh wants is to be remembered as a great and loyal servant of the mothers," Malini said softly, after a moment. "Not riches. Not a title. He will train these men, and fight the yaksa for me, and his name will be revered."

"And—the priests?" Lata's tone was skeptical. She'd made no secret of her feelings about the priestly warriors.

"Ah. They want to kill for their faith," Malini said. "And die for it. I can give them that. And if they turn on me, Mahesh and his men will deal with them. There's no trust there. I warned Lord Mahesh of their nature. He'll see them dead before they harm me."

All these traitors—these men who had chosen her brothers over her, time and time again—would serve her now. There should have been joy in that—that utter victory. But the satisfaction was muted. Her heart was steel and cold. She watched a moment longer, then turned on her heel, returning to her tent. The only thing that made her heart kindle with something like feeling waited for her there.

A black stone box was set at her bedside. A guard was on watch beside it. She departed at Malini's word.

Malini placed her hand on the box's stone surface.

One box of fire. One for her; a dozen for her army. What a paltry number. That was all that remained, from the hundreds if not thousands of women who had died on Chandra's pyres.

Soon she would see Ahiranya. She would set her army against its woods. Let them hack the trees, if nothing else. There'd be absurd satisfaction in that.

If she could, she would gut Ahiranya. She would kill Priya herself.

And if she could not...at least she could test the last of the fire she had. Women had burned unwilling for this at Chandra's hands. She'd find out if it had any use. Whatever she could destroy, she would. She *would*.

With a deep, steadying breath, Malini unlatched the lid.

10

PRIYA

Dawn light was threatening beyond the lattice windows. Khalida hovered as Priya dressed and hastily knotted her hair into a low bun. "Let the children keep on resting," Priya murmured to Khalida's anxious face. "They don't need to see what's coming."

Khalida's eyes darted to Rukh and Padma.

"They'll wake when they hear the noise," Khalida replied. As if in response, there was a rhythmic thud of a dozen footsteps outside. The noise swelled, then vanished.

Priya shook her head.

"Don't worry about that."

They wouldn't wake. All three of them had slept badly. Rukh and Padma often shared a bed with her now, the two of them curled up together like kittens. Rukh was still adamant that only he could care for Padma—but when Padma had woken earlier that night, crying and fractious as she so often was in the darkest hours, he hadn't fought too hard when Priya pressed a hand to his hair and hushed him. "I'll get her back to sleep," Priya had said. And he'd protested once, only once, then fallen into a dead slumber.

There were deep shadows under his eyes. He was too young for the burden he carried.

Priya had told Padma a nonsense story to soothe her—something about birds wearing boots. Padma was too young to give a shit if the story didn't make sense, surely? Priya had hoped so.

When that had failed, Priya had distracted Padma by growing flowers on her own palms and letting Padma examine them, her clumsy little fingers seeking the shape of petal and root. Padma had frowned seriously over them, comically studious under her mop of sleep-mussed curls. Then she'd started ripping them up, stubbornly pressing what was left into pulp.

"Destructive," Priya had murmured fondly, and felt an echo of Bhumika's love for her child in her own voice.

The wave of grief that had crashed over Priya had kept her awake long after Padma had fallen back to sleep on her lap.

The Parijatdvipans were coming. And for all that she and Ganam had built patrols and rationed out weapons, drained the mahal's stores for anything with a sharp end and anything that could be thrown, Ahiranya was not prepared for the might of an empire.

They needed power only Mani Ara could give them.

The thought of fire and arrows touching her people made her sick.

She plucked the crown mask from the high shelf where she'd concealed it.

"If any of the fighters come looking for me, tell them to go to Ganam or Kritika," said Priya, as waves of the mask's power lapped at her fingertips. "I need to go to the Hirana."

While the stone of the Hirana yawned open at her bidding, Priya put on the crown mask. She stretched her awareness into the green, feeling every inch of her home: each root and swaying branch, the worming and scuttle of insects under the dirt, steadily churning it into new shapes.

The deathless waters lay ahead of her. Priya stepped onto her own dark road and walked toward them.

On the soft soil that edged the deathless waters, Priya kneeled and prayed. She did so silently, hands clasped. Breathing slowly, she sank into the sangam in her mind. She reached through rivers of green and red gold for Mani Ara, always for Mani Ara.

She didn't know how long she remained there.

Pain rustled through her skin. She bit her own tongue reflexively at the sharpness of it—the way it erupted over her in a wave, radiating from her skull outward.

She wrenched the crown mask from her face and watched a spill of flowers tumble to the floor. She touched her face and felt new blooms threatening to rise under her skin.

Shit.

What did she look like? She didn't know anymore. Oh, she'd seen the horror in people's faces, and the awe too. And she'd been able to ignore it all, more or less, until now. But if she was growing stranger still . . .

It was a foolish impulse, but she didn't resist it; she knee-walked to the edge of the deathless waters and peered in.

The water shone blue. It shouldn't have reflected her like a mirror, but when she pressed her hands into the glowing surface, it stilled and dimmed, rippling into a sheet of silver.

Priya met her reflection's eyes.

She wasn't vain. She never had been. She knew her nose was crooked, and her face unremarkable—that she was small and strong and not particularly pretty. But she'd never needed or wanted to be pretty. She'd been comfortable in her own skin.

She thought she had accepted how changed she was. After she had—after *Malini*—she had walked home to Ahiranya with flowers growing at her feet and sap bleeding from her skin, and shed petals from her hair. But the woman she saw in front of her . . .

She did not have rot. That was clear. There was something cruel and twisted about the rot. What had become of her looked—natural. Like it belonged.

Her hair was still straight, but there were strands of dark leaves twined through it. Her eyes were still her eyes, but flecked in the whites with green—shards like algae blooms that dissipated when she blinked hard, then returned again.

On her face, at the places where bone sat closest to skin, lay a thin tracery of flowers—small blooms in pale rose and deep red alike. They shifted when she tensed her jaw, withering and then bursting into richer life when she forced herself to smile.

She looked almost like one of the yaksa. Almost.

She touched her fingertips to the side of her neck. The burn mark there was still a livid, bright slash of color against her dark brown skin. Perhaps her skin gleamed like bark or earth, and maybe her mouth was the deep color of a bruised flower, but that scar was all flesh, and all human.

She'd dreamt, a few times, of what it had been like when Malini had burned her. The scrabble of desperate hands. The pain, and the smell of her own flesh. Now when she touched the scar she felt nothing. The skin was nerveless.

Her reflection blinked away marigold petals, golden tears. But Priya's own eyes were dry. She touched fingers to her cheek and felt nothing.

Sapling, her reflection mouthed.

Priya took a deep breath and put the crown mask of sacred wood on her face, blotting her skin out once more.

Yaksa, she said in return.

Mani Ara.

Priya emerged from the Hirana to bright sunlight and a sea of pilgrims. They parted as she walked. Many bowed.

She did not look at them. She had no desire to. They were nothing to her. A sea of faces. A sea of flesh.

She was not like them.

Some of the guards from the mahal had gathered, waiting for her. Ganam was at the head, dressed for battle with a scythe hooked at his back. His eyes widened at the sight of her. He gave no other sign of shock. Swiftly, he lowered his head and bowed as the pilgrims had.

"Elder Priya," he said. "We're ready."

She swallowed. It was hard to find speech.

"I will fight from here," Priya said. Her voice was a rasp.

He nodded in understanding. Her weapon was her power. Not a blade, but what lay inside her.

"We're relying on you, High Elder."

"Yes," she acknowledged. She knew there were more words she would have said, if she'd felt more like herself and a little less hollowed.

She stood still, the soil under her curdling like milk as her Ahiranyi soldiers walked away. She drew a perimeter around herself: a thorny carapace, sharp enough to keep the watching people at bay.

She reached into the green and felt what she'd known would come, and feared.

Parijatdvipan soldiers. Coming closer.

And among them—

Something tugged beneath Priya's breastbone. A phantom ache. A loss.

Abruptly she was *herself* again, not hollow but overfull, heart pounding and lungs aching, fear and anger crawling up her spine. She was the ugly, human creature that loved Malini, and had to stand against her forever and always.

She knew who was coming. She knew who stood achingly close to Ahiranya's soil, and who had come to kill her and all she cared for.

Malini, she thought. And felt herself reach, through green and earth, an awful yearning and horror gaping inside her.

Malini. You're here.

11

MALINI

Ahiranya was a dark and imposing presence before them. At the forefront of her army, on her war chariot, Malini drank it in: the vast swathe of the trees. The utter silence surrounding the forest, a hush without birdsong or human voices to cut through it. Even the sound of her army—all groaning chariot wheels, heavy hooves, booted feet—seemed oddly muted.

The first time she'd come to Ahiranya, she had been a prisoner. She hadn't seen much of it when she'd arrived—only what she could glimpse when she parted the curtain of her chariot. Only what had filtered through her numb misery. But even her shallow recollections were enough for her to see how utterly Ahiranya had changed since then.

The dust-strewn road, surrounded by homes and blasted, wizened trees, was gone, swallowed by verdant forest. There were immense tree trunks, cleaved and sharpened like blades, ringing the deeper forest like walls.

Stay away, everything said. *Get out.* The way a venomous snake wore its colors on its flesh. Just the same.

She felt a whisper against her ears. A breeze, or her name. She resisted the urge to shudder. She felt watched.

"Send forward the men," she said to Mahesh. He raised a hand in signal, and a line of foot soldiers walked light-footed toward the forest, sabers in hand.

Of course Malini felt unease. She had expected to. She'd seen the guts and innards of that forest. Had walked through it, and survived it; had kissed Priya beneath a waterfall deep, somewhere, in its heart.

She knew there was a great deal to be afraid of.

What she had not expected was the other feeling that ran through her. It was not emotion. It was like a guiding star, tugging her blood as the tide draws the sea. The trees and thorns were a warning, but they beckoned to Malini all the same.

She wanted to walk between them. Into them.

Strange. Strange, and foolish. Her scarred chest throbbed.

There was a scream as one foot soldier suddenly plummeted, vanishing into the ground. Another fell, caught in a snare.

Traps, of course.

A gesture from one of her generals, and another cadre of soldiers moved to locate any traps they could. Blades were wrenched from the ground. Another man located a pit and marked it.

Once that laborious work was done, the next line of foot soldiers were sent toward the forest. She and her generals watched grimly as the soldiers slipped between the trees, melting into darkness. Malini gripped the hilt of her saber. The cool weight of metal grounded her.

There was a hush in the air. A heartbeat passed. Another. Then the cries began in the forest. Screams, then silence.

"The forest truly is impenetrable," Mahesh murmured.

Malini nodded once. Their sacrifice of soldiers had proven it.

Now she only had to test her flames against the forest.

"Arrange your archers," she ordered Khalil. "Make sure they're prepared."

"They'll be ready for my signal," he replied.

"Lord Mahesh," she called. On his horse, Mahesh turned. Inclined his head. "Bring your men forward."

The priestly warriors—her once enemies—moved forward on foot. They held their weapons. Before each of them lay a black chest. They were prepared.

Only Malini herself was left.

Prakash, quietly, cleared his throat. Malini looked at him. He was in the chariot beside her and his face was troubled.

"Empress," he murmured. "I still suggest caution. The Ahiranyi will have the advantage among the trees. Even if the trees were not...as they are...they know the terrain better. To enter is to walk into darkness, where blades and magic may wait for us. Even a single arrow could destroy you."

"I have heard you, Lord Prakash," Malini said evenly. "But I am Empress of Parijatdvipa. It must be me."

It must be me.

Not because of bravery, or because she possessed the desire to strive forward in battle in the way her brothers' teachers had always urged them to. Just and righteous warfare did not concern her. The battle tactics girls learned in court were by necessity cruel and viperous and underhanded, and above all, *clever*. But this was not cleverness, either. Her desire was driven by a rage deep and acrid, a rage that had swelled and deepened after Priya's betrayal of her.

If Ahiranya burned—even the smallest span of it—Malini wanted to be the one to strike the blow. She wanted to know if it could burn at all.

"Sahar, arrange my defenses," she said to the head of her guard. Then, turning her head to the left, she called out, "Rao. With me."

From horseback at Malini's left side, Sahar gave a nod. With a gesture of her hand, the women who made up Malini's personal guard fanned around her.

Rao, in his own chariot, had straightened from the forward-shouldered slump he'd been in. His bloodshot eyes met her own. He gave a firm nod. Malini's charioteer gave a click at the horse, and her vehicle lurched forward.

They went to the border of the trees.

The snarl of branches was menacing—leaves blood-black and profuse, limbs stretching their fingers to the soil. The horse drawing Malini's chariot whickered and resisted the tug of the reins as her charioteer tried to guide it forward.

"Stop," Malini said. She did not speak loudly—she felt like a prey animal, instinctually turning to a soft voice to avoid the attention of what lay beyond the trees. But her charioteer heard her, and with a nervous bob of his head, he stopped.

"What are you doing?" Rao asked. He had already alighted from his chariot, already had a chakram ready in his hand. It was foolish of him to ask.

Malini did not answer. She too alighted. Her feet met the soil with a thud that did not echo—the sound swallowed by earth and tree alike. She drew her saber, holding the gleaming moon-scar of it at an angle at her side, ready for the possibility of battle.

She met Sahar's eyes. If Sahar disagreed with her decision, she did not say so. "Stay close to me, my lady," she said.

In her left hand, against her hip, Sahar carried a black lacquered box.

Only one box of false fire. One burning, squirming thing stolen from a woman's death, to protect the Empress of Parijatdvipa.

She strode forward.

There were cries of alarm from her generals, who were still a sensible distance back. A voice yelled, *Hold.* Rao cursed, a soft thing under his breath.

"Malini," Rao began. And without pausing, Malini said calmly, "Will my warriors allow me to face Ahiranya's wrath alone, Rao? Or will you walk with me?"

She did not turn her head, but she heard it as he and her personal guard thronged around her—heard the clang and thud of boots, armor, maces being hefted up; the songlike sound of a sword whip being unraveled from a belt.

It was absurd to think any of their weapons could stand against what waited in the trees. But Malini had brought them here. Malini carried her own saber in a tight clenched fist like a shining lamp against the dark, a shield against horrors. She could not judge them for it. As long as they obeyed. As long as they followed.

One step beyond the line of trees, only one, and she felt the coldness of the air—sticky as tree sap, icy as a deep river. The ache in her chest twisted, yawned open. If her hands had been unimpeded, if she had not had her saber, she would have clutched her own chest—felt the scar through cloth, searching for the open wound she could feel in her soul, if not her flesh.

"Empress," Sahar said in a low, tense voice. "Shall we turn back?"

"No. Not yet."

That same tug in her chest, that same memory of how the forest had rustled, *breathed* around her when she'd escaped her imprisonment inside it. She looked down and watched as the ground shuddered. Green roots slithered through soil toward her. Moving, unwinding.

The roots . . . hesitated.

Grim satisfaction ran through her. The forest sensed what Sahar carried. It feared harming her.

A half step in front of her was a hewn tree, sharp-edged flowers growing red along its trunk. She paused before it, feeling that same strange tug in her scarred chest, in her heart.

Malini. You're here.

"The box," she said. Sahar passed it to her.

She opened the box. Set her own saber aflame.

Priya, she thought into the dark trees. Into the dark of her own chest, the void left there. *If you are here, I hope the fire finds you. I hope you burn.*

She struck her saber into the bark. It melted through the wood like a blade through flesh.

And Malini heard—her own name. In Priya's voice.

And pain.

It was madness, utter madness, Priya was *not here*, but Malini's scar was agony; her skin was soil where a root had been ripped free. She gave in and clutched a white-knuckled hand to her chest. With the other, she withdrew the saber, wrenching it free from the wood. It was easy enough; the wood gave way, with a crack like bone and marrow.

The flames spread wildly.

One step back, and another, with Rao's hand tight on her arm and Sahar holding her shield between them and the trees, and they were in the open air again. The fire was spreading like a sparking wheel, a sickle of flame. Around it the wood blistered and burned—birds flew screeching from the branches, and the whole forest rippled, alive and furious.

Thorns shot roughly from the ground. The air was thick, vibrating like a plucked string—and with a crash of pressure, an unfolding, the soil closed over the flames, smothering a vast swathe of them. Not all. But enough that one of Malini's questions had been securely answered.

So. False mothers' fire was not enough. Not enough to burn Ahiranya in a breath.

Not enough, most likely, to kill the yaksa.

But it was enough to begin the assault on Ahiranya.

Malini withdrew, back to her chariot. Sahar climbed on with her. The charioteer, with obvious relief, turned them toward the line of men.

Her waiting generals—Khalil, Narayan, Prakash—were visibly restraining themselves from comment.

A sharp nod from her was all it took. Khalil moved forward, raised a hand, and signaled the archers.

A golden flock of arrows flew, each tipped with what remained of Chandra's stolen, murder-borne flames. The forest burned once more, and the ground shuddered and roiled. The horses made an awful noise, trying to resist the control of their charioteers and riders; Malini gripped tight to her chariot and held on.

"Lord Mahesh," she called out. And her generals took up the cry for her.

"Now!"

In the gaps that burned through the trees, warriors raced into the forest, flames upon their swords.

Malini watched them go. Her tongue tasted of ash. Her chest

ached. It was like a thrum, a pulse inside her—a sinew strained, a string that could not be cut.

As the forest burned, so did something inside her. Where she had been stabbed. Where her heart had been stolen from her.

What had Priya done to her?

12

ARAHLI ARA

The forest was burning, and Arahli Ara was not afraid. He was exultant.

To be yaksa was to be part of green—enmeshed in its trees, its water, its deepest roots—and yet vaster. He kneeled at the zenith of the Hirana with his kin, the sunlight painting their bodies in golden light. But his will, his *self*, extended far beyond the limitations of his body. He was not the leaves that haloed his skull, or the striations of lustrous wood that braided his bones. He was also not the Ahiranyi trees that cracked and splintered from the heat below them as arrows wreathed in fire thudded into their marrow. But he watched through those trees as they burned, listened through falling branches and rotting wood to the cries and yells of mortal men. The heaving Parijatdvipan army swarmed helplessly on Ahiranya's border, as faceless and insignificant as ants.

They amused him.

The fire could not hurt him or his kin. He and his kin had laughed when they had felt the Parijatdvipans approach with their churning chariot wheels, their false fire.

The Parijati are not what they once were, his kin Taru Ara had whispered days before as their worshippers had bowed before them on the Hirana, pressing their faces to the cold stone, offering up gifts of flowers and fruit and golden coin, begging for safety from the coming army. *Even our own worshippers are less than they once were. Look how they crawl, my dear one. Look, sweet one, how they beg.* She'd clasped his hand with her own. Her skin had been cold, soothing as sap. *They do not understand how to kill us anymore.*

She had been right. He and his kin had changed under the earth and returned stronger, while humans had only grown smaller. He could feel the shared power of his kin now, rich in the sangam, rich inside him. Mani Ara had made them strong enough to survive anything.

Thinking of Mani Ara led him back to Priya, as easily as any sun-seeking green thing rooted in soil. He could feel her now, in the same green that held him—moving through the forest with her magic, twisting the traps she'd set into the soil to catch unwary warriors. She snapped limbs and throats easily, beautifully.

She moved like Mani Ara once had, as keenly as a knife, as strong as a storm.

What a vicious thing Priya is, he thought.

But then, she always has been. Even when she was small—

He quashed that thought like an insect. It was not his thought, and it had no place in his skull now.

He was not Ashok.

He met Taru Ara's eyes, and for a moment it was Ashok's vision that clouded his own. Sanjana's face stared back at him. Her mouth shaped into a smile.

"Dear one," she said—and that was not long-dead Sanjana's voice, but Taru Ara's wood-flecked rasp. He saw the solidity of her face—the curves of wood and stone—and felt comforted. She was not flesh. "She is growing stronger."

"Fear is a great teacher," he said. His other kin listened, liquid eyes unblinking.

"*I* am a great teacher," Taru Ara corrected.

Taru Ara was the one Priya had gone to in desperation, in fear, begging for the strength to protect Ahiranya. It was fear—and love—that had made Priya willing to reach for Mani Ara, to reshape herself. It was Taru who had given her the crown mask, so Priya would continue to change, growing stronger, nourished by its magic. He could not deny her role in making more of Priya than she had been.

He inclined his head in agreement. His kin's smile deepened.

"Next time she needs guidance, I leave it to you," she said, indulgent. "I know how you love your temple children."

He did not want Priya to be placed into his keeping, but he did not say so.

He saw Taru Ara's smile falter half a second before Arahli himself sensed Priya waver, flickering like candle flame. In the forest, in the marrow of a great tree, he felt a blade of fire pierce through wood—and felt her agony in its wake.

The blade sank deep into the tree, and Priya's presence among the trees extinguished, returning to the embrace of the sangam.

Something akin to a heart clenched its root-thick veins in his chest, pulsing with sluggish sap.

She is still too weak. Too human.

More arrows thudded into the trees, and Parijati soldiers raced into the forest, hacking through the green as they went. Waiting Ahiranyi warriors were caught under their blades. Blood reddened the soil, drowning it in its richness.

His kin, in their circle, hissed displeasure, rage unfolding inside them alongside his own. He was *angry*. At Priya, for hollowing so slowly—and at the Parijatdvipans for their temerity.

He felt his kin's rage stretch into the green, a furious tumult of churning soil and barbs rising from the ground to spear those men through. Ahiranyi or Parijati, it did not matter. Taru Ara rose to her feet, no longer smiling. At her left, Vata Ara's eyes sharpened.

"Do not," he said. But she bared her teeth, her sharp mouth a warning.

"I have not known war in so long," she said. "I would have their blood just once."

And then she was gone.

She was not the only one who fled. He did not intend it, no, but he found himself standing. His mouth tasted mortally of blood—the taste of fear. He could not remain where he was.

Arahli Ara descended the Hirana and raced to Priya's side.

She lay in her carapace of thorns at the base of the Hirana. Pilgrims were huddled around the thorns, but they scrambled away, bowing as they did so, when he strode toward them.

He ignored them. His fingers of wood-and-bone motioned like a knife through the air, and in answer the shell splintered open. He kneeled.

Her eyes were shut. She did not react when he clasped her shoulders, lifting her upper body from the ground beneath her to rest in his lap. She was not sleeping, not dreaming—her soul was safe in the sangam, cradled by cosmic waters. He had *known* she was. But he could not help but press a hand to her torso. She had believed for a moment that she was the tree, that her body had been stabbed through, and he half believed it himself.

He knew what it was like to be human. The pain of it, the fragility of flesh.

The skin beneath his hand was unharmed.

He looked at her face. Her closed eyes.

If she looks at me, a voice in his mind whispered, *I will remember what it means to be flesh.*

Horror wrapped itself in tendrils through him.

He had not been near Priya since her time beneath the Hirana, when she had kneeled and prayed and splintered, seeking Mani Ara. And this was why he had avoided her, in truth: She made something mortal rear up in him.

For a time he had believed himself to be Ashok. He had laughed and hated as Ashok did—had acted with Ashok's interests. He had sent Bhumika away as Ashok, gifted with her knowledge, in a desperate attempt to hold those last threads of humanity. He knew now what he truly was, but he still saw the mortal faces on his kin, and felt Ashok whisper in his skull; he feared what festered within him still.

But he could not avoid his responsibilities to Priya, or to

his kin. She would need to be taught. She would need to grow stronger than her pitiful mortality. She was a temple elder, their *only* temple elder, and Mani Ara's beloved. For his kin, he would reduce her to nothing but her worship and her bones.

The remnants of Ashok that still lingered within him faded once more. He laid Priya back down upon the grass, stood, and turned, following the path Taru Ara had walked, toward dark trees and golden fire.

He would kill a few Parijati himself and string their bodies upon the trees like a garland. A fitting welcome and farewell for their unwelcome guests.

13

MALINI

They moved her to the back of the army—to the wall of tents, behind a defense of elephant and horse cavalry and armed men. Safe.

Prakash kneeled before her, grim.

"You should not have risked yourself so utterly, Empress," he said. "If you die, what will become of Parijatdvipa? You are the last of your family. The empire stands and falls with you."

Raziya and Lata were watching Malini with disapproving—and worried—faces.

"My emperor father would have led his army into battle," Malini said crisply. "As his father would have before him. I must live up to their example, not cower behind my warriors."

She tried to hide how she was swaying. Her chest throbbed, and the ache had moved through her like mist, rising to fill her skull. It was so thick she felt as if it should have fogged her eyes, clouded her like a full cup of steaming water.

"There is no denying Ahiranya's cursed power," Lord Narayan said, his voice tentative. "And though we have faced defeat, we—"

"The battle was not lost," Malini said to him.

"Empress—"

"Surely you must accept, at this point, that I know something of war." She smiled around her words, pressing absolute faith into her voice. She was glad it was a sunlit day, the sky blue and expansive and the dust golden beneath it. It made it easier for her to sound confident and unshaken by what they had encountered, and how she had responded to it. "We knew the fire may not save us, Lord Narayan. We had to move swiftly to test its strength. Now we know, and we are prepared for the war ahead."

He inclined his head, but his expression was still troubled.

She didn't wait for him to speak. She already knew the shapes of his fears: mothers' fire, and yaksa, and battles or ambushes that could fall upon them anywhere, everywhere. She shook her head and said to him, "No more. You'll have chance enough to voice your views when I hold council. For now, see to your men."

"When will we meet, Empress?"

"This evening," she said, even as she turned. "So prepare yourself. We will speak then."

Raziya and Lata both moved to follow her, but she shook her head.

"Later," she said to them. Some of her pain must have leaked through her voice or her face, because Lata's gaze narrowed. She nodded and touched a hand to Lady Raziya's arm, silencing the protest that was already forming on Raziya's lips.

She couldn't banish Sahar and her other guards until she was safely ensconced in her own tent, so the guardswomen were there when Malini finally stepped into the cool shade of the fabric and exhaustion hit her like an arrow through the stomach. Numbness and fire began in her abdomen, radiating outward. Her legs felt weak.

"Leave me," she said to Sahar, and to Swati, who had been waiting for her. "I will rest."

Swati and Sahar shared a look. But the maid only nodded, and Sahar said, "I'll be just beyond the curtain, Empress." And then Malini was alone.

A bed beneath her. The smell of cedar around her, and the rising sweetness of sandalwood, from the incense left lit by Swati. There were thin curtains around her, clouds of frothing white. She closed her eyes and felt the coolness of the bedding beneath her.

Closed her eyes, and found herself dragged forcefully into sleep. She walked directly into a dream.

She dreamt that she was crossing the court of the imperial mahal again. The marble was colder than the bed and suddenly gave way to wetness. Water was running over the floor, softening the stone to sand. Above her the roof had vanished, leaving her surrounded by sky, trees, soil.

The fire at the heart of the court was still burning, blooming its flowers of flame. And Priya was lying next to it, her hair loose, dark tendrils fanned out around her, saturated with water.

Perhaps in this dream I will kill her before she can kill me, Malini thought, feeling oddly detached. She walked closer to Priya, taking in the shape of her—the lines of her body, the arm flung out, the head tilted away.

She looked at Priya's face and saw... not Priya's face.

Instead she saw a face carved of wood, so close to Priya's that it was almost perfect. If Malini had not known her, known her skin, perhaps she would have been fooled. The carved face was peaceful, strangely beautiful, haloed by roses.

Perhaps the person lying on the ground was not Priya at all. Perhaps it was a statue—as empty and lifeless as the wooden effigy of Aditya in the imperial temple.

Malini's footsteps faltered at the thought. In the silence, the figure on the ground stirred.

Malini had been mistaken, or her dreaming eyes had lied to her. Priya's face was not wood. She was wearing a mask. At its edges her real skin was visible. The eyes that stared back at Malini through the mask's sockets were warm brown, familiar and hazy with sleep. They fixed on Malini. Focused.

"Malini," Priya whispered.

Rage came over Malini like a tide. She kneeled over Priya, her knees and hands against wet stone. Those eyes through hollows of wood looked up at her in sorrow.

Why did she dream Priya sorrowful? What a cruel lie to gift herself. It made her angrier still.

"I felt you in the trees," Malini said, her voice shaky with anger. "You should have faced me. Isn't that my right? After what you did to me, after you stabbed me with a thorn knife, don't I deserve the right to aim a saber of fire at your heart in return?"

"You did hurt me," Priya said. She said it like she wanted to soothe Malini. As if any promise of Priya's pain could be a *comfort*. "Malini, you did. I was in the trees and you reached me, your soul to mine, piercing me through."

A wild fear ran through Malini. That she had burned Priya's skin away. That beneath that mask there was nothing, only gristle, or only flowers.

"Show me your face," Malini demanded. "Don't hide beneath masks. Show me."

Priya was moving too slowly, hands rising gently, skimming close to Malini's arms. So Malini reached for the mask herself.

The mask blistered her fingers. Not a mask of plain wood, or even a mask of sacred wood, but a mask of fire—

Her hands were burning. She was screaming, weeping, and Priya was whispering her name—strange, sweet whispering that was not wanted and yet terribly wanted, that cut harsher than any blade because of its softness, the way it was a balm. Malini could not stand it. Could not. She said more words, poisonous, furious words.

"You did this to me," she gasped. "You've changed me. What rot have you forced between my ribs? Why do I dream of you?"

"I don't know," Priya said, tender, tender. "I don't know. Forget me, Malini. Forget me—"

"How could I?" Malini snapped. Heart pounding, a wild bird caged in her chest. "How dare you be here in my dreams, and not under my hands, not where I can really hurt you?"

The mask was gone, and she could see Priya's face again. Priya's eyes held no guilt, no shame, not even sorrow anymore—only implacable determination, hard as stone.

"Malini," Priya said again. "If there had been any other way, I wish, but there *wasn't*—"

Malini pressed a hand roughly against her mouth, her nose, to silence her. Priya struggled—her teeth snagged against Malini's palm, then bit deeper. The pain was so bright it made Malini hiss out a breath and draw back her hand. Priya's mouth was red.

"I don't regret it," Priya said, defiant now. "I'm sorry. I love you. I would do it again."

Malini took her fiery hands and grasped Priya's scalp, drew her up. Whispered against her lips—

She woke.

It was still daylight. She could see the sunlight pouring in through a gap in the tent curtain. Distantly, she heard Sahar's voice in muted conversation. The air was heavy with the heat that gathered and settled after midday. It would break by evening.

She clenched her hands in front of her, pressed them to her eyes. She heard her own voice. Poison.

I can hurt you. I love to hurt you. Can't you feel it? All I want is your throat under my hands.

One day, I will take great joy in seeing you dead.

That was good. That, at least, was good.

"You cannot act so impetuously," Raziya said, her voice infuriatingly calm. "Lord Prakash was correct. If an emperor stood in your place, rather than an empress, he would have been offered the same counsel."

"In any normal war I would agree," Malini said. "But this is no normal war."

"In the battle against your brother Chandra you allowed yourself to become his prisoner," Lata said helpfully. "You could have died."

"That was also no normal war," Malini said.

"Tell me the shape of a normal war so I can ensure I recognize one when we meet it, Empress," Raziya murmured. She touched a hand to her creased forehead, then lowered it. "I am sorry for my rudeness, but you *cannot* risk your life in this manner again."

"Elder Priya has the power of the yaksa," Malini said calmly.

"I was sure she would recognize me and attempt to harm me through the forest itself. I was proved correct, and it allowed me to inflict harm in return. Sometimes a calculated risk is necessary."

Raziya still looked unconvinced, but there was no more time to argue. One of the guards—a new Parijati addition named Sanvi—announced that Malini's advisors were all arrayed in the council tent and waiting to receive her.

Malini had barely seated herself on her dais in the council tent when a single soldier rushed in. Her guards moved to protect her, but there was no need; he was Parijati, in her own colors, smoke and blood on his tunic, turning the white a dull rust in patches.

His eyes were wild and bloodshot. He was breathing shallowly, rapidly. For a moment his mouth moved without making any sound. Then finally, the words emerged.

"There are bodies," he said. "And—something else."

"Something else?" One of her military advisors had his brow furrowed. "Boy, what do you mean, *something else?*"

"Things are growing," the soldier said helplessly. "Please. I only know what I saw."

Malini heard the distant sound of a conch. She rose to her feet.

"Show us," she said.

To put Raziya's worries to rest, she allowed Lord Khalil and his warriors to provide her an extra layer of defense as she approached Ahiranya's forest. When she saw what waited for them, she was—despite herself—glad she had.

Soldiers had been impaled beyond the lines of trees.

Hundreds of bodies. She did not try to count them all. Even through thick soil and growing vines, their Parijati white-and-gold armor was visible. They hung skewered on living stakes of wood like festival flags—wavering, just slightly, in a breeze Malini could not feel.

One of their commanders had been pinned to a tree near the border of the forest, where fire had splintered a dozen trees to ruin. His body still wore his helm, but the face beneath it wasn't visible.

Leaves were growing from his eye sockets, lush and green. Where his jaw should have been were strangely pale ashoka flowers.

"Careful," murmured Khalil. He tilted his head sharply to the right. Malini followed the line of his gaze.

There, the forest had grown thicker, darker, more expansive. Before her eyes, new trees emerged—narrow, twisted things.

Even from a distance she could see the rot on them. They were flesh-and-wood—their stench was carried on the breeze.

To touch them, to move through them, was to court the rot and a terrible death.

She could not send her soldiers in. She was not sure anything could compel them to go. No faith could blot out the carrion stink of blood and meat.

There could be no real siege of Ahiranya. Not with the weapons they had. Clearly no fire could burn the forest faster than Ahiranya could regrow and overgrow, flourishing with violent speed.

They needed better weapons. And if Malini wanted to save Parijatdvipa—if Malini wanted to *not* burn on a pyre of faith—she would need to find them.

BHUMIKA

Weeks of travel in blistering heat and bitter night cold, sleeping in the open with a shawl draped over her upper body to ward off mosquitoes. Weeks of shared meals cooked over a fire, and water drunk from a shared flask. Weeks with no one but Jeevan for company; no one but Jeevan guarding her at night, his saber in hand, his voice gentle when he woke her in the predawn light for another day of walking side by side. She had to remind herself that *only* Jeevan was there, because her watchers returned again and again, water-drenched, their bowls upheld. They vanished as swiftly and strangely as they arrived, and Jeevan did not see them.

Of course he did not. They were tangled with the urgent knowledge inside her, that insistent drumbeat drawing her forward. In every place she and Jeevan walked or rested, she felt her knowledge call to her. *Once, the yaksa walked here. Once, an army marched through this village.*

The pain in her skull woke her one night. Her back ached. A stone was digging into her hip. She removed the shawl over her body and sat up, her spine creaking ominously.

The moon was full overhead. It shone against the bright metal of Jeevan's saber. He was sitting cross-legged, back straight, blade on his lap. His eyes were closed. He'd fallen asleep on watch.

She stood up. As the undergrowth snapped beneath her feet, he startled awake. His grip tightened brutally on the saber hilt, then released. He raised his head to meet her eyes. "Bhumika," he said, his voice hoarse with exhaustion. "Sleep."

She kneeled by him.

"You sleep," she said. "I can keep watch."

He shook his head. He said nothing, but she could see the stubborn refusal in the shape of his jaw, his shadowed eyes. How much had he slept on their journey? Had he been trying to stay awake every night, sleeping only when his body forced him to?

"If the yaksa come, a blade will not stop them," she said gently. "But they are not coming."

"They may yet," he said, his voice low. "And I am afraid a blade is all I have."

Flashes of knowledge swam behind her eyes—of cosmic waters. Magic winding from waters through skin.

The knowledge in her was stolen from a greater sea, cut off from those cosmic waters. *She* was cut off from those cosmic waters, and all the magic within them. In that lay the answer for why no yaksa had followed her.

They cannot find me. There is nothing to find.

"I am nothing to them," she said. "If they could find me—if they were searching for me—they would have me already. But I am as good as dead, in their eyes. A husk."

"You don't remember them," he said, his tired gaze sharpening.

"But I *know* them. Knowing is all I have."

He said nothing to that. She shook her head.

"If you will not rest, then I will keep watch with you," she told him.

She did not move from his side that night. Eventually, she slept once more.

When she woke, dawn's light was rising and Jeevan was asleep, leaning against her shoulder.

After that, they took turns keeping watch at night, and his exhaustion visibly eased. He focused his efforts instead on ensuring that they kept their distance from other travelers. There were many other people traveling away from Ahiranya—some toward

Alor, and others in any direction they could find. Ahiranya's borders had closed, the trees growing sharp and cruel.

Villages near the border with Ahiranya had become infected with rot, their crops destroyed, their people sickened with flowers rising through their skin. It was hard to avoid those strangers, but Jeevan did so carefully, leading Bhumika away from the main roads and trails. He told Bhumika about their plight with simple words, his eyes distant.

She knew it pained him to see them. But she did not feel for them, as he did, until they crossed paths with a family who had made camp by a river. One of the adults—an Ahiranyi man with green unfurling up his spine—was rocking an infant. The baby was screaming, hands curled into furious fists. Its cries were plaintive.

Jeevan's hand was on her arm, urging her away from the river to the anonymity of the trees. But Bhumika was frozen. A feeling was welling up in her—one she had no way to comprehend. It felt like grief. She turned and walked away, blood beating in her ears, and eventually found herself kneeling farther downriver, her knees in the water.

She pressed her hands into the river as if she were trying to grasp something within it. Somewhere there was another river, and it held the best of her. It held *before*.

Before was forbidden to her. She knew that, just as she knew hunger or tiredness or pain. It was a knowledge that lived in her flesh. *Before* was one memory alone. A rending. And after the rending—a knowledge that lived inside her. That ached in her skull and her teeth and her heart. The knowledge was what she carried, and it was what she was, and she could not rest until it was shared with a person fit to wield it.

Her reflection in the water was rippling, fractured. In its dark gloss she saw veiled faces—dripping water like tears.

She'd recoiled from them and felt Jeevan's fingertips settle against her shoulder.

"Drink," he urged, bending to offer her a water flask. She took it. "It's clean. Safer. You'll feel better for it."

She took it from him and noticed his hands: those strong, scarred, callused fingers, so much larger than her own; the paler strip of skin just beneath the sleeve of his tunic, untouched by the sun. She noted each small detail, grounding herself into her own body.

She lifted the water to her mouth and looked up at him.

His face was still lowered to her, which allowed her to look at her leisure. His face. The hard angles of it, the bristle of hair at his jaw, not quite a full beard, but something more unkempt and unshaven, as if he were used to a neatness that he had set aside. Had he been clean-shaven when their journey began? She could not remember.

"We will not travel any farther today," he said. "Let me prepare some food. You must rest."

He walked a little away from her. Then he crouched down and lowered his pack, and began to prepare a fire.

She rose from the water—her skirt uncomfortably soaked—and settled herself in the shade of a nearby tree. She was glad he had not cajoled her out of the water. He had allowed her the space to feel the great and awful thing she had felt.

She did not know how to cook, or at least, her hands did not know it. She and Jeevan had figured that out early, with only minimal disaster. But it occurred to her, as she crouched and watched, that perhaps she could teach her hands if she wanted to.

They ate. Potted achaar, roti. Then he began to pack everything away, blotting out the fire with dust and his boot.

"Wait," she said. He stopped.

"Is something wrong?" His forehead furrowed; his eyes fixed on her. She stood and walked toward him.

"Would you be honest with me?" she asked.

"I have always been honest with you," he replied.

"Tell me why I matter to you," Bhumika said. "Tell me why you travel with me."

He was silent for a long moment. He tilted his face away from her own, concealing his expression.

"I should not have asked," she said. "I'm sorry." She turned, preparing to continue their journey.

Another pause, and then his footsteps began to echo her own.

"Once," he said, his voice low behind her, "you won my loyalty. You saved my life. You gave it purpose."

"Is that why you protect me?" she asked.

A pause. A heartbeat of silence, as his footsteps stilled. Then began again. "Yes," he said.

At least now she knew what it sounded like when he lied.

"There is a wound in me," she said. "You know this, I expect. But I find I am constantly reaching, in my nature, for something…" Her hands twitched at her sides. Her chest was aching. Grief. That was what she had been feeling. "Something I left behind," she finished.

He was abruptly by her side. She realized, as he hovered beside her, not quite touching her and deliberately not looking at her, that there were tears in her eyes.

She wiped them away with her knuckles. He offered her cloth—clean bandaging fished from that bottomless pack of his. "Thank you," she murmured, a little stiffly. Daubed her eyes again.

"You do not have to feel pain," he said gruffly. She looked at him; through the blur of her tears, his stern face was softened. "I promised long ago that I would carry your grief for you. So lay it in my hands."

So I do have something to grieve for, then, she thought.

"Thank you," she said to him. She crumpled the bandage small in her hands. Such a small thing, a phrase of thanks. It did not encompass the tender thing in her chest—this grateful, wounded beat of her heart that knew him, relied upon him, as the parched soil relied on the balm of rain. "Thank you, Jeevan," she said again.

Alor lay ahead of them. With determination, she forced herself to stop crying and began moving again. Her knowledge thrummed with every footstep. Around her, between the trees, her ghostly watchers moved with her, and Jeevan's footsteps matched her own, solid and trustworthy.

15

PRIYA

Deep breath in. Out.

The fire from the forest was gone. The feeling of Malini's hands was gone too. Priya couldn't even feel an echo of them. There was no pain. Just the sound of water, a bubbling rush around her ears. Just the feeling of liquid slipping between her fingers. Just strange hands on her hair, cold as silt.

"Hush." A whisper of a voice. "You're with me, sapling. You're safe."

Priya opened her eyes. The sangam was nothing like that feverish dream, that mask of fire, those furious hands. Around her it was water and a winding, strange sky, speckled with stars. And above her, looking down at her, was Mani Ara. *Finally*, Mani Ara.

"The Parijati used fire," Priya said shakily, hoping if she focused simply on that memory the dream she'd drifted into with Malini would slip by unnoticed. "Fire like before."

Even on her shadow self, here within the sangam, the scars on her body were livid. They were a fiery gold at her throat, where Malini had burned her, and at her side, where false fire had touched her in the battle against Chandra. She could see herself reflected in Mani Ara's eyes, which were like deep waters, or a mirror.

"Yaksa," Priya breathed. "Where have you been?"

"Here," Mani Ara murmured. "Always here." Gentle hands on

her. "But even now, you're too weak to hold me. Even now, the fire almost took you."

The fire in Ahiranya's forest. Fire on Malini's sword, and in Ahiranya's trees.

She thought of the fire. The way she had felt it burn and had recoiled from it—and had found herself in a dream, with Malini standing over her.

"There may be more fire," Priya said, panic clawing through her. "They'll burn the trees. They'll—if they reach Hiranaprastha—"

"Their fire isn't as strong as they believe," Mani Ara said. Indulgent. "It is no mothers' fire. It cannot kill me."

"Their fire *will* kill our people," Priya said. "Yaksa, Mani Ara, please—Ahiranya and its people are in danger, *please* protect them. If the empire isn't stopped, they'll burn."

A finger touched her mouth, silencing her.

"Of course Ahiranyi people will die if the empire is not stopped." Mani Ara did not sound afraid. "But we are stronger than the empire."

The yaksa who wore Sanjana's skin had said the same thing. It did nothing to soothe Priya's panic.

"You wouldn't let Ahiranyi people die," Priya said. But even as she said it she knew the yaksa would. She felt it like a string plucked, a reverberation that ran all the way through her. "You must care," Priya said, choked. "They're your worshippers. They love you."

"Their love is sweet," Mani Ara said. "But they did not hollow themselves for me. They are only mortals, my dear one." Her hand on Priya's cheek was tender. "They may kill a thousand Ahiranyi, as long as you live," she said, smiling.

Priya shook her head beneath that hand. She must have said something, must have let the mournful *no, no, no* clawing at her throat spill out, because Mani Ara laughed, not unkindly.

"You can save Ahiranya, if you love it so," she said. "Grow strong before the empire can set your loved ones aflame. That is all you need to do."

"I am strong," Priya insisted, even though she felt weak—heartsick and small under Mani Ara's hands. "Haven't I found you, finally? I'm strong enough."

Mani Ara leaned over her. The yaksa breathed—an inhalation and exhalation against her hair, as light and as powerful as wind on still waters.

"You are still imperfect," Mani Ara murmured.

"How do I become stronger?"

"Keep reaching for me, sapling. Keep making a hollow of yourself. Become nothing but mine. That will make you strong."

Useless words. Priya had kneeled on the Hirana and deep beneath it beside the deathless waters and prayed and prayed for Mani Ara's strength. She'd worn the crown mask for so long and reached so deep that she'd changed herself, becoming more yaksa—more flower-skinned and green-veined—by the day. How was that not enough? What else could she possibly do?

The yaksa didn't care about anyone. Not Padma or Rukh. Not any other child in Ahiranya. They would not have cared for Priya either, but they needed what she was—temple raised and thrice-born, almost hollow enough, almost strong enough. And there was nothing she could do to change their hearts.

She should have felt helpless at that realization. Lost.

Instead, rage was kindling in her chest. They could not disregard everything and everyone that mattered to her so easily. Not after what they'd made her do. Not after what she'd given up for them.

She met Mani Ara's liquid eyes.

"If my people die," Priya said slowly, deliberately. "If Ahiranya dies, I will not be anything for you. I'll fill the hollows of myself up with grief and anger. There won't be any room for you."

Something flickered, a dark fish, in Mani Ara's eyes. For a moment, Priya did not know if Mani Ara would laugh sweetly or tear her soul to strips.

Priya did not look away.

"You are my priestess," Mani Ara said. There were echoes of

waters in her voice. "My hands. My power is yours. Wield it, if you like."

Can I? Can I truly?

She didn't ask. She didn't want this power snatched away from her. But somehow Mani Ara knew. Her face softened. She pressed one wood-whorled thumb beneath Priya's left eye socket, caressing the shape of it, close enough to gouge.

"If you cannot wield my power, then who else?"

She leaned down.

"Wake, sapling," Mani Ara whispered, the almost-kiss of her mouth tracing Priya's hairline. "Wake now. And grow strong and empty. For me."

Priya's eyes snapped open. She turned onto her side and heaved onto the ground beneath her.

She'd woken in a sickroom—made private by curtains, with one of the mask-keepers hovering anxiously over her. But there was nothing that any physician could do for her, never mind any once- or twice-born mask-keeper, so she waved away their questions and slipped out of the room. There were other bodies behind curtains—figures groaning in pain, and others utterly silent.

Hiranaprastha smelled of smoke. Underneath it was the sensation of the green, and *that* felt and smelled like charnel and decay to Priya's overwhelmed senses.

The yaksa had been busy after her collapse, and they'd been *angry*. The borders of Ahiranya were newly rich with rot. She could feel new trees, which were blood-heavy—feel the weight of the Parijatdvipan bodies speared violently on their branches. The power that had been poured into those trees was a rageful lash of magic—splintered and rotten to the core. It was only luck and an empty stomach that stopped her from being sick again when the sensation of it washed over her.

She dragged her body across the mahal to the armory and found Ganam outside it, nursing a pipe, crouched on the ground with his back to the wall. He lowered his pipe when he saw her.

Inclined his head. His expression was serious, tired.

"You're better?"

"I'm standing," Priya said, which she knew meant nothing. "I'm sorry, Ganam."

"For what?"

"For not defending you all. You were relying on me."

"We were," he said. "But you didn't choose what happened to you. There were enough pilgrims who saw the state of you to prove that."

"The fire did something to me," Priya blurted out. "That was why my magic wasn't there, fighting alongside you. How many people did we lose?"

He shook his head.

"We haven't counted all of the dead yet."

"Then I should help," she said. It was something to do, at least. Something better than remembering Malini's hands at her throat, or Mani Ara's lips on her forehead.

"There's nothing urgent about it, Priya. We'll bury the bodies later. Maybe we'll mourn them. Come and sit down. Smoke with me."

She didn't want to smoke, but sitting down did sound good. She joined him, pressing her back to cool stone as she slid to the floor. It felt nice to not move—to sit in silence. She closed her eyes.

But Priya had never been good at long silences. She was soon restless, words clawing at her throat. She opened her mouth and let some of them tumble out.

"I saw Mani Ara." She didn't open her eyes, but she sensed Ganam's stillness. Felt it, as his body turned toward her, attentive. "I've been seeking her all this time. It's what the yaksa wanted me to do. And I finally saw her again, and spoke to her, and now I know the yaksa don't care if any of you live or die. They don't care at all."

A beat of silence.

"I knew that," Ganam said heavily. "And I think you knew it too."

"Mani Ara said I am her hands. That her power belongs to me. That I can use it. So it doesn't matter if the yaksa don't care, because *I* care if any of you live or die, Ganam. And I have her power." She opened her eyes and turned to look at him, seeing the skepticism on his face—and the tentative hope. "The yaksa need me," she said. "Mani Ara needs me. I don't know why, but they do. So they'll care about what I care about, or they'll get nothing from me."

He swallowed. Nodded.

"So," he said. "All-powerful Priya. What are you going to do now?"

"I don't know yet," she whispered. "Anything I can. Even if it kills me."

16

MALINI

She arrived back to Parijat to so much celebration that she wondered if her people had somehow been misled and believed the war had been won. Even through the curtains of her chariot and the shadowy perimeter of guards on horseback around her, she could see the throng of crowds and hear their voices crying out.

Empress. Empress. Empress.

In her imperial court, seated on her raised throne, she could still hear the faint sounds of the city of Harsinghar celebrating her return. Drumbeats and cymbals echoed like wingbeats through the hall as kings and warriors seated themselves beneath her raised dais. The women of court were already seated behind her.

Varsha had joined them. She was close to the end of her pregnancy, and the strain was visible in every line of her body. Her pallu was drawn over her face; the hand not holding her sari was pressed to the swell of her stomach. She sat at the very back of the crescent of seated women, behind Raziya and Lata and Deepa, among the highborn wives and daughters and grandmothers of the kings and princes who kneeled below.

Servants closed the shutters. The sound grew muted until there was nothing but the noise of men's low murmuring voices, the rustle of silks, and the crackle of lanterns.

Malini leaned forward, and even the sound of those voices died away.

"There are wars," Malini said, "that cannot be fought by warriors alone. The rot grows. The priesthood have assured us that the yaksa will return, and what we all witnessed in Ahiranya—and the soldiers we lost—confirms their claim. The warriors who remain to watch Ahiranya's borders are brave," she continued, speaking of Mahesh and the priestly warriors—the ones left behind. "But we have an even greater duty: We must protect our food and fields from the rot, or all is lost."

She gestured to Lata, who rose smoothly to her feet and began to explain the inner workings of their plan: the essential harvests that had to be protected; the grain and rice in Alor, the herds in Dwarali, the Srugani orchards. The way soldiers uninfected with the rot would be directed and managed; the way harvests would need to be stored and distributed to ensure the empire's survival.

There were objections, of course. There were always objections.

"Empress," one quavering-voiced lord from Alor said. "Not all of this can be done. Not in an empire of our size. Not with perfection. We do not have the men. The war has drained us."

"Starvation would drain us much further," Malini said crisply. "We do not need perfection, my lord. Only willingness. Only bravery. All of you claim you would die by the sword for Parijatdvipa. If you are willing to do so, you can take on the smaller sacrifice of sharing food."

"There are many landowners and lords who will not wish to give their grain to the empire," another prince said. His gaze was steady. "They may resist."

"This is war," Malini replied. "They will do what is needful. And if they do not, you will convince them to do what is right."

He bowed. "Empress," he said. "As you command."

She went to the imperial temple. In these times, an appearance of piety was to her benefit.

She walked through the gardens of the temple under the cover of a parasol, with only Sahar to guard her. Hemanth soon joined her. He looked as unassuming as ever, an unremarkable figure in his plain robes, his ash-marked brow furrowed.

"High Priest," she said, inclining her head with a practiced smile. Then she allowed her face to smooth to graveness. "I have come to pray."

"You are welcome, Empress, in the temple of your ancestor," Hemanth replied. "Will you pray alongside me?"

"I have come for solitude," she said.

His jaw tightened.

"I am glad to see you safe," he said. "Is Ahiranya quelled?"

"I am sure you know how the battle fared," she murmured.

"I trust your word above all else, Empress." He met her gaze.

Every time she met his eyes she saw a sure belief in them. Not hatred—it would have been simpler if she simply saw hatred in his eyes—but a steady truth. Even as he bowed to her, she read the message in every line of his body.

One day you will burn.

Hemanth and the priesthood that served him believed the yaksa would return, and that Malini's willing death—like the deaths of the mothers of flame long before her—would give Parijatdvipa the strength to destroy the yaksa once more. When they had supported her brother Chandra's claim to the throne, they had done so for the sake of that truth. And when the High Priest had finally, *finally*, turned upon Chandra and backed Malini's rise to empress, he had done so for the same reason.

She had vowed she would not burn if she could not have her throne. The loyalty of the priesthood hinged upon that vow.

Aditya had bought her time with his death by fire. Because of him, many believed utterly that her rule was mother-blessed. But she knew how contradictory beliefs and desires could coexist in the human heart. And the priesthood held great sway.

She could not destroy Hemanth yet. Not until the power in his hands had faded.

"We tested the strength of Ahiranya, and our own fire," Malini said finally. "The war has only begun, High Priest. My advisors and I will carve a path forward and defeat the yaksa. They will crawl into the world, and we will purge them."

"There is only one way to purge the yaksa, Empress. I am willing—and able—to counsel you on how to face the future bravely."

"I will pray for Divyanshi's guidance," said Malini.

A heavy sigh left him. "Will you burn women, as your brother did? For the good of Parijatdvipa?" Those implacable eyes of his were pitying. "I understand that with the fate lying before you, it must be a hard thing to face your duty. But if you must fight the yaksa, if you cannot yet burn yourself . . ."

There were many things she could have said, the very things she had told herself in the dark, before nightmares of Priya's face swallowed her again. The false fire was not enough. Perhaps her own death would not be enough. And she wanted so much, so very much, to live.

The world was changed, riven with rot, and Malini wanted above all else to live, and taste vengeance.

"Thank you, High Priest," she said. "I will consider your words carefully."

There was a room reserved for her to pray in solitude. She'd used it many times during her recovery from her knife wound; she had arranged for its contents herself. It was small and bare. The walls were curved and carved from pale stone. The only items in the room were a hand-knotted rug, soft enough to kneel on, and a single item on a plinth: a yaksa's arm.

A severed arm from the Age of Flowers. An arm that had flowered, fleshlike, with new life. Its flowering had marked the return of the yaksa and Priya's inevitable betrayal.

Sahar remained outside the room, at the end of the hall. Malini kneeled and closed her eyes. She was relieved Hemanth had not tried to remain. She'd had enough of him.

She did not pray. She sat in silence, knees aching, her chest thrumming with a low-level, persistent pain. The mark Priya had left on her was impossible to ignore.

Time passed. She heard no footsteps, but she did hear the faint groan of the door opening and closing.

"Sahar told me to meet you here," Rao said. "I...did not expect to find you praying alone."

"I'm not truly praying, Rao," Malini said, amusement seeping into her voice. "I wanted to meet you without eyes on us."

"Ah," said Rao.

She opened her own eyes and turned her head, and saw that he had angled his body into the shadow between the door and the wall, where no passing guard or curious priest could walk by and catch sight of him. He looked tired but better than he had in a long time.

"What are you meant to be praying for?" Rao prompted.

"Success against Ahiranya, of course. I've assured Hemanth I intend to contemplate the nature of sacrifice." She clasped her own hands before her. "It wasn't entirely a lie. That is why I called for you, Rao." A fortifying breath to hold herself steady. "You were with Aditya. At the end."

He swallowed. She saw the movement of his throat. The flinch in his gaze.

"Ask," he said. "And I'll tell you what it was like."

She shook her head.

"Rao," she said. "I do not want to burn as he burned. And yet I know what the priesthood wants. What everyone will want in time."

The crowds may have lauded her when she'd moved through the city, but with the rot spreading and the yaksa returning, people would turn against her. Faith was slow to grow and quick to splinter. It was inevitable and only a matter of time.

"You saw him," she said quietly. "Would you want that for me?"

"You know I wouldn't," he said, his voice rough. "Even if I hadn't seen him. Even then."

She nodded. She'd known. But she'd wanted to be sure.

"Lata has been looking for alternatives," Malini said. "She has studied every book and scroll in the imperial libraries and beyond. And she believes there may be other ways to fight the yaksa. There are tales—myths—from the Age of Flowers that offer possibilities beyond flame. I want you to chase one of those myths for me, Rao."

His face was distant, as if he couldn't quite reach his own emotions.

"Where do you want me to go?"

"Dwarali," she replied. "I want you to go beyond the Lal Qila. Beyond Parijatdvipa, where the tribes of the Jagatay and Babure dwell. Lata will tell you more, if you choose to go."

Silence. She saw his forehead crease, his jaw tense. Then, carefully, he said, "I had hoped to go home. To Alor."

"You cannot go yet."

"Lord Khalil or Lady Raziya. If you spoke to them—"

"Lord Khalil must remain here to assist in my war. Lady Raziya will go to the sultan's court with a portion of my army," said Malini. "I promised her husband the sultan's throne, you see. By law it is not mine to give, but the sultan is old, and he has no heirs but a distant cousin. Raziya has my permission to ensure that power transitions smoothly into Lord Khalil's hands."

"That sounds a little like murder."

"Does it? How strange."

"Malini."

"I thought we were beyond your judgment, Rao," Malini said, baring her teeth into a smile. "You're missing the most important truth: I trust you more than I trust them. I know the price of their loyalty, and I know the source of yours. It lies in your sister's pyre, and my brother's. I know the strength of that grief. I trust you, perhaps, more than I trust anyone."

"Do you?" His gaze fixed on her. Sharpened. "Or are you sending me on a fool's errand? Perhaps you don't feel I am a fit general for your army any longer. I wouldn't blame you, Malini. I know what I am."

There can be more than one truth.

She didn't say the words. Didn't speak of Lata's troubled gaze, the way she'd whispered to Malini about him. *All I desire is for him to have peace.*

"This is no punishment," she said gently. "And no fool's errand. If distance provides you ease or respite...I would be glad. But I hope you will return with answers, Rao. And even if you do not, I hope you will return to be my general and my advisor again."

Vulnerability flashed across his half-shadowed face.

"I want to take Sima with me," he said. "Lata placed her in my care on your behalf, but I won't act without your permission."

"Do you not trust me to keep her safe?"

"I know you will only stay in Harsinghar until Lady Varsha's child is born," he replied. "Then you will go to war again. She can't be your priority."

"Is she yours?"

"She is a good person, or so I believe," Rao said quietly. "I'd like to make sure one good person survives this war."

"Do not return to me and tell me you've misplaced her," she said.

"I wouldn't do such a thing."

She felt nothing about Sima but an echo of her feelings for Priya.

But Rao. Well.

She didn't tell him what she knew. Sima's guards replaced with newer, kinder men; the efforts to arrange better food. The night-time visits. The list of small kindnesses and intimacies revealed his partiality to her. If another man had been so attentive, Malini would have wondered if he'd fallen in love or lust with his prisoner. But with Rao, she was not sure such concerns were necessary. She knew where his heart lay, and it was in ashes, not in Sima's bed.

"Remember what she is," said Malini. "She may be good-natured, she may listen to you and be kind enough, but she is Ahiranyi. She comes from our enemies, and no matter what she may say, her heart belongs with them. Remember she is a prisoner with good reason, and treat her as such."

17

RAO

After seeing Malini, he returned to his old rooms. He bathed, and tried to eat a meal, and tried to sleep. Only the bathing was successful.

He was wounded. He'd made no useful efforts to hide the truth of it. Did everyone know how much he drank? Did they distrust him for it?

He settled on lighting a pipe and sitting out on his veranda, where he could watch the sun lower in the sky, and the gold of dusk bleed over Harsinghar, turning the white city bloody.

To stay and fight in the coming war. Or go home.

Malini had not given any consideration to the idea of him returning to Alor. He could have begged, but he hadn't. He knew when she couldn't be moved. But now, breathing out smoke, he considered the idea of going anyway. Simply leaving on a horse without a word, taking nothing with him. The thought of it was sweet.

To go back to Alor, the place he'd left as a boy. Or to go to Dwarali, as Malini had ordered. To chase a myth.

He wanted to go home.

Dwarali would not be unfamiliar. He had lived in the Lal Qila briefly, when Malini's war against Chandra first began. He knew how the snow lay in a heavy white gauze over the distant mountains, and the way coldness of the air there bit more sharply than even the deepest nighttime chill he had ever known in Parijat. But he had not been born there, as he had been born in Alor, or reared there, as he had been in Parijat.

Once, he would have listened to the call of the nameless. The vision that had struck him in Sima's rooms—of white snow, bloodied mountains—was a clear message from his god. *Go to Dwarali.*

But he hadn't felt any love in his head or heart for the nameless god since Aditya's death. That was the truth he could not admit to anyone. It had stopped him like a hand to the throat when he had tried to enter Harsinghar's monastery garden and seek the gentle guidance of a priest of the nameless, in those first raw days after Aditya's death.

There had only been one priest that Rao had wanted to guide him, in truth. One gentle, blue-garbed priest with a smile on his mouth and eyes that could pin you—eyes gray and deep and sure. And that priest was dead.

Rao's faith had died with Aditya. That was the truth Rao acknowledged now. The nameless had guided Rao's every step; had shaped his fate, had given him a prophecy for a name, had set his feet on the path that had led him to his position now, as general to the empress. But it was the guidance of the nameless that had killed his sister Alori and made Aditya kill himself. The nameless god had left Rao utterly alone.

I have no more faith to give you, Rao thought—speaking to nothing, nothing but the heartsick void inside him. *I refuse.*

He began with the arrack. A bad choice. It was vile, milk-sour, filling his belly. But he didn't let the taste stop him. He drank more.

It was deep, dark night when the drink finally submerged him. Darker still, when he rose back up from its depths, eyes snapping open.

It was much like being out at sea had to feel. His head was swimming, his limbs light and heavy all at once. And his heart— his aching heart—was finally calm.

He felt in himself a tug that wasn't from the nameless but from himself. He rose up onto his unsteady feet and began walking.

He knew the mahal well. Had run through its corridors as a boy, when he'd first arrived in Parijat to be Prince Aditya's companion; had fought with Aditya in the training ground he could see through the windows to his left. The same latticed windows that his sister and Malini and their little friend Narina had once stood at to watch the fighting, their eyes birdlike, bright and curious. He knew the way to the imperial temple, too, although he had never had any particular reason to go there as a boy.

Sometimes the places you have not been are a hollow, an absence with a shape. He followed the emptiness.

The imperial temple was quiet.

Maybe he was simply lucky. There should have been priests around, sweeping the steps or lighting the lanterns that kept the temple illuminated all through the night. But the lanterns were bright in their sconces, and Rao could only assume that somehow he'd just missed the moment the priests had drifted through the temple, checking the flames and laying fresh flowers at the feet of the mothers. He was entirely alone, surrounded by cottony silence, as he walked on heavy feet into the temple.

The night was chilly, and the curtains that lined the central prayer hall were in motion.

At the end of the hall, he could see the gold-hewn statues of the mothers.

A new statue had been placed to their left. Male, tall. Smiling, hands open in welcome.

Aditya.

Rao drifted toward him. He was carved in wood. In the night's shadows, in the dark where the glow of torchlight gently illuminated him, his wooden form could have been flesh. He could have been alive.

"Aditya," he said. His voice cracked as it left his throat, and a spill of unwanted tears fell from his eyes. There was no relief or release in them. Just an ugly upwelling of grief that suffused him like fire. He strode forward and gently clasped that face, that cold carved face fixed into a smile, and thought, *I should have done this while you lived.*

He did not think. The drink had him, and the pipe, and the grief. It was simple enough to press his own mouth to that carved face. That ever-smiling mouth.

It was cold beneath his lips. It did not warm. It never could.

Later, he would not remember leaving the imperial temple, or crossing the mahal's grounds—or even consciously choosing his path. All he'd recall would be the coolness of wood against his face as he leaned his wine-flushed forehead against the door to Sima's rooms. The thud of his own fist against it. And his own voice, croaking out of his throat:

"Sima, it's me. I'm sorry." A pause. "May I come in?"

One of the guards standing to the side of the door shuffled from one foot to the other and said, in a low voice, "She cannot stop you, my lord. If the prisoner has done something—"

"I won't come in," he said loudly, clearly, anger giving his voice fuel. "Unless you say I may."

Silence. Perhaps it lasted only seconds, or perhaps it lasted a great deal longer. Rao, in his current state, could not tell. But he felt it when a hand rapped smartly on the door from the inside, and when a firm voice spoke through the barrier of wood.

"Come in, Prince Rao," Sima said.

He unbarred the door and stepped in.

She looked the same as she had the first time: tired and rumpled, and wary. But she wasn't carrying a makeshift weapon this time, which was good. She looked him up and down, and her mouth tightened.

"You're drunk, Prince Rao," she said. "Your soldiers should return you to your chambers. You won't get what you're looking for here."

"I am not here looking for anything," he said stupidly, shutting the door behind him. He leaned back on it. Not dizzy but—weakened. "What do you think I'm looking for?"

She pursed her lips, then said, "Tell me what you need from me, my lord."

Black exhaustion was blooming at the edges of his vision. He blinked it back. "I am going to Dwarali," he said. "I am accompanying Lady Raziya to the sultan's mahal, and then—I will go to the Lal Qila. And I will...stay there. For a time. Sima, I am here to ask—will you come with me?"

She gave him a blank look.

"Come with you," she repeated.

"Yes."

"If you say I must, then I will," she said. "And if you decide to leave me here again in this room—well. Then what am I meant to do? Your men said it themselves. I'm a prisoner. I go where you decide. Why are you asking what I think?"

He could not faint here again. He wouldn't blame Sima for killing him if he did. He'd been nothing but trouble to her—and to Lata. And to himself.

But he could do her this one kindness.

"Dwarali is far from Harsinghar," he said quietly. "Far from Parijat, and the empress, and all imperial concerns. And some say...some say the Lal Qila is on the edge of the world. A woman who vanished there...I think, if she wanted to, she'd never be found."

Sima stared at him silently, some terrible emotion rising on her tired face.

"Don't try to trick me," she said wretchedly. "If you're trying to find out if I'm a traitor, if I—I'm *Ahiranyi*, I can't and won't change that, so let your empress execute me, if that's what she wants—"

"No," Rao said forcefully, alarmed. "No, Sima, please, calm yourself—"

"Don't tell me to be calm." She was shaking, her voice rising in pitch—but she was trying desperately not to shout, and that turned her voice into something wavering and strangled. "You can grieve and drink and go anywhere and do as you wish but I—I'm not allowed to grieve all I've lost! And I have to stay in this *fucking* room until I die! I—" She stoppered her own voice, shoving one palm against her mouth. Squeezing her eyes shut.

He swallowed, forced himself to stand straight, and took a laborious step toward her.

"Sima," he said. No answer. "Sima, I am sorry. I..." Another step. "There are people even now, in Parijat, who care for you. I have been a bad ally to you. And nothing like a friend. But I am...I am one of those people who wish you well. Who trust you. I am not trying to trick or trap you. I am offering you a way forward. What you do with it...that, I leave to you."

Sima was breathing shallowly. Then she rubbed her hand over her eyes, freeing her own mouth. Gasped a deep breath. Another.

"Who else?" she said.

"What?"

"Who else cares for me? Wishes me well?"

"One of Prince Ashutosh's men came to talk to me," Rao said. "On your behalf. Romesh."

"Oh," she said. "Good."

"And Sahar, the empress's new guard," he added.

She nodded, once. Looked at him with teary eyes.

"I will come to Dwarali with you." There was determination in her voice. Somehow, in that paroxysm of feeling, she'd made a choice. Then, as if the words were being wrenched out of her, she whispered: "If I stay in here any longer, I won't survive."

"Dwarali, then," he said. "And a future where you'll live. That's what I promise you."

18

PRIYA

Priya knew she was dreaming. But this time she wasn't lying on the ground with Malini's hands on her face, her hair. She was standing and Malini was standing ahead of her.

Malini's back was to her. Blue light haloed her, veiling her body in shadow. But Priya knew the shape of Malini's body. She knew her narrow, firmly held shoulders and straight spine; the height of her, and the slimness, and the way she held her head— haughty, gaze direct, as sharp as an arrow.

Priya knew it all, and knew better than to approach her.

She did it anyway.

Just a dream, with her feet moving of their own accord across green-veined marble, the stone cold and grainy with river silt beneath her. Just a dream as she reached out a hand and pressed her fingertips to Malini's spine.

Malini stiffened under her hand. Priya felt the movement of her muscles. The sharp rivulets between the joints of her spine. She was marble-stone and ivory and a riverbed. She was a force of life under Priya's hand.

"Priya," Malini murmured. She said her name like a curse. Began to turn her head—

"Elder Priya." Priya opened her eyes. Her blurred vision cleared as she sat up in bed blinking. A mask-keeper, mask hooked at her waist, was standing at the doorway. It wasn't morning yet. The room was nearly black with shadow.

"What is it?" Priya asked, keeping her voice low. She didn't want to wake Rukh and Padma if she didn't have to.

The mask-keeper took another step into the room, her expression grave.

"There are people, High Elder. Strangers."

Fear ignited through her blood.

"Have the Parijatdvipan soldiers found a way into Ahiranya?" Priya demanded.

The mask-keeper shook her head frantically. "No, no. Not the soldiers. Normal people. Rot-riven. On the edge of the forest. They're—they're begging to be let in. We don't know what to do."

Priya stared at her, mouth open. She felt like a landed fish.

"They brought offerings," the mask-keeper said, sounding as confused as Priya felt. "They're kneeling. Some have weapons, but they've left them on the ground by the trees. I think—*we* think, those of us who were on patrol, Elder—that they're worshippers."

Priya rose to her feet, fumbling in the process of trying to tighten her sari. "Worshippers?" she repeated. "From—outside Ahiranya? Not our people?"

"No," said the mask-keeper. "What should we do with them?"

More mouths to feed. Outsiders. There was a voice that sounded distinctly like Bhumika's warning her that Hiranaprastha could not manage more people, and the mahal could certainly hold no more pilgrims. But Bhumika wasn't here, and Priya had always been too softhearted and lacking in sense to manage this kind of shit on her own.

"I'll see them myself," she said.

The mask-keepers who'd been on night patrol were waiting for her at the very edge of Ahiranya, where trees rich with rot grew thickly, and thorns like spears lined the rolling green of the ground that was once a track used by farmers traveling to and fro. They had their masks on, but she could feel how unsure they were. Their faces turned toward her as she strode toward them.

"Where are they?" Priya asked.

"Close," one mask-keeper said. He pointed outward.

Priya walked a few more steps and saw them. Maybe a hundred kneeling figures. Some young, some old. There were children among them. The people had no torches, and their faces were gray and frightened in the semidark.

There were Parijatdvipan soldiers in a perimeter all around Ahiranya. Priya had felt them in the green. Malini had left them behind. She didn't know how this group of people had managed to evade them, and it made her stomach knot trying to imagine it.

"Have you spoken to them?"

"A little," one mask-keeper said. "We told them not to get closer."

She swallowed. "Good," she said. "That's good."

No one could leave Ahiranya, the people in the mahal had told her. Anyone who tried to leave died, speared by thorns or swallowed by the soil.

And no one could enter, either. Walking into Ahiranya was just as deadly.

But Priya wasn't *most* people.

Taking a deep breath, she stepped beyond the trees.

She could feel those people. Their knees pressed to soil. Their mouths whispering prayers. They raised their heads when she crossed the boundary. Some scrambled back with gasps of fear. Others bowed their faces to the ground in reverence.

She turned for one brief moment to look at the mask-keepers behind her in the trees. In the moonlight, the mask-keepers looked eerie, the wood concealing their faces both gleaming and shadowed. She was glad she hadn't worn her mask; the crown mask still lay at her bedside.

She took a step forward into better light, and someone gave a shriek.

Ah. She'd forgotten her skin.

But... she assessed the faces in front of her. Leaves. Bark on fingertips and jaws. One woman had a flower growing from her throat.

The mask-keeper who'd woken her had been right. All of the strangers were rot-riven. Their skin wasn't so different from hers after all.

All of them were silent now. Watching her.

"I heard you," Priya said, forcing herself to be loud. Forcing her voice to carry. "I heard your worship. I am the High Elder of Ahiranya. Why are you here?"

The crowd moved uneasily. Then one kneeling figure stood. A man—broad-shouldered and scarred—stepped forward and bowed.

"Elder Priya," he said. "We are here for your help."

"You know my name," Priya said, surprised.

"You're the Ahiranyi witch," he said, without sharpness. "The one who tried to kill our empress. Everyone knows your name."

That shook her more than it should have. Of course people knew what she'd done. She should have expected it.

"What do you need from me?" Priya asked.

"High Elder," he said. "We seek a new home. We seek safety."

He spoke Zaban with a distinct accent.

"You're from Parijat," she said. "Why would you seek a home here?"

He hesitated. It was one of the women behind him who spoke.

"There's nowhere safe for us anywhere else," she said bluntly, meeting Priya's eyes. "Our own villages turn us away. Our own people try to kill us. Imperial soldiers hunt us down, saying we'll sicken the crops. Where else can we go?"

"We heard that if we pray hard enough, the rot can be cured," another said tearily. "That it may not kill us after all. We've brought all we have. Gold, coin, food—"

"Stop," Priya said sharply, and the worshippers fell silent.

A child was crying. She heard someone shush it.

"Please," the man said, voice wavering. "The soldiers will be back here soon—don't leave us here."

She exhaled.

"Wait here," she said. "I need to speak with the yaksa."

In Ahiranya the mask-keepers had their heads bowed. Between them, sitting on the sheared stump of a tree, legs crossed, was the yaksa wearing Nandi's face. He'd been waiting for her.

Priya bowed her head.

"Yaksa," she said. "I was coming to seek you out."

"We knew," he said. "We heard them. Their prayers. And you." The chiming rustle of leaves; the click of Nandi's neck as he looked at each of the mask-keepers, then looked at her. "They cannot enter," Nandi said. "They're not wanted. Ahiranya is a closed place. Our place."

"They need help because of what you've made of the world," Priya said, without thinking. She heard one of the mask-keepers hiss under their breath and bit back her own curse.

Foolish. She should have thought before saying it. But it was *true*, so she pressed on.

"They're rot-riven," she said. "They're what you made, yaksa. They belong here. So let me bring them where they belong."

"You are a temple elder," Sendhil said, from somewhere in the trees. He emerged, his wood-whorled face dark. "You do not question. You obey us."

She thought of Mani Ara, and of the way Priya had defied her. Mani Ara needed her, and the yaksa needed her too.

She thought of the people waiting for her permission to enter Ahiranya. Their terror and their hope.

"Mani Ara gave me the right to her power," Priya said, raising her head. "Mani Ara bid me wield it. This is part of her power too, isn't it? The right to order instead of obey. The right to *lead*. I'm letting them stay."

Nandi's pearly eyes were cold, his expression sharp.

"No," he said. "That isn't for you to decide."

Sendhil strode toward her. She felt his fingers at the back of her neck, rough-textured, pinching to the point of pain. He was going to lower her head. He was going to show the mask-keepers that obedience could be compelled from her.

Rage flickered up in her like a candle.

She reached into herself and grasped at the power inside her. She felt Mani Ara's voice rise behind her teeth, hot as blood.

"You do not tell me no, Avan Ara."

Behind her, Sendhil—no, *Vata Ara*, she knew his name now, as she knew her own—went utterly still. Before her, Avan stared at her with eyes that were twin moons, filled with light.

Something skittered away from Priya within her skull. Names and knowing, knowledge too big for her own brain or body. Mani Ara's knowledge.

"Release me," she rasped, and Sendhil—Vata Ara—did. He obeyed.

The rush of it was heady.

She heard the rustle of bodies as slowly, reverently, the mask-keepers kneeled. She watched them lower in a wave.

Vata Ara bowed with them, his great body elegantly lowering.

They were bowing to her, she realized. Because she had spoken the names of the yaksa in a voice vaster than her body, a voice that wasn't her own.

Shaken, she forced herself to remain calm. She had to use this while she still could.

She crossed the border of Ahiranya. The rot-riven strangers scrambled to bow again.

"Come," she said, and felt the trees behind her widen into a path, the yaksa allowing the way to part for them. "You're welcome in Ahiranya," she said. "If you are loyal to the yaksa, you will have a home here."

You should understand, Priya thought of saying, *that loyalty means hollowing. That loyalty may mean more than your life.*

But she didn't say it. It would have done no good. Instead she simply guided them into Ahiranya and let the trees close behind them.

19

BHUMIKA

Their food supplies had begun to deplete. They had no choice but to mingle with other people. As evening fell, they reached a caravanserai.

There had been strange, unseasonable rain. It was not monsoon season, but the rain had poured for hours. The road to the caravanserai was churned, thick with mud, and the guards at the perimeter fence looked tired and irritable, mud staining their trousers to their knees. They held up spears when Bhumika and Jeevan drew close but only in a desultory way. They were doing their job. There was nothing to fear.

Not yet, anyway. But she kept up her guard, making sure her eyes were demurely lowered, her pallu—wet though it was from the rain—drawn over her hair. She let Jeevan step forward and speak for her.

"Where are you from?" the guard asked abruptly. He looked between them. His scowl deepened. "Not Alor. I can tell."

Bhumika had tried her best to ensure they wouldn't draw interest. She and Jeevan had practiced speaking Zaban with a less pronounced Ahiranyi accent. She'd tied her sari in the Aloran style, and he had prepared a lie he trotted out now, claiming they were from a village on the far border of Alor, where languages and accents mingled easily. But she had known it was unlikely to be enough. They were not actors.

"Show us your arms," the guard said. "Both of you. Go on."

Jeevan rolled up his sleeves, and with a show of hesitation, she did the same. The guards leaned forward, inspecting their skin for rot. When none was found, a guard said, "Legs now."

"I am a married woman," she said in a small voice. She was *not* baring her legs. "I . . . I shouldn't."

"Tell your wife," another guard said lazily, gesturing at Jeevan.

Jeevan leaned forward, murmuring something apologetic, and clasped the man's hand. She knew he was passing coin between them and was unsurprised when the guard—without any visible change of expression—tucked away the coin, then nodded at his fellows. Spears were moved aside. The way was open to them.

"I should have made you pay double," the guard muttered, as the two passed. "An outsider's tax." But he did nothing more to stop them.

Inside, there were stalls selling food, many carefully covered to protect them from the deluge of rain. But it was not the market that snared her attention; it was the lake that lay at its center. It was vast, unchecked by trees or hills—a single flat sheet of waters ringed by the caravanserai's walls, and rest houses, and market stalls. Its surface was covered utterly in blue lotus flowers, which grew so profusely they were an azure blanket. The water between them was ringed by green algae. It was beautiful, and it called to her strangely.

"I'll get our supplies," Jeevan said, voice low. "Then we can leave swiftly."

It seemed a shame to leave a place of relative safety. But she didn't argue. She inclined her head. "I'll wait by the water," she said, and pointed to the water's edge, by an elderly lady's stall.

"I won't be long," he replied, anxious, and swept away.

There was no drop between the water and land. The lake was very high indeed. The rain had raised it rapidly, she was sure. She stood and looked down into it, gently adjusting her shawl, half expecting to see her watchers in the water once again. She listened to the threads of conversation moving around her. People muttering, concerned about crop yields. Talk of rot. The air was thick with fear.

The elderly lady at her stall tutted loudly; Bhumika raised her head.

"Keep away from the water, little sister," the older woman called in thick Aloran. It took her a moment to parse her words.

"Is it dangerous?"

"Old stories," said the older woman. "But old stories have grains of truth, eh? They say Utpala is the open mouth of the nameless god. Fall in, and you'll see the whole universe, and lose your life to it."

Bhumika looked down again, briefly. *This is not the mouth the stories spoke of,* she thought.

"The flowers are certainly beautiful," Bhumika said.

The stall keeper snorted.

"They are. And our only defense against being inflicted in holy visions, no doubt." Then she grinned, to show that it was more of a joke. "Now will you buy? No? Then give my stall some room, little sister. You're scaring my customers away."

It was said genially, but Bhumika took it as the order it was and moved away.

She walked leisurely away from the water and let her eyes thoughtlessly skim the land around the lake. She didn't let her gaze pause when she saw a group of men watching her, but internally she tensed and felt her unease increase. She cursed the foreignness she had not yet learned to hide. Whatever her old life had been, she'd had no need to melt into a crowd and vanish. It did not come easily to her.

Jeevan returned. A full bag of food was with him. He kept his face calm as he offered it to her, as she flaked golden pastry with her fingertips and told him lightly about her concerns, pausing between her words to make their one-sided conversation look casual rather than urgent. Easy talk between a husband and his wife.

"It would be unwise to stay the night," he said, "but also unwise to go. What do you suggest?"

"We leave now," Bhumika decided for him. "And we try to avoid them."

"You have your knife?" Jeevan asked.

Tucked against her side. Strong and sharp. "Yes," she said.

They left the caravanserai and received significantly less bother as they did so.

Bhumika did not watch to see if they were followed. To watch would be to reveal that she knew the threat existed at all. That would be like blood to a tiger.

They walked fast, moving off the path into trees. The air smelled of sweet fruit, of fresh rain-churned soil. They walked for ten, perhaps fifteen minutes, before Bhumika murmured, "Four of them."

Jeevan's gaze ticked to her, then forward again. He had never questioned her overly sharp hearing—the way she always knew what things lurked in shadows in the dark.

They turned. The men were approaching and making very little effort to hide. She moved to stand behind Jeevan, watching them with careful eyes.

The men held weapons. Chakrams, drawn from wrists. Daggers.

"We have nothing for you to steal," Jeevan said bluntly. Behind the cover of his body, Bhumika carefully drew her own dagger. Held it steadily. Memory or no memory, her body had an old knowledge of how to wield a short blade.

"You have food," one said. His expression wasn't particularly vicious. But he was twisting the chakram between his fingers, waiting to strike.

They had no way to defend themselves from a projectile thrown from a distance. Both she and Jeevan knew it.

Jeevan needed to get into proximity to them before they could act.

She considered what to do as the men and Jeevan traded barbs. He was not witty, her guard—but he knew how to play his role.

How to distract them?

Without overthinking it, she touched a finger to Jeevan's back. *Be ready.*

Then she opened her mouth and let out an earsplitting scream.

The men flinched, startled. It was enough of an opening for Jeevan to lurch forward, saber angled, and split the first man at the arm, then the throat. He caught the second in the chest before the other two managed to respond. One moved to stab him and slashed Jeevan on the arm; with lightning speed Jeevan turned on him and met him blow for blow.

Then a strike of ill luck. The last man threw himself bodily at Jeevan, grappling with him. Jeevan's saber was knocked from his hand, skidding into the soil.

The last man ran to seize it. But she was already moving, light on her feet.

She heaved up Jeevan's saber, her arms protesting, and angled it just in time for the man to fall upon it. His own momentum made the saber pierce his stomach. She felt the split and the bloody crunch of muscle and flesh as it went through his belly.

Just to be sure he would die, she wrenched the saber out.

She raised her head. The man Jeevan had been grappling with was facedown against the wet ground. He was unconscious, or dead. It didn't matter to her.

Jeevan was breathing hard. His eye was bruised.

"Thank you, my lady," he said. Then he corrected himself. "Thank you, Bhumika."

"Jeevan," she said, breathless with terror—and relief. "Come. Let me clean your wounds."

20

ARAHLI ARA

Taru Ara called to him through flowers. She seeded datura blossoms across the walls of the Hirana and the mahal, flashes of white at the periphery of his vision. One pointedly, viciously, grew its way through his right palm. It grew through blackened, its petals dying. He felt her in them. He understood.

You, her blooms said. *Secretly. Not the others.*

He drifted easily from the others. They were distracted with exultation. Priya had spoken their names; Priya had wielded Mani Ara's voice, a lustrous pearl in the ugly shell of her body. While they celebrated, he followed the sound of his kin. Taru Ara was crying pitifully: a sawing of wood sound, a creaking branch in a high wind.

He found her on a veranda carpeted in vines. She lay curved on her side, torso bared to the sunlight. Her cries eased as she felt him approach, as his leaves shadowed the curve of her body, where her wound lay.

Her stomach was seared. The burn upon it was a hole the size of a fist, blistered with heat and pus and the livid quality of mortal flesh. He lowered a hand to it.

"When I fought the Parijatdvipans," she said, voice still reed thin, "they caught me with flame. The flame was nothing, and yet it *caught* me."

"You concealed this," he murmured. "Why?"

"Our kin wouldn't understand. They would be afraid." *Or they would think me weak*, Taru didn't say. But Arahli Ara knew her nature and the harshness of their kin.

"And you think I understand?"

Her neck twisted. She gazed up at him.

"The remains of Sanjana must be inside me," she said, as he felt the contours of the wound. "Rotting me from the inside. You need to tell me how you laid Ashok aside. I cannot carry this upon me."

"Ashok fell away naturally, in time," Arahli Ara replied. A shudder ran through him as he recalled how untrue that claim was. Ashok clung to him still in so many small ways.

She heaved a breath, her chest rising and falling, then turned her head. "What do I feel, Arahli?"

Ashok's memories surged through him. This, Ashok had known.

"Pain," he said.

"I don't remember pain," she said, staring uncomprehending at her stomach. "Last time, when we were forced to burn by the Parijati woman, when we crept beneath the earth, when Ahiranya's soil let us sleep—I don't remember *pain*."

"I remember it," he murmured. He fed his green-toothed strength into her wound with the flat of his hand against her torso. His own hand was wood-whorled. Yaksa through and through.

"You are not like us, Arahli," she said, with a laugh that was all bitterness. "The sap in you practically runs red."

And in you, he thought as his fingers traced the shape of the gouge in her belly. Perhaps she did not understand what their sacrifices were making of them. But he knew.

They needed their temple elders. He felt the knowledge beat a drum within his skull. Once they had possessed so many. Elders, thrice-born and loyal, blessed and beloved. Temple children, small and strong and easy to mold. How easy they had been to love, once.

He should never have let Bhumika go.

Oh, his kin laughed indulgently over his folly. What a waste, they said, confident that Mani Ara's beloved would be enough.

But they did not understand how great Bhumika's worth had

been. He had known. Arahli had always known how to weigh the worth of a temple child, by the beating of their heart and their stubbornness, their capacity for pain and their ferocity. *Ashok* had known her worth, for all he'd loathed her as much as he'd loved her. That was why he had filled her with knowledge that could kill them all and sent her away. It had been Ashok's last folly— destroying his sister for a fragile, mortal hope.

Arahli Ara was not Ashok. But Taru Ara had been right: He was not like his kin, either. The mortality decaying Taru's flesh had shaken him at first, but now it only served to strengthen his resolve.

He left his kin. He moved through the city that surrounded the Hirana, seeding rot in his wake. Many Ahiranyi had fled the rot and their distant villages, settling in Hiranaprastha. The streets were crammed with a mixture of makeshift tents and ancient homes, the varnish of their verandas peeling, their lattice windows barely concealing cowering people within, reduced to fractures of fingertips and eyes peering through wood.

He found the first child soon enough. A girl, a small thing, hiding in her mother's skirts in the shadow of a ruined building. But there was strength in her. He felt it, as he'd felt it so many times in the past when he'd taken a child for the temple.

Once, Vata Ara had mocked him. When they were young, sap-green and fresh to life, when the Age of Flowers had barely bloomed. Then Vata Ara had been given easily to laughter. And he had laughed then, when he watched Arahli cradle a sleeping temple child on his lap.

You spend so much time with those mortal children, Vata Ara had said. *Do you enjoy it?*

Humanity? No. Arahli remembered his old voice, his stronger hands, rich with green and with power. *I do this for us.*

Now the child's mother trembled. The child did not. She stared boldly at Arahli, her eyes fierce.

Arahli Ara smiled.

"Your child," he said, "is no longer yours. Your child belongs to us."

21

PRIYA

The mask-keepers were working tirelessly to keep Ahiranya running, but somehow Kritika was not too busy to track Priya down and harangue her.

Priya wasn't shocked. She'd been waiting for it. The newcomers were hard to miss, after all. They'd taken over four dormitories between them. And Priya—in an effort to get the lecture over with—had placed herself helpfully in Bhumika's study. She was leafing desultorily through some reams of incomprehensible figures when the door crashed open.

"Outsiders." Kritika's voice was furious. "Parijatdvipans. Why would you allow them in here? What led you to this madness?"

Priya released the papers.

"They asked," Priya said simply. "They want to be here. They've got nowhere else to go. What other reason do I need?"

"They're liars," scoffed Kritika. Her gaze narrowed, reading Priya like a book. "Don't you think this is a trick of your empress?" Kritika asked. "Apparent innocents, sent to destroy us from within?"

A memory bloomed in her skull. Malini, imprisoned, fragile—her eyes huge, her mind caught in a snare. She'd always admired Malini's mind—its cleverness, its slow cunning. But this didn't feel like something Malini would have planned.

Malini wanted to break Priya herself.

"Are you listening?" Kritika demanded.

"I'm trying," Priya said. "But you know how I am, Kritika. If you look closely, you might see your words going into one ear and falling out of the other one."

Kritika hissed something under her breath—definitely a swear of some kind.

"We are at war, Elder Priya," she gritted out.

"Are we? Tell the yaksa to send me out with an army, then. That would be a proper war."

"Don't be a fool."

"Fine," Priya said, her patience finally snapping. "Let's call this a war, then. Why not? If this is war, we maimed those people, Kritika. Our yaksa, our power—we *changed* them. Destroyed their homes, their crops, their chance of survival. They're casualties of war. We should feel terrible for what they've suffered, and we should do everything in our power to help them."

"They are our enemies," Kritika said staunchly.

"No. They have the rot, Kritika. They were shaped by the yaksa. That makes them ours. They're going to be fed our grain and given work, and I promise if they try to harm our own, I'll kill them myself."

Kritika's mouth opened, but a skitter of noise in the hall and a series of hard knocks at the door silenced her. Priya was moving before she heard a familiar voice call her name.

Rukh was doubled over, panting. He'd clearly run, and Padma was still adhered to his hip, clinging on to him with a slightly alarmed and windswept look on her face.

"Rukh," Priya said. "What's wrong?"

"The yaksa," he said, voice shaking. "They—the one with Ashok's face. He—he brought children. Other children. I spoke to one—I heard—they're going to be temple children."

She stormed across the mahal.

She'd been avoiding the yaksa with Ashok's face. But now she followed the echo of him in the sangam. She knew even as she strode through the mahal, as vines brushed her face, as the corridors closed in on her in thick foliage and flowers as large as her fists, that seeing him would hurt. *Go back*, the green seemed to say. *Your foolish heart leads you here, your grief leads you here. But you will not find what you seek in him.*

Priya had always been too foolish and heart-driven for her own good. That wasn't going to change now.

He wasn't with the children he'd brought to the mahal. They were waiting at the base of the Hirana. She'd told Rukh to watch them for her while she dealt with him.

The room where Ashok's ghost waited shone with light. The windows had broken under the weight of roots, letting the sunbeams and birdsong pour in between leaves of emerald and jade. There were large-winged moths in the high branches of the trees clasping the ceiling. She could see the colors of their wings: gold and umber, red and lustrous carnelian.

The yaksa was lying in a bower of his own making. His head was turned away from her, the dark leaves of his hair swathing his face. She could see the tilt of his shoulder. One leg hung from the bower, almost touching the ground, which was cracked beneath his toes. Small white flowers were worming through stone, trying to meet him.

He looked entirely inhuman and therefore nothing like her brother. And yet Priya couldn't help but stop suddenly, grief clambering horrible and swift up in her throat. It was the thought of children that had done this to her. *Ashok. Ashok.*

She wished suddenly for that strange knowledge that had wormed through her on the edge of Ahiranya, when she'd suddenly known two of the yaksa's names. But no other name came to her now.

"Why are you here?" the yaksa asked, without turning his head. The leaves of the bower rustled at his voice. They turned to her, as if she were light or rain—watching her for him.

"Children," Priya blurted out. "Why would you bring children here?"

"You know why," he replied. "To create more temple elders."

"You have me. You don't need them."

"You are still imperfect," he said.

"I'm growing stronger," Priya said hotly. "I've reached for Mani Ara. I have her power, I've learned the names of your kin—"

"Names are nothing." His head turned, with a creak and whisper of wood. "We have always had many temple elders. Never only one. You cannot be alone."

"The mask-keepers are once-born and twice-born," she said immediately. "They're enough."

"They will pass through the waters again. But children are needed. Children are easier to shape and hollow," he said, and the rage swelled in her like fire. She wrestled to control it.

"I won't let them become temple children," Priya said tightly. "I won't let them suffer like I did. Like Ashok did."

The yaksa didn't flinch.

"And yet you must," he said. "It is our will."

"I am Mani Ara's hands. If you go against me, you go against her."

Those words were a mistake.

He moved, sudden and swift. In the blink of an eye he'd risen from the bower and grasped her by both wrists. His touch was unyielding, his mouth a bristle of thorns. And yet his voice came from him too human. It had a human's cruelty in it.

"Mani Ara," he said, "would forgive me for breaking her hand." A twist, a tightening, of his grip at her wrists. She didn't flinch. She'd suffered worse. "Mani Ara would make a better hand. Mani Ara would feel no pain," he continued. "You would, Priya."

You're only flesh.

She understood the message clearly.

"Don't try to frighten me," she said. "I know my value."

"Do you?"

"I know I'm needed. You won't break what you need."

His grip tightened. She ground her teeth to stop crying out, and tasted blood.

"You can't break me like that," she forced out. "Ashok tried. It *didn't work.*"

He released her. Her wrists were already purpling. She ignored the throbbing pain.

"They have been given to me by their families," he said, face blank and inhuman again, the cruelty leached from it. "I will raise them to be temple elders. They will grow strong and hollow, and they will pass through the waters. This is decided, Priya. It cannot be changed."

"Give them to me," she said.

"Your task is to reach for Mani Ara."

"Temple children should be raised by temple elders," Priya insisted. "By *me*. It's my right. I'll train them, rear them." *Protect them from the kind of pain you and your kin could inflict on them. Give them someone to defend them.* "You can't possibly want to raise them yourself, yaksa."

"I raised the first temple children," he said. "And many after."

"Human children are—they're *messy*. They scream, they cry, they fight, they die." She saw him flinch at that, or thought she did. "Give them to me," she urged. "I'll shape them so well. I know what it takes to be strong."

Silence. Then he said, "I will, if you perform one act for me. One test."

"Anything."

"You named my kin," he said. "Avan Ara. Vata Ara. You called them. Knew them. Tell me my name, Elder Priya."

She shook her head.

"I don't know it, yaksa."

"Name me," he said again, "and you may have them. Remain silent, and I will know there is not enough of Mani Ara in you to allow you to rear them. What is my name?"

Panic buzzed in her skull. But she was stubborn—she'd always been stubborn. She clenched her hands tight, and sucked in a slow breath, and reached through the panic.

To the waters of the sangam, and the green within her.

The waters washed her panic away and left nothing behind—just a vastness that unfolded inside her.

"Arahli Ara," she said finally. Her voice was an unnatural river-rasp. Water over stone. "That is your name."

He breathed, a green-rustling exhalation, and bowed his head in reverence. She'd passed his test.

"High Elder," he said. "Mani Ara's beloved. The children are yours. Train them well. But remember this: You have value, but the ones you love do not. Not to my kin. I could take the eyes of the boy Rukh. Or a tongue. Or a hand. I could steal away Bhumika's daughter and let the soil swallow her. And I am the kindest of my kin."

He had not raised his head. His voice was soft.

Priya's stomach knotted. Grief-sick.

He really isn't my brother, she thought.

"Wield Mani Ara's gifts with care," he said. "They are a knife that could cut throats and leave you with nothing but sorrow."

"I will, yaksa," she said. She inclined her head. "Thank you."

22

MALINI

All through the night she sat waiting for news. Oil lamps guttered and died, and new ones were lit. Swati yawned discreetly, leaning against the wall when she thought no eyes were on her. Deepa drooped in her seat, head propped up on one arm, eyes barely open—though she jumped upright whenever the doors opened and a new tray of tea was brought in and arrayed on the table.

Only Lata remained as awake as Malini.

It did not seem appropriate to play games of dice or chance when a woman could live or die, and a child along with her. Lata offered to play a singing game—"They don't all have to be filthy songs," Lata said, when Malini raised an eyebrow. "We could sing songs for good fortune. Healthy children."

"But you're so *good* at singing filthy songs," Malini replied with a smile.

"If dice games aren't appropriate—"

"—then dirty songs won't be either, I know." Malini sighed. "I'm afraid I don't know any songs for good fortune."

"Sahar would teach you if you asked."

"I don't think so," said Malini. "She's learned far too much about proper behavior for a guard since she left Raziya's service. A pity."

"Give her the chance to be bored, my lady, and I'm sure she'll be ready for mischief again."

They lapsed into silence. Malini could hear nothing but the quiet spit and smolder of the lanterns, the soft wheeze of Deepa's breath as her head tilted forward, almost a snore.

"Shall I wake her?" Lata asked.

"No. Let her sleep." She looked from Deepa to Swati to Lata. "I should let you all go to bed. It may be a long while yet."

Lata hesitated, then said, "I could go. Into the birthing chamber."

"I have eyes and ears and enough in there. No."

"You could have been with her, my lady," Lata said quietly.

"She will suffer enough in her life," Malini said, equally quiet and thoughtful. "I don't need to see her at her most vulnerable. It seems a cruelty too far."

There was a thud of footsteps from the hallway. Sahar opened the doors and stepped inside.

"Empress," she said. There was a hint of a smile at her mouth, despite the tired shadows under her eyes. "The baby's born safely."

"And Lady Varsha?" Malini asked.

"Healthy," said Sahar. "If you want to speak to the physician, Empress..."

"Later." Malini stood. "The baby," she prompted.

"A son," Sahar said, understanding the question implied in Malini's voice.

A son. A prince.

She didn't know if she felt relief.

An heir was a future—and a tool that would allow her to avoid marriage and childbirth. A son would be more readily accepted as her heir by the court than a daughter. There was some benefit in that.

But he was also a tool that could be used against her. He was a promise that even if Malini died, her family line—and the promises bound to it, that stitched the empire together—would outlive her.

He was all the more reason to let Malini burn.

Her instincts warred in her.

"I wish to see him," she said.

*   *   *

The birthing room was bustling. Maids swept in and out. A physician stood by the bed. The attendants bowed when Malini entered.

Varsha watched Malini from the bed. Her skin had a grayish pallor. Her hair was lank. Her eyes were dull, but she gripped the squirming bundle in her arms as if those blankets of silk and cotton held the world inside them. Malini could only see one small hand—wrinkled, shockingly small, spasmodically grasping at nothing.

"A boy, Empress," the physician said proudly, not waiting for Varsha to speak. "A healthy prince."

Was she meant to value a prince more than a princess?

Malini took a step closer. Now she saw a little more. Black hair. A scrunched face. He appeared to be sleeping. He did not look like her brother, or like Varsha, or in fact like anyone. He was too new to the world to carry echoes and debts, perhaps.

"Congratulations, sister," Malini murmured, meeting Varsha's eyes. "I wish you a swift recovery, and health for your son."

"Will there be celebrations, Empress?" Varsha's voice was a thin and wavering reed.

There were always celebrations on the birth of an imperial scion. Sweets and coin handed out across the city. And gifts carved for the infant: beaded bracelets to ward off evil, bangles of silver to commemorate the shape of small wrists, a feather to be placed in the child's swinging cot for sweet dreams. Varsha knew that. She was asking, in her own way, if her son would be acknowledged.

"He is a royal prince," Malini said. "An imperial prince of Parijat. All the correct rites will be held. Prayers will be made, and offerings. Of course I will do everything I must, and everything I should."

The baby made a hiccupping noise.

When Malini leaned closer, Varsha flinched. Her eyes closed. All her defenses had been ripped away, and the look on her face was a raw thing, weary and frightened and horribly resigned.

A hush fell over the room.

Malini did not say *I will not take your child from you,* even though the words rose unbidden in her throat. It should have horrified her that they all expected it, and yet—it did not.

It would have been the sensible thing to do. To take the only heir and make him her own; to mold him in her image, to make him love her, to place him beyond his mother's power. She was clear-eyed and coldhearted enough to know that it would be a wise path.

But she wanted to make something better than Chandra had. She did not want to simply enact his old cruelties.

Malini touched her fingertips lightly to the baby's forehead.

"He is beautiful," she said softly. "Your son. He looks like you, Varsha. And a little like my emperor father."

Lies, but they eased the tension from Varsha's face.

"Give him a strong name," Malini said, shaping her mouth into a smile. "Raise him well. But for now, sister—rest. I'll ensure that all the proper rites are performed."

23

PRIYA

Rukh was waiting with the children at the base of the Hirana, Padma on the ground next to him. There were so many people milling around: servants from the mahal, and soldiers, and pilgrims. But the mask-keepers were closest to the children, surrounding them in a crescent, holding the tide of people back.

"Where are the yaksa?" Priya asked one of them.

"Not here, Elder," the mask-keeper said. "When the one who...the one..."

"The one who looks like Ashok, I know. He left them here alone?"

The mask-keeper nodded.

"When he left, he told us to stay here. We were ordered to wait for you."

Priya could have sworn.

He'd always expected Priya to care for them, hadn't he? She'd begged to protect them for nothing.

Well. Never mind. Whether she'd played into his hands or not, she was where she needed to be.

She slipped between the mask-keepers.

The temple children the yaksa had brought her were all young. Fifteen in number. The oldest was a boy, tall and painfully thin in a way that suggested he'd recently had a growth spurt. Many were dressed in worn-out but cared-for clothing: stitches at the sleeves, patches in their tunics. But others wore fine cloth, dyed in deep blues, reds, greens.

"Bow to your Elder," a mask-keeper said sharply, and as the children scrambled, Priya said, "Don't. There's no need."

Some froze. The tallest boy was still standing tall. Arms clasped behind him, his blue kurta pristine. She met his eyes, and his jaw tightened a little, trembling with nerves and hate.

"You're highborn," she observed.

He gave a jerky nod.

"Yes, Elder."

"What's your name?"

"Ashish," he said.

"Tell me how you ended up here."

His jaw flexed. He looked away. "The yaksa brought me, of course," he said. The *obviously, you idiot* was heavily implied. She was pleased he'd managed to avoid saying it. "My . . . my parents were given the rot by the yaksa. For not being loyal enough. But the yaksa let them live, and they're grateful. Faithful. So when the yaksa came for me, I was happy to go."

He'd need to learn to lie better if he wanted to survive serving the yaksa.

"And you?" Priya asked, bending down to meet the eyes of the small girl next to him.

"I'm not a highborn," she piped up. "But my mother got spared from dying of the rot, and she promised me to the yaksa for it."

"And your name?"

"Pallavi." The boy kicked her, and she said obediently, "Pallavi, *Elder*."

Priya worked through the group, learning names and origins. The youngest of them was probably only four and couldn't answer Priya properly.

It made her sick.

Finally, Priya straightened.

"Do you know what it means to be a temple child?" Priya asked them, gaze sweeping over them.

A long silence followed, where they all stared in different directions.

"It means you serve the yaksa," Rukh said finally. Priya shot him a look, and he shrugged.

"It means worshipping," Ashish said, bolder now that someone else had spoken.

"To have magic and powers," another child said with a worrying amount of enthusiasm.

"Yes," Priya said after a moment. "All those things. But first, it means you obey me, you understand?"

They nodded.

"This boy Rukh is going to help keep an eye on you," Priya said, gesturing at Rukh.

"Is he a temple child like us?" a soft-voiced girl asked.

"No," said Priya. "But he's my family, just like you'll be. So you can trust him."

She refused to meet Rukh's eyes. *Family.* She'd never called him that before. But it was true. The only family she'd ever valued had been made by choice and circumstance, and never by blood. It was all she knew, and all that mattered.

These children were hers now.

"I'll show you somewhere to sleep," she said to them. She should have taken them up the Hirana to sleep, but the thought filled her with nausea. Smoke, and Nandi's dead eyes, and bloody terror worming through her heart—no. She wouldn't send them there to live, and wouldn't go herself. But she'd keep them close.

Padma was crawling toward her, so Priya leaned down and scooped her up. Padma promptly bit her arm. Priya swore, wincing as Padma kicked her for good measure.

"She wants to walk," Rukh murmured helpfully.

"Fine—Padma, if you want to walk, you can walk." She lowered Padma to the ground, holding her by the arm.

Padma did a smug, determined waddle forward. She looked up at Priya's eyes, and Priya drew on her reserves of patience and nudged her in the right direction.

"We'll go slowly," she said, and saw one of the temple children smile, from the corner of her eye. That was good. A step in the right direction.

She took the children to her own rooms.

She roped Khalida and Rukh into helping her arrange new bedding and makeshift curtains to divide up the room. By the time night fell, the children had been fed and given a few more clothes, and bidden to sleep.

The room was hot with so many bodies inside it. In the silences between the noise of insects and plants moving in the breeze, she could hear muffled sobs.

Priya hated this. There was nothing more she could do, or so she told herself. But it felt like a lie. It was a lie. She could have refused to allow the children to remain. Could have summoned Mani Ara's strength. Could have...

Could have let Arahli Ara hurt or kill the people she loved. And that was no choice at all.

She sat cross-legged on the floor by the bed where Padma and Rukh slept. Her skin itched with anger—at herself, at the yaksa—and there was no chance she'd sleep tonight. Instead she did the only thing she was good for, and placed the crown mask on her face, and tried to reach for Mani Ara.

It would have been better to go to the deathless waters. But tonight she didn't want to leave the children alone.

Deep, coiling breaths. Breaths winding her further and further into her body and *through* her body. The sangam waters rising in her.

Her shadowy body within three twining rivers. Her body of flowers. She remained there in the waters as the hours lengthened and melted around her.

She didn't know what else she could do to seek out Mani Ara. Her mind sank into darkness.

Arahli Ara's hands on her wrists, his face like her brother's. Malini's hands on her face, her scalp. The fury and salt of her tears. Bhumika gone—nothing left of her but a scrap of words, a child. She'd lost them all and still had more to lose.

Sapling.

Mani Ara's voice rushed through her like water breaking a dam. She fell hard back into her skin; sucked in a deep, gasping breath before pressing her mouth shut to hold the noise in. Power had followed her from the sangam, dizzying her. Her vision was swimming.

Roses had bloomed profusely around her.

She clumsily tried to brush them away—and felt them wither around her, turning to decay and then dust. Hands brushed them away. But they were not her hands.

Her head snapped up. The yaksa with Ashok's face—Arahli Ara—was crouched over her.

She hadn't sensed him. Her blood was burning hot inside her and her mind was an overfull cup, spilling magic. It made her vision dance. She took off the crown mask with trembling hands.

"Yaksa," she breathed out. "Why are you here?"

"The children," he said simply. "They should be on the Hirana. Close to the deathless waters and the stars alike."

"I wanted to keep them with me," Priya said, catching her breath. "And this..." She looked around her room. Bhumika's old room. "This is where I want to be. Will you make me take them there now?"

"No. They are yours."

"You were always going to give them to me, yaksa. Respectfully, you tricked me."

"Saying 'respectfully' does not make your words respectful," he murmured. But there was nothing sharp or monstrous in his voice. He'd pitched it low enough not to wake the children around her.

He watched her with deep, strange eyes—mirrors to the faint moonlight seeping in through the windows. But the darkness made the rest of him more human, concealing the leaves of his hair, the whorls of his skin.

"When I reared the first temple children, I began with their strength," he said finally. "I taught them to trust their limbs. To resist pain. To persevere. To run and to fight. Then I led them to the edge of the Hirana and bade them to climb down."

A difficult journey for any child.

"And then? What did you do with the ones who didn't fall? Take them to the waters?"

"It is a long path to the waters," he said. "Many years. As it was for you."

He wanted her to make the temple children strong. She swallowed back anger. Nodded. She thought of Ashok, and their shared childhood, and her grief threatened to overwhelm.

"After strength, what comes next? What did you teach those temple children?"

"Then," he said in Ashok's voice, "I taught you to use a knife and the power of your rage."

A flash of memory scythed through her. Ashok's hands on her own. A knife between them. Showing her how to move. How to fight. How to *cut*.

"They are yours, Elder Priya," he said. "But they continue to be mine, also."

And so do you.

"Ashok," she said.

A whisper of leaves. Then he was gone.

24

BHUMIKA

They were offered transport by a man leading an oxen-drawn cart of grain. The man was bearded, his face flayed red at the nose and cheeks by exposure to the sun. His gaze slid dismissively off Bhumika, but he spoke easily enough to Jeevan. As Bhumika tucked herself into the back of the cart, the man urged Jeevan to sit near the front between the sacks of grain and talk to him.

"Looks like you've been in some trouble, friend," the man said, whipping his oxen forward.

"Bandits," said Jeevan. His face was violently bruised. "They thought we had coin."

"Do you?"

"Not anymore."

The man laughed.

Bhumika, with their coin bound with cloth to her thigh, kept her head down and watched the fields blur alongside them.

Jeevan was not a natural charmer, and conversation between the two men soon withered. But Bhumika had expected that. She waited until the silence was particularly painful, then allowed herself to speak, shaping her voice into something timid, curious.

It wasn't long before the man began to soften and speak to her in turn. She managed to coax him into telling her about his grandchildren, first—in her admittedly limited experience, even men who thought very little of their wives and daughters were soft for their grandchildren, and this man was no exception. He told her about his four granddaughters and his five grandsons proudly.

"And you," he said. "Do you have any children?"

The words were aimed expansively at both her and Jeevan. She saw the telltale stiffening of Jeevan's shoulders. Unintentionally, unknowingly, the stranger had touched on a bruise.

She thought of the shape of her own body—the silver tracery of marks at her belly, her breasts—and then carefully thought no more of it. Her body remembered things she did not, and to dwell on them was to invite madness.

"One day, if the nameless god has written it in my stars, I would like to give my husband a family," Bhumika said, and the man hummed his agreement.

Jeevan did not look at her. She noticed that, too. Because she was looking at him.

By the time they reached a rickety set of roadside stalls serving tea and food to travelers, he was talking easily to Bhumika about the problems facing Alor. The men who had gone to war on behalf of the king of Alor, and the way the rot had destroyed field after field. Not enough to concern him yet, but she was sure in a month or two either he would have no grain to transport, or he would have to hire guards to protect it on his journey to sale.

She'd won him over so thoroughly, somehow, that he bought her and Jeevan a meal and waved away any effort to refuse him. "You said you have no money," he said gruffly. "What good would starving do? How will your wife have children if she's starving?" he said to Jeevan.

Jeevan lowered his head at that, and it was left to Bhumika to offer him a shy but effusive thanks. The food was good, and she didn't regret taking it.

The man hesitated when he rose to his cart. His gaze darted about. Then he said, "I could carry you farther. Another caravanserai lies ahead."

Bhumika brushed a hand against Jeevan's arm.

"We cannot," Jeevan said. "But I thank you, friend."

"The monastery…" The man trailed off, then shook his head. "Such a place isn't for people like us. They'll turn you away. But ah, if you want a god's blessing on your marriage, what can your elder say to you?"

"The monastery," Jeevan repeated.

"Where else could you be going?" A snort. "There's nothing else of worth here, friend. I'm no fool."

The rains began again, wild and unseasonal, as soon as his cart vanished around a bend in the road. Bhumika sighed, feeling the water trickle down her face and through her clothing with a resigned humor.

"He was only partially a fool," she murmured.

"He was kind to us."

"Kind only *after* we flattered him." A pause. "Yes. He was kind."

They moved under the canopy of a stall. It was barely any cover, but it was enough. There, they watched the rain pour down, beads of water arrowing through patches in the canvas into the ground around them.

"The monastery."

The question wasn't in his voice but in the way he turned his head toward her.

He did not say *We have passed a dozen monasteries of the nameless god*. But she understood.

She considered how he was just as beholden to the push and pull of her knowledge as she was. But he did not feel it beating, screaming, thrumming in his skull as she did in her own. She thought of telling him *I feel in every bone and every beat of my heart that this is where the one I seek will meet me. And if they are not at the monastery, where the waters show the way to the nameless, then I do not know where I will find them. I do not know if such a person exists at all.*

The yaksa are right to consider me nothing.

A soft wind touched her. She followed its grasp, turning her head.

In the shadows of the trees she saw her veiled watchers, bowls spilling bright water uselessly into the earth, the ether. They looked clearer than they ever had before, their limbs mottled blue with cold, their eyes hollows beneath water and cloth.

Drowned, she thought. *They are drowned, and yet they breathe still.*

"It must be this one," she replied quietly. That would have to be enough.

They stayed at the food stall long enough for the rain to abate, and for Bhumika to carefully eke information out of the woman washing the cups and pans behind it. She'd been talkative enough when Bhumika had offered to help, though she'd laughed over Bhumika's efforts.

"They must see worshippers," Bhumika murmured to Jeevan as they left. "That is the one requirement of a priest. To serve a deity, a god, a spirit is to be its mouthpiece. To offer comfort."

"Not all priests believe so," said Jeevan.

She had to hope these would.

Nimisa Monastery was ancient. Five hundred years had shaped its gray stone, erasing any human-made flourishes of beauty, making it one with the soil and the green that surrounded it. Its vast entrance arch, set above steps that curved like a crescent moon, shone as if emeralds had been carved into its walls. But lichen and vines were what bejeweled it, not gemstones. They were so oddly, beautifully lustrous that Bhumika had to pause momentarily in her walk toward the monastery's steps simply to stare up in awe.

She and Jeevan had walked along a path carved through the trees toward the steps of the monastery. The stone steps were silvery with pools of water. Perhaps it was the rain or the rot, or the looming threat from Ahiranya, but there were no worshippers waiting to enter Nimisa Monastery.

There was one young priest near the entrance, scrubbing the steps. He raised his head and looked at them with confusion in his eyes, even as a tentative smile shaped his mouth.

"Welcome," he said, his voice low and kind. He rose to his

feet, visibly hesitating. "Forgive me. In these difficult times we, ah, do not receive visitors. We are a...a monastery of solitude and contemplation."

She felt Jeevan's eyes on her for a second. Well, that was her answer. *Not all monasteries were open to worshippers after all.* No matter.

"Priest," she said. "I must speak with the head of your monastery. I come with a message for him."

The man's smile faded into utter uncertainty.

"I come from Ahiranya," Bhumika continued, not allowing herself to falter. "I come with a way to kill the yaksa. The name *Nimisa* echoes in the darkest of their memories for a reason. The head of your monastery will know why. Call him here. Please."

The priest still did not move.

She drew a step closer to where he stood, then another, until she could see his dark pupils, the whites of his eyes. Was it wishful thinking, or could she see a strange light in his gaze—a hint of otherness, a sign that he had the gift she sought? Surely if he had served here, worshipped here, he would have been touched by the magic of this place.

Bhumika had no weapon to sway him with but her words. So she turned to them once more.

"Let him ask the nameless god, if he wishes. His deity knows what I carry." She lowered her voice, cajoling. "*Your* deity knows what I say is true. The nameless speaks in your heart, yes? Please. Listen."

Finally, something flickered in the priest's eyes. He nodded slowly and turned to enter the monastery.

He was gone for some time.

There was a strange, uncomfortable desire in her to draw on something to convince him more fully. Some power that had once existed in her body—a magic, perhaps, or a cunning that losing her memories had stripped her of. But whatever it had been, she lacked it now. She stood tall with her hands gently clasped in front of her and tried to feel no fear.

The priest returned with five guards, who moved swiftly,

striding down the stairs to ring Jeevan and Bhumika, fencing them in. Jeevan's hand flew to his saber hilt.

"Remove your weapon," one said to Jeevan, his face grim.

"Step back, and I will do so," Jeevan replied.

"Ahiranyi bastard," the guard said, and Bhumika felt the mood of the men around her darken, as if his anger had given them permission to feel rage too. They were not going to allow themselves to be reasoned with. "How dare you come here, speaking of your monstrous yaksa—"

"Stop," a booming voice ordered. Bhumika raised her head.

Above them on the stairs stood a much older man in his blue robes, chest bare, long hair swept back.

"All of you. Lower your weapons," the head of the monastery said. And Jeevan did, slowly. The guards around them slid their own knives away. Bhumika, her dagger still safely tucked in her sleeve, bowed to him through the wall of guards.

"Thank you, priest," she said, infusing her voice with the appropriate gratitude.

The look the priest gave her was severe—empty of any compassion.

"I do not know why you have brought wild tales of yaksa to my monastery," he said. "If you are seeking food and shelter, we cannot provide these to you. If you seek to trick coin out of my young priests with sobbing and falsehoods, I will not allow it. But if you leave now, all will be forgiven and forgotten." He gestured with a hand, and the guards drew aside, leaving a gap for Bhumika and Jeevan to walk away from the monastery.

Neither of them moved.

"You think I am a beggar woman spinning falsehoods?" Bhumika shook her head. "Priest, if I sought your pity, I promise you I would tell a better story. If I were lying for coin, I would have run when your guards arrived. Only true conviction would make me face their blades."

"You are mad," he said.

"Determined," she corrected. "And ready to bare my neck to the mercy of your wisdom."

One of the guards made a noise of annoyance and reached for her, trying to encourage her to move away. She threw herself to the ground in a deep bow, hands to the earth—and in the process flung herself free from their reaching hands.

"Forgive me. You are head priest of the grandest monastery in Alor," Bhumika said loudly. "Men may forget why your monastery is great and grand. They do not know what you once were. But you have a grand holy purpose: to *listen*, as the nameless bid. So I beg you to listen to me. I come with a way to save you from the yaksa. I carry the knowledge in the empty vessel of my body and my heart. If you will sit with me, if you will take my burden from me, and tell your fellow priests—"

"Do not address our head priest, woman," another guard snapped.

She closed her eyes. Behind her eyelids she saw them again— her watchers, holding bowls of spilling water, bloodied and green and gold. Her body was overfull with truth, but there was more to be had.

Will you drink?

Not yet, she thought. *Not yet.*

"This is what I know." Knowledge roared like a tumult of water in her skull. And she, beneath it, was a stone worn smooth down to her purpose alone. Her voice left her mouth sonorous, strange—rich with power. "Long ago a woman came here, when your monastery was a hovel, a mere shell of stone. And she kneeled and she prayed and begged for a way to see the yaksa dead—and something *answered*.

"Divyanshi, first of the mothers of flame, came here and learned how the yaksa may die. The knowledge is gone along with her; the voice she sought has not returned.

"But even if the door to the void is broken and lost, a trace of its magic remains here. So you—and your priests—who live and breathe in this place, who seek the nameless god, must know I speak true. You must hear the truth in my voice. You have the authority and power to spread my knowledge. To be *heard*. Do you not hear the truth in me, priest? I seek someone to carry my burden. Is it you? It must be you."

She raised her head.

"Let me show you how it may help you kill the yaksa. Let me help you set all of us—Parijatdvipa and Ahiranya alike—free."

The young priest who had greeted them—and brought guards to remove them—was staring at her with wide eyes. Dark as the pools of water those priests used to seek the nameless god.

But the blue-robed leader of the monastery was still unsmiling and furious. No awe had softened his face. Her stomach plummeted. No matter how hard she hoped, or looked, none of that same dark knowing reflected back at her in his eyes.

"Old village tales," he said, with a curl of disgust to his mouth. "Leave here, woman. Wailing before our monastery will not help you."

You look into your pools of water and see nothing. I understand now. You don't refuse me because you think I am false. You refuse because you do not know your nameless god. You feel nothing, hear nothing.

"You do not hear the nameless," she said. She should not have spoken. She knew that. But she saw him flinch and at least knew, grimly, that she was correct.

She bowed her head and said, "I will return, priest. I promise it." And then she lifted Jeevan's saber from the ground before any guards could stop her, and grasped his arm, and strode away in defeat.

The rain began to fall again, bitterly cold.

"I should have known they would not listen to me," Bhumika said.

"You paid a high price for the knowledge you carry," Jeevan said, not disagreeing. "It should be given to people grateful to have it."

"I managed that badly," Bhumika said. She was angry—with them, and with herself. "I should not have been so honest or so forthright. Men with power do not respond to it. Especially from women." She closed her eyes and steadied herself, forcing the fire of her anger to quell. "What was I like before I chose this path, Jeevan? Was I wiser?"

"You were careful with your words," Jeevan said after a moment. "You would cajole. Mediate. For many years men with power did not listen to you. So you placed people in your debt, knowing they would help you not from fear but from gratitude."

"As I did you?"

"I was glad to be in your debt," he said quietly, after a moment. "That was your strength. You made people glad to be ruled by you." The rainfall was growing fiercer. Cold water poured down on them, blurring the trees. "You are still the same woman, Bhumika."

She shook her head.

"I have nothing to offer anyone now," she said, staring down at her own empty hands and the rain on them. "I have no way to compel those priests. What do I have now, Jeevan? I'm powerless. I feel it in me, that absence—I *know* I had power once. But it is gone, and my knowledge is nothing if no one will receive it from me!"

Her voice trembled, raised on those last words. Then she fell silent, clenching her jaw, turning from him.

"You could wield your own knowledge," he said, after a moment. "If this truth you carry requires someone powerful, someone who will be heard—that is you."

"I can't," she said, voice cracking. She had considered it. Amassing her own followers, sharing her knowledge before it drowned her. But those dreams were the desires of a ghost. She could not fulfill them. She was nothing but a painful, overfull skull. She was nothing but the ache of grief for something she couldn't remember. She was nothing but a hollow shaped by the endless push of an ancient tide. "I am nothing," she said.

"You have never been *nothing*. You could lead armies, Bhumika," he said, his voice full with such feeling it was like the sun. "Share your words, and people will follow. They always have."

Bitter grief curled through her veins regardless—and jealousy, for the woman she had once been. Perhaps that woman had been worthy of such love.

"Not anymore," she said.

She paused, staring into the distance. She thought of the younger priest's dark eyes that had seen her truth.

There was still hope. Her knowledge had brought her here. She would trust in it for now. There was nothing else she could do.

"We should find shelter," she said finally, blinking rain from her eyes. "Rest. I will have to try again, but first I need to—to *think*. If they say no once more, I will walk to Harsinghar and beg the Parijatdvipan empress directly to hear me."

The empress would kill her, of course. But at least Bhumika would have done all she could.

The rain did not stop, and the trees provided limited shelter. Under their feet, in a matter of moments, the ground turned to wet mud, then to ankle-deep water. At first Bhumika thought it was another illusion from her watchers. But then Jeevan gripped her arm and cursed. She followed the tilt of his head and saw, as he already had, that a river cut through the trees ahead of them. It was so high that it had flooded its banks.

"We need to find higher ground," Jeevan said, and Bhumika nodded her agreement. They turned away from the river.

The monastery had been on higher ground, but they couldn't return there now. Instead they tried to find their way back to the road.

The water was still rising when they heard voices crying out, arguing. Young voices. It took only a shared look for both of them to turn and follow the noise, wading through the sodden ground until they found two children, a boy and a girl, arguing outside a dilapidated hut. As Bhumika drew closer, she realized they were not arguing with each other but with an old woman standing inside the hut's doorway, who was clutching a blanket around her shoulders with one hand. The other hand was holding on to the older boy's wrist.

"What is happening here?" Bhumika asked in Aloran, as Jeevan stepped ahead of her.

The arguing died into abrupt silence. Three pairs of eyes turned on them warily.

"Old Auntie's refusing to come to our village," the girl said after a moment, darting nervous looks between Jeevan and Bhumika. "She's a widow. She lives alone here. But with the water— she can't *stay.*"

"She won't leave her wedding quilt," the older boy said, still gripping the old woman's hand tightly. "But she must. I keep trying to explain it to her, but she won't listen."

"What is her name?"

"Gulnar," the girl said.

"Auntie," Bhumika said. "Aunt Gulnar."

Something in her voice made the older woman meet her eyes.

"The young ones will carry your quilt for you," she said, carefully shaping the Aloran words. "And the man with me will carry you safely to your village." She looked at the boy. "Where is your village?"

The boy swallowed. "Across the river."

"The river isn't safe to cross," said Jeevan.

"There's a bridge," the boy protested. "It's safe enough. Safer than staying here. You can come with us. If you help—that would be enough thanks, wouldn't it?"

"The water will damage it," Gulnar quavered, still holding her quilt to her shoulders.

"It can be washed and dried," Bhumika said gently. "But if you die here, Auntie, it will not be loved as it is loved now."

The woman hesitated, then gave a curt nod. "Let him carry me, then."

"Get her quilt," Bhumika ordered. The boy scrambled to obey. "Treat it gently."

Jeevan picked the woman up.

The girl was the one who guided them to the bridge. It was a spindly structure of wood and rope, and the water was high enough now to brush perilously close to its boards. But Jeevan tested it with his own weight and judged it strong enough. "Go," he said to the children. They rushed ahead, light on the uneven surface of the bridge, clutching the blanket between them. Jeevan lifted Gulnar and carried her to the side.

Bhumika followed a step after him. The bridge rocked under her feet. The water was roaring. She lost her footing for a moment on the slick wood, slipping as the bridge trembled.

"Bhumika." Jeevan's hand was holding her wrist, helping her find her balance. The old woman stood on the opposite bank.

"Come," he said. "We're going to the village together."

She was suddenly, awfully, so grateful that he was here. That he had followed her from a past she could not see, and he trusted her still. That he looked at her and saw strength where she could find none, and worth where she only saw her own emptiness.

"What did you leave behind to come with me on this fool's journey?" Bhumika asked, voice trembling.

His grip tightened, infinitesimally, on her.

"Everything," he said. "Just as you did."

"Everything," she repeated. They took another step forward. Another. It would have been so easy to fall. "All this for duty? For a debt?"

Another step.

"I lied," he said. "I am sorry." His hand urged her forward. The bridge was swaying, the water groaning like a wounded beast. "I did not follow you for a debt."

She did not ask him *Why, then?* She did not push or prod. She met his gaze as he held her steady, as he guided her across churning, black water and did not let her fall.

He never looked away from her.

"Ah," she said softly. She knew.

25

PRIYA

The night when Arahli Ara visited her—when she heard Mani Ara's voice whisper again in her skull—Priya's fever began.

She hid herself in the only private place she could find—a storeroom in a particularly damaged corridor. But Rukh found her anyway.

"I've got some water and some kichadi, and some wet cloths too," he announced as he came in, balancing a truly alarming number of items in his arms. "Do you need anything else?"

"To be left alone," she groaned, but she took the cloth from him anyway and pressed it to her hot face. "Where is Padma?"

"I left her with the temple children. I...I know I shouldn't leave her alone, but..."

"With Ashish?"

"Yes."

She relaxed.

"That's fine, then." The oldest temple child was uncannily good with the younger children. "Go."

"I don't care about getting sick," Rukh insisted.

"Well, *I* care if you get sick," said Priya, but she didn't truly have the heart to send him away. Besides, she was almost sure the fever was part of her magic—a symptom of that broken dam of power inside her, that rush of strength that had made her eyes swim.

"You don't need to look after me," Priya said, in a last attempt to get rid of him.

"You've looked after me," he said quietly, after a moment. "You still do. It's only fair. Now sit up, Pri, and eat."

She dreamt of Malini again.

The fever burned in her. The fever was her power growing and growing, blooming to life inside her. Changing her.

In the dream, she felt her power crack wider. A cosmic egg, a golden yolk. She exhaled and watched the dream splinter around her. The imperial court's walls cracked. A fissure formed ahead of her—ahead of Malini, too. The fracture was a lightning burst through stone. It grew, and it grew.

Malini was not looking at the break in front of them. Her head was turned. She was looking at Priya.

Malini was watching her cannily, hungrily. Priya felt a tug in her chest, painful and strong.

"I can feel it," Malini said. Her rich voice was a hand at Priya's throat, drawing her another step forward. "Power. What are you doing, Priya?"

The walls of the court of the imperial mahal had splintered entirely. They should have fallen, but they stood, all their shards like cracked shell, light oozing through their frayed edges. And between the shards, between the light—

Priya took an unsteady step toward the path that lay before them both.

The path was green. It smelled of salt-rain, of somewhere distant where the sea pressed its strange hands to soil. Priya had never seen the sea. Only imagined it. Only heard it described in Malini's words. Vast, vast like a mirror of the sky.

She took another step forward. Heard a whisper of skirts beside her, and watched as Malini's shadow melded with her own. Malini came to stand close to her, brow furrowed, blood dripping from her chest, marking a path beneath her feet.

Priya turned her head. Their eyes met again.

"Tell me what you've done," said Malini.

"Paths," Priya said. "Malini, I think. I think somehow I've made new paths—"

Priya woke up.

She walked into the depths of the forest with her hair still wild, her feet bare, clothes rumpled. She went to the bower of bones.

The seeker's path lay before her: that ancient path through the forest where time moved strangely and a person could become lost for weeks or reach Srugna in the blink of an eye.

There were new paths visible between the trees. She could *feel* them—as if she were a tree and the paths were her own roots. Above her the bones bound by ribbons to the trees were utterly still. There was no wind here. No noise at all.

Her fever was fading. She could finally think.

She hadn't chosen to make these paths. But Mani Ara's magic had made them through her. She was Mani Ara's way into the world—her hands, her beloved. And so Mani Ara had used her.

Thudding footsteps behind her. There were mask-keepers there—one once-born, another twice-born. They must have felt the paths appear too.

"You took a while," she said.

"We—we went to find you. But the boy Rukh said you were sick, and when we went to your sickbed—"

"I'm not sick anymore," Priya said. "Don't worry. You don't need to explain. You're here now."

She took a step closer to one path, feeling it out with her bare feet and in the taste on her tongue. Salt-rain. Strange winds. She'd dreamt this, and it was real, and Malini had dreamt it too.

Somehow Malini was part of this.

There was a cough behind her. An uneasy rustle of bodies. She turned and saw the patrol of mask-keepers waiting expectantly, their anxiety palpable.

"Elder?" one prompted.

"Ignore it for now," Priya said. "It's the work of the yaksa.

Nothing to trouble over."

They didn't relax at her words. Their eyes were wide, black and frightened in the flicker of their lanterns and the night-dark.

"Keep on patrolling," she said.

"We should walk you back, Elder."

Priya snorted and shook her head.

"No, I'll be fine." She wasn't going anywhere they could follow anyway. She needed to go to the deathless waters. "Keep away from the bower tonight," she said.

"Of course." They bobbed their heads, eyes wide.

She walked away from the new path—the salt of it, and its mouth, all thorn-toothed trees, silver-striped, waiting to swallow bodies whole.

A voice in the forest called her name. The green around her shivered. Turned as if called.

Yaksa, she thought. And turned with it.

She found Chandni in a lake within a clearing. The green led her, and there Chandni was: silver-skinned, bark-whorled. Deep in the water.

"It's almost the dark of the moon," Chandni said. Her voice was a silvery ripple. "Priya. Little elder. When it comes, tell your mask-keepers that my kin and I have decided it is time for them to enter the deathless waters again, where they will become true elders. Tell them we'll await them."

"I will, yaksa," Priya said. A thud in her chest. So there would be more deaths, soon. And maybe—finally—other thrice-born. True elders.

"You've opened paths," the yaksa said. "Where do you wish to go, little one?"

"They're Mani Ara's paths," Priya said. "I'll go where she wishes me to go, of course."

A musical hum. "Then you must speak to her."

"I will, yaksa."

Priya looked at the yaksa's reflection in the water. Her

mirror-self was even less human: silvery, liquid, and changing. She thought, not for the first time, of the real Chandni, who'd maybe been her mother. Who had killed her siblings, and given her the chance to live.

There were things stirring beneath the surface of the water, things growing, blooming in shadows, breaking her reflection into nothing but ink.

"Come into the water," the yaksa called. The water rippled again, a beckoning hand.

Priya didn't bother to argue. She'd expected this from the moment she'd been drawn into the clearing, under the hushed arch of those trees. She knotted her sari so it wouldn't billow, then lowered herself in.

The water was blood-warm. She tried to ignore the feeling of the silt under her feet, uneven like teeth, silken-rough like tangled hair. The yaksa held out her hand, and Priya took it.

"Look," Chandni ordered gently again. And Priya looked— down at Chandni's palm, and the flower held within it.

A lotus. But not a lotus. A thing that had bloomed in shadows under the water, summoned by her presence, her magic, her call. Its petals were perfect, its roots long and coiling. It was rot-riven, there was no denying that; she could see it in the puckered sheen of it. In the way its roots pulsed, like something with a heartbeat . . .

"It took us so long to return," Chandni said. "So long to sacrifice pieces of ourselves so that we could change the world to fit us. But look what we've made. You think the rot is a curse. An ugliness. You recoil from it, all of your kin and kind. But it is beautiful, little one. Can't you see it?"

The yaksa pressed the lotus into Priya's hand. Priya felt the weight of it. Blood ran between her fingers. She stared down with a detached kind of horror, very far from her own body, outwardly calm.

"You don't understand the beauty and fragility of your own bodies," the yaksa was saying, with singsong softness. "You see the beauty in an ancient tree, a flower, and fail to see it in yourself: in the architecture of your lungs, the veins and bones that make a thing of you. Can't you see how beautiful it is, for us to be one?"

Priya should have lied. But she could not make her mouth move into a yes, could not force herself to nod. The yaksa closed Priya's own fingers over the lotus. An inexorable pressure.

"Can't you see what a beautiful thing we have made of you, Priya?" the yaksa asked, with great and terrible tenderness.

A shuddering breath left Priya.

"What do you want from me, yaksa?"

"Reach for her here," the yaksa said. "Mani Ara has created a miracle through you. New paths. The world altered a step further. Let her in again. Yield."

The yaksa's hands pressed onto Priya's shoulders. There was no option to refuse their pressure or the yaksa's commands. Priya closed her eyes and let herself be submerged.

The sangam greeted her like an old friend. Joy rippled through her. It wasn't her own joy, she knew that. It was vaster, like the sweep of wind over grass, the sun on bare earth. Was this how immortals felt happiness?

"Sapling." Mani Ara's rich, laughing voice. "Can you feel it, as I do? The paths, the sangam, the cosmos?"

She could not see Mani Ara, but she could hear her—and feel as she felt too. Once she'd felt her siblings in the sangam. Now she could feel the mask-keepers, and the wound where Bhumika should have been, and worlds bursting and withering...and something great and terrible stalking her kin through a thousand eons.

"Yes," Priya whispered. "I can."

"Good. Feel what lies at the end of my paths, sapling. Feel what I want you to seek."

The yaksa, in the sangam, like clusters of bright stars. And beyond them, further, sleeping in the earth...

Images flashed through her mind. A ring of vast stone-like trees. A lake of blue lotus flowers. Two yaksa.

"Other yaksa," Priya breathed out. "Sleeping. In the soil. Awakening in the places where they died."

"*Yes.*" Exultant.

"One in—Alor," Priya said. The words poured from her. "One in Srugna. She's waking. I feel her."

"She will be awake very soon," Mani Ara agreed, and her voice was in Priya's ear, her lips soft, her hands at Priya's throat. "Go to her. Be there to usher her into the world, so she arrives without fear, with her kin watching over her. Be where I cannot be. My heart, my hands."

"Your kin," Priya said, dazed. "They're returning."

"Our kin," Mani Ara said. Her laugh was rippling, delighted. The very stars shuddered with it. She turned Priya by the shoulders, the throat, and pressed her mouth to Priya's own.

"You are exactly what you are meant to be," Mani Ara whispered to Priya's lips, like breathing a secret between them. "A herald, a storm, my hands, my feet, my sword."

Abruptly, Priya was back in her skin, standing in murky water, swaying. Clutching a beating flower-heart, sluggishly pulsing in her hand.

Tentative fingers touched her cheek. There was a question in the yaksa's eyes.

Bhisa Ara, Priya thought.

She wanted to say *I know you now.*

Wanted to say *Mani Ara loves you all so much. She loves you in a fathomless way my brain can't comprehend. She loves you like... rivers and mountains and oceans love one another. It's impossible and ancient, and I don't know how such cruel beings can love so much.*

"Yaksa," she said instead, and saw the question wither in the yaksa's lifelike face. "I saw her. I know what to do."

She sought out Ganam. He was waiting for her at the mahal. Maybe he'd felt her coming. Her magic was a thrum now, pulsing through Ahiranya. Impossible to ignore.

Hair still dripping, a bloody lotus clutched in her fist, she went to him at the mahal's entrance. He barked orders, sending the mask-keepers around him away. The words slid from her ears like water. He met her eyes.

"The yaksa," she said thinly. "They have orders."

"Priya," he said. "Tell me what the yaksa need."

"You need to tell the mask-keepers the time's come," she said. "You'll be passing through the deathless waters again. All of you. And…" The lotus was still pulsing in her hand. Still gasping for life. "And when this is done—those who survive are coming with me to Srugna. You're coming with me to Srugna."

His gaze was steady. "Are we finally going to fight a proper war? Soldiers and swords?"

"No," said Priya. "We're going to watch a yaksa being reborn."

26

RAO

He had a headache for the entire first week of travel toward Dwarali, a pounding, burning ache that settled in his temples and behind his eyes and refused to fade.

The simple light of the day often felt painful, and when he closed his eyes there was more light: gleaming embers behind his eyes, and Aditya's wavering ghost, haloed in fire and smoke, and distant mountains, white, bleeding bright blood. Every conversation grated at his already strained nerves. Even the pounding of hooves disturbed him. He'd tried to prepare for his journey, filling his skull with Dwarali's particular tangle of politics: the aged sultan, and his lack of heirs, and the relative power of the Lal Qila, a gold-rich fort guarding the edge of the empire; the innumerable, interwoven Jagatay and Babure tribes and clans that hounded the fort, scrabbling over the scarce resources of the mountains beyond the Lal Qila, warring with one another in complex patterns that only Lata had been able to sensibly explain to him. But all of it spilled from his memory like water. He could hold none of it.

Perhaps the nameless still held some love for him, even if he held no love to hand in return, because he was left largely alone by his traveling companions. His men were obedient but not talkative, and the Dwarali riders seemed simply happy to be able to ride freely on their horses under an open sky. Life in the imperial capital Harsinghar clearly had not suited them.

Lady Raziya was polite and kind, her eyes on him thoughtful—but she too respected his clear desire for solitude.

Only Sima seemed interested in breaking his self-imposed isolation, and that surprised him. She had no reason to like him, after all. Hadn't he left her alone—simply abandoned her—to her imprisonment?

She turned up one evening at his tent, startling him. She slid inside, entering calmly as if she had every right to be there.

"Did my guards not see you?" Rao asked.

"I told them you asked for me," she said with a shrug. He paused, then decided not to think about what assumptions those men had made about his prisoner coming alone to his tent in the night darkness. Better not to contemplate it.

She moved toward him and sat cross-legged across from him. For a moment she seemed content to simply watch him pour his wine into a small glass.

"You drink too much."

"Thank you," he said slowly, "for pointing that out. I'll stop, then."

She huffed a laugh. As she watched him drink, her eyes grew grave.

"Does it help? Does it dull—all of it?"

"It does," he said. "And doesn't."

"Let me drink with you, then, Prince Rao."

He hesitated.

"You should go," he said finally. "There will be talk."

"And what does that matter to me? I'm not trying to find a good marriage to a nice Parijatdvipan man." She wrinkled her nose. "Or a nice Ahiranyi one. Besides, I'm a prisoner. My reputation is already dirt."

"A prisoner for now," Rao corrected.

A flick of her eyes to him, then away. She took the wine, grabbed a spare glass, poured and drank. So did he, not stopping her.

"So how should it be done?" she asked. "My potential escape, I mean."

Her look was guarded, behind the rim of her raised cup. She was testing him. Not quite ready to trust him on this. He could see that.

"Shall I slip away when you're not paying attention? Or will you arrange it for me? Should we have some kind of signal?"

"I don't know," he said. She frowned at him. He tried again. "If you choose to slip away, I can't stop you. But..." He gestured vaguely around them, not to encompass the tent but to suggest the sheer size and business of the camp—and the impossibility of escaping it unseen. She nodded, understanding.

"Teach me how to play catur," she said. "Or something else. Anything you like. It's boring to drink in silence. So teach me."

He hesitated again. But ah—what could it hurt?

"Let me get the board," he said.

After that, they played regularly. Some of the wariness left her eyes and the lines of her shoulders. Something uneasily like friendship began to sprout between them.

It did not stop his gnawing grief, or the need for drink to ease the hard edges of the grief-knife digging into him; but it helped lighten his burden, and there were nights that he slept more easily in a tent than he ever had on a soft bed in the imperial mahal.

He accompanied Raziya to the sultan's court.

The sultan was ancient, wrinkled and wizened, eyes pearly black beads in his face. But he accepted Lady Raziya gracefully, as a daughter. He was no fool. He knew the way the winds were blowing.

There was a feast of welcome, where Rao sat with the company of a handful of Dwarali lords and administrators, who treated him with courtesy and gentleness. Clearly tales of why he was traveling to Dwarali—to take him, broken as he was, comfortably away from the empress's war and the political heart of the empire—had spread.

For one night, he rejected liquor and let himself feel everything: grief, and fire behind his eyes, but also the smell of incense rising from the edges of the room, where cones of powder burned; the music of a flute in a young musician's hands, where he sat alongside a tabla player beneath an arch of white jasmine flowers, in subtle honor to the empress and empire. He let the gossip of the nobles flow over him too, and heard them talk of attacks by the tribes that lived beyond the Lal Qila's borders, and obliquely of the sultan's growing frailty. He stored all that information away. It could perhaps be useful.

He stayed as long as he could, among Dwarali's lords and ladies, then gave his apologies and rose and tried to make a discreet exit.

He thought he'd managed it. He was at the entrance to his chambers when he heard a voice call his name. He turned. Walking toward him, one guardswoman trailing her, was Lady Raziya.

"You're leaving us, Prince Rao?"

"Leaving the feast, Lady Raziya—yes." A smile, a bow of his head. "But I will go to the Lal Qila, with your permission, in the morning. If there is anything you wish for me to take...?"

"No." A smile of her own; a tilt of her head. "And what does our empress seek for you to do in the Lal Qila, Prince Rao?"

"The empress sends me," he said, "to recover from my grief."

"The Lal Qila is not known as a soft place for the sick and stricken." There was amusement in the curve of her mouth, a thoughtful and probing look in the eyes turned on him. "I think she does trust my family with your care—and cares for you, deeply—but I also have no doubt she has other motives that guide her actions. What awaits you there?"

"Nothing that will bring ill luck to you and yours," he said, and Raziya laughed.

"You won't deny it, then? Well, you have always seemed an honest man guided by honest stars."

She placed a hand lightly against his shoulder.

"My daughter Asma rules in my husband's stead. She will take good care of you, I promise. Rest easily in her care, and if you need anything from her or my family to aid you, simply ask."

"Thank you," he said.

Raziya released him and turned in a swirl of skirts back into the feast, leaving him alone.

There was a noise behind him: a quiet, pointed cough.

He turned and saw Sima watching from the archway of the door. She must have been standing silently out of sight, listening.

"Are you really going to the Lal Qila just to rest?" Sima asked.

"Do you think I am?"

"Lady Raziya certainly doesn't."

"Well. I am being sent," he said, "to chase a tale." He walked into his room and she followed. He itched for some distraction—he thought of Prem with his pipe, soothing smoke, and wished for the first time not for liquor but the bliss of needle-flower smoke.

Instead, he said, "Let me tell you a story."

He told Sima what Lata had told him: a tale in one of the languages from beyond the borders of Parijatdvipa. It had been poorly translated, or so Lata had claimed with some displeasure. "But even poor translations from beyond Parijatdvipa are rare as pearls," she had told him.

"In the snow lies the corpse of a king," said Rao. "He died for his people, when monsters came and ate their land. And from his chest, after his death, his people cut free his heart. But it wasn't a heart."

"What a twist," Sima said blandly. Rao glared at her.

"I didn't write the tale!" He threw up his hands. "I won't tell you about the battle with monsters, then. Just know his heart was a ruby with the power to murder beasts—and that is the falsehood I've been sent to chase across the empire."

"It *could* be a ruby," Lata had told him, riffling lightly through the book, her brow furrowed. "Or that could be a translation error. The root word in Jagai—never mind. I can see your attention wandering, Rao. It's just as likely to be a pomegranate. That's all."

That had only confirmed his fear that this was a fool's errand: a search for a smear of a tale, a scratching that could be no more than a mistranslation.

An excuse to remove him—and his drunkenness and his grief and his visions—from court.

Sima looked thoughtful.

"You trust me enough to tell me this?" Sima asked. "The story of a weapon you could use against—the yaksa?"

"If you wanted to destroy Parijatdvipa, you would have left a long time ago. Besides," he said with a smile. "A tale like this is a fool's errand, I told you. I am being sent away to rest. Or because I am not fit to serve the empress as she requires. It doesn't matter."

"Well, don't treat it as a pointless task. Treat it like something that matters. I've seen strange things in my life—done strange things. A ruby with magical powers doesn't sound impossible, and it might be an adventure to look for it. And if not..." She hesitated. "I've never been to the Lal Qila. I'd like to."

He couldn't hide his surprise. "I thought..."

"Thought what?"

Instead of using his words, he went to one of his travel chests and opened it, removed a pack, and placed it in her hands.

She opened it. Her eyes widened.

"Food was simple to arrange," he said. "Coin, too. Clothes were harder, but I hope they'll do."

She touched the edge of the bag reverently.

"You really want to help me," she said.

"One good thing," he said curtly. She raised her head. He swallowed. "I want to do one good thing," he said. "In a sea of shit."

She nodded. Closed the bag.

"I'll go to the Lal Qila with you," Sima said. "I couldn't stand being trapped. I don't feel trapped anymore."

His heart twisted at that.

"You still are," he said slowly.

"No. Not exactly." Her hands were still on the pack. "But I can't go home. And if I get to choose where I'm going to be, well." She shrugged. "I think you could use a friend, Prince Rao. And so could I."

He swallowed, unable to speak.

"Get out the catur board," she said gently. "Unless you're tired?"

"No," he said. "I'm not tired."

As he arranged the catur board, he thought not of Aditya or Prem or even his sister, but of Lata when she'd said goodbye, when he'd told her he saw no worth in chasing foolish, broken stories of rubies and false hope.

She'd taken his hands in her own. Her hands were far smaller but held his steadily, firmly—and her eyes were just as firm.

"I do not want the empress to burn, Rao," she'd said to him. "I want her to live. I want an answer—a tool or weapon—that will save her. But I want you to live, too. Go to Dwarali, go far from all this, and learn how to live again. Then come back. Whole, or broken, it doesn't matter. There is nothing worthless about a broken thing—be it a tale, or a man."

One of Lady Raziya's guardswomen sacrificed a shawl and a lined tunic to Sima for the journey ahead. As they drew near the Lal Qila and colder climes, Sima changed her clothing, clearly grateful. She wore her pack at her back, like a charm for luck or safety.

Her eyes rounded with awe as they approached the Lal Qila at dusk; the sun setting made the vast fort look even more bloodied and imposing than it usually did. At its gates, flanked by guards, Lady Asma waited for them. She looked a little more like Lord Khalil than her mother, although she had her mother's smile—confident in its welcome and its strength.

"Prince Rao," she said. "Welcome back to the Lal Qila."

27

MALINI

She was holding an audience when a rider arrived. He was announced and strode in still in his traveling clothes, stained with dirt. He prostrated himself, then gasped out, "Empress. There's danger. Near the border with Saketa—"

She raised a hand and quelled him to silence. Behind him, Deepa slipped in and gave Malini a wide-eyed look. All Deepa's looks were nervous, but Malini had learned to read them all, and this one made her say, crisply, "I will speak to this man alone. Immediately."

She rose to her feet and swept from the public court toward a private audience chamber. Her lords and princes bowed as she passed.

The rider, with Deepa's gentle urging, stumbled through an explanation. A cadre of guards near the Saketan border of Parijat had found something they could not understand. Something that had changed the landscape, cut through the rice field they were guarding like a sickle. It was not rot—he was sure it was not rot. One of his fellow soldiers on patrol had investigated and said it seemed like a path.

"He vanished into it and returned in hours," said the rider. "But, Empress—he said he had been gone for days. He was thin and thirsty. We could not understand. We took lots, and I left with my horse to come to you immediately."

An image reverberated through her like a plucked string. One of her terrible, restless dreams. Cracked walls. Priya's voice behind her. A path, opening.

Certainty settled in her blood. She'd seen a true thing once again.

Once it was clear the rider had no more to say, Deepa's gaze darted up to meet Malini's. Malini nodded.

"Thank you, soldier," Deepa said, wringing her hands together, smiling. "You have done well. If you'll come with me, there is a place you can rest..."

Her own soldiers investigated. By the time they returned, other riders had made it to Harsinghar. They had come from all corners of the empire with news of strange paths, where time coiled and bent. The worst news came with a lord from Srugna, who informed her heavily that Srugna was riddled with such paths.

"From end to end, Srugna is infected," he told her. "Our king has sent you a request for aid, Empress, written in his own hand. He..." He hesitated. "He fears that our proximity to Ahiranya has placed our country in great peril. There is rot all over the land. No matter the guards sent, it cannot be stopped. And people claim, now, to have seen the yaksa among the trees, and faces hidden under masks of wood."

A murmur ran through her advisors. She read the request. Handed it to one of her officials.

"There was one such path in Ahiranya called the seeker's path," said Malini, trying not to recall Priya and their journey through that path—that moment of both terror and the purest joy she had known. "Carved, I was told, by yaksa hands. It led to Srugna. I am unsurprised, but deeply sorry, to know that Srugna has suffered so greatly from yaksa magic."

She met the eyes of Lord Prakash. Her Srugani general looked tense and deeply worried.

"I will go to Srugna to witness these new paths directly," she said, and saw relief cut through Prakash's fear. "To face these enemies and offer King Lakshan my aid. Lord Prakash, as my Srugani advisor you will travel with me."

"It will be a balm to visit home," Prakash replied. "Even in such dark times."

"Lord Narayan—I would have you and Low Prince Ashutosh also. If we face yaksa, his rot-riven liegemen will be safe from further infection."

Narayan inclined his head in understanding.

"I will inform him, Empress."

"Good," she said. "We will not let any of our lands suffer at the hands of Ahiranya. We will protect our own."

"I don't like you traveling without me," Lata admitted later.

They stood in the nursery, over the crib where Prince Vijay slept. Varsha was walking in the gardens with her maids. In her absence, a physician had examined the child again and assured Malini, his eyes respectfully lowered, that the prince was healthy and growing as he should be.

Now Malini and Lata stood alone. Lata was stroking the child's hair gently.

"Sahar and the guardswomen will keep me safe," Malini said. "Swati will make sure I eat. There's no need to worry. I value your mind, Lata—but I will be clever enough to manage this foray into Srugna without you."

"You're a cunning woman, my lady," Lata said, tucking the blanket around the sleeping infant with care. "But no one can know everything."

"And you can?"

"I am a sage still," Lata said, staring down at Vijay. "I would prefer to guide you, but if you leave me here . . . I will care for Parijatdvipa. And I will continue to try to find a way the yaksa may finally be dealt with."

Without you burning. She did not say it, but Malini heard it all the same.

She thought of the magic worming through her own heart, unwanted and strange. She thought of her dreams.

This was the moment to tell Lata. *I dream of Priya, and not the dreams of a betrayed lover. I dream of her and her power, and I dream true. Perhaps the answers lie there. Perhaps it is in the power and knowledge of my enemies that I can save myself.*

"Thank you," Malini said softly, instead. "For all you've done."

She left Varsha's rooms. With her guards trailing her, she headed to the imperial mahal, lost in her own thoughts.

She'd known about the paths before the rider came. She hadn't understood what the dream meant until he spoke, but still. She'd *known*.

She could see Priya. Reach Priya. Whatever the dreams were, they held some truth. Truth she could use.

Perhaps more than truth lay in her dreams.

No one questioned her desire to pray in solitude again. She banished her guards, and she went to the room where the yaksa's arm lay on its plinth; she lit an oil wick lamp and looked at it.

The lamp flickered. Shadows congealed on the arm's length— the overlong fingers, the gold-green veins at the wrist. Her chest, her healed wound, throbbed.

Without allowing herself to flinch, she stepped forward and touched the arm.

The moment her skin touched wood-flesh, something rushed through her. It raced through her veins, her muscles, her bones. It was a pure burst of energy, stealing her breath and filling her with something greater than air.

Power.

She snatched her hand back. She clutched it to her chest, fingers tingling on the verge of pain.

"Turn to me," she whispered to the arm on the plinth. "Toward me."

The wrist... twisted. Fingers splaying toward her. Then it shuddered and went utterly still.

The air smelled of flowers under rainfall, and Malini's chest throbbed, and Malini covered her mouth and laughed, and laughed.

28

VARSHA

Vijay loved sunlight. At night he was fretful, weeping and weeping, his cries insistent enough that Varsha could only weep with him. It was only when her maid Parul suggested lighting oil lamps—enough to brighten the room and draw every flying insect to its walls—that he quieted.

So Varsha began to make a point of carrying him around the mahal, to every single veranda or rooftop or garden that she could find. She had never moved freely during Chandra's reign—she had been far too frightened to risk angering him—but the empress had told her she could go where she wished within the mahal. She'd told Varsha she was part of the imperial court.

Well, then. Varsha would test that.

She found that one of Vijay's favorite places was the garden of the imperial temple. Here, the light was soft—turned gentle and shadow-touched by the high walls of the temple and the low, wide-branched trees that seemed to be constantly fragrant and flowering.

She was in the gardens, seated on a bench beneath a tree, when a priest approached her.

"Lady Varsha," he said. He leaned forward, gazing down at her son. His eyes crinkled in the corners as he smiled. "He is a fine boy, my lady. A true scion of his father's line."

He did not say *He looks like his father.* But she wondered if that was his intent. Her stomach curdled. She had looked at Vijay again and again and searched for his father in his face. He had her brother's nose, and her father's ears; her mother's eyelashes and her own mouth. He was heir to Parijatdvipa, to be sure, but he was a Saketan child through and through. Or so she had convinced herself. Perhaps she was wrong.

"Thank you, priest," she said, and lowered her eyes.

He sat down beside her. "May I bless him, my lady?" he asked. "Simply a mantra for his good health."

"Of course." What else could she say?

"If your maid could give us privacy," he said cordially. Varsha raised her eyes to meet her maid's. Parul, gray with terror, nodded and bowed—and stepped away.

The priest touched his fingertips to her sleeping son's forehead and began to murmur a mantra. She held her son and listened to the cadence of the prayer, waiting for it to end.

"The empress will die, Lady Varsha," the priest said. His tone, his cadence, did not alter. He could still have been praying. "She will burn, as the mothers demand she must. She will see, one day, that she must rise to the pyre. She cannot be an ally to you. For your son's sake, you must ally with us. Trust in the priesthood, Lady Varsha, so that you may raise your son to glorious rule."

She could not look at him. Her maid was not far, and her son was beginning to stir.

"Return here tomorrow," he said, rising to his feet. "And we will talk, you and I."

That night, in the lamplight, she rocked her son and pondered her choices.

The priest claimed the empress would die. If he said so, perhaps it was true. And in her absence, her son would be under a new power: the priesthood.

They would not be kind to Varsha if she stood against them.

They are all the same, she thought bitterly. *Those who wield power.* And not for the first time she hungered for what she did not have. Power of her own.

She met him the next day. Bowed her head, worshipful. She knew how to play at subservience.

"Priest," she said. "Tell me what I must do."

He smiled at her, a kind, gentle smile.

"My name is Mitul, Lady Varsha," he said. "And all the High Priest asks of you, my lady, is information."

29

RAO

Lady Asma took the task of caring for Rao far too seriously. She and her crowd of maidservants and guards were like a swarm of mosquitoes, ever-present. Would Prince Rao like to rest? He wanted to *walk*? Surely not. A walk on the ramparts sounded rather dangerous. Would Prince Rao like some gentler entertainment instead? Perhaps he would like to see the library—in fact, she needed help with the library, and had he not assisted the empress's favored scribe? Yes, the library was certainly ideal!

At one point, when he protested, Asma steered him herself with a hand clamped to his arm. She was a head shorter than him but moved with the determination of a mother cat holding a kitten in her jaws.

"Come now, Prince Rao," she said, cheerily determined. "Books will provide you good comfort."

He'd seen the like of this before: young lords new to power wielding their authority clumsily, without any of the subtlety or restraint their elders had cultivated. Asma's manipulations in her position as lady of the Lal Qila were unsubtle. Inexperience was her greatest flaw.

If Lady Raziya had been here, she would have walked with him along the corridors of the fort and arranged meals with visiting lords; she would have cajoled him into helping with some laborious but somewhat interesting task, better suited to his talents than organizing ancient Dwarali tomes, with the household scholars hovering anxiously over him for fear he would ruin their hard work.

If Lady Raziya had been here, it would have taken him days, or even weeks, to realize he was being carefully watched and managed. As it was, he'd realized on the first day. It hadn't made it easier to slip Asma's notice, though.

And besides, what point was there trying? She did not act out of any malice. There was genuine concern in her eyes when she looked at him. Her mother had clearly sent messages strongly advising her of his worth to the empress, impressing the need to keep him safe. She'd practically panicked when he walked along the paths carved into the fortress roof and walls.

Rao had no purpose here. He made a desultory attempt to ask about a ruby—and received a frown in response and then a lengthy explanation of what could be found in the mines beneath the mountains, so dull his eyes practically crossed.

So he gave up and allowed himself to be set down in the library to read and nap over pages. In the evenings, after awkward dinners with the household, he spent time with Sima.

He asked her again if she'd go, and she refused.

"Not yet," she said. "I'm not done with this adventure."

"We've been trapped in this fort," he pointed out.

"Exactly," she said, grinning at him. "I won't consent to run until we've done something worthwhile."

Change came suddenly, in the smallest form: a shared silver platter of fruit and sherbet glasses. Lady Asma chattering mildly to him, as she instructed a servant to carve some new delicacy and place it on the platter before them. He watched as the servant peeled the rind from a pale segment of fruit and lightly scattered salt on its surface.

"What kind of fruit is this?" Rao asked.

"A rare kind," she said. "Grown from a gourd. Enjoy it."

She nudged the tray toward him, urging him to eat.

He did. It was mild and sweet, unfamiliar. There was an edge of rind to one that she warned him not to eat.

"Where does this grow?" he asked out of no particular curiosity, simply to make conversation. "I have not seen it before."

"Many things grow here that do not easily in the rest of Parijatdvipa."

"Your mother and father should offer them in trade," he said, to compliment her.

A thin-lipped smile. "I don't think so. They're an unreliable crop, my lord. Very hard to cultivate."

A spark of a memory ran through—of ink on scraps of paper he'd dully riffled through, in the hours he'd been trapped among books.

"In your books, there is talk of the agriculture of the tribes beyond Parijatdvipa's borders," Rao said lightly. "Who farm and harvest across vast swathes of land and travel with the seasons. What did that book say..." He frowned, clicking his tongue in his throat. "Ah. *The Babure and Jagatay carry muskmelons across the hills, a sweetness for trade for cold winters.*"

"We do *not* trade with them," said Lady Asma. "The tribes are our enemies." She shook her head. "In the past it was done. But that was during the Age of Flowers, my lord—before we were one empire."

Her cup of half-emptied sherbet clinked against the table. "Perhaps you would be more comfortable outside the library, Prince Rao. To think that you've resorted to reading about agriculture!"

Clumsily done, he thought. Perhaps time would make a better politician of her.

He nodded, agreed, and drank.

Now that he was looking more closely, he noticed what they perhaps didn't want him to: cloth that could not come from Dwarali, never mind any other part of the empire, made of some unfamiliar animal's fur; fruit and meat that also screamed *elsewhere*.

He'd spent hours in the depths of the war against Chandra tracking supplies from every city-state of Parijatdvipa. He knew that these items were not traded by Dwarali—and certainly had not been obtained from Srugna or Parijat, Saketa or Alor.

All these years of protecting the border... it was no surprise that some intermingling of trade had occurred between the residents of the Lal Qila and the people who lived beyond its walls. It would have been surprising if that had *not* happened.

Something about this called to him, and he didn't know if it was the nameless or his own gut instinct. But he couldn't let it go.

On a quiet night, he asked a servant for a basin of water.

In a temple of the nameless, he would have had the guidance of a priest. He would have gazed into a still pool of deep waters and sought the guidance of his god.

The water in the bowl before him was not deep enough for darkness. He could see the ceramic through it, slightly fractured.

In the past, he'd actively reached for the nameless with joy and hope. Now he looked down and waited, staring at the dark with a sense of grim resolve. He knew a vision was coming for him. A vision had been waiting all this time in the fire behind his eyes.

All he had to do was let it out.

A long moment of nothing. He stared foolishly at his own reflection. Then he turned away in disgust, poured himself a drink, and went to the narrow window—wide enough to let in nothing but a sliver of the sky.

The sky was dark outside. Flecked with stars.

His eyes burned once more. He saw snow again, bloodied. And then a jewel—glowing like fire, dulling to ash. And Aditya's face, wavering. His hand reaching through fire—

He returned to himself. He was sweating, his eyes damp with tears. His drink had tumbled to the floor. With one sleeve he wiped his face and breathed with all the steadiness he could find in himself.

He snuck into Sima's room before morning. She shot up in her bed, untangling herself from her sheets with a swear. Then she gave him a bemused look. Already, just on their journey together, he'd lost the power to frighten her. Good.

"You're planning something," she said. "*Finally.*"

"What makes you think so?"

"Your eyes looked like that before," Sima said. "When you came to my room, when you were drunk—your eyes were like gold. Nothing in them but light."

He swallowed. "I'm going beyond the Lal Qila," he said. "Following a vision from the nameless. My men will keep you safe. But if you want to leave, I can take you to a horse now. Whatever you need."

She snorted delicately, then said, "Don't be absurd. I'm coming with you."

He shook his head. "You don't want to follow a vision with me," he said heavily. "It never ends well."

"I followed Priya, didn't I? For less than a vision. And I can see it's real." She gestured at his eyes. "This is the adventure we wanted, Rao."

"I never wanted an adventure."

She huffed, ignoring him. She began to pack and draw on her warm long jacket, tightening it over her tunic.

"How are we getting out?"

"There must be exits," he said. "The Lal Qila is meant to be impenetrable, but if someone is exchanging fruit or cloth, there has to be a route through..."

"Oh," she said. She grinned, baring her teeth. "I know one of those."

At his stupefied look, she said, "Do you think I've been hiding in this room all the time? When I'm not with you I have to find something to do." She shrugged. "We agreed I'm not a prisoner anymore, and no one here is watching me as closely as they did in the empress's palace. I've seen where the warriors go when they want to trade—or smoke where their superiors can't see them."

"Show me," he said. "Please."

She led him to a narrow corridor that wound out to a hall just beyond kitchens used by the servants. Gesturing at him to be quiet, she showed him a door.

Beyond the door, the mountains were swathed in white. Rao took a step outside. Snow was falling steadily.

"It doesn't look safe to go out there," Sima said nervously.

"I have to," said Rao. "You should stay here, but I must go."

Fire and snow were clouding his vision, and through them he saw a figure—Aditya perhaps, standing in flames. Aditya, holding out a hand...

He heard Sima yell, but it was too late. He was already striding confidently out into the cold, into a heaving wind colored white that pressed against him like cold water without the wetness of rain.

A hand caught his tunic. Sima was stumbling after him.

"I've changed my mind," she heaved. "I won't follow your vision, and I don't think you should either, you absolute idiot."

"I told you not to come."

"But you knew I would, didn't you?"

Her teeth were chattering. He turned to look behind them—but the path was gone, swallowed by white. Internally he cursed.

"I've never seen snow before," she said. "I... I thought it would be different." A pause. "It's like home."

"In what way is this anything like Ahiranya?" he asked.

"Oh, beautiful but liable to kill you," she said. He couldn't help but laugh.

"I guess we have no choice," she said. "No way back, is there? Let's follow your vision and see where it takes us."

They walked, and walked. A storm rolled in over them, bringing howling winds and more snow.

"It's so fucking cold," she said. "Did your vision bring you out here to make us so cold we'd die?"

"The nameless has done worse to me," he said in a low voice.

"We're turning back, Prince Rao."

"I don't know where back is. You know that."

"Ah," she said. "Well, shit. Neither do I."

They found no shelter, but there was an outcropping of rocks tall enough to hold the wind at bay. They huddled together, wedged close for warmth.

It was growing darker.

"Rao," she said, into the howling wind and his silence. "The prince. Did you... Who was he to you?"

"My friend," he said.

"You grieve him very deeply."

"Everyone grieves friends deeply," he murmured. His toes were beginning to grow numb.

"They do." Silence. She trembled beside him. "I like women, you know," Sima said, speaking through her shivers. "If you judge me—I don't care, really. I know what Parijatdvipans believe, and us Ahiranyi, we don't feel the same. But I..." She paused, and he didn't know if it was from cold or from the weight of her own thoughts. He took her hand in his. It was icy. "Sorry," she went on. "I just wanted to say that if you felt more for him—I understand. I can listen."

He swallowed. He thought of Aditya's statue, of a kiss. Aditya's smile.

"I knew I loved him," he admitted. "When he was alive, I knew I loved him... more than I should have. But the shape of it—that wasn't something I let myself see. I didn't know."

"Did you really not see?"

"It was like staring at the sun," Rao said. A shaky laugh. "Really looking at it would have destroyed me."

"I-I'd give anything for a bit of that sun right now," said Sima. "It would be so nice to be warm."

"Agreed." He closed his eyes. There was no fire behind them right now. Just his own mind, and that was almost worse. "What good would it have done to tell him?" he whispered. "Tell myself? We couldn't have done anything. Been anything."

"It's not tragic to love like we do," Sima said gently. "To be like we are. You... you should know that. Although I'm sorry you've had so much grief."

He laughed again. Shaking.

"I think," he said, "that if we weren't currently freezing to death I'd cry."

A trembling huff from Sima.

There was a crack of noise. Voices.

He scrambled up the rock. Through the white haze he saw figures in thick furs and dark cloth. He saw one of them point and cry out. Bows were raised.

His eyes suddenly burned as the panic rose in him like wildfire.

"Stop!" He stumbled out and fell to his knees on the snow. "I am Prince Rao," he called out. "A nameless prince of Alor, a servant of the Empress of Parijatdvipa, and I was brought here by a vision." He shouted louder as the wind howled and howled. "A vision of blood and snow and fire—and a ruby like a heart! A stone ripped from the earth!"

The figures stilled. Some lowered their bows.

A man emerged from between them. A slight man, with eyes as sharp as a hunting bird's, crossed the moonlit snow.

"Prince Rao," he said. "No longer fear. I am Ehsan, kai of the Jagatay, and you are safe with us."

30

PRIYA

"How long do you want them to run in circles?" Khalida asked. "Will this...help them? To be temple elders?"

The children were running in circles around the orchard. Priya and Khalida were watching them from the shade with Padma at their feet, Rukh crouched beside them.

Khalida sounded dubious, which was fair. One of the youngest was lying pointedly on the ground, face-first in the soil, limbs starfished.

"One of the yaksa told me this would work," Priya said with a shrug. "At least it should keep them distracted."

"They're worried about the ceremony later," Khalida said, voice hushed now.

"Then maybe I'll make them run a bit longer. They can't think if they're running."

"You should make them climb trees," Rukh said. He had his elbows propped up on his knees, his chin in his hands. "Jeevan made me climb trees. He said it'd be good for my balance."

"Why don't you go climb trees now, then?"

He looked up at her, suddenly bright-eyed.

"Can I teach them?" Rukh asked eagerly. "Can I?"

Another child had slumped on the ground. The rest were flagging—all but Ashish, who was still running steadily.

"Why not," Priya said, giving in to the impulse of chaos. "You there!" Priya yelled, raising her voice. The children stumbled to a stop. "Rukh will be leading the rest of your training today. When it's time to get ready, Khalida will stop you."

There were groans but no real protests. Rukh grinned at her and ran over to the group, already yelling orders.

"Keep an eye on him?" Priya asked Khalida.

"You've released a monster," Khalida said dryly. "But I'll do my best to manage him."

Priya would have liked to run in circles, honestly. Maybe climb a tree or two. But she couldn't. The journey through the deathless waters was approaching. She had a duty to the mask-keepers.

She found Kritika's room, knocked on the door, then nudged it open without waiting for a reply.

The older woman was brushing her oiled silver hair into a plait. She gave Priya a nod as she entered. Kritika's mouth was thin, bracketed by lines of tension. She wore a white salwar kameez. Beads of wood were wound into her hair.

"You look ready," Priya said.

"I am, Elder," Kritika said stiffly. "I'm prepared."

Priya crossed the room toward her.

"There's no shame in being frightened," she said.

"I'm not. I have faith in the yaksa."

Priya nodded. She wasn't here to poke at the fraying edges of Kritika's faith today. She was here to be kind.

"I'll be there too," Priya said quietly. "I'll be watching. And I'll pray for you all. You're strong. You'll make it through."

"Strong," Kritika repeated. The lines around her mouth deepened. "I have tried to be."

Kritika reached a hand out. Surprised, Priya let her hand be gripped. Let Kritika look up at her, eyes shining with fervor, faith.

"Today Ganam and I will become twice-born," Kritika said with determination. "And I have hope that the twice-born among us will survive their third journey. Soon you will have real help, Elder Priya. Fellow elders. And the yaksa will listen to more voices than just your own. You will not be alone. We will save Ahiranya together."

There was real hope in Kritika's voice. But fear, too.

Priya grasped her hand in return.

"I know it," she said.

Evening came, and dusk fell. The temple children lined up for the ceremony. Priya and the mask-keepers had agreed to try to make the journey through the deathless waters as traditional as possible: children in white, and mantras being softly sung; lanterns lit, and the effigies of yaksa surrounded by flowers. The moon above them was only a sliver, a hand sickle against the black night sky.

Priya kept her focus on the mask-keepers. Nervous twice-born, faces gray with fear, were trying to look strong. Ganam had vomited in a courtyard just before they'd begun their walk to the Hirana, but nothing in his bearing betrayed his nerves. Little Pallavi had run off to the kitchens and brought him back water, which he'd thanked her for. Afterward he'd said to Priya, in a mutter, "I'd prefer liquor."

"Wouldn't we all," she'd said, feeling that want down to her bones.

Now they stood before the Hirana together. Waiting.

There was a rustle, nearly a sigh, as the tree shuddered, and the ground shifted, and the yaksa emerged as if from nothing, simply rising from the night dark. All of them were here.

It was Arahli Ara who opened the way, who whispered through the green and made the Hirana yield open for them, providing them a path into its heart.

"Go," Priya said. "Become twice-born and thrice-born. Take your place as elders."

She felt sweaty. Uncomfortable in her tunic. Not at all like a proud and confident temple elder. The mask-keepers drifted past her, entering the tunnel, following the yaksa into the dim and dark.

Priya looked at the children. "You stay here," she said. It wasn't their time.

They nodded. Ashish was looking at the tunnel, his face wan and resolute. He, more than the rest, seemed to fear the fate that lay ahead of him.

Priya stepped into the tunnel, followed the dark until finally blue light began to bleed through it, overcoming the shadows around her. The deathless waters lay ahead. It was time.

A hand grasped her own, clammy with sweat.

"Priya," said Kritika. Her voice was a gasp. All fear. Priya turned to her and saw her fractured shadow face: her trembling mouth, her wide eyes. Her terror, all the hope and faith stripped clean. "I do not know if I will survive it."

She thought of telling Kritika she could turn back. But she knew Kritika wouldn't, no matter how much she wanted to. There was a lump in Priya's throat, fresh nausea in her stomach. She gripped Kritika's hand tight. "None of us know," Priya said quietly. "But you won't go alone."

"Kritika." Another voice ahead. Ganam, waiting for them. His expression was resolute. He held out his hand.

Hesitation. Then, with a gasp, Kritika wrenched from Priya. Her mouth went firm. Her spine straightened. She took Ganam's hand and walked toward the water.

There were, perhaps, things Priya should have said or done. But she could only stand with her feet in damp soil, blue water-light shining on the walls. She could only watch, as Chandni said in her melodious voice, "Go. We wait for you."

Twice-born—a bare handful, only three mask-keepers—walked into the water. Their white tunics billowed around them. She saw their bodies sink. First torsos. Then necks. Then their heads were immersed. Hair rose, a cloud around them. Then even that vanished, and there was nothing but the light of the water. Not even the shape of their bodies remained.

Ganam and Kritika entered together.

And then—silence.

It stretched, and stretched. She waited, counting her heartbeats. But they were too swift, too unsteady to be a reasonable measure of time. She took another step forward, and another, and felt Nandi's—Avan Ara's—fingers grasp her tunic, holding her fast.

"The water isn't for you," he whispered. "Wait."

She waited, and her mind was empty, blank. She couldn't think. If she thought, she would feel her fear not just in her body but in her mind, and then she wouldn't be able to stand here with a yaksa grasping her skirts, waiting for the living or dead to rise out of the water.

The first body to emerge rose like a flower—blooming, each limb rising at a time, feet first, and then a torso, and finally the head. Mouth open, eyes sightless.

Avan Ara let her go then, allowing her to stand on the wet edge of the waters and heave the body out. A woman. One of the mask-keepers. She would be no thrice-born.

Priya thought she would be sick.

Silence again. A steady sure grief began to rise in Priya. It had been too long. There would be no one else. No survivors. Only, if they were lucky, bodies to bury.

And then, a shadow—something rising. Someone broad, strong, and her stomach twisted violently at the sight. *Dead, dead, and all my allies are gone—*

Ganam rose with a gasp, and a swear, and scrambled for the bank, and heaved himself out. She ran over to him, helping, dragging him by the shoulders. She was crying like a child and she didn't give a shit.

"You're alive," she sobbed.

"See," he said, teeth chattering, water in his hair. "P-Priya. See. You're not the only one who gets to survive."

"Get up," she said, and slapped his arm. "Up, now. You need to get warm."

"Where are the rest?" he asked.

"None yet," she said. "But there will be more."

She waited. Waited. The joy turned bitter. Her vision went narrow and small. Her false confidence shriveled and faded away.

Nothing and no one.

There were no other survivors.

The yaksa were speaking. Their voices above her were like storm-bent trees, furious and fearful and strange.

"How is this possible?"

A murmur, in response. She couldn't understand it.

"Everything has changed too much."

"...betrayed," another whispered. "We need strength. We need what was murdered and should have lived."

"Only *her*—"

Priya didn't look up at them as they argued around her. Out on the grass surrounding the Hirana, where the yaksa were ringed around her, she was growing and plucking flowers to weave into garlands to lay on the bodies that would be buried. She pressed her magic into the soil. *Grow,* she urged. *Live, flourish, so that I may crown the dead.*

The mask-keepers deserved better than a funeral of fear and shame and quiet. They deserved a reverent burial. They had entered the deathless waters to make themselves strong enough to protect Ahiranya, to become powerful enough to make up for all the ways Priya was weak, unable to defend and protect and govern Ahiranya the way it deserved. Kritika had been frightened, but she had still gone into the waters. She'd done it for Ahiranya, and she'd done it so Priya wouldn't be alone.

She'd never liked Kritika, and Kritika had never really liked her. But they'd come to rely on each other.

I need you here, Priya thought. *You deserve so much more grief than I can give you.* A flower, woven with another, and another. *But I can give you this.*

"I lived in this earth," Sanjana was saying, her voice a wild bird, a saw to bone. "The soil ate me and I ate it in return. Bones buried within me, and bodies drowned, and I am telling you this, my kin: I will *not* die now."

"You should never have let the other one go," Avan Ara said. "Bhumika was ours. You were too human, Arahli. Rotten—"

"Hush," said Vata Ara, the yaksa who wore Sendhil's face.

"We need temple elders reared from babes." Chandni's voice. No. *Bhisa Ara's* voice. She could not let herself forget what they were. "That is what we need and what we shall have. The ones who entered the water were imperfect. We will have better."

Priya's hand stilled on the flowers.

"The children aren't ready," she said.

Silence.

"Speak again, child," Vata Ara said. "If you must speak, then speak."

She did not turn to face them. Did not bow. She only sat, her hands and her lap brimful of flowers.

"Arahli Ara can tell you how long it takes to make a child hollow and strong," she said. "If they enter the waters now, the children will only die. Give me years to teach them and they might live. Instead of using them, give me the deathless waters broken from their source. Let me feed my warriors those vials of poison and strength. And . . . let the best of them, the ones who prove their strength, try the waters. It's another chance for all of us. A way to turn strong worshippers into strong temple elders."

An approving noise, a murmur that moved through the yaksa.

"Spoken like a leader," Vata Ara murmured.

Spoken like a desperate woman, Priya thought.

"The waters are yours," Avan Ara said. "Take them. Feed them to your people." Then he leaned down and tugged her by the braid, as Padma so often did, a childish, urging hand. "Go and bury your bodies now," he said imperiously.

She walked back toward the mahal, holding flowers—wearing them around her arms and shoulders, a living cloak. It took her a moment to realize Arahli was walking with her. She'd been too numb to really care.

"Yaksa," she murmured.

Was he here to comfort her or show her another cruelty? His eyes met her own. His wood-whorled face was unreadable.

"You did well," he said.

"Thank you."

"It is a plan your brother would have approved of," Arahli said, and ah, there it was—the sting, the words meant to poison and cut.

31

MALINI

On the journey to Srugna, Malini saw forests and fields rich with rot. Despite the work of her army, the rot was spreading.

One of her guards claimed that at night, in the wind, the trees sang, like their branches were strung through with the cords and sinew of human throats. Malini stayed up one night until dawn and heard nothing, not even the natural groan of trees, and was glad.

Sahar taught her a new game involving dice, and two other guardswomen—Sanvi and Shri—helped Malini practice with her saber, and later with a bow.

Her strength grew.

There were nights when she did not dream of Priya, but there were more nights when she did. Priya haloed by flames; Priya lying on marble carved by rivulets of ever-running water. When she woke she felt a sure knowledge in her bones: They were drawing closer to one another.

Lord Prakash had a haveli on the edge of Srugna and offered his land up as a resting stop for Malini's army. Malini was grateful for the respite. She was lucky her tent was comfortable and her maid Swati attentive, but traveling day in and day out was exhausting, and even within a perimeter of armed soldiers and her chosen personal guard, she could not avoid the realities of the strain that Parijatdvipa was under. Blasted, empty fields and abandoned villages met them at every turn, and every day they seemed to have to change their path toward Srugna in order to avoid a new outcropping of rot.

As her army settled outside the haveli, within it she and Prakash, Narayan, and Ashutosh shared a carafe of wine. They spoke of lighter topics than usual, and Malini had just managed to cajole Narayan into a game of catur when a Srugani military official interrupted, apologizing and genuflecting even as he leaned over Prakash and whispered a message into his ear.

"There have been fires sighted in a neighboring village," said Lord Prakash, after the official had scurried out. "If you will excuse me, Empress—I wish to discover the cause."

"Of course, Lord Prakash," she said, rising to her feet a second behind him. "Allow me to join you."

"I am sure this is beneath your notice," he said gently. "Please remain here. Rest."

"No emperor worth his salt turned his back from battle," she said, offering him a firm, thin-lipped smile. "I am no less than my forefathers. I will come."

The heat in the village was blazing. The size of the fire was vast, golden on the horizon.

When they drew closer, Malini realized it was a large pyre. Her skin instantly grew clammy. She gripped the edge of her chariot.

On the ground, there were warriors corralling a group of people. There were too many people for them to be simply residents of this village—and every one of them was in some way riven with rot. There was someone—a lord, from the look of him—yelling orders at the warriors. Prakash set eyes on him and jumped from his chariot with astonishing nimbleness for a man of his years. By the time Malini had more elegantly alighted, they were deep into an argument.

She took a moment to study the face of this new lord.

She knew it. Once, this lord had been insolent to her. *Rohit*, she thought. Now, as he stood before her sweating, the firelight reflecting on his face, she could feel nothing but disgust for him.

She should have dealt with him sooner. Her instinct for vengeance hadn't failed her yet.

"...killing innocents," Prakash was saying, furious. "What were you thinking?"

"They were not innocents," Lord Rohit said hotly. "They're rot-riven. They were attempting to steal food. We do a service burning them."

Malini took a step closer. Her guards flanked her and barked, "Is this how you welcome your empress?"

A startled silence. Finally, Lord Rohit bowed.

"Empress," he said. "I did not know you were in Srugna."

"Clearly," she said. "You claim these people are criminals, Lord Rohit?"

"The rot turns people into traitors, Empress."

"And yet there are people in my army who are rot-riven," she said coolly. "You called them thieves."

"They have no place in our villages, Empress," he said. "They have no right to eat our food." He straightened, squaring his shoulders. "You ordered it so," he continued. "*No rot-riven near our grain.* That was your edict, was it not? My soldiers are doing what is expected of them."

That was not what she had ordered, when she had commanded each city-state to protect its harvests from the rot. She had intended for the harvests to be protected from rot in order to defend the empire's people from famine, *not* for the rot-riven to be starved and burned. But horror ran through her in a wave regardless, as she considered how her orders had been interpreted and utilized, how her voice had set this pyre alight. She should have been clearer, she should have been careful.

"Lord Prakash, arrange a military official to speak to the survivors," she said, gesturing at the corralled, terrified people. "Put a stop to this, Lord Rohit. Immediately."

He ground his jaw. Bowed again. "Empress."

There was a cry from near the pyre. Not from the pyre itself, and not a cry of horror. A cry of joy.

Mothers' fire, someone screamed, and Malini was turning, moving toward it before she could stop herself.

The crowd parted for her, and she saw it there. In the ashes, in the dying flames. A glowing, squirming thing—a thing that pulsed, breathed, shone like the sun.

A flower of fire.

"Sahar," she said, whirling. "Send someone back. To my chambers. Swati will have it, a black chest, it will be able to carry it—"

"Yes, Empress," Sahar said, breathless. She turned and yelled an order. Her hand gripping her saber hilt was white-knuckled, trembling.

Not mothers' fire. False fire. But still—more fire they could use.

Malini was not sure if she felt sickness or relief.

There were more flowers of fire. Two. Then three. They were all collected and carefully stored away.

And Malini watched it be done. Watched, her stomach knotted, and tried to decide what must be done next.

Could any death create the flames? Was this all it would take—a willingness to mark certain lives unworthy, and place them upon a pyre?

"Prakash," she said quietly, beckoning the Srugani lord toward her. "I do not want this news to spread. You understand? We know, and we have seen, that false fire is not enough to destroy the yaksa or Ahiranya. We cannot have our people turn on one another or those they believe deserve to die. We hold sacrifice holy. What has been done here is an abomination. For his crime, Lord Rohit must be imprisoned on his lands." *Where he cannot spread what he has seen*, she did not say. She knew Prakash would understand. "These people will be freed."

Prakash nodded, but his jaw was tight.

"Empress," he said quietly. "If these people are thieves, if they are criminals—"

"Then they have been forced to it," said Malini. "I do not want the rot-riven exiled and starved. I want messages sent across the army to instruct my warriors in the strongest terms that the rot-riven are our own."

"Lord Rohit has claimed that some were attempting to run to Ahiranya."

"If they were trying to run from hunger and fire, then we are at fault," Malini snapped.

A pause. "The fire," he said, after a beat. "If it can be used...If we may fight the yaksa. Empress, there are things you must consider."

"I will not repeat Chandra's errors."

"You do not listen to your generals with the same trust you give to your women, Empress," he said heavily. "But I would counsel you now to consider the needs of war. This fire, made here or elsewhere, with people already condemned by rot..." He trailed off, then said stiffly, "If they must die, it is better they die for Parijatdvipa. The fire of their deaths could save us."

"You believe I should murder my own people," Malini said dully. "I assure you, Lord Prakash: I have done it before. I will do so again if I believe it is needful."

"It is needful, Empress."

"Yes," she said. "Chandra certainly thought so. I'm sure he would be jubilant to see me continue his work."

"When the war is won, when peace comes, we will grieve our actions, Empress. We will honor the dead and raise effigies to them. A new generation of mothers, saviors of Parijatdvipa. We will do it all, Empress, I promise you. But now, we must put grief aside. Do you see it? Surely you must." His voice was pleading.

"So many women died at Chandra's hands that we will never know all their names, Lord Prakash." Malini did not know how she spoke. Her emotions were a distant star of fire, and she was the black void around them, cold and empty. "We could build a forest of golden carvings for all those women who died unwillingly and still we would not have enough. And still, the rot is here."

"There are women who would die freely if you asked it of them, Empress."

"Perhaps there are," Malini said. "But they are not the people who died on the pyre today. Thank you for your counsel, Lord Prakash. But I am afraid I must spend time alone in prayer now. The mothers must guide me in this."

There was silence on the journey back to the haveli. When Malini reached her room, Sahar drew the doors gently shut behind her. Sahar's mouth was a thin line, her brow creased. Malini could tell she was ruminating.

It was one of her other guards, Sanvi, who broke the silence first.

"I don't think it should be done, Empress." Her voice was trembling. "Burning people like that, people who don't believe, who aren't willing. It's wrong."

"Hush," Sahar said. "You're tired, Sanvi. Go and get water for all of us."

"But—"

"*Go.*" To Malini she said, "I'm sorry, my lady."

"No need," Malini said. They were all overwrought.

"If your sage were here she'd give you useful advice," Sahar went on. "But me, all I can say is…" A sigh. "You're our empress. Mother chosen. You'll know what to do. Trust yourself."

Malini could have laughed. Trust *herself*? She didn't even know if she wanted to burn a field of bodies for her own life or throw herself on the flames. She had no reason to trust her own heart.

Finally, even her guards left her alone. If she'd had any faith she would have prayed then. Instead she lay on her bed and closed her eyes and tried to convince herself she could not smell charnel smoke.

She could not pray to the mothers. But.

Alori, she thought. Called, a cry to the dark. *Narina. Aditya. If you're more than gristle and dust, send me a weapon I can use.*

I don't want to die as you did. I don't want to kill as Chandra did. Please.

Give me a weapon without such a terrible cost, before I must pay with what remains of my rotten heart.

RAO

Rao woke and fell unconscious and woke again. He was being dragged through snow; he was in a tent, surrounded by the smell of warm bodies and smoke; he was being forced to drink something warm and sweet that made the shivers in his body fade and his consciousness fade once more too. When he woke after more time than he cared to think about he saw things in flashes: a circle open to the sky, snow swirling in and smoke rising out; blurred figures in long wool robes; walls of dark canvas. Then he felt the warmth of a body close to his own. The body kneeled.

"Raise your head to the firelight," a low voice ordered. There was a finger under his chin, gently urging his head up. There was a man in front of him with pale, hawkish eyes. Behind him in the tent a campfire burned.

"Perhaps I imagined it," the man murmured. His thumb came to rest beneath Rao's left eye. "I saw two fools in a storm. Strangers in Dwarali clothing. I thought of letting my soldiers shoot them—and then I saw your eyes. I thought they glowed like flame. Was it a trick of moonlight on snow, Prince Rao?"

"Kai Ehsan," Rao said croakily, dredging the name somehow from his skull—from a fresh memory of snow, moonlight, a lowered bow. "You did not. The nameless god guided me here."

"And why did your god guide you here?"

"To seek a ruby," said Rao. There seemed no worth in

concealing the truth. Yelling about his vision had saved his life, after all. "But it may not be a ruby. The nameless showed me—snow, and blood rising from inside it."

A strange look passed over the man's face. For a moment he did not speak.

"I believe you," he said finally. "Only a fool following a god would walk to his death in snow." He released Rao's face. "You no longer look like you're going to perish, Prince Rao. That is good."

"The woman with me—"

"She is recovering," said Kai Ehsan. "If you can stand unaided, you can speak to her yourself."

It wasn't easy, but Rao rose to his feet. He took a moment to regain his balance and take in his surroundings. His weapons were gone. There were no chakrams at his wrists or daggers at his waist. He was wrapped in a blanket of fur and embroidered wool. One staggering step forward, then another, and he finally saw Sima on the other side of the fire, gray-faced and bundled in a mound of blankets so thick she looked like a swaddled-up infant.

The sight of her gave him the strength to stumble to her side. She mouthed his name, then mouthed a curse so vile that it made him laugh in surprise and then laugh again in relief as he lowered himself to his knees in front of her.

"Sima," he said, his voice rough. He clasped her hands in his, drawing them out of her cocoon of blankets. They were very cold. "I'm so very sorry."

"N-no need," Sima managed. "W-we're both idiots."

One of the women clucked at him and batted his hand away.

"Bring your hands closer to the fire," she instructed Sima, who complied.

"My sisters," the kai said, nodding to the women. "Bahar, Qutlugh."

"You're welcome here, Prince Rao of Alor," the younger of the two women said. The elder nodded in agreement.

The leader of the Jagatay—that was what the term *kai* denoted, or so the scraps of knowledge Rao had gained in the Lal Qila's library had told him—placed a hand on Rao's shoulder. "Rest," he said. "My sisters will watch over you."

"Thank you," Rao said, looking from the two women to their brother. "For your kindness, and your compassion. I am indebted to you."

"I do not need thanks," said Kai Ehsan. "But I will take your debt. When the storm dies and you are recovered, Prince Rao of Alor, I am going to ask you for knowledge. And you will answer honestly."

The storm eased eventually. No more snow flurried in through the roof, and Rao's shivers had stopped. He and Sima didn't talk in the hours that passed—not with eyes on them. But eventually Sima wriggled her hand free from her blankets and touched her knuckles to his arm. That comforted him.

One of the kai's sisters—Qutlugh—stirred, turning toward the entrance of the tent with narrowed eyes as the tent flap drew back.

Kai Ehsan stood at the entrance, the sky and ground blue-white behind him. "I want you to come with me," the kai said. "It is time for us to talk."

Rao's gaze turned to Sima. She looked back.

"She'll be safe with my sisters," said the kai. "Come."

"Go," Sima said croakily. "I'll be fine."

So Rao rose to his feet and followed.

"You'll like this wine," Ehsan said, as Rao sat across from him at the low table in the kai's own tent. The fire was burning low, but the closed tent and the furs and blankets around them kept the chill at bay. "This is my last bottle," Ehsan said as he poured. "My grandfather lost his eastern ancestral lands, where our grape-vines grew, in war with his cousin. Now my heritage is reduced to this. Two cups of sweet liquor." The bottle hit the table with a soft thud. "My father later lost his fruit orchards to a Babure kai," Ehsan continued, pushing the cup to Rao, who took it obediently. "But I never cared for peaches, so it was no great loss to me, beyond my pride." A beat, and then he murmured, "The losses afterward were harder."

Rao touched the cup to his lips. He didn't drink deeply, but what little he tasted was rich, warming. It was like nothing he'd had before.

"What knowledge do you want from me?" Rao asked, lowering his cup.

A thin-lipped smile from the kai, who lowered his own cup.

"I want knowledge of the empire," he said. "Of Parijatdvipa."

Knowledge could be many things. Gossip. Secrets. And Rao knew more about Malini's court—and her army, and her secrets—than he would ever share with a stranger.

"I know you trade with the Lal Qila," said Rao. "You speak Zaban. You know as much as I could tell—perhaps more."

"A few Babure tribes trade with the fort," Kai Ehsan corrected. "And only sparingly. Only when they seek more weapons to fight us." Another thin smile. "You understand, perhaps. The Lal Qila arms one impoverished border tribe against another, ensuring that we are too busy killing one another to fight the Dwarali or turn our faces toward the empire. A clever defense strategy, but not one that has benefited me or my kin. I know many of your languages because my people, like yours, believe in the value of learning." A fluid shrug of a single shoulder. "A common soldier could bring me knowledge I don't have. But I am sure you, as a *prince*, can give me truth as precious as gold."

"I must apologize," Rao said, his voice steady despite the pounding of his heart. He was painfully aware of how vulnerable he and Sima were here in this camp where they did not belong. "But I will not share any knowledge that places my empire in danger or works against the lord and lady of the Lal Qila. If that is what you seek, I cannot pay my debt."

"Did the lord and lady of the Lal Qila allow you here? Surely not, or you would have approached my camp with an army. You already act against them." Ehsan leaned forward, his hawkish eyes unblinking. "Nothing I ask you to share with me will harm your empire. I am not going to torture you for knowledge—there's no need to look so hunted, Prince Rao—and there is no need for you to withhold it from me. I have something you want, and all I ask in return is to know how the empire fares beyond the border of mountains and fort. Tell me about your new empress. Tell me what danger sends you running to follow a god's voice."

He was dangerously convincing.

"What do you have that I want?" Rao asked, trying to buy time.

"The end to your quest, of course," Ehsan said. "The truth of your ruby. Though we call it heart's shell."

Rao's breath caught like a claw in his throat. For a moment a vision of fire, an insistent call, burned behind his eyes, then faded to smoke.

"You are a desperate man," Ehsan said, low. "I see in you an echo of myself. I am a man with barely enough food to feed his soldiers. My people are decimated. I know what desperation looks like. What hunts your people? What beast hounds Parijatdvipa? Tell me."

Rao held his cup of wine simply to ground himself. Cold metal under his hands. His own blood thundering in his ears.

"There is a danger in Parijatdvipa," Rao said. There was a hush inside the tent. Nothing but the crackle of the low fire and the light of it glancing off the planes of Ehsan's attentive face, his narrowed eyes. "Yaksa—ancient beings—are returning. And a strange rot destroys our crops and our people. Those beings want to destroy us. Our empire. And it is my duty to find a way to save us all. I hoped my vision would be an answer."

Ehsan's smile faded. His expression was solemn now.

"We were meant to meet. I prayed for an answer to my desperation, and here you are." He stood abruptly. "Come with me. And put on this coat, Prince Rao," Ehsan ordered, offering him a lined jacket as he drew on his own, drawing the high collar tight at his throat. "It's bitter where we're going. Cold that rises from inside your bones. You'll need all the warmth you can get. And one last thing..."

Rao paused as the man briskly drew out a cloth and held it up to Rao's eyes.

"You will have to trust me," the kai said.

Rao closed his eyes and allowed himself to be blindfolded.

He would never have been able to chart the route if asked. He was led on a winding path: up a rough surface, then down again; over soft ground onto jagged stone. He felt foolish and uncomfortable, convinced at any moment that he would fall and crack open his skull. But Ehsan led him calmly, giving straightforward instructions even as he steered Rao with hands at his upper arms.

"Lower your foot. There, good. You likely know little of the politics of people beyond your empire's borders," Ehsan said mildly as he urged Rao to follow him down a steep incline. "But among our tribes, land can be gained or lost in a generation. If you are not strong enough, cunning enough to keep it, then it will be taken by wiser and stronger leaders. That is why my tribe is so reduced. My father's and grandfather's failures haunt us, and I . . . have not been able to change our fortunes." His voice tightened on those last words, restraining feeling. "Turn to your left. There is a wall there—stone. Hold it for balance."

"Where have you brought me?" Rao asked.

"To the heart's shell," Kai Ehsan said, putting a hand on Rao's shoulder, urging him forward. "My father could not sell this knowledge, nor could it be stolen from him. No one knew it had any worth to a prince of Alor." Amusement in Ehsan's voice. "The location of this mine was passed to me, from father to son. It is my inheritance."

As they descended, Rao felt the air change, growing heavier. Even without his sight, Rao was sure they were under the earth, the weight of mountains above them. He desperately wanted to peel his blindfold off, but he resisted.

"Have you heard of the philosopher Sunata, Prince Rao?"

"Everything is the void," Rao said promptly. Ehsan chuckled.

"As Sunata espoused—we believe in the void, the great

nothingness. And we believe that the void is home to innumerable gods." Ehsan's hand circled his arm again, drew him onto ground that crunched underfoot, rocky and uneven—then abruptly, suddenly, as smooth as rainwashed stone. "We know of your yaksa because my ancestors feared them once too. How could they not? But they prayed to the void, to any benevolent immortal listening in the dark, and received a warning from a kind god: All magic from the void has a terrible price. All magic can only touch the world for so long before it twists the world and itself into monstrous shapes. So one of my ancestors, a great kai, made a sacrifice. He meditated, and strengthened his mind and transformed his body by sheer will alone into weapons to hold the yaksa and all dark magics at bay."

Rao felt a tug at the back of his skull. The blindfold was removed.

Disoriented, Rao blinked until his vision adjusted to the flare of the single torch held in Ehsan's hand. The sight in front of him made his breath stop in his throat.

Ehsan's forefathers might have lost their vineyards and orchards, but here lay a far more powerful crop. He could see no bodily remains of a long-dead ancestor, but he could see strange stones fused into the vast walls of the cavern around him. The stones were blooming like flowers of rock—fistlike, curled shapes by the dozens, each a fragile weft of black stone.

"Heart's shell," said Ehsan, holding it to the light of the torch in his left hand. In the glow of his left hand one of those dark, fragile stones gleamed a liquid black as deep as blood. "It was used by my people, in the Age of Flowers. It negates the strength of the yaksa, traps them, and reduces them. Take it."

Rao took a piece of stone.

Heart's shell. Empty. A hollow thing, light and strange in his hand. He gazed at it and felt no magic inside himself. No light, no voice from the void. He was entirely empty. Entirely human in a way he realized he had never been in his whole life.

There were no voices inside his skull but his own.

"What proof do I have that your stone acts as you say?" Rao asked. His voice shook faintly.

"None but what you feel now," Ehsan said. "None, but that your god guided you here, and guided me to let you live. I prayed for help. I prayed to the void, hoping something benevolent within it would answer; perhaps it was your nameless god who heard me and brought us together." Ehsan took a step closer. "I knew we were meant to meet," Ehsan said, hushed. "When I saw your eyes, I knew. You were my answer. And now, ah—your eyes are lightless." Humor in his voice, and awe. "You look like a mortal man, untouched by fate."

Rao shook his head, wordless. The nameless had never filled his eyes with light before Aditya's death. No priest of the nameless had ever spoken of that power. The nameless's power lay in prophecy—in names and messages that steered the heart.

It was Aditya that Rao thought of when he thought of light. Aditya and fire.

On the heels of that thought came a suspicion, a fear—what if it was not the nameless who spoke to him at all, but something else—a being of fire, of light, a being wearing Aditya's voice?

"I…do not know," Rao said, his voice a little raw. "Perhaps two gods work through me, or even a dozen."

Ehsan's mouth quirked into a smile. He thought Rao was jesting with him.

"Perhaps all the gods of the void share one cause," Ehsan agreed. "Perhaps they seek to help us, or perhaps they seek to use us. But all that matters to me is whether you will help me, Prince Rao, in return for a supply of heart's shell to fight your yaksa."

"How can I help you?"

"I am tired of war, and tired of running," Ehsan replied. "My people need peace. In return for a supply of heart's shell, I want land for my people. I demand a place for us in the empire. A home we may keep for generations."

"You ask a high price," Rao said evenly, "for something we need to survive."

"I am asking for a chance to survive in return for giving your empire the same chance," said Ehsan. The light of his lantern painted whip marks of gold across his face. "We both know that well. And you may refuse me, of course. But I promise you, Prince Rao, you will never find the heart's shell again. Even my own sisters do not know the way to this mine. That knowledge is passed from father to son, and only I possess it. I would die to keep it in my hands, and my hands alone. But give me what I ask for, and your empress shall have all the heart's shell she desires. So, Prince Rao. Will you bargain on your empress's behalf?"

Whether the nameless had brought him here, or another being in the void Sunata had once written of, there was only one answer Rao could give. He had come here to save Parijatdvipa, and to stop Malini from burning.

He carefully curled his fingers around the heart's shell in his palm.

He would not return to Malini empty-handed.

"I can," Rao said steadily. "Let us return to your camp, Kai Ehsan, and discuss terms. I'll put the blindfold on myself."

33

PRIYA

There was no one to bully Priya into taking a palanquin now that Bhumika was gone. The yaksa certainly didn't care. She walked through the city of Hiranaprastha in her plainest sari. She didn't need a palanquin or gold or the garb of a temple elder to demonstrate her authority, after all—flowers grew where she walked. She was pretty sure that was enough.

The city was still bustling. It seemed like nothing—not even the return of their gods—could make the people of Ahiranya stop the difficult business of surviving. Priya passed familiar food stalls and homes, pink-lanterned buildings, and families sitting on verandas, shaded from the rising heat of the sun. The crowds parted around her, faces uneasy. Some bowed.

There were many, many more people with rot than there had been before. There were effigies to the yaksa everywhere, surrounded by offerings. Glints of gold, and fruit black with ants. She bowed her head too as she passed. She'd been told to show reverence, and she would.

She reached her destination. The guards at the gates of the haveli clearly recognized her, because one paled and fumbled with his saber, lowering it as he kneeled.

"I'm here to speak with Lord Chetan," she said. "Get him for me."

They did. The first guard ran ahead to warn the household. By the time Priya had crossed the relatively small courtyard and was inside the open hall of the house, where a pool of flowers-in-water sat beneath colonnades open to the sky, there were maidservants bowing, and offers of sherbet or wine. The highborn lord of the house was hurrying out, adjusting his brocade jacket into place. She must have woken him from rest.

He didn't look well. There were great shadows under his eyes. And his arms—partially concealed under his jacket—were so rot-riven they were more fern and vine than flesh. He swallowed, visibly frightened, his eyes all black pupil.

"High Elder," he said, sweeping a bow. "How can my household assist you?"

Priya felt supremely uncomfortable. She tried not to let it show.

"Lord Chetan," she said. "I need your help."

He ushered her to a seat. She told him what she required: more warriors and guards. Anything his household could spare. Weapons. Money. Assistance in maintaining some semblance of government. He poured her sherbet, and a small glass for himself. They both left them untouched.

"Elder, anything you require, I will give. Anything the yaksa need I will hand over wholeheartedly. The yaksa allowed me to live, when my loyalty was lax. I will not fail them again." His hands, in his lap, were trembling. "All my fellow highborn will feel the same. I can assure you. If you wish me to speak to them on your behalf…"

"I'd be grateful," Priya said, a wave of relief washing over her. Bhumika had told her, once, about the connections Lord Chetan had. This was exactly what Priya had been hoping for. "I'm pleased, Lord Chetan," Priya said to him earnestly. "I know the yaksa will be too. They won't allow your rot to progress further. In fact…will you give me your hand?"

He held it out, and she took it. Closed her eyes. She felt for the rot in him—that blooming kernel.

She opened her eyes.

"The yaksa have frozen its course," she said. "Nothing new grows."

"Thank you, Elder," he said, and withdrew his arm. Visibly, he hesitated. Then said, "There is a boy in your—care. A temple child. My son, Ashish."

A dark feeling shuddered through Priya. Oh.

Temple children were meant to have no family but the temple. But she didn't tell him so, only nodded her head, clasping her own hands now.

"Is... is he well, Elder? His mother worries for him." His voice wavered. "I know the yaksa may use him as they see fit..."

"He is well," Priya said softly. "He's a smart boy. Stubborn. He's good with the younger children. He's well taken care of, Lord Chetan."

The man blinked rapidly, his eyes wet.

"Thank you," he said, then cleared his throat. "If I may ask. I beg of you, Elder—one small favor."

Rukh found her. She was sitting in the empty storage room that had been her sickroom again. She'd left her bedding in there. Sometimes her rooms just felt a little too crowded and she liked to come here and be alone. Rukh always knew where to find her, though, and he turned up soon enough.

"You look sorry for yourself," he said. "Very grim. Like a proper war leader."

"Shut up," she said. "How did you find me?"

"People are always watching you," he said with a shrug. "I just asked. What's wrong?"

She met his gaze; his eyebrows were furrowed, his face serious. He was so young still—it felt wrong to pour her problems into his ear. She wished Sima were here. She missed her so much it was like an ache.

"Adult problems," she said. "Nothing for you to worry about."

"Why don't you have a drink?"

"Don't tell me to have a drink!" She reached out to play-act at cuffing his ear and let him leap out of the way.

He grinned at her. "What about Billu's hashish?"

"Shhh. I can't do any of that and you know it."

"Why not?"

"I might be needed, Rukh." She sighed and drew her knees up so she could prop her forehead on them and groan in a proper dramatic fashion. "I'm always needed."

She heard the scuff of his footsteps. He sat on the ground beside her, mirroring her. When she raised her head his own knees were drawn up, his chin on his hands.

"What are you holding?" Rukh asked.

Priya unclasped her fist. It felt stiff. She'd been grinding her fingers down tight all the way back from the haveli, across Hiranaprastha.

In her palm lay a little ribbon—a knot of red and orange cloth, bound with a bead shaped like an eye. Just large enough to be hooked around a wrist and tied tight. "It's a good-luck charm," she said. "Made by a boy's mother to keep him safe."

It was from the father too. Maybe he'd made it and lied to her. She didn't know. But she'd seen the grief and fear in his eyes.

"It's pretty," Rukh observed.

"It is." She ran her thumb over it: the soft cloth, the knots in it. "Maybe it would be better not to give it to him at all. Maybe it would be better to...to let him focus on getting strong. This might just visit hurt on him. Remind him of the family he can't go back to."

Rukh pressed a hand over her own. The roots under his skin were a sharp pinprick that made her breathe deeper, feeling the heat of the air in her lungs. She raised her head properly and looked at him.

"You need to do it," he said. "Whatever hurt that boy feels... he's going to have to be strong enough to stand it, isn't he? If he's a temple child."

"And if he's not strong enough?" Priya whispered.

"Then you'll be here," Rukh said. "You'll protect him. As you've protected me."

Priya huffed a laugh. "When did you get so grown up?"

"When you were away," he said, his smile a little lopsided. "And maybe a little when you got back, too." He drew away his hand, sprawling out against the wall. "I'm really glad you're back, Priya."

She brushed a hand over his hair. He let her.

"Me too," she said.

She gave Ashish the braided thread. Then she kissed Padma good-bye and ordered the other children to listen to Khalida. "Or I'll do something awful to punish you," she'd said. "Like shave your eyebrows off."

"You'd never," Pallavi said stoutly. Her fear had worn off fast. Behind her, still seated on his bedding, Ashish was watching quietly, clutching the braid of ribbon around his own wrist.

Priya rolled her eyes.

"Just *behave.*"

Priya had dressed in a serviceable salwar kameez. She bound her hair back in a tight knot, so tight it made her head ache a little. She appreciated the pain, though. It was grounding.

There was a yaksa being reborn in Srugna. It was time for Priya to find her, as Mani Ara had bid her to.

She and Ganam walked together to the bower of bones, a cadre of soldiers following behind them. One carried a box of vials for her, each glowing blue with water broken from the source. Many were guards and warriors who'd been trained by Jeevan, and ex-maidservants with arrows and scythes. And there, at the very edge of the group, were a few of the rot-riven outsiders who now lived in the mahal.

"We've lost nearly all of our mask-keepers," Priya said. "Only Ganam remains. I am the only temple elder left. We need more strength. More power. And this is the weapon we have." She held up a vial of deathless waters.

She explained the deathless waters to them, and what drinking them broken from the source would mean.

"When you're a temple child like I am and you survive passing through the waters, you gain strength and magic," said Priya. "But surviving's not promised."

Murmurs and lowered heads, from her listening crowd. They knew how many had died trying to pass through the waters and rise.

"When you drink water broken from the source," Priya went on, "you gain some of that strength. For a while. But it's poison. Eventually it kills you. Unless you become once-born, there's no chance of living out your full life. I won't force you to drink. But if you're willing to—you have the chance to carry this with you. To drink it when you need strength."

A deep breath. "And if you must drink...this is your chance to grow strong and pass through the deathless waters. To perhaps become thrice-born, one day, like me. I promise you that chance, even if I can't promise you your life."

She held the vial out. "You don't need to decide now. But you can carry the waters with you."

"Elder." A rough voice. One of the outsiders. A man, she remembered, called Shyam. "Would you trust those of us who came from beyond Ahiranya with this?"

A rumble of unease from the crowd. Priya met his eyes.

"I want to," she said. "But tell me why I should."

"I fought in the war," Shyam replied. "I saw what you did. You're stronger than the empire." He said it bluntly, fiercely. Like he believed it. "I'd rather risk my life for the home you've given my family than side with an empire that left us to die."

"That's enough for me," Priya said.

"If you turn on us, we'll kill you, of course," Ganam added. Priya had to work very hard not to roll her eyes.

They took the vials from her.

She led them to the seeker's path. Above them, the bones on their ribbons wavered and spun. Some, absurdly, had sprouted flowers. It was like being in a macabre highborn lady's garden.

Priya met Ganam's gaze.

"How does it feel to be twice-born?" Priya asked.

"Terrible," Ganam replied quietly. "The price was too high."

"Ganam," she said. He stopped, then turned, a questioning look in his eyes. "You don't have to try to become thrice-born."

"I do," he said. "For Kritika. For all of them. I have to try. They'd want me to."

"And what do you want?"

He shook his head.

"What good is wanting going to do either of us? Come on, Priya. Walk with me. Let's talk about other shit until we get to Srugna."

All these new paths, and here they were following the oldest of them.

"Can you feel any Srugani?" Priya asked Ganam, after a time. Parijatdvipa had left armed forces at Ahiranya's borders. There were many in Srugna's forests, too.

She could feel them. But she wanted to give Ganam the chance to test his own skill.

"I can feel mosquitoes biting me," Ganam said, hacking his way through the snarl of branches that riddled their path. Once, he would have needed a hand scythe for that work. But now he only needed the sweep of his hand. His twice-born magic made the branches wither and splinter around him, parting to allow the two of them to pass. "That's what I can feel."

Priya rolled her eyes. He couldn't see it, but that wasn't the point. Derision bled into her voice when she said, "Can you feel the warriors waiting for us?"

"Not the way you can," he said. "So maybe you do the seeing for both of us. I'll focus on clearing the way."

She could have cleared the blockage with a breath, with a single brush of her mind, bending the green on the path around them to her will. But Ganam's shoulders were bunched with tension, and she was pretty sure he needed this: an outlet, a focus. Something to home in on that wasn't the fight that lay ahead of them.

"Fine," she said. "But don't exhaust yourself, all right? Your strength is going to be needed."

A crash. A rumble. A tree fell to the side, vanishing through the haze that edged the seeker's path—where time melted and changed before returning to its normal shape.

"You'll be fine," Ganam said. "You don't need my brawn. I've seen you in a fight, Priya."

"It's not me I'm worried about."

She could hear the warriors behind her, clutching their scythes and sabers. Some of them were shivering with fear. Others looked nothing but determined. None of them had drunk from their vials yet.

She closed her eyes for a single breath, feeling the song and swell of the green. "A whole contingent of Srugani warriors," she murmured. "Armed with maces, mostly. But some have sabers. And some have arrows. And others... fire. But not mothers' fire."

"Fire's fire," Ganam muttered. "We could wait here until the patrol passes."

Priya shook her head.

"They're not moving," she said. "Their camp is at the end of the seeker's path. We'll need to go through them."

They were nearing the end of the path—near Srugna itself, where the forest receded and its power began to gently ebb. She could feel the warriors arrayed, waiting for them.

Behind her, one of her soldiers took a step forward. She was timid, square-faced and strong but trembling.

"Elder," the woman—the *girl*—whispered. "What do we do now?"

Priya could hear everything, feel everything. The uneasy shifting from foot to foot of her own soldiers; the creak of hands on scythe handles and bows; the drag of heavy boots from beyond the forest. The grunt from a throat as someone hefted a mace. The eyes watching the forest. Waiting.

"We start," she said, addressing the people huddled close around her—trying to sound authoritative. Trying to sound ready. "By pretending to be prey."

34

ARAVIND

"It's a thankless job," Aravind's commander told him before their force set out to the border between Srugna and Ahiranya, where the trees loomed and old monsters now walked. "But you have to do it, boy. It'll be good for you." A pat on the back, oddly gentle.

The commander was often kind to him because he was the youngest warrior in this patrol. Too many men had died in the war for the imperial throne, or from the rot, which meant even boys had to fight. But Aravind was glad to be in the army. He wasn't as much of a child as everyone seemed to think he was.

Aravind hadn't argued, because it didn't seem like anyone cared if he wanted to go to the border or not. That wasn't what it meant to be a Srugani warrior. He hadn't built his strength hefting river stones and, later, heavy carved maces so that he could stay home and be comfortable. His job was to be a loyal body, and that was what he was going to be.

He was fifteen. Old enough for war.

Patrolling the border with Ahiranya was still not a job he wanted to do for long. The forest was old and dark and soundless and rotten. Sometimes, at night, some of the other men swore it sang, trying to call them in. His mother had warned him about the forest when he was a boy, fed him warnings in the sweet milk of a bedtime story. The last time the yaksa had walked the subcontinent, they had come to Srugna with feasts and promises.

Sometimes they'd tempt people with gifts. Fruit that split open into flowers, or gold and jewels that could only be won by combat or marriage. Sometime people took what was offered.

People who went with them never came back.

Now Aravind shuddered. His armor wasn't heavy, and part of him wished it had a bit more weight and cloth to it. The trees here blotted out the sunlight, leaving the air uncomfortably cool. All he could hear was the creak of leather, the muttering of his fellow soldiers, sharing more of those stories that settled like stones in Aravind's guts. Even the birds didn't sing this close to Ahiranya. There was nothing to distract him.

Because he wasn't sharing stories—because he was looking at the birdless trees—he was the first one to spot the woman who stumbled out of Ahiranya's forest. She was in a light-colored salwar kameez, stained up to the calves in forest dirt. She was rot-riven, which wasn't a surprise. He knew that local villages hounded out their sick, sending them into exile.

He was reluctant to approach her. Like most folk, he feared catching the rot. "You," he called out. "Move along."

She took a stumbling step forward. Aravind clutched his mace tighter, then let his grip loosen. She was just one girl.

She went to her knees. She wasn't as young as he'd first thought—nor was she old. She was just short, narrow-boned, her face visibly tense, even in the dim light. "I need your help," she called back. Her voice was low, almost rasping. "Will you help me, brothers?"

"What kind of help?" Aravind's commander asked. He was frowning. He reached for his belt. "I have a water flask here, little sister. You can drink."

She whispered her thanks, looking between them. She held out a hand—and the commander grasped her hard by the wrist, wrenching her forward.

"You're not Srugani," he said flatly. "What are you doing here? How did you get out?"

The woman's expression flickered. Gone was the soft look on it. Her mouth firmed.

"Well," she said flatly. "I've never been good at this sort of thing."

The world exploded around him.

Trees, soil, green—all twisted, all strange.

The solid world around them was like water in her hands. Every time she moved, it moved with her—branches splintering and dirt roiling—and he could only think, wildly, *So this is what a yaksa is.*

He grappled for his mace. It fell from his hands.

A hand wrenched him around by the back.

"I have one," someone said. A man's voice.

Aravind threw a wild punch. But for all his training—and he'd truly done his best—the man who had him was even stronger. Aravind found himself slammed down to the ground. A hand grasped his throat.

Distantly, he heard screaming. The sound of bones breaking.

Above him was a masked face—carved, cruel whorls of wood, and black eyes behind it.

The masked face spoke.

"You're just a boy, aren't you?" The masked man's breath was hot. The skin of his throat gleamed with sweat. He looked vicious and animal, and Aravind wanted to shut his eyes from terror, wanted to die without seeing that mask over him. But when he turned his face away, the Ahiranyi man slapped a hand against his cheek, hard enough to hurt. "Look at me," the man snapped. "Tell me who else waits us out on your lands. Is the empress's army there with fire?"

"Yes," Aravind gasped out. He grasped the lie. "Yes, there are more soldiers coming and they have fire. They'll destroy you."

A shadow fell over him. The woman from before crouched down. There were small flowers tracing her throat.

"He's lying," the woman said. "If the empress had sent forces they'd be here." Her eyes were flat, grim. He didn't know how he'd ever thought she looked fragile or small. Crouched, she was all coiled muscle.

He looked beyond her. All he could see of his patrol were still bodies.

All dead.

"Ganam," another voice called. "Elder Priya. I've caught the commander. He's still alive."

"Bring him here," the woman ordered.

Aravind watched his commander being dragged over. The man's lip was split. A bloody wound was dripping from his side.

He was forced down onto the ground next to Aravind. The masked man stood tall and said to Aravind in a deadly voice, "Get onto your knees. Wait there."

Without his mace and with his friends dead—what else could he do but obey? Better to die kneeling, he supposed, than flat in the dirt.

The masked man asked the commander the same question he'd asked Aravind. Aravind's commander narrowed his eyes. Spat on the dirt. "The empress will destroy you. I can promise you that."

"They don't know anything," the masked man said, turning to the woman again.

Silence from the woman. The rustle of footsteps as figures surrounded them.

"How old are you, you?" the masked man asked. It took a moment for Aravind to realize he was being questioned.

"F-fifteen," he said.

The masked man said nothing.

"I'll do it," the small woman said.

"You shouldn't," the man said. "And neither should I." His hand on his scythe was trembling. "Fuck the yaksa," he said. "I won't kill children for them."

"Let him go, then," the woman said. Her voice was soft. "Spirits, Ganam. I'm not asking you to do it."

"He'll tell someone we're here," the man said. "They'll send more warriors."

"You think I can't fight them?"

"I think if they have their magic fire, none of us can. Your empress will come running when she knows you're here."

The woman closed her eyes.

"If anyone must die," Aravind's commander said heavily, "let it be me. Let the boy go."

"Stand, boy," the woman said to Aravind. He rose unsteadily to his feet. He looked down into her eyes. The look she gave him could have cut his soul. "Run," she said.

"Listen to them, son," his commander said softly.

Aravind hated himself for his own cowardice. He turned and fled.

Aravind ran. He didn't look back. He heard a noise—a sharp, terrible noise. The snick of metal. The spill of blood. He ran. And ran, and ran, and ran.

35

PRIYA

In the aftermath, with blood drying clammy cold on her skin, its metallic stench filling her nose, she went to a woman who'd drunk the deathless waters.

She hadn't seen her do it, but that didn't matter. Priya could feel the writhing power in her, a green and living thing severed from its source. She took the woman's hands.

"Ruchi," she said. "How do you feel?"

There was a fleck of blood on Ruchi's cheek. Her pupils were huge discs of black. She laughed, a little hiccupping thing, and said, "Amazing. I've never felt so strong before. I see why the mask-keepers tried it." Her mouth was shiny with water still. Gleaming. "It feels like it's worth risking death for."

Her grip on Priya was strong. Priya gripped back just as hard. Grounding.

"The feeling is going to pass," Priya said. "When you begin to feel weak, or ill, speak to me, all right? I'll make sure you have the waters broken from the source as long as you need. But even then—the waters will only make you powerful for so long. Do you understand?"

"When will I go into the deathless waters?" Ruchi asked eagerly. "When can I prove myself?"

Priya swallowed. "When the yaksa will it," she said.

Ruchi barely seemed aware of what Priya was saying—and

not saying. Her death loomed over her, but she only nodded frantically, and smiled, then whirled around to face the other warriors. They were watching her with fear and a little awe and drew her into their circle swiftly. Some of them were shaking; one was retching noisily into a bush.

Ganam wasn't in their circle. So Priya took a firm breath, squared her own shoulders like a woman going to war, and turned in his direction.

She walked over and put her hand on Ganam's back, and rubbed circles. He was crouched by the body of the man he'd killed, head lowered.

"Get up," she said, low. "The rest are scared. We need to look strong for them."

He looked up at her.

"We used children in war," he said, low. "Ashok. The rebels. We did what we needed to do. I never minded it then. I've gotten soft."

"No," she said.

A shudder of breath out of him.

"Those temple children. Rukh. Little Padma." His hands clenched. "I've accepted that we don't get a better world," he said. "But this. I won't go back to this."

One day, she would have to take those temple children through the deathless waters. One day, some of them wouldn't survive and she would have to bury them in soil, knowing a yaksa could rise wearing any of their faces. One day, and another day, and another.

She felt a wave of nausea pass through her.

"I agree," she said, just as low. She raised her eyes—saw the people around her. "Get up," she said again, gently. "We have a long way to go."

The Srugani knew they were here now. They would need to move swiftly.

They traveled deep into the night, until she could hear the yawns behind her.

"I can hide us," said Priya. "Ganam, help me."

"As the High Elder commands." Ganam rose to his feet.

With a little urging, he drew on his twice-born strength. They wove a camouflage for their group—a hollowed basin of soil hidden beneath a canopy of leaves. From a distance, no Srugani soldiers would see them. And up close, Priya would have an array of weapons to draw on. She sharpened one branch into a series of thorn knives, tucked beneath the leaves ready for use, then settled on the ground to hold vigil.

The warriors fell asleep around her. The vials of water at their waists gave off faint light.

Ganam settled next to her.

"Sleep," she said to him. "You're going to need it."

He shook his head.

"No. I'll keep watch."

"Grief is like an extra weight you have to carry around wherever you go," Priya said, tucking her chin against her knees. "Sleep. Let the weight go."

"I've got no right to grieve," Ganam said wretchedly. "The yaksa chose me. They let the rest of the rebels—my *family*—die."

The yaksa had made no such decision. Priya had seen their panic.

Maybe strength doesn't matter to the deathless waters after all, Priya thought with disquiet. Kritika had been strong. So many of the mask-keepers had been strong. Maybe it was all chance. Maybe she and Ganam were here and everyone else was gone because of luck alone.

That didn't make her feel better, and she didn't think it would help Ganam either.

"Just close your eyes for a little while," she said. "See. I'll close mine too."

"Someone should keep watch."

"I'll feel it if anyone comes," Priya said. "The green speaks to me. There's nothing to be afraid of, all right? Now, sleep."

It took Ganam a long time to sleep, but eventually he did.

She listened to his low, even breaths and buried her face against her knees. She wept silently, misery forcing its way out of her like blood, like poison. Bhumika was gone and Sima was gone; the mask-keepers were dead. The people around her would all eventually drink the water from their vials and die too. Even Ganam would enter the deathless waters for a third time, and in her heart she didn't believe he would return.

No harm had come to her today, but she felt like a hollow thing, scraped clean. No organs, no bones to hold her together, no joy, no strength. A single touch would be enough to break her.

She slept.

The imperial court was shattered.

The stone had crumbled. The stone was being carried away by swift, strong waters. Three rivers roared and swirled, merging around Priya's knees. Somehow, she still stood upright. This wasn't the sangam, although it looked very like it. Above her were the arches of the court's ceiling, shining from within with the golden light of fire. Around them were vast trees, bending in a fierce wind Priya couldn't feel. There were paths all around her, breathing, calling her. But the strongest song came from the waters around her. It was like a plucked string—a resonance. *Here you are.*

From behind her, she heard a sharp inhale. Heard the movement of a body through water.

Felt fingertips against her arm. The resonance ran right through her, and she knew.

Those were not Mani Ara's fingers. She would know these hands anywhere. They had held her and traced the shape of her body; they had been inside her. They had closed around a dark flower carved from her own heart.

They were hands that wanted her dead.

She squeezed her eyes shut. She couldn't dream of her tonight. She *couldn't.*

"Malini," she said, voice choked. "Don't."

36

BHUMIKA

A single day in the village stretched into two, then three, then four. After that, Bhumika put aside counting.

"You'll go nowhere until the floodwaters recede," one villager had said on their arrival, rain- and river-soaked and shivering. That woman had soon been proven correct. The waters rose until the village was circled, and no one could safely leave.

Bhumika made the best of it when they first arrived, instructing the two children to help Gulnar to shelter, as Jeevan rounded up the strongest villagers to build a makeshift dam from felled trees. As the days passed she put herself to good use, stoking fires and washing flood-soiled clothes. She sat with Gulnar and hand-fed her a thin kichadi to restore her wavering strength.

When the children she'd met on that first day of flooding visited and hesitantly thanked her for helping them, she set them to work tidying and sweeping and watching over Gulnar in her stead whenever she had other tasks to tend to.

The village was small—a set of ramshackle buildings, flat-roofed and set high on a hill. Almost all its people were women or young children, many of them rot-riven. The headwoman of the village, Manjeet, had told them in her own terse but not unkind words that the men of the village had gone to war, or left in search of work, or become sick with rot and left to seek a cure. None had returned.

Gulnar's home was farthest from the center of the village. When Bhumika questioned this, one of her new helpers told her that widows were bad luck. "Usually she wouldn't be in the village at all, but we couldn't leave her to drown," the boy said, shifting uncomfortably on his feet. "Truthfully, ma'am, if you didn't feed her I'm not sure any of the women would risk it. But maybe for outsiders there's no ill luck?"

"I'm sure," Bhumika agreed. "You were right to help her," she told him, which made the boy relax. But long after he was gone she pondered the information he'd given her. On her pallet, Gulnar shifted uneasily in her sleep, her wedding quilt wrapped around her in a messy shroud of cloth.

Jeevan had claimed again that he and Bhumika were married, and they had been given a portion of a house, made private by a curtain, to share. It was warmer than Gulnar's new abode. Too warm, perhaps, with Jeevan's body next to hers and radiating its own heat.

She'd learned her lesson, she hoped, from her disastrous meeting with the priests of the nameless. She would speak on Gulnar's behalf but quietly, in the privacy of the headwoman's own abode. The headwoman Manjeet had so far proven herself to be sharp but not unreasonable. There was hope.

Bhumika walked by Jeevan and a group of younger women and boys cutting wood. He looked up at her as she passed. He nodded, his eyes soft. She nodded in return.

The headwoman wasn't alone, to Bhumika's dismay. Women surrounded her, kneeling on the floor and grinding grain into flour. They looked up when Bhumika entered. Some greeted her vocally, and others only nodded, still wary of this stranger in their midst.

"You shouldn't be in here," one woman said. She was curly-haired with rot growing visibly on her right arm. "You're ill luck."

"Our ways aren't custom across Alor, Bidisha," the headwoman said, still grinding with long sweeps of her arms. "She doesn't know any better than to leave a widow alone. Don't berate her."

"She isn't from Alor," Bidisha replied. "I don't know where she's from, but I can guess. You think we don't have enough trouble to deal with without you here?" She brandished her arm pointedly.

Manjeet lowered her pestle with a thunk and a sigh of breath.

"Is she troubling you that much? Ah, fine, fine! Leave, the lot of you," said the headwoman to Bidisha, waving a hand irritably. "I'll talk to the outsider alone."

Bidisha frowned but didn't argue. The other women filed out quickly, clearly pleased to have a break from their work.

"Sit," Manjeet said. Bhumika sat.

The headwoman was silent for a long moment. Bhumika clasped her hands neatly in her lap and waited.

"You're used to ordering people about," Manjeet observed finally. "You expect to be listened to. Telling the children to save the widow's bedding, getting your husband to order my folk to cut the rosewoods and dam the river, for what little good it will do…strange."

"You asked the children about me," Bhumika observed.

"I asked old Gulnar too," said Manjeet. "Though some might say even a word from her could curse me. I asked about your husband as well, but the children had less to say about him. Gulnar told me he has lovely strong arms. Why are you here, little sister?"

"The flood—"

Manjeet clucked her tongue. "Never mind the flood. Why are you in Alor? In this forest? You're not Aloran. You come with your foreign highborn voice and your ragged clothes, your man with his saber and the way he looks at you, like the nameless wrote loving you into his fate, and you order about my village children and stranger still—they *listen* to you. It's the listening I don't understand. The obedience. Why do they do it? What makes you, a slip of nothing, worth trusting? If I didn't know better, I would say you were a witch, or some ancient being sent to play tricks upon our minds."

"I am none of those things," Bhumika said evenly.

"I said I know better, didn't I? I traveled in my youth. I know what you are." Manjeet leaned forward. "You've got no rot on you," she said. "How did you avoid it in Ahiranya?"

There was little use lying about her origins now.

"Luck," said Bhumika, who did not know. "But it cannot pass between people. If anyone in your village touches a crop with rot, tell them to wash their skin with salt water. It is the only thing Ahiranyi believe can help."

Manjeet nodded, satisfied to have her suspicions proved correct.

"Salt water we can make and try," said Manjeet. "Now tell me honestly why you're here. Go on."

There was something in Manjeet's eyes that made Bhumika pause, a canniness that was not the faraway, deep dreaminess of the young priest at the monastery but was still akin to it.

"I came for the monastery," said Bhumika. A half-truth would do, here. "I had heard the monastery holds a special magic. A way of reaching the nameless not just for moments in a pool of water—but deeply, powerfully. I hoped to find a wise person there who would listen to me." Bhumika paused, then said carefully, "I fear that the world is in great danger. Insignificant though I am, I hope to do some good."

"What could you hope to say to a wise priest that would make anything better?" Manjeet asked. "Well, you'll find no listeners in that place, sister, and no lecturers either. Even when they welcomed visitors, they liked ones with more coin than you have. There are smaller, more welcoming monasteries that will take you and pray with you if you like. But that place is too grand for outsiders. Don't bother trying."

That warning was far too late, but there was no reason for the headwoman to know that. Bhumika nodded. "Thank you," she said.

She could hear the children playing outside. The hiss and thud of an axe felling wood. She thought of Jeevan out there, callused hands on the axe, the way she knew—as she knew the sun would rise tomorrow and tomorrow—that when she emerged from this house he would look at her with that solemn face, those searching eyes again. *The way he looks at you—*

She tucked the thought away.

"Headwoman, your men are gone," Bhumika said, quiet and even. "Many of you are likely widows like Gulnar, even if they do not know it. Why obey old traditions that no longer serve you?"

"Foolish of you to come here and judge us so," the headwoman said. But there was no anger in her voice. She was listening.

"I mean no harm," Bhumika said. "I want only to help. I don't want to cause problems for you or your people. But I have been forced to change to survive. I gave up everything to flee my old home. I have changed so utterly my old self would call me a stranger. But my choices have allowed me to live, where others have died.

"Your old village is gone," Bhumika continued. "But you are all here. Let my husband and me take Gulnar's hut, and give her a safe bed close to your village's heart. We are strangers, and she is one of your own. You will need to hold each other close to survive what is to come." She gave Manjeet a smile. "I think your village's children would support you. They're fond of her."

The headwoman's look was piercing.

"I'll consider it," she said. "It would be better if we wait long enough for it to be my decision alone. I won't have Bidisha harping at me." She lifted her grinding stone again and turned to her grain in dismissal. "You and your man will want to leave when the flood ends, I expect."

"Yes," Bhumika said. Polite, but nonetheless a door closed. "Jeevan and I are grateful for your kindness. I promise when the waters fade and go, so will we."

37

MALINI

"Malini. Don't."

Her hand froze on Priya's arm. Under her fingertips, Priya's dreamt skin was cold. There was dirt on her, and the veins under her dark brown flesh shone faintly, the iridescence of leaves under a spill of light.

Water roiled around them both. There was something exultant in Malini's blood—a singing brightness. Priya was close. In flesh, in dreams. But the pain in Priya's voice gave her pause.

"What do you fear, Priya?" Malini asked. She lowered her arm slowly, curling her fingertips to her palm, resisting the compulsion to touch. "Do you think I'll show you the kindness you showed me?"

Priya turned to face her, water swirling.

"I know what you're capable of," Priya said. She smiled, but she was crying, face wet. Her lip wobbled. "I know what I'm capable of. Hurt me if you like, Malini. It doesn't matter. I'll dream you and I'll dream you, and I'll never see you in the flesh again in my whole life."

"You cried when you stabbed me too," Malini observed, unable to look away from Priya's face. She wanted to brush those tears away with her fingertips. She wanted to murder that tender instinct inside her, that soft wanting. Her own eyes ached.

"I did," Priya said. "I did, of course I did."

Priya covered her face with her hands.

"You don't understand," Priya said, choked, "how alone I am."

Alone. Malini on her throne, her heart sisters dead, her brother burned, and Rao shot with an arrow of grief, gone somewhere in Dwarali; Malini, with her empire, and the promise of a pyre ever at her feet, with allies aplenty and no one she could trust entirely.

"You would not be alone if you hadn't betrayed me," Malini said, angry again. *I wouldn't be alone.*

"I did it to save you. I told you I don't regret it. I did it *for* you." Priya dashed her own tears away and raised her face up, eyes bloodshot. "It's awful, but it's the truth, Malini. The only thing I have ever done with these hands is love you."

"If you'd acted with love, you wouldn't have taken my choices from me," Malini said, voice shaking. "If you'd loved me, you wouldn't have stolen *yourself* from me. You wouldn't have hurt me."

"I don't regret it," Priya said, as she'd said so many times before. But this time...

This time Malini took a step closer. Softened her voice.

"Why did you do it, Priya? Why did you betray me?"

Priya met her gaze, head tilting up.

"So you would live," Priya said simply.

Explain, Malini wanted to command. *Tell me why. Tell me everything.* But Priya was drawing closer to her. Malini tensed instinctually, waiting for a knife through the ribs, that moment of pain that she had dreamt of over and over, like a wheel that never stopped turning. But Priya only curved her hands around Malini's arms and pressed her face to the crook of Malini's throat. She bowed into Malini, like a woman at prayer before an effigy, like a creature taking shelter from the storm.

Malini should have shoved her away. But she pressed her forehead against Priya's hair instead. She closed her eyes and let her lips touch Priya's forehead.

"This isn't real," Malini lied. To herself, to Priya. If this wasn't real, she could allow herself to have this: Priya in her arms. Priya loving her.

"I said I'll never see you in the flesh again," said Priya. "But I know this is real. All our dreams are real. They wouldn't hurt so much if they weren't."

Priya rose up and pressed her mouth to Malini's. Unbearably gentle, unbearably tender. Her mouth tasted of salt, of life. She was cold like she'd been swimming—like she'd been wading through water, laughing with her sari knotted to her knees, then climbed onto the bank to press a kiss to Malini's mouth. It was like an image plucked from another life they would never live, sweet and bitter all at once.

Malini touched her hands to Priya's back, palms flat, and drew her closer. Priya was thin, all corded muscle under soft skin, and she came to Malini's hands easily, wrapping her arms around Malini's shoulders. She made a thin noise—an almost soundless gasp—when Malini's hands moved over her body. Her hips, her buttocks, her waist, the softness of her stomach. The hollow of her thighs, warm under her river-tangled cloth. Her nails dug into Malini's shoulders. She tipped her head back, and her eyes were brilliantly bright—shining brown under gold-hued lashes, full of want and wonder.

"Malini," she gasped. No tears now. "*Malini.*"

Malini saw light ripple over her own arms—a green lattice glowing under her skin, a flowering of want in her chest, her belly. It felt like worship. It felt like coming home.

She leaned forward and slotted her mouth over Priya's again.

She woke. Aching, between her thighs, with want. Tears in her eyes.

Some instinct grasped her. She struggled out of her own clothing—sleep-soft cotton parted easily and there was her own bare torso. Her stomach, her breasts—the knot of the scar at her chest. In the dimness of her sleeping she touched her hand to her chest.

She felt the sting of it when her fingers met ruptured skin over her heart. Not her scar, which stood untouched, complete—but a new wound. And through it...

A flower. A single flower, black in the dim light and lustrous and *alive*, growing from her own flesh.

Her heart lurched. She heard, through the rush of her own blood in her skull, a distant noise, and saw a light.

"Empress," said Swati, setting the lantern down. "It's time to wake."

Malini saw her move through the curtains that surrounded the bed. In a moment, Swati would peel the curtain back, and then she would see.

She could not see.

"Leave me for a moment," she ordered, forcing her voice to remain even. She felt like an animal searching for human speech—her mouth better suited for the scream that wanted to rear out of it. "I'll rise on my own."

It was an unusual request. But after a heartbeat of hesitation, Swati obeyed. "I'll bring your breakfast, my lady," she said. Malini heard the sweep of the tent's curtain, a slice of birdsong— then silence.

She covered her mouth with her hand, struggling for breath. In, out. In. Out.

There was no time, and no one she could turn to. Alone, she drew on her blouse and dressed, and prepared to meet the world.

The mahal of King Lakshan, ruler of Srugna, was a squarish, colonnaded set of buildings set on different tiers hewn into a cliff face. An easily defensible home for a king. Once, every tier of the palace had been decorated with flowers, or so Prakash told her as they approached its entrance. But the fast spread of the rot had made the king cautious, and he had ordered all vegetation to be hacked away. Without it the mahal looked severe—cold, with its bare stone unmarked and lacking in beauty.

Inside the mahal, his court was little better. The courtiers were tired and frightened, and King Lakshan had the exhausted look of a man who had not slept in months and did not expect respite to ever come. One feast of welcome was all it took for her to judge that the rot, the new unnatural paths that had carved their way through his lands, and the constant threat of the yaksa had drained his resources and his will. He spoke anxiously about his army. "It is not that we lack men, Empress," he said. "It is that they are cowardly and run from their duty. They fear the rot and they fear death."

"I have brought soldiers to help you," she said soothingly. "You have not been abandoned. The empire does not forget your aid in the war against my brother."

A little of his tension eased at that, but it returned with a vengeance when she delicately dipped her hands in attar and wiped them clean, leaving her plate of appam, and said, "I do have questions about the treatment of the rot-riven on your lands. I have heard troubling reports..."

All through it her chest ached. A sore wound.

When she was alone once again in her rooms she refused the offer of a bath or the assistance of her maid, and opened one of her trunks herself. She withdrew from it everything she thought she'd need: bandages, thread. Liquor of a high enough potency to be used on a wound.

Then she lit her oil lamp, sat upon her bed, and removed her blouse.

The flower was still there.

Malini closed her eyes. Breathed with her mouth open, sucking in air. Her lungs felt tight, and horror had left her cold.

Then she closed her mouth. Gritted her teeth. Curled her fingers around the flower and with a wrench tore it free.

Blood under her fingers and clear, clarifying pain.

Without thought or feeling, she reached for the liquor and the bandages. She cleaned and wrapped her chest clumsily, relieved she would not have to sew her skin shut. She was sure, in a strange way deep in her bones, that by morning the wound would have closed again, leaving nothing behind.

Kissing Priya had been a mistake. But.

She could use this. She would have to use this. She would find a way.

38

MALINI

Rao's arrival was a welcome relief and the first surprise that had brought her joy in a long, long time. She greeted him herself on the mahal's grand marbled bridge, standing beneath a parasol held by an attendant, a smile on her face as he lowered himself from his chariot and bowed to her. It did not even bother her as much as she had expected to see Sima still on the chariot he'd left, doing her very best not to be noticeable.

"I am glad to see you, Prince Rao."

"And I you, Empress. Please forgive me for rudeness but—I must see you alone." There was a light in his eyes she hadn't seen before. A fierceness. "It is very, very urgent."

She examined the stone, turning it back and forth in her hands.

It was just black stone, but it felt unlike any other stone she'd held before. Oddly cold. Like ice—though she knew it was not.

She winced as she lowered it back to the table. Her chest ached oddly, a twinge along the rope-knot of her healed scar.

"You didn't see the way to the mine?"

"No," Rao said. "I was blindfolded. I'm sure he also took me a winding way, so that I won't be able to recall the route by sense memory either."

She nodded, thoughtful.

"So this kai wants land. An ambitious man, is he?"

"He wanted the Lal Qila at first," said Rao. "But he'll accept a portion of Dwarali soil instead."

"He still demands a great deal. But if this stone does as he claims, of course he will have it."

"He sent one of his sisters to negotiate on his behalf. She remains with some of my men beyond Srugna's borders. She can bargain for him. He's promised that her word is his bond."

Relief was coursing through Malini, far too early.

"Does this heart's shell have any worth against the rot?" Malini asked.

"They didn't know," said Rao. "There was no rot on their land. Not yet."

"Then we will take it to the Srugani fields and see what it does to them. If it serves in the fields and in battle, then the kai will have all he wants," said Malini. "You did well, Rao."

"I'm glad," he said. "We traveled hard, Malini. I...I will be glad for rest, if you'll allow it."

She wanted to ask him if he was well now. Healed. But the question would not leave her lips. It was, after all, absurd. Of course he was not. She was not.

"Yes, rest. We'll test this heart's shell," she said instead. "If it's of use, I'll begin my bargaining with the kai's sister."

Malini had her opportunity almost immediately.

There were rituals to an imperial visit to a Parijatdvipan court. But these were not normal times, and Malini had chosen not to indulge in them. She had come to support King Lakshan in a time of crisis, she assured him. Multiple feasts and dances and hunting trips were not required and were certainly not wanted.

When he held court, she did not take his throne, or raise her own throne above his. Instead, when he sat upon the raised platform of his throne, on a silk knotwork cushion with rose-salt incense burning in alcoves behind him, she sat on her own cushion to his far left, surrounded by her personal guard and by her generals.

She was glad she had come here today for his audience with

his courtiers. It allowed her to delve even deeper into the woes of Srugna. The growing panic, and the ever-depleting state of their coffers was on full display. It also helped her understand how they could be helped: the food and weapon supplies that would need to be diverted to them. The soldiers, in great numbers, that would need to be funneled to the border with Ahiranya. The ones she had brought with her would not be enough. She would need to leave Prakash here to organize what was needful.

She was listening closely to a report on Srugna's eastern farming villages when there were a tumult of noise at the grand arched entrance of the hall. It had no gates or doors to bar shut, and no curtains, so there was nothing to impede Malini's view. She turned her head and watched as a handful of Srugani warriors— one of them clearly barely a child, for all that he had a mace hefted at his side—demanding entry. Two of the courtiers of King Lakshan were trying to dissuade them. The voices of the warriors rose, but the boy—and only the boy—remained silent. The others were ringed around him in an obviously protective circle.

"If they are not allowed entry, bring the boy to me later," Malini said quietly, turning just slightly to speak into Prakash's ear. He murmured his agreement.

The noise was not relenting, only growing. With a darting, near-panicked look at Malini, Lakshan finally raised a hand, palm out. The sound quelled.

"Bring my warriors forward," he said in his rumbling voice. "They may speak."

They all walked forward onto the circle of carnelian-flecked marble where petitioners were always bidden to stand.

They bowed together, low to the ground, then stood.

One of the older warriors nudged the boy forward. "Speak, lad," he urged.

"M-my king," the boy managed to say, his voice reed thin. His gaze darted about the court and fixed briefly on Malini. He was clearly overwhelmed, unfamiliar with the grandness of a highborn court. "I..."

"This boy," one of the other warriors said, stepping in when the boy's voice trailed to overwhelmed silence, "is the only survivor of a patrol along the border with Ahiranya."

He was young to be a warrior, and young for such a dangerous duty. Circumstances were more dire than Malini had first judged them to be.

"I saw something on the border," the boy said. At first his voice was a whisper, then stronger, as he clenched his fists, raised his head, and found his courage. "She had others with her. People like her with magic in them. And they... they entered Srugna. We tried to stop them, but we couldn't. They're in our country."

A rising murmur of discontent swelled in the room.

Malini leaned forward. In a voice that was clear and sharp and cut through the swell of noise like a knife, she said, "Describe her."

The boy looked at her, startled. But he did as she'd asked.

"Not tall," he said. "Not... I thought she was a child, but she wasn't. And she—she had flowers on her."

It was not a lot of information, but Malini did not need more. She knew the truth in her bones.

He'd seen Priya.

"King Lakshan," Malini said. "I have brought my people to help you. Let my generals speak to your warriors and assist you in facing this terrible threat."

King Lakshan gave his assent and his thanks.

As Prakash moved forward to gather the warriors, Narayan leaned forward to speak into her ear.

"Low Prince Ashutosh has offered his liegemen," he said. "Seasoned warriors, well trained. They are trustworthy men. I will send them to test your stone against this threat, Empress, if you allow it."

"Yes." As he rose, she continued. "Narayan."

He stopped and turned to listen to her voice.

"Impress upon them my orders," she said. "If they capture someone with the magic of Ahiranya—be they yaksa or mortal—I want them alive. If the stone works, a knife through an arm or leg should hold a prisoner well enough."

"Alive," he repeated. Almost disbelieving. He did not ask her why, but she read the question in his eyes.

"Dead men cannot tell us what lies at Ahiranya's heart or fuels its strength," she said softly. "And I find more and more that I must know what the Ahiranyi are capable of and how I can stop them."

39

BHUMIKA

The rain stopped abruptly. It left behind a day that cracked the sky yellow. As the flooding began to recede, Bhumika knew it was time to leave and face the monastery again.

She was given a kind farewell. Gulnar kissed her cheeks, and the children hugged her and offered both her and Jeevan a little food to take with them. It wasn't easily spared, and Bhumika would have liked to refuse.

She thanked them instead, and professed real pleasure in the small gifts of dried fruit and seeds. Let them have their pride. They deserved it.

The forest felt different in the aftermath of the flooding. Stranger, and unfamiliar. Many trees had fallen, leaving the wet ground bare. The birds and insects, so loud before, were silent.

They crossed the bridge and walked between the trees.

Her time snared in the village by the flood had felt like a respite—from her ghosts, from her knowledge, from the weight of her task. But that time was over, so it did not surprise her that once they had crossed the bridge, her watchers appeared again. She felt them before she saw them: a churning of water in her heart and her skull that made her lower her head from the heaviness of their presence.

When she raised her head, there they were: a dozen figures, young and old, mottled with water. In the sunlight their edges were hazy and soft.

She felt as if she were underwater too—floating, unable to control her limbs. She distantly heard Jeevan call her name as one figure walked toward her.

"Will you drink?"

A figure had stepped forward. Slim and small—maybe a child.

"You must," the watcher insisted. *"Just a taste."*

Fingertips touched her lips. A single drop of water—green as leaves. No more than that.

She felt new knowledge in shards. A warmth in her belly, squirming; a golden egg splintering open; life and life and life blooming and being born; and an ancient and new thing stirring beneath the soil, sap seeping from its root-gnarled flesh as its eyes slowly, inexorably peeled open.

"Bhumika."

She returned to herself. The world around her swam for a moment, until her vision settled and she knew her body once more. Jeevan was holding her steady, his hands warm, eyes worried.

"Something is wrong," she said. "Let me go, Jeevan."

He released her, near-vibrating with tension, and she kneeled on the ground and pressed a hand to the earth.

Her ghosts watched, water swirling from them.

One shard struck her again—

Grief welled up in her, as it had when she'd heard a child crying so long ago. But now her grief wasn't alien or formless. That droplet of strange water had carried something in it—laughter, and a life inside her, and the desolation that losing it had left behind.

She could hear Jeevan's breathing and it made her grief swell, somehow. She couldn't help but speak.

"The child I gave birth to," Bhumika said. "Was it yours?"

He stilled. "The child," he repeated.

"I've seen my own body, a time or two," she said. The hand she hadn't pressed to soil was curled against her stomach. She'd mapped the marks on her skin with her hands, silver where she'd been reshaped, not hollowed but molded to cradle another heart-beat, another life. The water she'd drunk had only clarified what she already knew.

"No," he said, finally. "She was not my daughter."

She. A daughter.

"Is she still alive?"

"Yes," Jeevan said immediately—eyes suddenly soft. "Yes, Bhumika."

She nodded. A jerky, wordless nod.

"Good," she said. She swallowed around the sharpness in her own throat—a feeling like glass. "That's good."

She splayed her hand more firmly against the ground.

Underneath her palm, the life beneath that soil thudded like a heartbeat.

She must have moved, because Jeevan called her name, low and alarmed.

"It feels me," she said, hushed. "It thinks I am calling to it."

Jeevan kneeled beside her. She looked at him, meeting his gaze.

"There is a yaksa sleeping beneath this forest," she told him. "I can feel it awakening. When it does so, the entire forest will flower with rot, and the people..." She paused, trying to shape her horror into better, calmer words.

"They will die," he said. "I understand. Can you stop it?"

She shook her head. Maybe she'd had that power once, but not now.

He rose to his feet and offered her his hand. "We'll go to the village and warn them. We can lead them from the forest to safety."

"That will only save one village," Bhumika said. She knew the enormity of what a yaksa could do. She *knew*. "What if they don't listen, Jeevan?"

"We will convince them, Bhumika," he replied. As if it were so simple.

She took his hand and stood.

Manjeet was already waiting for them, standing between the fallen trees at the base of the hill where the village stood.

"I don't seek to bring you trouble," Bhumika said. "But I fear your village is in danger."

Manjeet walked toward her, and Bhumika realized she needed no convincing. The headwoman's face had a gray pallor.

"It came so suddenly," Manjeet said. Her voice trembled. "We don't know what to do."

She led Bhumika and Jeevan up the rising hill to the village. The people were huddled together in the center of the cluster of homes, whispering. They watched Jeevan and Bhumika pass them, no smiles on their faces now.

The old hut at the edge of the village where Jeevan and Bhumika had slept beside one another was gone. In its place was a rictus of trees, shaped into an arch. Bhumika walked toward it, one step, then two, then stopped. Every inch of her body felt cold in its presence. She knew what the arch was, and she knew what lay beyond it—even if she did not know where it would take her.

A seeker's path.

The words came to her in a whisper. Bhumika bit down on her cheek hard enough that she could now taste blood, metal-sweet, flowering in her mouth.

"Don't go any closer," Manjeet said. "There's rot in those trees and in the soil. You don't want to get sick."

Bhumika wouldn't get it. Couldn't. But it didn't seem wise to say so.

"You can't stay here," Bhumika said. If a path existed, anyone—and anything—could walk through it. And surely they would. A yaksa was sleeping under the ground. Someone would come for it. The yaksa loved their kin too much not to. "We need to hide somewhere safe." She turned to meet Manjeet's eyes. "The monastery."

"They won't help us," Manjeet said wretchedly. Then she cursed, rubbing her knuckles roughly against her forehead. "Those religious bastards, they won't *care*. You understand that, don't you?"

"It doesn't matter," Bhumika said. "The danger here is coming for them too. Soon they'll see we may only stand a chance of surviving it together."

40

PRIYA

As a group, they moved deeper into Srugna. Like Ahiranya, it was thick with trees, but as they moved farther from the border the trees began to open into dipping valleys, cut through with shallow streams and low hilltops.

They avoided villages and paths and walked through silence broken only by their own voices and soft footsteps.

Once, they crossed paths with two hunters searching for deer. They were young—no older than the warrior Ganam had spared, perhaps. When they saw the mask-keepers their eyes went wide, faces ashen. She thought, for a moment, they would freeze like prey—but then one darted off, swiftly followed by the other.

She could feel fallen twigs and branches snap under their feet. The pressure of their racing footsteps in the soil.

It was easy to snare their feet and make them crumple to the ground.

She turned to who'd drunk the waters—Ruchi—and said, "Go and find them. Tie them up." She swallowed, battling with herself. "Somewhere they'll be found eventually."

Ruchi nodded sharply, then raced after them, light on her feet. Next to Priya, Ganam murmured, "Good."

"Sometimes," Priya said, "I like to pretend I'm still a good person." Then she started striding forward again.

Obediently, her people followed her.

She was following a thread. A fine root, wending its way through Srugna's soil. She could feel the yaksa waking, a restless thing.

It was dreaming, somewhere. Waiting to be reborn. It was Priya's job to find them.

The trees around them grew larger. Thicker and taller, with roots that snarled the ground in knots of latticework. Priya stepped over them lightly; the roots moved around her, an awakening, a shudder of motion that greeted her like an old beast rising from sleep.

"These are ancient trees," Ganam observed. "Older even than the Age of Flowers. That's my bet."

"We'd have to cut one open to know for sure," Priya replied. "Count the rings inside them." Then she stopped and raised a hand to her lips. The mask-keepers went quiet.

She could hear the wind. A high, keening whistle.

It sounded like the wind upon the Hirana.

"Ganam, with me," she said. "The rest of you—create a perimeter. If anyone comes, yell for us."

Murmurs of understanding. Her people fanned out. And she and Ganam walked through the cover of trees out into an open clearing.

It was vast. A stretch of land baked brown by the sun. But it was far from empty. On its surface stood vast pillars, so high that she had to crane her neck to view the full length of them. The noise she'd heard was the wind moving between them. On the ground, it was oddly cold, and Priya felt small and insignificant, overawed.

"This was a special place once," she said to Ganam as he came to stand beside her. "I'm sure of it."

She walked forward and kneeled at the base of one pillar. She pressed a hand to it.

She'd thought from a distance that they were stone. But the pillar before her was fossilized wood. Inside it would be too many rings to count, preserved in amber, but she did not need to see inside them to know that once yaksa had walked here, and in the

time since the Age of Flowers, the Srugani had deliberately chosen to forget.

"They've allowed nothing to grow here," said Ganam, when
she told him so. "You can see signs." He pointed at the ground—
at a place scarred and tilled. "They've burned the soil. Over and
over."

"Then they remember," Priya said. She pressed a hand deep
into the soil. Beneath it, she felt that familiar thrum. An awakening thing.

"There's something I must do," she said. "To make this new
yaksa welcome. Ganam, will you check on the others?"

"They'll be fine."

"I'm not convinced. The Srugani have to know about this
place. Would they really leave it unprotected?"

He frowned. Then he said, "Maybe you shouldn't do this now,
then."

A laugh cracked out of her. "What do you think the yaksa will
do if I don't? I do this now, or it doesn't get done."

"Then I'll stay and protect you."

She shook her head impatiently.

"Do I look like I need coddling? Go."

He rolled his eyes and walked away.

And Priya closed her eyes. Breathed. Reached for her power.

Calling the rot was a rush of strangeness through her. The
green in her blood and skin coiled and withered and flourished in
recognition, cycling through its lifespan as the smell of iron and
blood seeped from her hand, as the ground softened and changed,
thickening like flesh. As rot worked its way through the soil.

"Wake," she whispered. "Your family are waiting, yaksa. They
sent me to seek you. Wake soon."

She felt the sun sink above her. She felt—

Pain.

Her body staggered. Fell backward. An arrow through her.
She clutched her side but found nothing there.

Something had happened in the sangam.

Priya felt the shadow of it, a cold dart, like an arrow through her ribs. She gasped. The cold stretched through her chest for one brief strange moment—then vanished.

She found herself in her skin again. *Mostly* in her skin. But it was like the sangam was nestled close, pressed to her ear, a song inside a shell.

Somewhere in the sangam—somewhere inside her—the yaksa were howling. It was a high, mournful chorus that reverberated through her skull, and with it came fragments of images: soil, vast leaves, bodies, strangers, shifting through the shadows. Blood, and a gleaming silver whip, and a stranger's bared teeth, and Ganam drawing up the earth with his hands.

Ganam, and a dagger at the chest.

Ganam and then—nothing.

Ganam is dead, she thought, and the realization was a punch that went through her more harshly than the first arrow-dart of cold. It was more awful, by far, than the song of the yaksa. Ever since she'd returned to Ahiranya he'd been her only ally. She'd guided him through the deathless waters. Dragged him out with her own hands, and cried over him, laughed with him. *Look,* he'd said, teeth chattering, water in his hair. *You're not the only one who gets to survive.*

She was already moving. She hadn't consciously taken a step, but she was striding forward regardless, the ground shifting under her, roiling in response to her emotions. The green was her, and she was the green, and the soil splintered as the moisture leached from it; the trees bent to her, and the flowers withered, and she strode on, until the great leaves she'd seen in the sangam loomed around her. She had made a seeker's path from nothing, nothing but her own will, and she had brought herself to him in a heartbeat, and she knew she was where he had died.

Except.

There he was.

Kneeling. Head bowed forward. Tunic torn. The earth around him, a crater, jagged with stone. And his slumped shoulders rising and falling, rising and falling, as he struggled to breathe around the sharpness of the dagger through his chest, the hilt visible to her, ringed by a spreading stain of rose-black blood. She couldn't feel him in the sangam—couldn't feel that strand of strength that ran through cosmic waters, that bound them both—but that didn't matter. She could *see* him.

He wasn't dead. He was very much alive.

She swore, a helpless noise, and saw him jerk. He raised his head.

"Priya," he said hoarsely. "Go."

She took a step forward, and he shook his head wildly.

"Parijatdvipans," he gasped out. "Danger—*you*."

Behind him there was a noise. The crunch of soil. And then she felt them. How had she not? Panic, perhaps. Or the cry of the yaksa—still ringing painfully through her head—had masked the delicate chime of their mortal hearts and lungs. Ever since her power had grown, human flesh had grown less significant. Less noticeable. If she survived this, she would have to put that oversight right.

Perhaps the soldiers had come here hoping to set a blade through an Ahiranyi's ribs. Perhaps they had come here specifically for her. She could imagine them deciding it over bottles of wine, eyes wild and lips wet with drink. *The Ahiranyi witch tried to stab our empress through the heart. It's only justice to stab her heart in return.*

Perhaps it was Malini who had decided it.

A wound for a wound, a heart for a heart. Maybe if the blade were in her chest she would accept it as her due. But the dagger was in Ganam's chest, and he was staring at her with wide eyes, the pupils tiny pinpricks of black against the whites.

Get up, she thought—urging him with her own eyes as she took one steady step forward. Two. Three. There was nothing chaining him to the ground. And she knew he could fight with a dagger through the torso. She'd seen him fight through worse. But he was wavering on his knees. He wasn't standing.

Did he have a head wound? Was he injured in other ways that she couldn't see? Something had caused the echo through the sangam. Something was stopping her from feeling him in the sangam now.

"No closer," someone said, the voice a hoarse bark of Zaban. It took her a moment to place the Saketan accent—and a moment longer still to see the figure in Saketan green stride forward and place a saber to Ganam's throat, their own arm trembling. Behind them, a dozen Saketan liegemen emerged, uncoiling their sword whips, their weapons spools of liquid silver against the shadows.

Knowing they were there didn't soften the blow of the sight of them. Priya's stomach still swooped. Her body still felt hot with fear as she forced herself to stand entirely still and said, "Give him back."

"He stays where he is," the soldier said, his voice clipped. His mouth was a grim line. He didn't look as afraid as he should have. "And you—you stay where you are. If your feet move—if your hands move—I promise you he's dead."

She stayed still. Her feet were squared against the ground, her body as steady and rooted as an ancient tree. The earth held her. Waited with something like bated breath for what she'd do next.

Slowly, the Saketan soldiers were edging farther out—a semicircle of sword whips and wary eyes. The other Saketan soldiers did not look as grimly, forcedly calm as the man with the saber to Ganam's throat. Their fear was so palpable she could almost taste it. It would be so easy to destroy them. The earth could collapse around them, dragging them under. Thorns could spear up from the sod and pierce them through. That kind of work was easy for her.

As if the soldier holding the saber had sensed the tone of her thoughts, he spoke up.

"We know how quick you are, Elder," he said. "I fought at the Veri river, so I know exactly what you can do when you set your mind to it. But my hand and this sword are still faster than you can be. You try to use your witchery and he'll die in a blink under my blade. There won't be a thing that'll save him."

Priya watched—and felt—the men around her keep moving. Slow, so slow, as if she were a tiger and they were hunters.

"You're not planning to kill him," she forced herself to say. Forced her voice calm. "If you wanted to kill him, he'd already be dead."

"But we will," the man stressed, "if you don't behave."

"You don't have any reason to think I give a shit about him."

She saw one of the soldiers swallow, his throat bobbing visibly. The one with the saber said, with a calm that matched her own, "If you didn't give a shit, temple witch, then we would all be dead already. I told you. I know what you can do."

"Then what do you want from me?" Priya demanded. "Negotiate."

"Come with us quietly," he said, "and we won't end his life."

Why would they want her alive? Why did they want Ganam alive? And what had they done to make him so quiet—so biddable, despite the knife through his chest?

It was hard to think through the yaksa's howling.

"Give him back to me," she said slowly, "and I let *you* leave here alive."

"No."

"If you know me, you know I'm not a political creature," Priya said bluntly. "So I'll be clear. There won't be a negotiation. You give him to me, or you all die."

An ugly laugh from one. "I don't think so," he said.

"Leave her be," came a voice. Steady. "Let me talk to her."

A figure stepped forward. An older man. A hint of rot at his hairline.

She knew him.

"Elder Priya," Romesh said. Low Prince Ashutosh's liegemarks were emblazoned on his tunic. His familiar, steady eyes were fixed on her. "It's been a long time."

"Romesh," she said. "Are all of you Low Prince Ashutosh's men?"

"You won't know the newer faces," he said. "But you know mine."

He moved around the curved line of men. His footsteps were

steady. His sword whip was coiled at his waist. In reach, but not yet in his hands.

"You saved my life, and my lord's life, in the war for the empress's throne," said Romesh. "What you did to the empress is a crime you must answer for. But I don't want to hurt you."

He took a slow step closer.

"Your advisor," he said. "Sima. She's safe."

Sima. Her heart was pounding. "She's really safe? Well?"

"Prince Rao took responsibility for her," Romesh said. Another step. "Come with us," he said, low. "You'll get to see her yourself. I'll make sure you're not harmed. The empress doesn't want you dead."

"What does she want me for, then?"

"What you know, maybe," Romesh said gently. "Or to take you off the battlefield. But what does a soldier like me know about what an empress thinks?"

A shuddering breath left her. She could feel the eyes of those men on her.

"I don't care about my safety," she said. "But you can't keep him."

Romesh shook his head.

"That's not for me to decide, Priya," he said.

"I'm not for the empress to take," she said, just as soft. "Let my friend go. We'll leave."

His jaw tightened. "I'm sorry, girl," he said.

He drew a dagger from his sleeve. Black stone.

Before she could move, it slashed her arm—the barest brush of stone on flesh—and she felt a strange, awful jolt run through her. She stumbled back.

For a second, when the blade had touched her, she'd been cut off from the sangam. For a second—perhaps not even a whole second, maybe only the thinnest, cleaved strand of time—she'd felt no more than human.

She turned vines onto him. Cracked his wrist. She dragged him in front of herself as he made a noiseless sound of pain, using him as a shield.

"Give my friend to me," she said sharply. "Or I take his life. I don't need a blade. I just need my magic."

A breath of utter silence. Then one man said, teeth bared, "We can take your magic from you."

He shot an arrow. Priya moved, shifted.

Heard a sickening thud, and a gasp.

"Romesh," she said raggedly.

The arrow had gone through his chest.

She felt it with her hand. Touched trembling fingers to his throat, where his pulse should have been, and felt—nothing.

He fell dead from her arms.

The saber was still against Ganam's throat. One of the men was shouting. Another was drawing his bow again. Her ears were full of the sound of her own blood, which roared like a fast-moving river, like deep water with deeper currents.

A strange reverberation filled her voice. Something ancient, powerful.

Sapling.

Mani Ara's voice, a whisper and a dream in her ears.

For so long, she had only been able to grasp at Mani Ara in dreams. She had recoiled from her: from her thorn mouth, the flowers of her eyes, the viciousness of her love. *Beloved,* Mani Ara had called her, but Priya had never wanted to be her beloved. She wanted her heart to lie in different hands, or at least safely in her own chest.

But this time, as Romesh bled on the ground and Ganam stared at her with blank eyes, she did not care for her own revulsion anymore.

Yes, Priya said in response, and welcomed her. Her ribs were an open door.

It was not like in the war, in the fire and the Veri river, at the borders of Harsinghar when her chariot had overturned and Mani Ara had come for her in her moment of darkness and despair. It was like the water rushing in where it belonged. Priya was hollow. It was meant to fill her to the brim.

She moved, but it was not just her. She was bigger than her own skin. Memories that weren't her own skittered at the edges of her conscious mind. She remembered running, crawling. Desperation, and the blue light of a distant shore, the curving edge of a world, knowing she would do anything to make sure her kin survived—

The men before her were so small. Kneeling between them, the temple son was a glowing thing, shot through with the deathless waters.

Kin.

A negligent raise of her left hand. The soil moved with her, throwing them from their feet. Arrows, mid-flight, flowered and collapsed, withering against the earth. She had sacrificed to be part of the green, sacrificed and bled starlight like water, like blood. It followed her bidding.

She buried the men. The ones on the topsoil she choked with roots. An easy thing. All mortal flesh was meant to die eventually.

When it was done, the only one left was the temple son.

She breathed, and breathed, and—was not all that she'd been, for a moment.

She was Priya again.

She doubled forward. Shaking. Forced herself to straighten, and stumble over to kneel in front of Ganam, as the wave of otherness washed over her again. Between it, she breathed, and remembered to care about the wound in him, the knife, his survival.

"Ganam," she called. "Ganam, answer me."

His mouth moved. One noiseless motion.

"Hold still," she said. She wrapped her hand in cloth. She drew the dagger slowly free, terrified she would kill him in the process. It dropped to the ground. Blood followed, ruby dark.

41

PRIYA

Priya grasped part of Ganam's torn tunic and pressed a hand hard to his wound, staunching the blood.

"Shit," he said, his voice shaken. Light was returning to his eyes, but his skin was still horribly dull. "I thought I was dead."

"So did I." She swallowed. She wasn't trembling, but she felt as if she should be.

"That weapon," he rasped. "It—did something to me."

"It would be better not to speak of it to anyone," Priya said. "We need to leave. Can you stand?"

"I'm not sure."

She lifted him up a little; he groaned. He was heavy in her arms.

He'd been alone when she'd found him. He shouldn't have been alone. The vastness of her new power yawned open. She reached for it.

She found her warriors—*sensed* them through the green, their heartbeats and their footsteps—and ripped a path through the green to lead them to her. *Come,* she called, and the green beckoned them: rot-riven plants turning their vines and their leaves, trees bending with the pressure of her command.

It shouldn't have been so easy. She'd marveled at the paths Mani Ara had created through her, that labyrinth spiraling across Parijatdvipa from the bower of bones. But this came to her with savage ease. She wanted the path, and there it was. It was simple, now that her mind understood what it was to be a yaksa.

A moment passed, and the Ahiranyi warriors emerged in a group.

She turned her head to look at them. She didn't know what expression she wore, but the warriors went very still.

"Where were you all?" Priya asked.

A long silence.

"*Speak*," she demanded. The ground trembled faintly.

Shyam stepped forward, standing tall, arms behind him. Ready to take a blow.

"We were fighting the Parijatdvipan soldiers," Shyam said. "When Ganam drew their attention and led them away, we couldn't follow."

"You'd be surprised," Ganam said with difficulty, a grimace of a grin on his mouth, "what a few bushes of thorns will do to slow them down."

"I'll need to train them harder," Priya said.

"I led the Saketans away," Ganam said, breathing heavily. "When I realized what their weapons could do."

Priya looked at her warriors again. Ruchi was bleeding from her arm. Her eyes were glassy with pain. The broken waters should have healed her. They hadn't.

Priya could guess what kind of knife had carved her.

Her gaze dropped to the dagger she'd pulled free from Ganam's skin, lying on the ground near them.

The blade was wet with Ganam's blood, but even through the sheen of viscera, Priya could see the black stone of the blade.

She crouched on her palms and peered closely at it. The stone almost seemed to swallow the light.

She looked away from it.

"We're returning to Ahiranya."

"We haven't found the sleeping yaksa," Ruchi said in a thin voice, her eyes fervent despite her blood loss—or perhaps because of it. "We can't simply leave."

"We can," snapped Priya. "Ganam is injured." *And I have*

power I never had before. And the empire has a weapon we can't fight. Too many things have changed, and I won't risk you all. "Help me with Ganam. I must see the yaksa."

They rushed over to pick him up.

They were carrying Ganam toward the new path. They weren't looking at her.

Her hand was still wrapped in Ganam's torn tunic, wet with blood. She bit down on her own tongue, wrapped her hand tighter, and picked up the blade that had stabbed him and taken his strength away.

It was, in a way, no different from handling sacred wood. Although it did not burn, as sacred wood could, its coldness was a different kind of fire—a numbness against the skin. The cloth provided a barrier to its power, but an imperfect one. Even through cloth, it cleared Mani Ara's memories from her head like dissipating smoke—and left her weak and trembling on the dirt, more human than she'd been in a long time.

But the new path would get them home. She didn't need her strength right now. What she needed was to keep this weapon— this thing that could negate a yaksa's power—close, until she could work out how to use it to her own ends.

She tucked the weapon into her kameez. Then she stood and followed them.

She could feel the yaksa waiting for her on the Hirana. Priya, at the end of the seeker's path beneath the bower of bones, looked at her warriors and decided the yaksa could wait a little longer.

"Go," she said to the warriors. "Take Ganam to the sickroom, and Ruchi too. I'll be there soon."

"Where are you going?" Ganam asked.

"To the Hirana," she said. "I'll talk to the yaksa alone."

When the warriors had left her, she buried the knife. She didn't know what purpose it would serve yet—she didn't know if she would speak of it to the yaksa. They'd been dismissive of mothers' fire, but *this*—this was an unknown.

She climbed the Hirana, stone melding together beneath her feet, all its rough edges, its carvings, turning to steps beneath her, making her ascent smooth.

In the triveni, open to the sky, the yaksa waited. Priya kneeled smoothly in front of them.

"We fought the Parijatdvipans," Priya said evenly, her head lowered. "They ambushed us. In the process, your only twice-born elder, Ganam, was injured. A warrior who drank the death-less waters broken from the source was injured, too. But the Parijatdvipans are dead, and I will return to Srugna to save your sleeping kin. I *will* be there when they awaken. The fault was all mine, but I can fix it, and I will. If anyone has to be punished it's me." She raised her head, steeling herself for their cruelty and disapproval.

That was when she saw the smiles on their mouths.

"Oh, look at you," breathed Sanjana. She drew Priya to her, fingernails sharp. "You carved a path. You brought yourself home."

"You killed so many men, and so swiftly," Bhisa Ara said. She sounded proud. Pleased. "Finally. You grow stronger."

"Of course war is a good medicine," Avan Ara piped up. "War and cruelty."

"Mani Ara will want you," Bhisa Ara said. They were speaking over each other so swiftly, a song like birds. "You must go to her."

"I'll seek her in the sangam," Priya said, hoping she could grasp a little time before she sought out the first yaksa again.

"You must seek her near the deathless waters," urged Vata Ara. "You will be closest to her there, in body and in your soul."

What could she do? They were watching her with such hunger.

"Yes, yaksa," she said. "Of course."

She entered a prayer room alone. She kneeled and covered her face with one hand. She was still stained in blood and dirt, so tired she could have cried, but her life wasn't her own. She had her orders.

She opened the way down to the deathless waters.

The light was, at least, oddly soothing. Blue reflected on the walls, a deep luster emanating from the waters themselves. She breathed in the scent of the waters: sweet flowers, petrichor. Salt.

With a breath, she entered the sangam. Within it she saw the same light, but stronger, colder—the stuff made of distant stars, stitched into the water and the rippling mirror of a sky above her.

"Sapling."

She did not see Mani Ara in the water until Mani Ara had risen from it and pressed her cold, wood-whorled hands against Priya's jaw.

Priya saw, for a dizzying moment, through Mani Ara's eyes—her own shadow flesh, starlight-flecked; her own mortality. For a moment she was not simply Priya. She was more, vast. She was Mani Ara.

"Wh-what," Priya gasped, not able to quite form a question.

"We are becoming one, sapling," said the yaksa, joy rich in her voice. "My magic to your hollowness. Your heart to my ancient cruelty. Your natural belonging to the world and flesh, to my cosmic nature, my roots and green." She was still holding Priya. "You have fought and grown," she said. "Soon you will be strong enough to hold me."

"You told me you wouldn't erase me," Priya said, shaky. Struggling to comprehend it. "That you wouldn't turn me into a shell."

"There are many things that are green and living, that belong to your world, that can only exist because their life is twined with another life," Mani Ara said. "Think of the banyans of your forest, sapling. How one being grows upon another, and together they make a great life."

Sapling. She was a plant, a seed, a tree that could act as Mani Ara's host—the living, breathing bones that would allow her to slip into the world and grow from Priya's skin.

Was that what the not-rot upon Priya was? Her sap-heavy blood, and the flowers at her collarbones—the flecks of green at her eyes. Were they all Mani Ara slowly eking out her space, her presence in Priya's flesh?

"You have not been destroyed," said Mani Ara, tenderly clasping Priya's face, hair, skull—as if she could reshape her gently. As if she already had. "You will never be destroyed. You are a precious thing. You are my beloved, carved and hollowed for me. So slow you've grown, but now you're close. So close."

"Was I so difficult to create?" Priya asked. "Am I such a rare thing?"

"So many of you burned," Mani Ara murmured. "Poor children. Nothing but husks." Mani Ara's hands released her. "The last one who was anything akin to what you are to me burned in mothers' fire too," Mani Ara said.

"I am surprised you don't lock me away, if I'm so precious," said Priya.

"How will you grow strong if I do so? It was only fighting and suffering in Srugna that allowed you to become so much more mine—so utterly complete."

Panic was clawing up in her.

"How long until I am ready?" Priya asked, voice shaking.

"A few spans of days," said Mani Ara sweetly. "Sunrises and sunsets, and you will be fit for me. And we will be one and yet not. Two halves."

"One half eclipsing the other," whispered Priya. "We won't be equals, will we?"

"I am your god, sapling. Is that answer enough?"

It was in a way. It was.

"Look," Mani Ara urged. "Look at the water."

Priya lowered her head and looked.

The water beneath them, for a breath, stilled. And Priya saw one reflection in the water—one being, bigger than either of them. Her face, wrought strange, with a skin of bark whorled with stars; one mortal eye and another of flowers. Mortal skin at the throat and the shoulders, then a riot of flowers again at the heart. As she watched, it rippled and changed—flesh, to flowers, to utter cosmic starlight.

It was awful, and it was beautiful.

"What do I want you to do, sapling? Where must you go?" Mani Ara urged.

And for a single span of a heartbeat, a blink of an eye, she knew Mani Ara as she knew herself.

"Our children sleep in the earth," said Priya. She raised her head. She filled her voice with determination. "I need to wake them up. One, and two, and then I need to return to you and become whole."

Mani Ara smiled.

"Yes, sapling," she said. "Just so."

Maybe love and grief were light and shadow, and Priya a sundial. That must have been so, because the first thing she did when she returned to her skin was seek out Arahli Ara. He was alone, thankfully.

"Will Mani Ara wear my skin?" Priya asked. "Will she take it from me? Does she lie when she says we'll *share*?"

His body went—still. She hadn't known how much the yaksa moved—how their leaves swayed and vines rustled—until they stopped.

"Your skin is your own," he said. "You live inside it."

"You knew then," Priya said dully. She wanted to look at his face. Read his expression. But what use would that be, when he only wore something like a face? Could she read the leaves gilding his skull—the inky waters of his eyes? Was there language in them, just like there was in a smile, a tight jaw, a crinkled eye?

He was not Ashok. He was not hers to read.

"Do not think she does it lightly. It was a sacrifice to make us part of this world," he told her. "A…I cannot describe it. Your mortal tongue has no words." A pause. "A wrenching," he said finally. "We were creatures of stars. Then we were not. It was enough, until we burned. When we were dirt and wood. Unable to die and unable to truly live.

"We become more human because it is a sacrifice. It is one that allows us to survive, even after what the mothers' fire did to us. It allows us to come back. But it hurts us, Priya," he said. "It hurts her to become you, as it hurts you to become her. But she does it so she may walk the soil and lead us. So we may all survive and bring your Age of Flowers again."

"The way you wear the skins of my temple siblings—"

"We are not as old as her, or as powerful." A strange tight smile, drawing his mouth, and joyless. "Our burden is lighter."

"You told me you're not my brother," she managed to say.

"He is like a limb I have lost," he said. "I feel him, even though he is not there. His absence is language. Maybe I grieve him."

One vessel. An image—a memory—ran through her, bled its color behind her eyes. That ever-changing body Mani Ara had shown her. The way the world had shifted already. Rot making it flesh and green, and humans the same, and all of it full of magic.

The yaksa were shaping the world for them, as best as they could.

"You will live, Priya," Arahli Ara said. "You will live with her. As all the green sings and moves, so you will sing and move."

The world would become forests of rot. People of green. The yaksa would be flesh and green, and they would rule it all. Only the most blessed people, and the chosen, would be allowed to continue to live with the rot inside them. The rest would die, cut through with flowers. It wouldn't be a world that belonged to humanity anymore.

The world Priya had known would end.

And Priya wouldn't be here to see it. Priya would be a hollow shell, a carapace of meat for Mani Ara to wear, to bloom within, to rule from. Arahli could say she would live, but that didn't make it true. She'd felt what it was like when she really, truly let Mani Ara in. The yaksa's magic and memories were overwhelming.

Mani Ara wouldn't love the people she loved. Mani Ara wouldn't care about the Ahiranyi. She wouldn't protect the temple children. She wouldn't tell Padma nonsense stories until she slept.

She would let Ahiranya die, as surely as Parijatdvipa would. Because Ahiranya was not the glory of the Age of Flowers, or worshipping the yaksa, or the magic of the deathless waters, or temple elders standing on the triveni under a blanket of stars. Ahiranya was its people. It was the life they'd cobbled together and the culture they had built after the yaksa had first died. It was the love they had for one another. It was Ashok's ruthless determination, and Bhumika's steadfast cunning, and Sima's practical kindness. It was scraps of the Birch Bark Mantras, and the crush of people in the market, and family, and the love and duty that bound them.

It wasn't anything a yaksa could understand.

She couldn't let the yaksa win. But she couldn't let them lose, either. Both roads led to the obliteration of the Ahiranyi.

There had to be a third way. And if there wasn't, she was going to *make* one.

She nodded, and breathed, and reminded herself she was still human. For however long she had, she was still that. And that meant there was still hope.

"Priya," Arahli Ara said softly. "What will you do now?"

"What Mani Ara has willed," Priya said. "It's time for me to seek her children out once more."

That night, when she dreamt, she thought of it. A third path.

In the twilight of sleep, in the darkness where she dreamt and Mani Ara couldn't quite touch her, where a cord bound Priya to Malini, and Malini to Priya in return—she carved a path. A way. A welcome.

Come and find me, Malini.
If you want me, I'm yours.

42

MALINI

Malini heard the howl when the news came. A single wail of grief carried across King Lakshan's court, making heads turn. She rose from her seat and made her way across the court toward the entrance.

Beyond the doors, on the vast entrance staircase, two men kneeled. They were clutching each other, foreheads pressed together. One wore the garb of a Saketan liegeman, but ripped and bloodied almost beyond recognition; the other was Low Prince Ashutosh, in his usual finery. He was weeping. As she watched, he howled again—a wretched, impossible sound of grief. He was holding the shoulders of one Saketan soldier tight enough to make his own hands mottle white.

One liegeman. Only one. She understood instantly that the rest were dead. Her stomach plummeted.

The weapon Rao had brought her was useless after all.

The disappointment was so intense she could have screamed.

But the liegeman was standing. Wrenching away from Ashutosh and stumbling toward her, where he fell back to his knees.

"It worked, Empress," the liegeman was saying, his face blood-ied and streaked with the aftermath of tears. "The weapon works. My brothers died to test it. But it works." He lowered his own sword to the ground and then lowered himself, bowing his head to the stone as a roar of noise exploded from the watching courtiers around them.

Malini felt weightless. She lowered herself with the man. She raised his chin with her hand, astonished at herself, at the way her hand did not even tremble.

"Tell me everything," she said.

A battle. A single Ahiranyi man leading them astray. A knife in him. And then—

Priya.

The liegeman had seen Priya, even if he hadn't known her. Some of the other liegemen had recognized her, and threatened her, and even softly cajoled her.

She'd killed them all.

"She didn't look human, Empress," he said, in the private room she'd ushered him into. Behind him, leaning against the wall, Ashutosh listened without moving, barely even blinking. "The Ahiranyi are truly monsters."

He'd brought back all the weapons he could find. He wanted to return to the place his fellow liegemen had died, but he was afraid. Priya had buried the remains of his compatriots. He wanted to see them respectfully, properly burned.

"Empress," Sahar said. "If I have your permission—I'd like to help find and burn the dead. Make sure they get their proper rites."

"Of course," Malini said. She gave Sahar a considering look. Sahar's eyes were red, her mouth thin. "Are you well, Sahar?" Malini asked gently.

"I knew one of the soldiers who died," Sahar said. Her voice thickened. She cleared her throat. "Romesh. He served Low Prince Ashutosh. We—we were friends."

"I'm sorry for your loss," Malini said. She placed a hand on Sahar's arm, then released her. "Go. Rest for a while. I will stay here. The other guards will stand at the door and protect me."

Sahar nodded shakily and left without protest.

Malini turned back to the liegemen—and met Ashutosh's eyes, over the liegeman's bowed head.

"Low Prince," she said. "I am sorry for your loss. Your men were brave."

He looked back at her. His eyes were red-rimmed.

"Our liegemen are not simply soldiers to us, Empress," he said. "In Saketa, they grow up alongside their highborn, sworn at birth. My men were more than family to me. When they first became infected with rot, I told them they would always have a place at my side. 'You wear my liegemarks,' I told them. Those meant something to me, and to them." His voice was rich with grief. "One of my men begged me for this task, Empress. He knew you ordered for the Ahiranyi to be brought in alive, and he wanted to make sure that would happen. He *liked* the Ahiranyi witch. He believed there was good in her. And I agreed." A bitter, trembling twist to his mouth. "Look what price he's paid for his foolishness. I cannot make sense of my own loss. I feel like I've lost myself."

He crossed the room and placed a hand on his surviving liegeman's shoulder. It was gentle.

"I am glad your heart's shell has power," he said to Malini. "But next time, I beg you—kill the Ahiranyi before they can kill us. Order the witch's throat cut. I deserve her blood. My dead liegemen deserve her blood."

Priya, dying in dreams. Priya, a water-drenched dream in her arms, speaking of loneliness. Priya, kissing her.

It was there, staring into Ashutosh's red eyes, that Malini finally acknowledged the truth of herself: She could not kill Priya. She hated Priya and she wanted her and she hated wanting her. She wanted Priya to stop existing but couldn't live in a world where she didn't exist. Perhaps it was the cruel magic that bound them that made it so, but Priya was not simply a part of her that could be burned away.

She wasn't going to use the heart's shell to kill Priya. She was going to use it to claim her.

"I will do what is best for Parijatdvipa," Malini said. "Always."

43

RAO

The highest rooms of the Srugani mahal were so far up the cliff face that standing at their windows made Rao feel as if he could touch the melting blue sky. Malini was not looking at the sky. Her head was bent over a map.

Rao slipped past Raziya, who gave him a nod, then left the room, leaving him and Malini alone.

"No pretense at praying alone today?" Rao asked.

"The High Priest has no eyes on me here," Malini said. "And if he does, I find I cannot care. Why did you want to meet, Rao?"

He looked at her gaze—her knowing, piercing eyes. She'd guessed at what he wanted. She always did.

"I will take you to Lady Qutlugh," he said. "I will stay until your negotiations are done. But then, I beg you, Malini. Let me go to Alor."

She said nothing. Her silence spoke for her.

Convince me.

"You send your generals where they're needed. I want to go to Alor. I admit it." He did not say *I am still broken.* Did not say *When Sima and I were alone on the snow I realized how much I loved your brother, how much I loved Prem, and the grief of what I never said or did is driving me mad. Let me have the peace of home. Let me have at least that.* Instead he said, "I can also serve you better there than anywhere."

"And how will that serve me, Rao?" She did not sound displeased—or at least, no more so than she usually did. "I have your father's loyalty. And Alor's rot cannot be defeated by battle."

"The priesthood of the mothers supports you, but they also stand against you," Rao said. "But the nameless god proclaimed your right to the throne—through me. We have no High Priest, as the mothers of flame do—but there are influential, *powerful* temples in Alor, and I can seek out their support. The priests of the mothers gained too much sway in the time of your brother," he went on. "It wasn't so, before. When your father ruled. We both remember. Bring priests of the nameless into your court. It may help you."

"Or it may drive High Priest Hemanth to behave entirely like an animal with its leg in a snare," Malini said. But she sounded... thoughtful. "Yes," she said, after a moment. "You may go. Bring me back worthy priests, Rao, but if you can't, I'll accept more coin from your father. Heart's shell is going to cost us dearly, and what it doesn't take, famine will."

He bowed his head.

"Sima won't go with you this time," she added.

He raised his head abruptly.

"She's proven her loyalty," he protested.

"I know. But I have need of her," said Malini. "She's proven herself to you. I accept that. But it's time for her to prove her loyalty to me."

Malini's voice was mild, but there was iron in it.

"As you say," he replied through gritted teeth.

He found Sima looking out at Srugna.

"All those trees," she said, looking out from the balcony of the cliff-face mahal. Her arms were on the edge, her gaze fixed on the distance, where the trees were so thick they were like a spill of green ink. "It's almost like being home.

"Don't ask me if I'm going to run away again," she added, as he propped his arms on the edge of the balcony beside her. "My answer hasn't changed. Priya told me not to follow her. I don't think she'd want me to try now. I'm staying with you."

He looked at her face. It was only then that he realized Sima was crying.

"Romesh and the others—they cared about me." Her voice was choked. "They *liked* me. And now they're dead. I know you won't believe me, but Priya is a good person. She's always been the best fucking person I know, and she's my friend, and she killed one of the only people I could trust in the imprisonment she told me to choose. What am I meant to do now? How can I be angry at her? How can I not?"

He hadn't known that Priya had told her to remain, but now did not seem the time to say so. Instead, he placed an arm around her shoulder. Let her weep.

When she'd quieted he said, "I... I have some bad news. I'm sorry."

He told her.

"You're leaving me behind." Her expression was shuttered, but it was the exact absence of expression on her face that told him how hurt she truly was.

"I have to go home," he said. "I... I have to go to a monastery and reach for the nameless god again. I can't continue like this, Sima. I have to talk to the nameless god. I need a priest to guide me." *I need to know if the voice inside me is the nameless god at all.*

"Insist on taking me with you, then."

"The empress will take you back to Parijat with her. Lata will protect you then."

She scoffed.

"Go then. Listen to your god. But I think you should listen to your own heart a little more, and your god a little less," said Sima.

"I'm afraid," Rao said quietly, "that I don't know my own heart."

"You do. You listened to it in the snow, when we almost froze. You told me what your heart said." She stepped abruptly away from him, arms crossed. "You won't find your answers in Alor or with the nameless god. But I can't stop you. Go, Rao. Just go."

44

ARAHLI ARA

Priya was the one to build the path. He could feel her in the sangam—as she could likely feel him, if she dared to reach out. But she had no interest in him. She guided the way, walking forward as he followed.

In Srugna, they kneeled on the earth and watched a yaksa peel their way from the dirt. A yaksa, baring her teeth, breathing as if she had mortal lungs.

Distantly, he knew that Ashok would have known the face that rose from the soil—that face that tipped toward the sunlight, catching its fading rays like a flower in bloom. But it also felt wrong to think of Ashok in this moment. *Riti*, Ashok's voice whispered in him. He banished it. A mortal had no place in this, the birth and return of one of their own.

"Cira Ara," Priya said tenderly. "You live again."

"There was fire," the yaksa whispered. "And then a long sleep, where I saw nothing and dreamt nothing. If I thought, it was of soil and darkness." Her eyes were all strange sclera. "What did I give up in order to return here?"

You will become more and more flesh, thought Arahli. *Your heart will beat strangely in your chest. You will feel, as you have never felt before. Small, encompassing emotions, born of the body, but so vast they could have drifted with us out of the cosmos.*

But Priya said none of the ugly things drifting through his head.

She held Arahli's sister with her hands. Cradled her. A hand to the skull. A hand to the cheek. She looked at Cira with all the infinite love and strangeness of Mani Ara.

"It doesn't matter," she murmured. "You're here now."

She glowed as darkly as his mother, as if her skin were a paper lantern to the starlit void of Mani Ara. It was like a cold hand passing over him, witnessing it. Ashok grieved, horrified. But Arahli felt something sharp-edged and beautiful. He felt hope.

45

MALINI

She wanted only her most trusted people for this negotiation, but she couldn't wait to summon Lata. She took her Parijati warriors and Rao's forces along with her. She directed Lord Narayan and Low Prince Ashutosh to return to Parijat.

Lord Prakash she left in Srugna. He would counsel King Lakshan on her behalf.

The kai's sister waited in an encampment on the road from Srugna. Rao had left her with a significant number of his men, guarded in her own tent. She bowed immediately when Malini entered.

"Lady Qutlugh," Malini greeted. "Please. Stand."

She raised her head. Qutlugh was fairer skinned than Malini, with thick black hair bound in a braid. She wore the kind of clothes typical of Dwarali, with its bitterly cold winters and mild summers: a salwar kameez and jacket and shawl, thick fur-lined boots. On her wrists, ears, and throat she wore heavy golden jewelry, and her eyes were lined with kohl.

"Prince Rao has told me what your brother and your people desire," Malini said, without pleasantries. "I'd like to hear it from you."

"We desire a home, Empress," Qutlugh said. Her accent was thick, musical—but she knew court Dvipan, the language of the empire's highborn, and wielded it now instead of the common

Zaban that Malini had used. Her choice of language said, *I am highborn. I was born to power, just like you.* "Land that is ours. In return, we offer heart's shell."

"You will give us the location of the mine?"

Qutlugh shook her head.

"The location is secret," Qutlugh said. "Only a few members of my family line possess the knowledge. I am not one of them." A dimpling smile. "We will bring the heart's shell to you whenever you command it, of course."

"It will be inconvenient for your family to cross the Lal Qila regularly," Malini observed. "Especially if your new home is deep within the empire. And we will need a great deal of this stone. Our empire is at war."

"We will make the journey gladly, as many times as Parijatdvipa requires it of us," said the kai's sister. "But we will not part with our knowledge. My clan recognize that we have been weakened. My brother lost our lands when he was a young ruler, and we have limited military power. But we have the heart's shell. Our knowledge is our greatest resource, and we will not squander it."

Malini inclined her head.

"Will you vow your obedience to Parijatdvipa, and to the descendant of Divyanshi who holds the Parijatdvipan imperial throne?"

"Will you refuse us if the Jagatay do not? If we will not vow, will you reject us?" Qutlugh raised an inquisitive eyebrow. "If we have no home from you, Empress, you will have no heart's shell from us.

"You have threatened nothing," Qutlugh continued, "but I will tell you this anyway, because I understand the nature of those who rule: My brother will not bow or bend if you hold me hostage or kill me. I came here as any warrior going to battle. I knew I risked my honor and my life. If you torture me, I have no knowledge I can share that will lead you to heart's shell. But I am willing and able to bargain with you, Empress."

"I can offer nothing without a vow of loyalty," Malini said.

"Ahiranya was part of your empire once. They made no such vows."

"Ahiranya was a conquered nation. Do you wish your people to be treated similarly? Lady Qutlugh—this vow I ask for does not chain you. It makes your people equals among equals."

"Equals beneath your throne, yes." The woman tapped her lip thoughtfully. "A vow can be a hollow thing, Empress. You know this, don't you? If I choose to lie, the vow of the Jagatay will be worth nothing. How can you trust me? How can we trust you?"

"My throne, my empire, rests on the vows of the kings who serve me," Malini said steadily. "Betraying those vows would betray myself. As for my trust in you...Lady Qutlugh, you and your brother have given me a weapon that may save my people." She filled her voice with feeling—let emotion flit, for a moment, across her features. "How can I not extend you trust?"

Qutlugh gave her a long look. Then, finally, she nodded.

"We may bargain, Empress. You will need heart's shell urgently, I think."

"You're correct."

"I carried a supply of heart's shell with me," said Qutlugh. She touched a light hand to the heavy gold at her throat, then swept the hand up to the large earrings strung through her ears, bound with chains to her hair to ease the burden of their weight. She met Malini's eyes with a smile. "Heart's shell painted with gold," she said. "I guessed it would go unnoticed."

Clever.

She removed her bangles—heavy links of stone bound together and placed them each into Malini's waiting hands.

Malini looked at them. She felt their weight and thought of how easily the strings that had bound them to Qutlugh's wrists could be crafted into locks. Something to hold a yaksa's powers at bay, and a human woman's hands chained.

"Come," said Malini. "My guards will bring us food and drink. We have negotiations to conduct."

*   *   *

When negotiations came to an end, Rao departed. Half his men would take Lady Qutlugh to Dwarali and arrange her safe passage beyond the Lal Qila. The rest would have to travel with him.

He left at dusk, gold light grasping his shadow as he rode away from her camp. He'd bowed when he'd said goodbye to Malini. To Sima, who would remain with Malini, he gave a soft farewell, his eyes huge with apology.

Sima gave him a stiff farewell in return. She was clearly upset at being left behind. But she watched his departure for just as long as Malini did, her eyes fixed on the distance, arms crossed protectively over her body.

"Take care of her," Malini said quietly to Sahar. "Make sure she causes no trouble."

Sahar inclined her head in understanding.

A rider with a message arrived hours later, kicking up dust under his horse's hooves. His face was sickly under his helm; his hands shook when he drank the water that was carried to him.

"Soon after you left, Empress," he said, in a grim voice held steady by stubbornness alone, "something unnatural pierced Srugna. A quake shook the earth. And the rot...the rot spread in the blink of an eye. And something in the forest, among the trees, killed hundreds of soldiers. It took less than an hour, Empress, for the devastation to spread." He bowed his head. "Lord Prakash begs more aid on behalf of King Lakshan. More soldiers. Food supplies. Anything that can be spared."

"There are no swords I can offer that will be able to fight the rot," Malini said finally, once her horror had settled. "But I will send a message with you ahead of my retinue to Parijat. Our stored harvest will be shared with Srugna, and the priests of the mothers—and I—will pray for Srugna's dead."

She left the audience tent.

She paused, one breath, one heartbeat. That was all it took for her to see what lay around her, and how the landscape had changed:

The leaves of the fronded plants surrounding the tent had all turned toward her.

She could not save Srugna from the rot. But there was something else she could do.

She could dream.

When Malini returned to her tent, shaking and strange, she smelled something sweet on the air. Something like green things after the first flush of monsoon rains. No incense had been lit, and Swati had left no flowers in bowls of water to fragrance the room. The scent was a beckoning, a call.

Priya.

You knew I would come for you after all, Malini thought. *How could I not, after what you have done?*

Malini did not sleep. For some reason, she knew she didn't need to. She remembered the way Priya had reached for her magic at times; the closed eyes, the slow deep breaths. She kneeled on the ground, on the softness of a rug over tent canvas, and closed her own eyes.

Inside her skull lay a door. The distant sound of rushing water.

She stepped through it.

She was not in the imperial court. She was in a shadowy place where leaves rustled and insects whined, a place where Priya kneeled in front of a vast lake, black in a dreamlike darkness beyond day or night.

The lake was covered in a thick carpet of blue lotus flowers.

"They're beautiful, aren't they?" Priya said. She turned her head and met Malini's gaze. "I've never seen anything like them. But I will soon."

Malini walked toward her. There was still distance between. Too much to cross with hands, touch. Malini kneeled down, soft grass beneath her.

"You killed people you once claimed as your allies," Malini said. "People who were your friends."

Priya flinched. She turned back to the water.

"I could have died because of you, Malini," Priya said. "That weapon you have could have killed me."

"I ordered them to capture you alive."

"You can tell a man what to do with a weapon," Priya said. "That doesn't mean he'll obey. You know that." Her shoulders bowed forward a little. "They should have killed me before I could kill them. Why didn't you tell them to?"

Malini's heart thundered in her chest, a roar in her ears.

"You know why," she said. She didn't know what emotion seeped into her voice. Only that it made Priya's hands curl against the ground and her head tilt forward, as if she could shelter herself from it.

"What would you do if you could see me again, Malini? Touch me?" The water rippled. The blue lotuses glowed. "Would you kill me? Imprison me?"

Malini said nothing. If she spoke, she would say something she did not want to—something that revealed her rotten, wanting heart.

"I think we should find out," said Priya.

Malini returned to her body with a gasp.

She knew of those lotuses. She'd studied the geography of Parijatdvipa, marked on maps of war and maps of famine, in the course of her rise to the throne.

Utpala Lake. Alor. That was where Priya would be.

46

RAO

His luck was rotten. A flood had struck Alor. "Strange rains, my lord," one of his soldiers had told him, after interrogating a lone farmer walking along the edge of the road they were traveling on. "He says no one will travel until the ground dries and the river recedes fully."

There were barely any travelers on the roads. Combined with the homes and villages emptied by rot, Rao found the roads eerily empty. The only large groups he saw were refugees from the edges of Ahiranya, many of them rot-riven—and they scattered at the sight of his men. He couldn't blame them for that.

Even the caravanserais had been abandoned. There was some grumbling from his soldiers at that. Trading posts were good for fresh, warm food and an excellent place for stocking up on liquor.

The ground would have been unpleasant at best to pitch tents on, so he decided to take advantage of his princely status and descend on the lands of a local landowner. The man welcomed him effusively, arranging accommodation for his men.

They shared a meal and a hookah pipe.

"Will you be heading to your father's mahal, prince?" the man asked.

Rao shook his head. "No, I am seeking the priesthood. There is a great monastery near here, in the forest. Nimisa."

The man clucked his tongue.

"You will struggle to move through the forest in the aftermath of flooding," he said. "A river bisects the woods."

"Nonetheless I have to try," said Rao, smiling.

The man hesitated. "And those priests...ah, it will not impact you."

"I would still like to know," Rao said earnestly, sensing a story there.

"They are not welcoming as other monasteries. Too ancient, too powerful. Even your father goes to them, they do not go to him." He chuckled. "They feel the weight of their history, Prince Rao. We do not go there to pray or seek prophecy—though I send fine offerings regularly," he added hastily. "But you are a prince. They will see you."

"Yes," said Rao. "I hope so." Internally, silently, he hoped they would be willing to ally with the greater power of an empress and support Malini's claim to the throne. Or his journey would be worth nothing.

As they reached Nimisa's border, they passed another empty village.

"There's rot around," said a soldier nervously. "If we turn back, my lord..."

"We know it's spreading across the empire," Rao said calmly. "This is all the more reason to make this trip swiftly."

A bigger problem immediately faced them. The flooding had turned the forest floor to such thick mud that their horses struggled to move forward; worse still, the horses resisted, eyes rolling wildly, legs rearing.

"They fear the rot," one soldier muttered, not meeting Rao's eyes. But he was right.

Rao bit back a curse.

"You," he said, gesturing at the closest group of soldiers. "With me. We'll walk. Make sure you carry heart's shell with you."

The monastery was as grand as he expected, and he felt a thud of his old faith—a reflexive, instinctual love—in his chest, as good as a heartbeat at the sight of it.

The faith was short-lived.

Guards swarmed out of the monastery at his arrival, holding bows and spears. "No one is allowed to enter!" one yelled from the stairs, his spear held threateningly in front of him.

"I am Prince Rao of Alor. Is this the greeting Nimisa Monastery offers a son of Alor's king?" Rao called out.

One guard hesitated, but another yelled back, "How do we know you're a prince?"

"Lower your spear, you fool," a tired voice said. A figure emerged from the monastery and strode down the stairs, bowing low to Rao. "Apologies, my prince," the head priest said. "Forgive my men. We have been facing unforeseen danger. It has made children of us." He straightened, meeting Rao's eyes. "I met you once when you were a young boy—before you were sent to Harsinghar to be raised alongside Prince Aditya. You have the look of your father."

Rao had not seen his father in years. "My thanks," he said.

"Come," said the head priest. "We will talk alone."

He took Rao to a private chamber, poured him a clear cup of water, and offered him dried fruit, a pleasingly sweet fare to welcome him to the monastery. Rao ate a little out of politeness, but even his mouthful tasted more and more like ash as the priest talked.

The head priest—Sunder—told Rao that rot had grown virulently across the forest ever since floods had drowned the woods. One of his priests had stumbled onto a strange path of flowers and never returned. Another became ill, growing flowers from his skull.

"We have not been able to leave," said Sunder. "There is too much danger beyond our walls."

"My men and I will accompany you to safety, of course," said Rao.

The priest shook his head.

"We cannot abandon this place. Caring for this monastery, worshipping within it, is our sacred duty."

"Then we will remain here to help you."

"You would be wiser not to," Sunder said immediately, but he did not mean it. Rao could see the wretched relief in his eyes. "Matters are more dire here than they first appear." He hesitated. "I have . . . a regret."

The priest drank his own water. His glass clinked as he lowered it.

"A woman came to us," Sunder said. "She was Ahiranyi. She told us she had a way to destroy the yaksa. We drove her away. She returned, begging for safety for her and a number of villagers, claiming a single yaksa would soon come to destroy us. We turned them all away. I did not understand—as none of us did—how terribly these paths have riddled the forest. I fear she told us the truth—that a monster will soon be the ruin of us. And I fear she is dead and cannot be helped."

Rao listened, frozen.

"I cannot stop thinking of her words," Sunder continued. "She haunts me. I think, perhaps, the nameless punishes me."

Was it Priya? Had she arrived here, of all places?

Maybe this was proof that the nameless was the one working through him after all, like it or not.

"This is the holiest of places," said the priest. "And I fear that evil forces seek to destroy it. Anything you can do to help us, Prince Rao." He exhaled, shame and fear in his face, his voice. "I have not felt the nameless in voice or heart in a long time. It is my great shame. But I see and know that you do. I should not ask, but I must. *Help us.*"

Rao could not leave the monastery unprotected. He would defend it with heart's shell. If a yaksa was coming, it was the only possible protection they had.

He had to hope it would be enough.

When he left the room, shaken, he saw eyes watching from the shadows. He almost jumped—almost reached for his heart's-shell blade—until a figure came forward.

"Prince Rao," said the young priest. "My name is Ishan. And I . . . I think you're looking for a woman. I can take you to her."

The priest led him from the monastery to the land behind it, cleared of trees.

"I have been taking them what I can," Ishan said, shamefaced. "We have stores for offerings—for food, grain, oil—anything we don't wish to keep on monastery grounds. They're staying here."

He took Rao into a low-walled building, opened the large doors, and called out, "It's me!" Rao heard rustling and saw crouched figures move. So many figures.

"I've brought someone willing to listen," the priest said earnestly.

"Ishan told me he would gently cajole his fellow priests," said a woman, hidden in shadow. Her voice was low and musical. "I did not expect a highborn lord."

She stepped into the light, and she was not Priya. She was beautiful and plainly dressed, with wide, soft eyes. Unfamiliar.

But the man who walked forward into the light was not. He'd seen that face when he'd first tried to save Malini in Ahiranya—an Ahiranyi soldier's face.

That was all he needed to know.

Rao drew his heart's-shell blade. People screamed. The Ahiranyi man reached for his sword. The woman stood smoothly in front of him, shielding his body.

The priest Ishan grabbed Rao roughly, and Rao dropped the heart's-shell blade; suddenly he felt fire behind his eyes again, pressing insistently against his skull. The Ahiranyi woman looked at him. A strange look passed over her face.

"We are not enemies," she said, placating. "No weapons are needed here. We have a shared purpose, do we not, my lord? You feel it. I know you do."

"Please, my lord," Ishan said shakily.

Rao urged his heart to calm. Opened his hands.

"I'm listening," Rao forced himself to say.

"Let us have a proper introduction," she said, polite as any highborn woman over tea. "We have very little time left before the yaksa comes. My name, my lord, is Bhumika."

47

PRIYA

After the dream, she thought of the stone knife constantly. Malini's new weapon.

It had extinguished her powers when it had touched her. She knew what that meant.

Malini could fight the yaksa without burning herself. Malini could fight, and Priya...

Priya was going to throw herself into the hands of fate.

The yaksa awakening in Alor was a sluggish heartbeat in the base of her skull: a slow, sullen, dreaming creature, roiling under soil. She tried to ignore it as she gathered the temple children and told them to climb the Hirana. "Not to the top," she said. "Just until the height of that ribbon." She gestured at the ribbon she'd tied a tree's height up the Hirana, on the outstretched arm of a carving.

"I don't want to climb the Hirana," Pallavi said in a wobbly voice. "I'm frightened of it. What if I fall?"

"Then you'll get back up," said Priya. "Or I'll catch you."

"What if you miss?"

"I won't miss," said Priya.

Pallavi stared at her. Then she pointedly sat on the floor.

Priya sighed.

"Come on. It's the only way you'll learn."

"Maybe we need an easier task," Ashish said, his hands on the younger child's shoulders.

"You need to do *this* task," Priya snapped.

"We don't want to—"

"That doesn't matter." Priya knew her voice was harsh. Some of the children flinched. "You don't want to listen to me? There are so many things worse than me. Some of them are yaksa, and some of them are people. The empire wants us dead, and our own gods don't care if we live or die. Our own gods want to put you to a test that could kill you. But I want to teach you so that you'll survive. So what are you going to do?"

Silence fell.

"They're going to make us go through the waters, aren't they? The yaksa," said Ashish eventually.

"One day," Priya said. "Yes, they will." Deep breath. "I was always told you need to be strong to survive the waters. I don't know if that's true. But it's all I can teach you to do. You have to try to climb the Hirana. You have to try to scrape away your fear. You have to be brave. It's the only power you have. Please."

Another silence, and then Ashish stepped toward the Hirana and began trying to climb.

She caught him with vines as he fell.

"Try again," she said, thinly.

They didn't know this, but this was the last time she could help them.

She thought of Mani Ara, and her fate, and theirs, and felt dread coil in her belly. A snake. A poison that lived in her.

Rukh was feeding Padma a mash of lentils and rice in the kitchen courtyard. She crouched down next to them.

"Rukh," she said. "If you ever have a chance to leave Ahiranya, take it."

"Hi, Priya. I'm fine, Priya." He shook his head absently, wiping Padma's face clean even as she wrinkled it in protest. "I've never been anywhere else," he added. "Ahiranya's my home."

"Do it for Padma's sake, then," she said.

She thought he'd ask questions. Instead, he raised his head

and looked at her . . . and nodded. Eyes piercing, too understanding by far.

"You're going to Alor?"

"Today."

"Come back safe," he said quietly. "I'll take care of everyone while you're gone. I promise."

She, Ganam, and their followers went to the bower of bones and stepped onto a new path. The first path she'd dreamt of.

The path that smelled of salt didn't lead to the sea but to one of Alor's churning rivers. Light flecked the water, and fish were leaping from its wild surface. A few fighters laughed with delight at the sight. She looked into their faces and felt her own heart lighten at the sight of their joy.

They walked across Alor. It reminded her a little of Saketa's vast green and gold rolling landscape. But unlike Saketa, Alor was lush, with dark soil and rich fields, vast rivers snaking across the landscape. The trees curled into the water, deep roots coiling into the silt.

As they walked, she teased Ganam—tugging a smile out of him, and then laughter.

"Let me show you how to make paths," she said, nudging her shoulder against his arm. "Go on."

"That seems like a thrice-born skill to me," he said dubiously, squinting against the sunlight.

"It isn't," she insisted. "Now that I've learned it, it's pretty simple." She reached for him in the sangam—half in the waters and half in the world—and began to show him the trick of it.

Their joy dimmed as they passed fields cut through with rot. They saw villages shuttered and abandoned. Priya saw a few emaciated, hollow-eyed figures in the distance. They ran when they saw the Ahiranyi.

This was the world the yaksa were creating.

Priya looked at the people around her.

This was the world *they* were creating.

Night fell. They made camp, the warriors asleep around them. Priya took herself to the very edge of the camp, far enough away that she felt near enough to alone. She settled on the ground.

Ganam soon followed after her.

"Are you all right, Priya?"

"I need you to listen to me," Priya said. "I'm going to be maudlin and you're going to have to be patient."

"I think I can do that," Ganam said. He sat on the ground beside her.

"Is someone on watch?" Priya asked.

"Yes," said Ganam. "You can just talk."

"I've hidden vials of deathless waters," she said. "In Bhumika's study, and in Kritika's old rooms. Ruchi's already used three, and I know that a few more fighters have drunk waters broken from the source. They're going to need it, and it's only a matter of time before the yaksa realize they can control all of us by withholding the waters from our people. So keep the vials hidden. Use them carefully."

"Priya." His voice was urgent—aware. "What are you trying to do?"

"What do you mean?"

"Teaching me how to make paths, giving me vials of deathless water... Is something going to happen to you?"

She didn't want to answer him.

"I grabbed the knife the Saketans used to stab you," she said instead. "I buried it near the bower of bones. You'll be able to find it easily—I marked it with ashoka blossoms. If you ever need to fight another temple elder or once- or twice-born, or someone who drank the waters, or a yaksa, you'll find it useful. It has some kind of magic it in that stops our own."

"*Priya.*"

"I'm leaving," she said. "I'm sorry."

A pause. His voice was low.

"Like Bhumika left."

"No. Maybe." She shook her head. "I don't know why or how Bhumika left. I don't know if she's even alive anymore. But I'm leaving because if I stay, the yaksa will win and we'll die." She clenched her hands into fists. Grounding herself. "I need you to take care of them all when I'm gone," she said. "The children. Our fighters. Everyone."

"Priya." His voice was harder. "I can't let you do that."

A deep breath left her. "You can't stop me, Ganam."

"The yaksa won't let you go," he said. "And...shit, Priya. I'll be honest. We all need you. What would they do without us? Without you?" His voice softened, cajoling. "Don't do anything stupid. Please. Let's talk about this."

"Fine," she said. "Let's talk."

She told him what Mani Ara intended for her. She told him what the world would become.

He listened, and under moonlight she saw his face grow grayer and grayer.

In the end, he said, "What do you need from me?"

"I need to make it clear that you're loyal," she said. "That you didn't help me."

She bound him by the legs and throat to a tree with thick roots. "The others will find you in the morning," she muttered, working. "By then I'll be gone. As far as they'll know, you're loyal to the yaksa. And that's what the yaksa will know too."

"Where will you run to?" Ganam asked, watching her. "Where can you go that the yaksa won't find you?"

She shook her head. "It's better you don't know."

She tightened his bonds.

"I'm not going to awaken the yaksa sleeping in Alor, and neither are you," said Priya. Then she leaned back and swallowed, reaching for the iron in her spine. "This is going to hurt," she told him. "I'm going to break a bone. If you're too injured to move through Alor or go through the deathless waters, it will give you time. And save your life, I hope."

His mouth thinned into a grim line.

"Give me a cloth to bite on," he said. She grabbed one. Pressed it between his teeth.

"Build paths," she urged, circling his arm, upper and lower, with her hands. Gripping him firmly. "Build them secretly. Make them small. The yaksa won't notice immediately—there are too many paths already for that. And then help our people get out. If they want to run, help them run. I know it's a lot to ask for. I'm *so* sorry, Ganam. But you and I, we're all there is."

He nodded as far as his bonds allowed. *Do it*, his eyes said.

"I'm sorry," she said again.

He fainted when she broke his arm.

48

VARSHA

The priest Mitul had asked Varsha for information. He had not told her what, exactly, she was meant to seek. Whenever she met him in the temple gardens or wrote him letters in the deep night, she told him a string of true tales that to her mind amounted to nothing. Stories of the squabbles between some of the women in the empress's inner court. The coldness of the empress's sage, Lata, who cared more for books and administration than she did for the finer things of court. And she told him about the soirees the women held, where they drank wine or sherbet, or smoked their pipes, and gossiped about nothing and everything. Local estates, who had birthed an heir and who had not, and what they thought of the empress's choices.

Over time, she began to understand what these tales might be worth to him—how they could be mined for truth, raw and powerful, that could be used to shift the balance of power within the empire.

But it was not Mitul who taught her this. It was Deepa.

Deepa assisted Lata. Deepa was a highborn woman—a daughter of Lord Mahesh who served now at the border of Ahiranya. Her father had betrayed the empress once, but Deepa had been loyal to her. As a result, Deepa was a wealthy and powerful woman in her own right.

But she did not wield her power as the empress did—in jewels and swords and cold, knowing eyes. She was mild and gentle, and welcomed Varsha into her company with a smile. She was never annoyed when Varsha brought Vijay with her. Even through his crying or his sickness—and oh, Varsha wished someone had told her how often some babes could vomit—she allowed Varsha to accompany her on her tasks. Often they sat together in Deepa's study, looking through messages from outlying city-states and from Parijati landowners, as they shared sliced fruit and laughter.

"You are very insightful," Varsha once said to her. "Very clever indeed."

Deepa blushed and said, "I was not my father's favorite. Nor was I pretty. I had to notice things to survive."

Perhaps Varsha's life would have been better if she had been less pretty, less powerful, less loved. But she knew better than to say this. Instead she tried to learn by example. She listened, and began to understand the currents of power that flowed through the empire.

Then she heard it. Information like gold, or something more precious still.

She was feeding Vijay, tucked in a corner of Deepa's study, when Lata entered. The sage did not even glance at her. She kneeled down by Deepa's desk and began to speak hurriedly, her fingers tapping on the surface. Deepa's eyes grew steadily more worried.

"…Dwarali land," Lata was saying. "Lady Raziya will not accept it, Deepa, nor Lord Khalil. They will be at war with the empress before we know it."

"Land—to the Jagatay?" Deepa frowned. "I can't believe it. I—"

She stopped as Lata's gaze fixed finally on Varsha. Varsha pretended not to notice. She brushed a hand gently over Vijay's hair.

"She's no trouble," Deepa murmured.

Varsha did not wait to hear Lata's response. She lifted Vijay from her breast, arranging her blouse as he fretted. Then she stood, and made her apologies, and left.

Ferment in Dwarali. Displeasure with the empress. Knowledge like gold.

She felt eyes on her back as she left, but she paid no attention to it. Her excitement was too big for such petty concerns.

The priest would want this knowledge from her, she knew.

But why, she thought, *should I hand power to the priesthood? To another man in power?*

She thought of the empress, and thought of what the empress had—power and allies of her own. In the cage of her life, Varsha clung to this new information, this small power she had...and then she exhaled and began to write.

She sent her letter—with a hefty bribe of jewelry for the courier—to Dwarali at dawn.

She would make her own allies. When the empress was gone, she would be her son's regent. She would keep him safe.

49

PRIYA

It was first light, the blue-white of milk, when Priya drew near the lake.

She could feel the water—deep, stagnant, and still, with hundreds of lotus flowers blooming from silt-tangled stems. *Utpala Lake.* She'd seen it in the knowledge Mani Ara had gifted her of the sleeping yaksa and where to find them. It was the place she'd shown to Malini in a dream, so that Malini would know where to seek her out.

She could not feel Malini's presence, no matter how she searched, all the tendrils of her magic seeking Malini out. Instead beyond the lake, far beyond, she felt dense forest. Beneath that forest, the yaksa Mani Ara had shown her was shifting restlessly—a consciousness awakening, uncoiling under soil, responding to her presence.

The yaksa would have to awaken alone. Priya could not help them now.

The lake was ringed by a caravanserai—a place for travelers to rest, and a market all at once. It should have been bustling, noisy. But it was silent.

No one was here.

It was not a trap. Traps were meant to be subtle. The silence of the caravanserai was an invitation. Malini had prepared the way. Malini was expecting her.

Priya walked through the gates of the caravanserai, which were open and unguarded. The caravanserai was a ring of empty tents and stalls.

At its center, the lake was a vast blue disc, rich with flowers the color of wrist veins. She walked toward it, stood by the water's edge, and watched the lotuses.

She could sense no rot in them. She sat on the edge of the lake and placed her legs in the water. Her clothes grew wet—the end of her tunic billowed, white going blue-black in the murky dark.

Time passed. And passed. There was no sign of Malini. She breathed out, and in, and made flowers grow around the edges of the caravanserai's walls. Jasmine flowers, mostly, darted with needle-flower.

Maybe she had lied to herself. Maybe the dream had just been a dream after all. Perhaps Malini hadn't understood.

Perhaps the only future that truly lay ahead of her was as a hollow gourd—a perfectly formed vessel for Mani Ara. Herself, and not herself. There would be no escape from those shining thorn teeth, that voice that called her *beloved* and *sapling*, and asked her to break and break and break.

"Thank you for announcing yourself so clearly," a voice said. In the quiet of the empty caravanserai it carried—a dark, winged bird, settling in Priya's ears, Priya's heart. "I wasn't sure when you would come."

Priya lifted her feet out of the water, stood, and turned. And there she was. Malini.

The same, always the same as Priya had dreamt her: slim and tall, with that braid of curling black hair, those gray eyes that could pin you and hold you. She was unsmiling. She wore white—a white sari, pleated to a knife edge—and armor over her torso.

Priya reached for her power. There was no need to make the earth tremor or force thorns through the soil, not yet—but she held them ready. Malini's gaze was unwavering, but there was something in her eyes—something that said she *knew*.

"There's no need for that, Priya," she said softly, confirming it. "Come out of the water."

Priya stepped from the water. In the green, she could feel nothing and no one.

"Where are your guards?" Priya asked. "Your warriors? I can't feel them. I can't feel you." A step closer. "Why can't I feel you?"

"I'm alone."

"You wouldn't have come here alone. Not to face me."

"I faced Chandra without my guards or warriors," Malini said calmly, her face lovely and empty. "I faced him on faith alone."

"You took a risk facing him, but you knew it gave you the best chance against him. You had... allies..." Priya's voice trailed off. Malini was walking toward her, alive and real and in the flesh before her.

"I think perhaps you are my ally against yourself," Malini said, drawing closer. Priya heard the clink of the saber at her hip. The gold at her throat and wrists shone. "Why did you tell me where to find you?"

So Mani Ara could not use me. So I could be taken beyond her reach. So I could carve a third path.

"Maybe I want to see what you'll do, Malini," she said. "Now that you have me."

"Ah, Priya," she said. "I do not have you yet."

"You think I'll fight?"

Malini exhaled and smiled. She reached up, carelessly touching the gold at her throat. "Will you?"

"Will you try to kill me?"

Malini's eyes were black as pitch, her expression soft in a way that told Priya her hatred ran deep, as deep as the deathless waters beneath the Hirana itself.

"I will treat you with exactly the same courtesy you extended to me, of course," said Malini. "What else?"

Priya clenched and unclenched her hands. Preparing. Not her body, perhaps. But her heart.

"You have more right to my death than almost anyone,"

Priya said. "If anyone could kill me...But I won't die yet. I don't want to."

Malini's body moved, swiftly, and Priya didn't wait to see what she'd do with their closeness—what saber Malini would set through her stomach, what needle she'd jab into her throat. The ground erupted around them both. A wall of earth and rock to keep Malini at bay, and more thorns erupting from the ground to push her back, back, back. Priya was a fool, she knew it, but even now she didn't want to hurt her. Even now...

Malini leapt forward and looped the necklace of gold that had been around her own throat over Priya's neck with all the reverence of a wedding garland.

Then she tightened her fist, turning the necklace into a noose.

The second it touched her skin, Priya felt what lay under that gold. Something cold and dark that grasped her power and strangled it. The weapon that had hurt Ganam. The stone on the knife.

The ground went still. She gave a choked breath, and another, and the necklace loosened but did not leave her throat.

Figures appeared out of the darkness. Soldiers.

"You're right," Malini said. "I lied. I didn't come alone. Will you yield, Priya?"

"No," she bit out. She looked around for an escape. But Malini, clever Malini, had her trapped already.

"You made this so simple," Malini said. "I thought you would try harder."

The soldiers drew in closer.

Priya hadn't felt their approach. The stone they carried—the stone around her throat—had concealed them from her magic. Just like it had concealed Malini. She tried to jerk away, but Malini's hand did not relent—and her other hand was rising, holding a blade by the hilt.

Holding the blade to Priya's throat.

"I know you don't need your gifts to fight," Malini whispered. "Move, and I cut. So, my love. Will you come with me?"

The only answer was yes.

50

BHUMIKA

The villagers were not invited into the monastery until morning, which left them to a night of worry and speculation. They sat in groups in the grain store and waited for dawn and for judgment.

Manjeet took the wait stoically, but Bidisha was furious. She said nothing to Bhumika, but her glare was ferocious, and her whispers to the other women weren't subtle. She blamed Bhumika for their plight. Bhumika had encouraged them to break village taboos; Bhumika had brought herself and her Ahiranyi blood to their village, and what had followed in her wake? Strange paths, and rot, and displacement from their home. Nothing but wreckage and grief.

Bhumika knew breaking taboos had not brought the village to ruin, but she still wondered if Bidisha was correct for blaming her for their ill fortune. Perhaps Bhumika's presence alone had been enough. She held her silence through the night, Jeevan's body a warm and solid comfort at her side.

When Prince Rao arrived once more, guards from the monastery behind him, the villagers scrambled to their feet. Their fear was palpable.

The priest Ishan stepped forward, holding his hands up in a placating manner.

"Come with us," Ishan urged. "I promise no harm will come to you."

After a brief hesitation, the villagers gathered their courage and followed him.

Beyond the grain stores, the forest had grown even more rot-riven. Bhumika could smell the faint stench of meat. The distant trees, hazy in the light, were mottled like cold flesh.

There was a thunderous crack of noise. The trees bent and swayed above them, although there was no wind to move them. The ground shook.

Bhumika's knees buckled. She caught herself just in time, finding her balance even as her vision swayed violently.

She felt the yaksa under the earth, waking, its eyes of sap peeling open, its mouth open on a rattling scream. And she felt something else. Something had touched her for a moment—a dizzying image of a younger woman with pin-straight hair and a crooked smile turning to her, and a yaksa with a mouth of thorns, and then abruptly nothing. It was as if a great presence had brushed against both her and the newborn yaksa, then vanished.

"*She was close,*" a watcher whispered. A girl, water dripping from the long braid of her hair. Yearning in her voice.

"Who?" Bhumika asked. She did not think her ghost spoke of the yaksa. Jeevan looked at her sharply.

The watcher shook her head, then faded into morning mist.

Bhumika took a fortifying breath and straightened up. "The yaksa," she said to him. "We have no more time. It wakes."

The ground shook again. Prince Rao took an abrupt step toward her.

"Can you stop this?" he demanded. "As an Elder—"

"She does not remember herself," Jeevan said sharply, cutting through Prince Rao's words. "My lady can give you the knowledge of how to kill the yaksa, but beyond that she owes you nothing."

"I made a sacrifice of myself for this knowledge," Bhumika said. Her vision was beginning to settle, nausea in its wake. "Any power I had, I no longer have. You seem angry at me, Prince Rao. I am sorry for it. But any debts I owe you, I cannot pay." She held her palms open. "In many ways, what you see before you is a ghost."

He looked stricken for a moment. Then the look passed, settling into something far more determined and focused, and devoid of softness.

"Move quickly," he barked. "All of you."

Quickly was difficult, with elderly and small children in their group. But they soon shuffled up the stairs of the monastery and into its gray-stoned corridors. Flickering torchlight guided them to a doorway. An older priest was waiting.

"Take them in there," he ordered the guards and Ishan. He bowed his head in respect to Prince Rao, then swiftly walked away.

They entered. The room was large and circular. But the first thing Bhumika noticed was how it felt—like the lake in the caravanserai. Like a dark pool, a door, a gateway vaster and stranger than any seeker's path. Her heart thrummed. How powerful would it have felt when the waters still stood here?

"This hall," Bhumika murmured, awed. She turned, a slow arc that allowed her to take in the curving walls, the tessellated stone of the floor, opening like a flower—and the ring of ghostly water-drenched figures that now circled her. At her side, Jeevan saw none of them—only tracked her movement with his eyes, as his other hand rested close to his saber, wary of threats. Ever since the Aloran prince had raised his dagger, Jeevan had been on alert.

Beyond the crescent of her ghosts, the villagers huddled together, no threat to her at all. Only the Aloran prince carried a weapon, sheathed at his belt with his hand on the hilt, and he was looking at her—and her slow, awed movement—with confusion.

"Do you not feel it, Prince Rao?" Bhumika asked.

Rao shook his head.

"No, Elder Bhumika," he said. "I don't understand."

Elder. That word again. She let it slip away unquestioned. Now was not the time to worry about her past.

It was not the watchers who guided her this time but her own good sense. Her gaze lowered to the strange stone dagger still at his waist. It was only when he'd dropped the blade that his eyes had shone, and she had felt the knowledge in her stir in recognition of that light.

"The dagger you carry," Bhumika said. "The one made of dark stone. Lay it on the ground."

Rao did not move. So Bhumika said mildly, "Do you think I will seize it from you? Give it to one of your soldiers if you prefer."

Another heartbeat passed, and then he removed the dagger from his belt and held it out to one of his men, who took it from him. She saw him inhale, and saw his eyes widen. Starry light flared in his eyes, then faded once more.

"What is this place?" Rao asked.

"This is what makes the monastery sacred, Prince Rao." The head priest entered the room, his vast voice preceding him. "A sacred lake lay here in the Age of Flowers. Those who gazed into it fell directly into the arms of the nameless—into visions vast enough to drive them to madness." He shook his head. "Common folk claim that it lies beyond the forest, in a caravanserai. But what remains of it lies beneath us."

He walked farther into the hall. Without pause and without awareness, he stepped through one of the ghostly watchers. He did not feel them. He bent forward, reverently touching a hand to the ground. "Divyanshi prayed here," he said. "When she departed, the water departed with her."

From the corner of her eye, Bhumika saw Manjeet sharply nudge one of the women beside her. Bit by bit, the group lowered their heads in reverence.

The head priest did not appear to have noticed their previous lack of piety, or its sudden arrival. His focus was on Bhumika.

"My priests say you claim a yaksa is coming," he said.

"I only claim the truth," Bhumika said, inclining her head in respect. "The forest speaks more strongly than my words could. You see what has become of it."

"Yes." A pause. She saw disgust and hope war on his face. "You can kill a yaksa?"

"I can share the knowledge of how it can be done," she said. "I cannot do so myself."

"Daughter," he said formally. "You came here to seek the help of the holiest priests of the nameless. If you can demonstrate your power, you have it." Behind him, more priests entered the room—blue-garbed and solemn.

She should have been exultant to have the trust of the head priest. But her eyes were drawn inexorably to Rao—to this man with eyes that held a flame, who felt the power of this dead lake so strongly that even now he trembled, unable to look away from her in turn.

"Prove yourself," the head priest said. "Prove you are no trickster, no charlatan or madwoman." A twist to his mouth. "I implore you."

"The yaksa will wake and come here," said Bhumika. "It will come to destroy your sacred monastery, and this sacred space." *It will come for me*, she did not say. That was the truth that would serve her like a knife to her own throat. "I can give you no proof that will not require you to face it."

The head priest's face hardened. But Bhumika looked once again at Rao.

"Prince Rao," she called, and felt the strangeness of her own voice—as rich as it had been when she'd begged outside the monastery, when only the young priest had heeded her. "What do you see?"

"Fire," he said. His voice sounded rough. "I see fire. And I see the dark of the nameless. And I see the—void. I see terrible danger ahead." His voice broke a little upon that word. He met her eyes. "And you, Elder Bhumika?"

"I see your faith," said Bhumika. "And I know it will guide you."

He flinched at that. He swore, shaping the words without sound. Then he said, abruptly, "I believe her."

"Prince Rao," the head priest said, his voice low with concern. "Do you—"

Rao shook his head, speaking again.

"The nameless speaks in many ways, in many forms. Through visions, yes. But through other means, too. Through instinct. Through our sages and our teachers. Our parents. Through a man's flesh, and a woman's voice." He stopped, turning to face the head priest—who flinched, as if struck by the flames of Rao's eyes. "The nameless speaks," he said finally. "And you—*we*—are failing to heed our god." He touched a hand to his chest. "I feel it."

The earth shuddered again. One of the boys whimpered, and Manjeet clenched him tight, looking at Bhumika and only Bhumika with a demand in her eyes.

"I feel the nameless too," Ishan said. He took a step forward. "Lady," he continued. "When you prayed I felt our god. I know I am not alone." He looked at his fellow priests then. "Brothers. You felt it. How could you not? We were meant to be here. We were meant to learn from her, and save our people from the yaksa."

A ripple of agreement ran through the priesthood. Not all. But enough. The head priest's expression was unreadable, his eyes hard. But he said, heavily, hopefully, "I obey my god."

The villagers were told to leave the room, urged away by guards. They would be hidden away in the far end of the monastery, where they would hopefully be safe from what was to come. The younger priests insisted the head priest Sunder join them. "For your safety, and the future of the monastery," Ishan insisted earnestly—and the head priest relented.

Manjeet gave Bhumika a grave nod in farewell as she guided Gulnar out. Bidisha waited until last—and walked a few determined steps toward Bhumika before stopping.

"You are a curse," Bidisha said. Her voice trembled. Her gaze darted from the priests and soldiers back to Bhumika. But there was defiance in her eyes, too. Bravely, she said, "You drew this evil here. I am no priest, no noble lord or lady, but I know we cannot trust you."

"You should not be in this room for what will follow," Bhumika said gently. "Go with the guards. Keep your people safe. You will not see me again, and I am grateful for the kindness you and your people showed me."

Bidisha's mouth thinned. She shook her head, then turned and walked away. As the villagers shuffled from the hall, Prince Rao made his way toward her.

"Speak with me alone, Lady Bhumika," he said. It was an order, not a request. She nodded and followed him from the hall. She gave Jeevan a brief glance. *Wait for me*, she tried to say with her eyes. *Trust me.*

His mouth was thin with tension, but he inclined his head subtly in understanding.

Prince Rao led her to an alcove room. In the distance she could hear the footsteps of the villagers and low voices from the Aloran soldiers and the priests.

"Prince Rao," she said, before he could speak. "Your weapon. Your blade of stone. It deadens magic, does it not?"

"I was told the stone is powerful enough to fight the yaksa," he replied. "I *know* it is a tool that can hurt the servants of yaksa." He said the words levelly, his gaze probing. When she stared back at him, unable to give him the reaction he was clearly seeking, he shook his head and continued. "I had already vowed to myself that I would protect the monastery with all the weapons I have, before the head priest told me about you. I *can* fight the yaksa, and I shall."

"And yet," she said, "you spoke to the head priest on my behalf. Why use my knowledge at all, if you believe you have the key to destroying the yaksa already?"

His smile was joyless. "I cannot ignore the nameless when my god speaks," he said. "What right do I have to be so foolish?" From his tunic, he withdrew the dagger of stone. He must have taken it back from the soldier he'd handed it to and concealed it for this moment, though she did not immediately know why. It was only when he held it out with the blade toward her that she realized he planned to threaten her. His eyes, lusterless and human, were cold. "But, Lady Bhumika, I promise, if you prove yourself to be a traitor and a liar, I will put this blade through your heart myself."

She held out her hand, palm open.

"Let me see this weapon that will kill me," she said. When he did not relinquish it or place it through her heart, she said mildly, "Do you fear me so much, Prince Rao?"

"I've seen what your kind are capable of," he said. But he placed the dagger on her palm.

She felt—nothing.

Utter nothing. She was silent inside, her head no longer aching, no longer roaring with waters. The absence of magic was absolute.

She returned the dagger to him. Her hand was trembling faintly.

"The yaksa will come here," she said, after a beat, when her voice returned to her. "But I will need it pinned. Can you do so, with your weapons of stone?"

"I will try," he said.

"The yaksa will fear the stone once they feel it," Bhumika said. She hoped her own horror did not show on her face, but she was sure it did. "That will give you some advantage. And—it will be young. Newly reborn. That will help too."

He tucked his blade away, moving to go. But she could not let him leave yet.

"Prince Rao." He paused, looking at her. "Whatever happens here, I hope the villagers who traveled with me will be cared for. Their home has been destroyed. If they survive the yaksa today, they will starve tomorrow without assistance."

His cold gaze finally thawed a little.

"If we survive, I will speak to the head priest," he said, "and to a nearby highborn lord. I will ensure that they are cared for."

"Thank you," she said quietly.

"Come," he said, looking a little uncomfortable. "We need to return."

She returned to the hall. The villagers were gone. A handful of priests were waiting for her, many of them young, fervent light in their eyes.

"Kneel," she said. "We'll begin with prayer. Reach for your god."

"And you?" Ishan asked.

"Reaching for the nameless is your task. I have no gods to reach," she said. "What I need lies inside me."

She kneeled too and closed her eyes. And breathed. And breathed.

She did not leave her body. She did not, indeed, pray. She closed her eyes, and she was kneeling in darkness—empty and vast and velvet beneath her.

A lake that had once opened to the nameless god—and to the void the god resided in. Kneeling on its remains, a part of her felt the void too.

Her watchers surrounded her. Against the darkness, they glowed with deathless light.

"Will you drink?"

"Tell me what you are to me first," Bhumika said calmly. She was within the confines of her mind, where such things could be spoken.

"We are yours," said a watcher. "Your kin, temple born and temple drowned, tangled forever in the weeds of magic, carrying the knowledge you cannot carry. We are your oldest grief, forgotten."

She swallowed, seeking strength inside herself.

"I am ready to feel the weight of the knowledge now," she said to them.

"It will hurt you," said another watcher, with the voice of a terribly young child. "It will make you weep." The face that stared at her through cloth had deep black eyes, miserable hollows. "We know."

"Thank you for carrying the burden of it for me," she said gently. "Ask me your question now. I am ready. I will answer."

A chorus.

"Will you drink?"

"Yes."

"What will you drink?" Green water, red and gold flowed from their bowls and their skin.

Heart's blood. Immortality. Soul. She knew them.

"This one," she said, holding her palms open to a boy with his bowl. "I will drink this one."

A sigh like a song ran through them all.

But the boy grasping the bowl held it tighter. His knuckles, beneath the pearling water on his mottled brown skin, were pinkish with tension. "If you give them this knowledge, you condemn your own kind," he said, his voice rich with urgency. "Do not drink, sister."

"I condemn the yaksa," Bhumika said. "Only the yaksa."

"You will give these outsiders the knowledge of how to destroy Ahiranya," he said. "Not the yaksa alone. But all that Ahiranya is. All that you love." He leaned forward, and on his breath she smelled salt water. "They spared the Ahiranyi once," he said. "Human and degraded, they allowed us to continue when the Age of Flowers withered. They will not make the same mistake again. The Parijatdvipans will obliterate our people."

"I must have known this before I sacrificed all that I am," Bhumika replied, finally. "I must have believed it worth the price."

"You have a daughter." A baring of teeth beneath water-drenched cloth. "Will you be another temple-born who sacrifices her children for a greater good? You *know* what they did to us, Bhumika."

"I don't understand," she said, oddly numb.

He laughed. "One day you will. Do not give them everything," he begged. "Once you know all, keep a shard of knowledge from them. Make them vow that Ahiranya will be safe before you place the whole truth in their hands."

"Of course," she said softly. "I will make them vow, and I will also go back for my daughter. I will go back for the Ahiranyi, and I will protect them. Now. Let me drink."

"Drink if you like, then. But I know now: You will grieve, sister. Whether you know why or not, you will grieve."

Let me grieve, then, she thought. *Only let these people live.*

She held her hands out, palms cupped. Red water poured into them, spilling, falling. But she raised what she could carry to her mouth like a woman in prayer and touched her hands to her lips.

She drank. It was agony. She drank again. She thought she would choke—she could not continue. It was like swallowing knives. Her skull would split. She was grateful, suddenly, for her watchers. If she had carried this screaming ache every day of her journey, she would have died.

She drank more. More. *More.*

And finally her knowledge spoke freely to her. She knew what had to be done.

She opened her eyes and looked at the kneeling priests around her. At Jeevan standing at the entrance door, saber drawn. At Prince Rao, dulled of his light by his blade of stone. Her knowledge, full and complete, made her nauseated. She wished she could weep.

But all power required its price. When the yaksa came, everyone in the monastery would perish. Better this. Better the awful thing she carried than the death of all.

Perhaps she had been a woman capable of making hard choices once. Perhaps she still was.

Her heart twisted like a knot. She breathed deeply and released all the grief and love wound through her like gold. She looked at the priests around her and their eyes that saw deep and far. Their eyes heavy with faith.

And she said, "Let me show you how to kill a yaksa."

51

RAO

The priests had been praying for what felt like hours. Torches had guttered and been relit. The air smelled of smoke and bodies. There were no windows in this hall. Rao did not know if night had fallen or if the sun still shone beyond the dark walls. The priests and Bhumika were a crescent of bodies, gold and dark in the flickering light.

He stood at the entrance of the hall with Jeevan and his own soldiers, his heart's-shell dagger clenched in his fist. At his urging, his men had taken what heart's shell they had and bound those daggers and arrowheads to spears taken from the monastery's own guards. But he could not bring himself to do the same with his own weapon. The closer the stone was to his skin, the less he felt the pulsing voice of the nameless in his skull.

He wished he had more of his men with him. He wished he had more heart's shell. But he'd done his best. He had left one of his best archers on the monastery roof, ready to shoot a heart's-shell arrow if he saw a yaksa approach.

If the heart's shell could kill the yaksa outright, that would be... easier. But he did not think it likely. Still, better to try than not.

Rao moved his dagger hilt back and forth in his palm: slow, even motions, as he tried to keep himself calm. Jeevan did not seem to need anything to ground him. He stood there calmly, one hand on his saber, the other neatly behind him.

Rao gestured to one of his men. At his unspoken urging, the soldier removed a spare heart's-shell blade from his belt and placed it in Rao's hand.

"Here," Rao said, and held it out to Jeevan. "Make your own spear. You'll be of more use properly armed."

Jeevan eyed it without any expression, but he took it after a moment and nodded his thanks.

Rao turned away, fixing his gaze on Bhumika again. Her eyes, previously closed, were now open and fixed on the door.

The ground shook—a deep tremor. In flashes of shadow and golden light, he saw green things begin to worm through the stone walls. His men hissed and cursed, stepping away from the edges of the room.

"The yaksa is coming," Bhumika said. "Do not stop praying."

The priests were chanting mantras, their voices swelling to fill the room.

There was a groan like the splintering of wood and stone. A guttural cry followed, so wild and alien that it made a chill run down Rao's spine.

The man Rao had sent to the roof had possessed a conch to sound in warning. No warning note had been blown. Either the man was dead, or the yaksa had crawled through the stone foundations of the monastery into its innards without ever walking across the threshold. Rao had been a fool to think it would approach like a person.

The ground shook harder, cracks spidering along the ancient walls. Rao gripped his dagger tighter and watched as the soldiers around him readied their spears. Sweat was crawling down his neck.

The yaksa appeared at the entrance of the hall, limned in shadow. It smelled powerfully of petrichor and blood. It had a human shape and an uncannily human face, but its eyes were clusters of shells, its body all roots packed with wormy soil.

Rao could not have moved if he had tried. A cold horror settled over his limbs, holding him for one second that stretched like lifetimes.

The yaksa only had eyes for Bhumika, who kneeled calm and unmoving in her crescent of priests. Their prayers had faltered, ebbing like water.

"I feel you," the yaksa said. Its voice clinked like bones, rattling in his ears. "Temple child. Broken husk. I felt you from beneath the soil. Where is the other?" A turn of that head; a snapping, creaking noise of stone. "I felt the stronger one but they are—gone. There is only you. Will you take me home?" the yaksa asked, stumbling forward. It sounded as hopeful as a child. "Why are you here, kin? Above dead waters?"

Bhumika met the yaksa's eyes.

"Surely you know," she said. Her voice hardened. "Hold the yaksa in place. *Now.*"

Her order broke their awe and terror as well as a blade. Rao's warriors surged forward.

The yaksa *screamed*, and the ground trembled so violently that Rao almost lost his footing. He heard the clang of at least one spear falling. Roots burst through the walls, lashing out at anything and anyone they could touch. There was a bang as one of his men was flung bodily against the opposite wall, then dropped to the floor. The priests were still kneeling, praying frantically.

Rao went cold, then focused. He had trained as a warrior in Harsinghar alongside Aditya and Prem, trained in sabers first and foremost. But he had still been a prince of Alor, bred to Aloran warfare, and he had kept his heart's shell in dagger form for a reason beyond fear. He knew how to throw a dagger.

He aimed for a difficult target—the throat. The dagger left his hand. For a moment he was not sure it would meet its mark. Time stretched into vastness.

Then he heard the thud of the blade. The yaksa stumbled, blade jutting from its throat.

His men leapt.

Four spears pierced the yaksa, and four soldiers held those spears in place, their knuckles white with tension and their faces blanched with terror. Jeevan was one of those men, arms trembling with the strain. The heart's shell made the yaksa howl. Around those spears it bled green-black blood, thick gouts that spilled and flowered into vines on the stone floor.

"We cannot hold it for long," Jeevan bit out.

"We don't need long," Bhumika replied.

"You," the yaksa gasped. Its hand stretched out toward Bhumika. "Why would you betray your own? Your kin?"

"Think of the nameless," Bhumika called, not meeting its eyes. "Call upon the nameless in your heart."

"I felt Mani Ara," the yaksa said, its voice a wet creak of splintered wood—of insects in wood marrow, eating it whole. "I felt my mother. Where is she? You are not her. A single flicker of her, and now she is gone."

"Open yourself to the nameless," Bhumika said, her hands tight upon her knees. "Think of nothing else. Be *empty*."

"Temple child," the yaksa gasped. "You're broken from the waters—torn from your roots. You are empty, and dead in all the ways that matter." It tried to worm closer; it was weeping, its tears sap and rot and blood. "But I came here for you," it said, its voice yearning—frighteningly human. "I came here for kin. Are we not bound, little one? Are we not family to one another, born from the same waters?"

The pressure in the temple was growing stronger and stronger. It reminded him of the snowstorm he and Sima had been caught in when they had traveled beyond the Lal Qila: a sudden dimming of light, a hush in the air, a growing silence, heavy, like a breath waiting to be exhaled. There was no darkening sky here, but the glow of the lanterns looked oddly blue. In its lights, the priests and the worshippers were colored in the indigo of deep waters. Most of them had their eyes closed, hands clasped, and faces lowered.

In the center of it all, the yaksa writhed like a landed fish, all its limbs contorting at awful angles.

He kept his eyes on it. He knew it was foolish. And yet...

No heart's shell was touching him anymore. Fire, as if it had been waiting, began to bank behind his eyes. It was the fire that urged him to tilt his head toward Bhumika instead.

Bhumika was sitting straight and tall, knees tucked beneath her, her shoulders back. Her expression was not calm—it was tense, her brow furrowed, her jaw set.

The shadows were moving strangely around her. He watched them move, flickering with the lantern light. Twisting, reshaping. Figures, they looked like figures, veiled and strange.

Those are not real shadows, his mind whispered. *You are not seeing them with your eyes.*

The vision is within you.

"When you have faith, you become a vessel," said Bhumika, her voice stretching across the hall. "You empty yourself. You became a living void where a god may land—as easily as a leaf on waters. Pray as Divyanshi prayed over the waters of your monastery. You have in you what she possessed—not holy blood, but *faith*. It is all she had, and all you need. Pray for this yaksa's death. Pray for cleansing fire." Her voice trembled, and Rao realized she was weeping. "And—and know that the price is all that you are. If you are willing to pay it, then *pray*."

He blinked sharply, his pupils burning. Then he squeezed his own eyes shut.

Darkness built behind his eyes, in his skull. Not pain but a pressing, inexorable thing. A storm, an inevitable coming—

He had shared a vision of the nameless with Aditya once. In it, he'd seen the yaksa. Their flowering eyes, their bodies pressing through the soil. Now he saw no soil, no plants, no monstrous deities. Only the darkness, pressing upon him, trying to crack him open, to seep through him. It felt like it could destroy him. All he had to do was welcome it. Lay down his whole self and say yes. Yes.

The darkness was the nameless. Surely it was. He heard a sound, impossible and vast, a hundred thousand voices twining together as one. *Let us in, let us in, let us—*

No.

The pressure evaporated.

Rao's eyes snapped open.

At the outer edge of their circle, one of the youngest of the priests of the nameless was convulsing. Ishan, he realized. It was Ishan. Hands scrabbling the ground, opening and closing. His head beating the soil. Someone cried out in alarm. Bhumika held up a hand, and they fell swiftly silent.

More convulsions. The sound of heaved, desperate breath escaping a throat. Then Ishan abruptly stilled.

Slowly, he raised his head.

His eyes were blazing. All light. It hurt to look at him, so Rao lowered his head and watched the shadows writhe instead. He felt nauseated.

He hadn't let the nameless in. Ishan had.

The priests bowed immediately. They knew the nameless as Rao did: in their marrow, their lungs, their beating hearts. Rao bowed with them, placing his palms against the cold ground. He heard the rasp of Ishan's throat; heard the god in the skin of a priest begin to speak.

A voice left Ishan. It was the voice of the nameless, grating and deep, a wild thing so huge it made Rao freeze, like an animal in a snare.

The words made the ground tremble and the world... *rewrite*.

A gurgle of blood. The sudden roar of a body engulfed by flame. The yaksa and Ishan were both wreathed in fire. The yaksa screamed, a wild and ruined noise.

Rao scrambled up onto his knees, then his feet. It was too late. Ishan lay dead, his eyes bloody holes, his mouth tongueless, his body burned almost beyond recognition.

Around them, the rot was gone. The yaksa was dead too—a husk of charred wood, empty of life. A set of sapless limbs. A face hollowed out and empty. A face that was a mask.

"There, you see," Bhumika said, her own eyes open now, her face calm under the salt tracks of her tears. She met Rao's own gaze, and he saw the exultation there, but also sorrow. "It is straightforward enough. All magic demands sacrifice. A life for a gift." She rose and crossed the temple. Leaned down, and with grave tenderness shut Ishan's empty, ruined eyes. "To destroy a god," she said to her hushed audience, her worshippers, her people, "you require the strength of another god. And now—if you are a true worshipper, if a god holds your heart—you have it."

She looked up. At him.

"This is the knowledge you must carry, Prince Rao," she said. "To your empress. To your priests. This is why the nameless sent you."

A shudder ran through Rao as he looked at the body.

Aditya. The gold light of fire. The gold light fracturing his dreams—

This should have been your burden, Aditya.

But Rao was all that was left.

He was suddenly sure, deep in his own marrow, that the nameless had a purpose for him yet.

Bhumika did not even flinch when he stumbled to his feet, when he ordered his men to restrain her and Jeevan for travel back to Parijat. She told Jeevan not to attack even as he reached for his sword, his jaw tight and face thunderous.

"She saved you all," Jeevan said. "To imprison her for it—"

"She is still what she is," Rao snapped. "I can't simply let her go."

"Lower your weapon, Jeevan," Bhumika ordered, her voice even. "There are too many of them."

Jeevan hesitated. But he lowered his spear and removed his saber, laying them on the ground under the watch of Rao's soldiers.

Rao met Bhumika's eyes. "The empress will have need of you," Rao said. And, wretchedly, "I'm sorry. Your power...I have to take you."

One of Rao's men brought a heart's-shell blade forward. "My lord," he said, voice low. "We don't have cuffs of heart's shell, but if we bind a blade to her clothing..."

"No," Bhumika said immediately, blanching. "Prince Rao, I beg you. No."

Guilt thumped sickly through his body at the sight of her fear.

"Leave her be," he ordered. "Metal to bind her is enough. Elder Bhumika, if you harm us, we will use the heart's shell on you. Do you understand?"

"I do," she said.

Jeevan was bound first. As Rao's men brought in a second, smaller pair of cuffs, Bhumika stared at Rao with exhausted eyes, swaying on her feet.

"I knew I would meet someone who would help me," murmured Bhumika. "I thought it would be a priest. A person of the faith of the nameless. But it was you, in the end," she said, with a mirthless smile. "Is the nameless the one who speaks to you, Prince Rao? Or does another god call you across the void?" She looked away, closing her eyes. "I suppose we will know soon enough," she murmured as the cuffs closed around her wrists.

52

PRIYA

They were taking her to Parijat. They had to be.

Malini's soldiers had placed her in an enclosed cart. The one high lattice carved crudely into the wood wasn't close enough or large enough to let her see the landscape they were passing, and the jolt and rumble of the wheels and the clatter of the horses made it hard to hear anything that would allow her to orient herself—no rush of river water or noises of local villages.

And thanks to the magical stone cuffs now at her wrists, no green.

She hadn't expected how losing it would make her feel, but it was...disorienting. She knew what she was meant to feel—but when she reached for it, constantly and compulsively, there was nothing there.

She slept a great deal. She was fairly sure the food she was given wasn't drugged, but boredom made it hard to do anything else. The only time she saw other people was when her food was brought, or when she was taken out at swordpoint to relieve herself. Which was a kindness, she supposed.

Over time, her guards grew more lax. Sometimes she heard them talking as they directed her cart—voices rising and falling in casual murmurs. She learned the name of the stone that controlled her.

Heart's shell. Why was it called that? It was a strange name.

Perhaps it sounded different when it was said in a language that wasn't Zaban.

The cuffs at her wrist and the single ankle chain of heart's shell were impossible to ignore. They clanked whenever she moved—and because she was on a literal moving cart, she moved frequently. Once, in a thin knife-slant of sunlight, she'd examined the links. No metal—apart from the lock at her ankle bone—held the chains together. It was pure, whittled rock, smoothed to a gleaming shine.

What was even harder to ignore was the pressure in her own head. She could feel the yaksa trying to reach her. Sometimes she woke and felt the ghost of their touch on her still—flat, lidless eyes, and hands reaching, and mouths of bark and thorn shaping her name. Trying to call her back to them.

They couldn't. Not with the stone at her wrists.

Malini was clearly making good use of her heart's shell. The guards carried it; their blades were edged with it, and they wore it around their throats. Just like Ahiranyi once wore beads of sacred wood, Priya realized, and almost laughed at the realization. They were no different from each other really, underneath the thousands of ways that they were. They all feared something in the dark, something they could only keep at bay but never vanquish.

The door opened. A figure entered, up onto the cart's creaking wood. And Priya—straightened.

"Sima," she breathed.

Sima took one step farther in. Joy shot through Priya. Sima was alive. Sima was *safe*. Sima was—

"Pri," she replied. Her smile was strained. Her eyes were damp, shiny. Both her hands were curled into fists at her sides. *Careful,* her face said.

The cart was still. It was quiet enough that Priya could hear the movement of bodies around it. Guards, listening in.

Sima was dressed like an Aloran woman, in a narrow churidar and a loose man's-style tunic. No shawl. Her face was sun-dark, golden at the nose and cheeks. She looked as strong as she'd always looked, but she also looked...

She looked like she didn't smile as much anymore.

"Are you hurt?" Sima asked, after a beat of silence. "Do those... are they hurting you?" She gestured at the heart's shell at Priya's wrists.

"No," Priya said. "They just chafe a little. Sima, I'm so glad you're safe. And I've missed you." She swallowed. "I really have."

"Oh, Pri. I..." She stopped and shook her head. "You killed Romesh," she said. "Or I was told you had. Did you...?"

A thump of grief and guilt in her chest.

"I did," Priya said. "It was not my weapon, but it was my fault."

Sima lowered her head.

"I'm not going to make excuses," Priya said quietly. "But I am sorry. You have the right to be angry with me."

"Of course I am," Sima said, her voice low. She raised her head. Her eyes were damp. "I'm so angry at you. I don't think I could ever forgive you. You—you did that. And you *left* me."

Priya nodded, her own throat tight.

"I did," she said.

"You're awful," Sima said. "An absolute shit." She rubbed her knuckles over her eyes, her wet face, roughly. "Try to do what the empress wants. Please, Pri. Don't die now. I'll never forgive you."

Priya wanted to reach for her, wanted to draw her into a rough hug so both of them could cry in the ugly, awful way you could only cry with a friend. Instead she raised her hands and clumsily wiped her own eyes.

"I'll do my best," said Priya. "But for now... tell the guards, or the empress, or whoever let you come here—I won't offer you anything useful. If the empress wants answers, she must speak to me herself."

She'd seen Sima alive and healthy. She knew Sima was well.

That was enough.

53

PRIYA

Her prison in Parijat was more comfortable than she'd expected. There was a bed. A window. Slack on her ankle chain. Really, she couldn't complain.

It took two days, judging by the movement of the guards and the rise and fall of the sun, for Malini to come to her.

Malini waited until it was late night, dark apart from a few crackling lanterns, the glow of a guard's cheroot. The door was thrown open and something pushed through it. She heard Malini's voice:

"Leave us."

No protests. Only footsteps.

She heard the whisper of skirts. A clink of something against stone. She stood. Stepped forward.

On the ground, beyond the door, under a slant of watery light from through the bars...

"Wine," Priya said out loud. She'd never hungered for wine, not really—but now she craned forward and snatched up the bottle. It was cold in her hands; it had clearly been stored in darkness, just like her. She opened it, the smell meeting her nose: sharpness, acid, and beneath that, something deep and mellow that made her mouth water.

She raised her head, meeting Malini's eyes through the lattice. She offered her a smile, sharp with teeth. "Be honest with me,

Malini," she said. "Is it laced with needle-flower? Poisoned? Have we swapped roles? Will a sip of this kill me?"

Malini did not speak, but her shoulders did stiffen. Her face went tight. It made Priya laugh, something bitter and malicious cracking in her chest. What else could she do but laugh? "You have to admit it feels like something you would do," Priya said through her own laughter. "I know you well enough to know that."

She lifted it to her mouth and drank. And drank. She could only hear the blood in her own skull. The click of her own throat.

"Well? Have you decided if I've poisoned you yet?"

Malini's voice.

"If you wanted to kill me there are simpler ways," Priya said, leaning her head back against the wall. The stone was cool under her skull. "You could have strangled me. You could have slit my throat."

"Yes." Malini's voice would have been unreadable to someone else. But Priya could hear the anger in it. She'd learned the song of Malini a long time ago. The language was still with her, in her. "That would be simple. Swift."

"Oh, and you don't like swift, do you? Not for your enemies." *Not for me.* She took another deep slug of wine. She hadn't eaten much earlier of the food her guards had practically kicked into the room. She knew the wine was going to hit her hard, like a fist. She wasn't entirely sure she cared. Seeing Malini there had already set a fire in her blood—left her furious and elated, a sharp and shivering nerve of a woman. "Well, there are other ways to kill me slowly too. You could leave me down here alone to starve. You could torture me. You could hold the knife yourself. You'd probably enjoy that."

Malini said nothing. Perhaps she was imagining the pleasure of that act. Perhaps she was disgusted.

"Don't pretend you wouldn't," Priya said finally.

"I didn't say a word," Malini replied. Her voice was terrible in its calm—in the anger rising under that apparent serenity, a dark fist, a clenched thing. "You dreamt with me. You know what I want. What I feel."

Priya thought of Malini's hands on her mouth, and her knife parting Priya's ribs, blood and flowers blooming in its wake. She thought of the gentleness of Malini's mouth, the demand of her hands on Priya's waist, her thighs.

"I've read what I can of your Birch Bark Mantras," Malini said. "Are there any tales beyond the Birch Bark Mantras, Priya, of the cruelty of your yaksa? The evil of them?" Malini was leaning forward, all the tension in her face sharpening her gaze, her voice, to a blade. "So many soft, tender tales of love, and none of them true."

"Tender? Soft? I thought you of all people would understand the tales better than that," Priya said. "You can love something knowing it can destroy you. Maybe you love it more for it."

Malini's mouth tightened.

"Once, I read those tales to better know you. And now—"

"Now you still don't know me," Priya cut in.

Malini stared back at her. "Then *let* me know you. Why did you let me take you?"

Maybe that was why Malini had given her the liquor. Not out of kindness—Priya had never truly believed it was out of kindness—nor out of a desire to poison Priya. Maybe Malini had just wanted to unspool her, untether her—to leave her light and open and more likely to speak foolishly. To let something slip that she couldn't afford for Malini to know.

Something like *I let you take me. I let you. I'm using you too, Malini, my love, biding my time—*

"I learned firsthand in Srugna that you finally have a weapon that will kill us without killing you," Priya said. "Congratulations." She drank again. Courage. Leaned forward. "Your heart's shell might be enough to kill the yaksa. I want to help you use it."

"You want to help me," Malini said flatly. "*You.* I know how the yaksa are written into you. In your magic, your nature, your faith, and your history." Her hand curled around one of the bars. "Don't lie to me, Priya. You're no good at it."

"I'm not lying," said Priya.

"You betrayed me for your yaksa. Rot spreads across Parijat-dvipa, and my people are dying. You should be happy. Why would you help me now?"

"Because the rot infects Ahiranyi people too," said Priya. "Our fields. Our flesh. I've learned...I understand..." A deep breath, mind swimming. "If the yaksa succeed, everyone will be rot-riven. Everything and everyone that matters to you and to me will be lost. I can't allow that. So I'm here."

"When I win, Priya," Malini said slowly, "there will be no Ahiranya. My people want to obliterate your land, and I see little reason not to allow it."

"*When*," Priya repeated, mockery curling her mouth. "There's no *when*, Malini. You've lost your war. The yaksa already have the world, don't they? You told me yourself. The rot is all over the empire. If you want to destroy the yaksa, you need my knowledge. No one in the world knows the yaksa like I do. You need me. And in return, you'll need to ensure that the Ahiranyi people survive. How can you reject a bargain like that?"

Malini's mouth thinned.

"Fine," Malini said. "Let's play at negotiating. Let's pretend there is a way through this, where I do more than leave you to molder here in the dark, forgotten."

Priya grinned at her and watched Malini stare at the shape of her mouth—the gleam of her teeth in the half dark.

"Thank you, Malini," she said. "That's all I want."

54

GANAM

Ever since Priya had vanished, the yaksa had turned into monsters.

"They were always monsters," Khalida whispered when he told her. She was sorting through the temple children's laundry. She'd roped one of the youngest into the task of scrubbing, and Pallavi was doing a great job of *not* washing anything and simply swimming in the bucket.

"They can hear you even if you whisper," he told her, and she glared at him and vowed not to speak to him again. She broke that vow seconds later, of course.

But the yaksa had become worse. Crueler. When Ganam and the others returned from Alor without Priya, Ganam had groveled. *We couldn't find the yaksa in Alor without her, ancient ones. We looked for her, searched, but she was gone. Please, forgive us. I fought her, I begged her to come home, but she broke my arm, fled from me. I don't have the strength of a thrice-born; there was nothing I could do.*

Please.

And still, the youngest yaksa, dragged free from Srugna's soil by Priya's own hands, had taken one of Ganam's men and torn him apart like an insect. Ganam could still smell the blood, hear the screaming.

He pushed the thought away, and the dark nausea that came with it. He wasn't much for wallowing, but it was hard to avoid it.

The yaksa often had their eyes on Ganam. Hungry. Desperate, maybe. He was their last twice-born. But he made a good show of his broken arm, telling them he was in pain. He could not fight with a broken arm, and he could not enter the waters again. What did they know of human suffering, human bones? It wasn't hard to convince them.

When they left him alone, he did what Priya had begged him to and built paths.

It wasn't easy. It was hard, winding the magic throughout the forest, bending routes that would lead Ahiranyi out of the country. Every attempt left him covered in sweat, nauseated with his mind full of roaring water. But he marked each path carefully, and spread the word with even more care: There were now ways out of Ahiranya. If people were quiet—if they traveled in small groups and took little with them—they stood a chance of escaping.

Common, normal people stood a chance of slipping away beneath the yaksa's notice. He knew the rest of them didn't. And yet he looked at the temple children and wanted more for them. He looked at Rukh and Padma and felt his heart turn over, hot like a coal.

It would be nearly impossible to get them away from Ahiranya without the yaksa noticing. He was pondering the problem, staring at the children, when Khalida gently touched his arm with a laundry-damp hand.

"You're talking to me now?" Ganam asked.

"If you need help, Ganam, you should talk to us," Khalida said. "To me."

Fuck. Well, maybe he hadn't been as subtle as he'd tried to be.

"The yaksa," he said. "I wasn't joking, they can see everything, hear everything." At least when he'd been rebelling against the empire, he'd known when people were spying on him. People, he could spot. A god listening through the leaves was a trickier prospect. "Sometimes they will and sometimes they won't, but I'm not putting you all at risk."

"I am afraid every day," Khalida said, voice shaky. "Aren't we all? If there is something I can do—if you *are* doing something to defy them—I want to do it. I want to help. Billu has said the same. There are so many of us, Ganam. Let us try."

Ganam swore under his breath. He didn't want to say yes, but the truth was he was tired. He needed the help. And who was he to decide who got to fight and who didn't?

"The next time Billu needs supplies from the bazaar, tell him to get them himself," he said. "And tell him if he sees anyone who wants out of Ahiranya to take them to the trees to the east— where the banyan grows. Tell them to wait there until nightfall. I'll do the rest."

Group after group of people fled Ahiranya through the paths Ganam built. Groups of strangers, thin and frightened, huddling between the trees, flinching when Ganam arrived without even a torch in hand to guide them. He led them to the paths—told them to go without looking back, to walk until they were free.

He wasn't good at putting people at ease or persuading them to do what he wanted. But they were desperate folk, and even a big man with a broken arm telling them to run into the forest was better than nothing.

He returned one night to find Ashish waiting for him. That temple child, the oldest of them, was trembling.

"Khalida told me to wait for you," he said, and Ganam cursed Khalida internally. Why was she involving the children? "Ruchi's dying," said Ashish. "The yaksa says she's too weak to become once-born, and they won't give her any more waters broken from the source. You need to help her."

He went to the yaksa first. They were often on the Hirana, or *in* the Hirana, and today the waters of the sangam led him to the remains of the orchard. Three of the yaksa stood together. A fourth was kneeling, her body bare. The sight made him pause. He could see the shape of it—the curve of breasts, and the angles of hips and chest—and didn't want to see any more, especially if he'd be gutted for it. But there was something strange about her torso. A redness; a sap more red than green.

"...fire," one was saying, and the word made the trees shudder, recoiling.

"Felt the death..."

"What do I care of fire? Look what has become of me," the woman yaksa was wailing, her voice jagged. "And it will come for you all, I know it. We changed the world for us, but the world is changing us back, and I *cannot*—"

The leaves rustled around him. Ganam froze.

"Leave," said the yaksa with Ashok's face. His gaze was flatter than ever—cold. "You are not welcome here."

Ganam bowed his head. The yaksa glided past.

As soon as the yaksa was gone, he fled.

He had not asked for a vial of deathless water.

Too late now. There was no point begging the yaksa. He ran to Bhumika's study and searched the room, clumsy and one-handed, until to his relief he found the last of the vials Priya had hidden, a cracked and half-full thing. It would have to do.

He went to the sickroom. Khalida and Shyam were by the woman's bedside. Ruchi's head rolled as she tried to look at him, so he walked into her line of sight.

"I have something for you, Ruchi," Ganam said.

She tried to speak. Her mouth made no sound.

When he'd been a rebel against the empire, he'd seen other rebels die from the broken waters. Many had reached the point where no water could save them.

That was how Ruchi, hazy-eyed with pain, looked to him.

But he kneeled down by her charpoy anyway, gently raised her head in the cradle of his palm, and fed her the vial of deathless water.

"There," he said, lowering her head. "Rest."

Shyam leaned against the wall, his eyes fixed on Ruchi. His face was bleak. Khalida stroked Ruchi's hair. Ganam watched the oil lamp on the window. The flicker of the flame.

Ruchi was gone before the light died.

*   *   *

They were all running out of time. He knew that.

It wouldn't be long until the yaksa flung him into the waters again. And he'd die. He was sure of it. Then the yaksa would turn to the children—fling them into the waters to see who'd rise and who'd drown. They would kill so many, and there would be no one left to protect them.

He caught Rukh alone.

"You know I've been building paths out," he said. Rukh looked away. "Rukh, don't lie. I know you've followed me."

"I thought I was better at spying," Rukh muttered.

"I'm afraid you're shit at it," Ganam said a little gruffly, to hide how he wanted to bury his face in his hands and never move again. Fuck the yaksa. And fuck Priya too for leaving this mess to him.

"Rukh," he said. "It's not going to be long until it isn't safe here. You have to go. Take Padma." Rukh opened his mouth, and he gripped Rukh's arm with his good hand. Let his desperation bleed through. "Do it for Padma," he said. "Survive. There's no hope here."

"How are we going to survive outside Ahiranya?" Rukh asked. "I've got rot. And Padma's so small. We'll die."

"You're stronger than you realize," Ganam said. "I believe in you. Priya believed in you. Hold on to that, boy. You'll make it through."

"You're just saying that to make me go," said Rukh. "You don't really think that. What about the others? Ashish? And the smaller ones? They should come too."

Ganam shook his head.

"The yaksa watch them more closely than they watch you and her. You're not temple children. Use that in your favor."

Rukh frowned.

"We'll go when we've got no choice," said Rukh. "Not a second before. You can't force me to run, Ganam. I won't leave them. I've got to help them. They miss their families and they're not strong yet, you know? Not like Priya is—was. They need me."

"When I tell you that it's time—"

"I'll go," Rukh said. "But not before."

"Fine," Ganam said. "Fuck. Fine."

There was a blade still buried near the bower of bones. Something that could, perhaps, hurt the yaksa. Something that had hurt him.

He'd dig it out tomorrow. He'd ask Billu to carry it for him. It wouldn't hurt Billu like it had hurt him. Rukh and the others were going to need all the protection they could get.

55

MALINI

She ordered Sahar to rest, despite her own sleeplessness. She knew she would not close her own eyes tonight.

Deepa had come to her. Her quietest advisor had slipped into her chambers with serious eyes and a copied letter, carefully transcribed, at hand.

"Lady Varsha wrote to Lady Raziya," she said, watching Malini read the missive. "I think... Empress, I think she assumed Raziya would be so angry about the Jagatay that she would betray you. But it was a foolish thing to do. I do not think Lady Raziya would betray you for anything."

Foolish was right. And disappointing. It proved how sheltered Varsha had been as the High Prince's daughter, and then as Chandra's bride. *If Chandra had lived, his court would have eaten you whole, sister-in-law*, Malini thought bitterly. *You are lucky that I am kinder than he ever was.*

"The original message was still sent?"

"Yes, my lady. Weeks ago." Hesitation. "Lady Raziya and a retinue have been seen at the borders of Harsinghar. If you..."

"I will meet her," said Malini, "whenever she comes."

There was no other reason for sleeplessness. Certainly not Priya. She hadn't dreamt with Priya since the moment she'd placed heart's shell around Priya's throat, but now she'd seen Priya in the flesh and heard her barbed voice—

Ah, she could not lie to herself. She feared what dreams or nightmares sleep would bring her. That was the truth.

She heard a sharp rap at the door. Sahar opened it, her face flushed from running.

"I told you to rest," Malini said.

"Lady Raziya is here," Sahar said. "She says she must speak to you urgently."

Raziya must have exhausted her horses and her retinue to reach here so swiftly.

"Let her in," said Malini. "Wait outside."

Sahar stepped to the side and allowed her old mistress entrance.

Raziya swept into the room alone, no attendants with her. She was not dressed in light cloth suitable to Srugna's weather but in Dwarali clothing—a thick salwar kameez, draped over with a blue wool-lined jacket. Her clothing was stained at the hems with dust. Her cheeks were red from wind and heat, her eyes fierce when they settled upon Malini. She bowed.

"Empress," she said. "We must speak."

Malini nodded once.

"Sit," she said. "I will have someone bring you tea. Something to eat."

"I don't require food or drink," Raziya said.

"Will you face me at such a low ebb in your strength?" Malini asked. "I know why you're here, Lady Raziya."

Raziya sat, stiff-backed. When a servant brought her refreshments she drank and ate without looking at what lay before her.

"I told my husband I would speak with you first," Raziya said.

"And what," said Malini, "will you tell him we discussed?"

"My daughter sent me a swift courier some time ago," said Raziya. "The courier carried a message that told me Prince Rao had left with a woman from beyond the walls of the empire. That he had made promises, on behalf of his empress, in return for a gift. Promises of Dwarali land, to an outsider my husband's bloodline have loyally kept at bay. Tell me. Have you offered the land you granted to my husband, my children, to a Jagatay king?"

"A portion of land," Malini said steadily.

"It was not yours to give."

"The sultanate was not mine to give either, Lady Raziya," Malini said. "And yet I did."

She explained the need of it, and what the Jagatay had given in return. But Raziya's ire did not fade.

"On the journey here I had many dark thoughts," Raziya said, her low voice trembling. "I was exultant when you promised my husband the sultanate. I was glad, too, that it could be done without war, only a transference by death—but I would have accepted war, for that glory. But I thought, ah—perhaps the empress does not wish my family to have the power of the breadth of Dwarali, the Lal Qila to the city-state where the sultan's mahal sits. Perhaps she wishes to carve up our power to weaken us."

If Malini had intended such a thing, she would have acted far more subtly and slowly. It did not seem entirely wise to say so.

"No, Raziya," she said, placing courtesies aside. "You and Lord Khalil have fought loyally by my side. Your people have died for me. You and I—I have thought of you as my friend." She said it honestly, letting some of her true feelings shine in her words. "I would not take the power that is rightfully yours. This cruel circumstance has fallen upon us. It cannot be helped."

"There is one thing you must consider, of course," Raziya said after a moment.

"Tell me."

"The Jagatay have made no vows to you and yours," she said. "All of us, born and reared in Parijatdvipa, know the vows made to Divyanshi upon her death. We serve your bloodline because we know she burned for us, and we venerate her great sacrifice. We honor her last wish. The Jagatay have no reason to."

"The Jagatay have promised to make their vows to me," said Malini. "They will not join our empire without solemn promises of loyalty to the empire."

The clink of Raziya's glass against the table was overly loud. "Elder Priya kneeled before you in a temple of the mothers,"

Raziya said. "She did not vow to serve the empire, but she vowed to serve *you*. And still, she harmed you." There was compassion in Raziya's voice, despite the harshness of her words.

"The vows that made us as an empire are holy," Raziya continued, gaze unflinching. "The Age of Flowers, the burning of the mothers, shaped vows between us that cannot be sundered. A vow made from fear, or for the sake of power or political gain—even a vow made for love—cannot compare. The Jagatay will be traitors one day. No matter how closely they are watched, they will turn on you, and you will be forced to break them. It is inevitable, and in the nature of humankind. It is an endless wheel, Empress. You cannot change it, nor can you stop it turning."

If Malini flinched, no one could blame her for it. She bit her own tongue. Sharp, but not enough for blood or even true pain. A simple grounding.

"It is lucky that you will watch the Jagatay carefully," Malini said. "I am indebted to you."

"Indeed," Raziya said. "You are. And I come with other news."

She drew a missive from her jacket and laid it before Malini.

"Your brother's widow seeks to commit treason," she said. "She couches it beautifully, Empress, in carefully tailored words. But nonetheless it remains true. She assumed or guessed I would be angry. She tried to make an ally of me, and of Dwarali, to support her son's early rightful claim to the throne."

Malini took the missive.

"Empress," Raziya said. "You're testing the limits of your power. The very vows it rests on. The enemy we seek to destroy. People like Lady Varsha will test your throne accordingly. She may be a fool, but you will face wiser and cannier enemies. You must be careful." She was silent for a moment, watching Malini with something like grief in her eyes. "It is a hard road you walk, as empress," she said finally. "What friends can you have, when you must always place the empire above the very people who have bled for you, fought for you, wept for you? I do not envy you."

She rose to her feet.

"Khalil will continue to serve in your army," Raziya said. "And I...I will return to Dwarali, to make sure his throne is ready for him. I know the scale of the war that lies ahead of you. I know you fight an enemy we have not seen since the Age of Flowers. But I must protect my own, Empress. And I have done my duty. On the vow made by my ancestors to yours, I always shall."

56

VARSHA

Her son had been washed and fed, wrapped in cotton, and cooed over by his mother and by a maid with a little silver rattle-drum, who shook it over his head as he tried to grasp it with clumsy little hands. "When he is older, he'll be strong, my lady," the youngest maid marveled. She was watching with a sweet smile on her face as little Vijay grasped Varsha's finger. "Look how tight he holds on!"

"He can't even grab the rattle properly," Varsha protested, but she was pleased. She wanted her son to be special. She knew her son was special. He had to be worth the trouble she had gone through for him: the physical agony of her changed body, the grief-lash of her marriage, the loneliness of her widowhood.

He had to be worth all her loss.

"He's far too small yet," one of the older nursemaids said comfortingly. "You'll see, my lady. He'll grow into a fine prince."

Crown prince, she thought. She held him tighter.

When he refused to sleep, fussing, his nursemaids placed him in his cradle and rocked him to sleep. She watched from her own bed as the older maid placed her foot to the cradle's lever, making it swing softly; as the younger one, Parul, sang a Parijati lullaby. It was some nonsense about hunting golden deer, and a tiger with a belly full of jewels, slit from throat to tail by a clever hunter with a sharp sword. A good song for her son. Something to daub his sleeping mind in the promise of glory.

She would sing him her own lullabies, she told herself. She closed her eyes, exhausted by the heat and little Vijay's demands upon her—and, always, the dull shroud of her grief. But the grief was lighter than it had been in all the long months since her brother and father had perished, and through it she grasped that small, shining possibility: Saketan lullabies for her son. Lessons hidden in small tales. The chance to shape him into an heir who would make Parijatdvipa better than the cruel thing it had become under Divyanshi's scions.

She was woken by the sound of a voice calling her name.

"Varsha," the voice said. "Sister. Wake up."

Even in the grip of sleep, Varsha knew that voice was not her brother's. She woke with her heart pounding, sweat on her skin. That voice belonged to Empress Malini, who had come in unannounced. She was sitting in Varsha's favorite chair by a low lattice window, where songbirds often came to her, flitting around in bright comfort.

There was no one else in the room. Varsha made a sound—a low, heaving thing she couldn't restrain—and scrambled up onto her feet.

"Where is my son? Where is—"

"Prince Vijay is with his nursemaids," Malini said calmly. "Walking the corridors. They are going to take him to the orchid garden, where they will show him the flowers and sit with him in the shade. I've instructed a servant to take them sherbet." The empress was entirely still in her seat, her sari a sweep of ivory and silver around her, the light carving her face into facets of brown and effigy gold. "He won't be harmed. Sit, Varsha."

Varsha, trembling, sat. She grasped for a semblance of calm. But she struggled to find it. Something was wrong. She knew something was wrong. What she did not yet know was how much danger she was in.

The empress looked unchanged. Still thin, and hollow beneath the eyes, as if exhaustion had carved itself into her flesh and bones—but also elegant, in her pale silk, her crown of white jasmine, the gleaming weight of gold draped from her ears and throat. Vaguely, Varsha had thought war would make something harsher of her, that she would return to Harsinghar in armor, smelling of blood and smoke.

But blood and smoke could be washed away, of course. And armor could be removed.

What could not be changed was the iron in Malini's eyes. Her gaze was unflinching, her mouth firm and unsmiling. There had been no softness in her voice when she'd spoken. And there continued to be no softness when she said, "You should have trusted me."

She clutched her own skirt in her hands. Tight, a tether to hold her to her own flesh.

"I do trust you, Empress," she said in a small voice. "I...I would like my son. Please."

"I was my brother Chandra's prisoner once," the empress said. "I know his nature. He hurt me. No doubt he also hurt you. I am sure your life as his bride was frightening. Even when he was kind, you feared he would turn to sudden anger. He was a storm, my brother—and he had a taste for cruelty he could not quench. I am sorry you suffered him. I am sorry we both did." A pause. "And yet you see me as your enemy," the empress murmured. "And when I visit you, you offer me only lies."

"I..." Throat dry. Heart pounding. "I have never lied to you, Empress."

"Pleasantries are lies, Lady Varsha, when they hide ill intent and a honed knife."

"I hold no ill will toward you, Empress—"

"Now *that* is a lie," the empress replied. "You are a traitor, Lady Varsha."

She knew.

Varsha was sure of it now. Her stomach dropped. Her head was light, a scooped-out void of fear. But like a drowning man opening his mouth for air beneath water, she parted her own lips again and said, "I am not, Empress, I am not. Please!"

She began to cry, and hated herself for it. But she couldn't help it. Her body was acting without her say-so, heaving out sobs as she twisted her hands back and forth in her lap.

The empress was silent, and as her silence stretched, Varsha found her fear growing into anger. She had never been allowed anger. But she had nothing to lose any longer.

"You think you are different from him," she said, low. "From Chandra. But, Empress, you are not. I am still beholden to you—still your property. I know my worth to you. I was—I am—a womb, a carrier for your heirs, so you may never have to place yourself under the power of any king or lord who wishes to rule the empire in your stead." She clenched her trembling hands. "I may be foolish," she said. "But how could I trust you when I know that? When I know how little I matter? How can I place myself wholeheartedly in your power when I know you will use me as callously as any man for the sake of your empire? It is your power that makes you a monster," said Varsha. "You cannot change that, and I don't think you want to."

The empress sighed and rose gracefully to her feet. A moment later, Varsha felt a hand on her own, and something cool pressed into her palm. Her hand was urged up, and she found a metal cup pressed to her lips. Thoughtlessly, obediently, she drank. Cold lemon water, sweet and sharp enough to shock her into swallowing, and breathing. Her tears petered out.

"Drink again," the empress said, and Varsha took another gulp.

"Good." A clink, as the cup was lowered down. The empress turned, returning to her seat. She looked utterly unmoved.

"Letters between you and Lady Raziya were discovered. And you spoke often with a priest, who guided you astray."

Varsha shook her head, silent.

"I have a witness," said Empress Malini.

Who could it be? One of her maids, surely. The knowledge hit her with a sickening lurch. Which one? Parul? She'd trusted those women. With her son, her son, how could they—

The empress sighed.

"Don't weep, Varsha," she said again. "I won't take your son from you."

"Y-you won't?"

"No," said the empress. She kneeled by her side. "What will my heir do, in years to come, when he learns that I murdered his mother? He will learn to be cruel. He will learn that power is destruction, and to wield it is monstrous. He will be correct, of course. You see me clearly, Lady Varsha. But I find myself hungry for an alternative." She stood again. "Either become clever enough to depose me, or teach your son to be worthy of my throne. That is your task. You will have no power in my court beyond what he gives you. Raise him wisely."

"The priests say you will burn," Varsha said, her voice thin. She was not sure if it was safe to feel relief yet. If *she* was safe.

"They're wrong," the empress said simply. "Rest well, Lady Varsha. If you betray me again, I will not be so kind."

57

PRIYA

Waiting was hard.

Malini didn't visit. Of course there was no chance that Sima would come to see her, but Priya still felt unwanted hope shrivel in her chest as days passed with no sign of either of them.

Malini would come back. She had to see the worth in negotiating with Priya. But until she returned, Priya had nothing to distract herself from the excruciating boredom of imprisonment. She counted the links of her ankle chain, and the stones that made up the walls. She slept and dreamt of nothing at all. She tried not to claw her own hair out.

Usually, in the evenings, her guards were a man and a woman—the woman broad with a serious face, the man thinner and much more fidgety, always adjusting from leg to leg or tapping his fingers in a drumming cadence against his saber hilt. Today, as Priya sat in her corner and contemplated whether she could do a cartwheel with her leg chained, two unfamiliar guards arrived. Both of them were men.

Maybe Malini had simply changed who was on duty. But wariness prickled up Priya's spine and made her stand in the corner of the room, cross-armed, her ankle chain snaking across the ground by her feet.

"Food," one said shortly. He shoved the tray across the ground. The thali was full of the same uninteresting food as always: a little rice and a roti, stale at the edges; a smattering of dhal; and yoghurt that looked on the edge of congealing from heat. She crouched and took the tray.

There was an odd sheen on the dhal. Her gut churned.

She raised her head. It would be smart to simply pretend to consume it, maybe—but both guards were watching her, one standing in the room with her, the other barring the door with his body.

"Eat," said the one in the room, his eyes and voice flat. "Go on."

"No," she said. "I don't think I will."

His nostrils flared.

"Fine," he said shortly. "We'll do this the messy way, then."

He strode in farther and grabbed her by the arms, pinning them behind her back. The other drew a dagger.

She didn't pause to think. She fought like a wild creature, squirming, the chain rattling as she craned her neck back at an angle that made her spine scream, and dug her teeth viciously into the first part of the man she could reach—his exposed jaw. Blood filled her mouth, and the taste of meat, and he gave a howl of pain.

The guard with the knife was still coming toward her. Trusting the strength of the grip on her arms, she used the support to kick up her legs and catch the man not on his armor-clad chest but his exposed jaw. He stumbled back and she bit her captor harder, and finally—finally—felt the man's grip on her falter.

Just enough for her to wrench free. Just enough for her to scramble to the door, even though she knew the chain would stop her from escaping.

She grasped the door. A hand grabbed her by the hair, dragging her back. Her face knocked against the floor—a dull thud she only managed to cushion by throwing her arm in front of her, the stone abrading it. She heard one of them fumble for a blade. Heard a grunt, and the heave of a body over her own, and knew the blade was going to go into her back—

No.

She grasped the power inside her with all her strength. Blood in her mouth, blood in her ears, a howl clawing its way out of her as she fought inside with everything she had. The heart's shell was a fist around her wrists, her ankle, strangling her power, but she couldn't allow it to win. Its grip on her trembled, its coldness seeping in her bones—and abruptly she pushed its strength away and found her own rushing over her.

The ground shook, throwing both the soldiers back off their feet. She leapt for the door.

One man was already scrambling up. Quick, she had to be quick. The door was open. The door bar—that long, heavy piece of metal, slotted back into place every morning and evening— was in her hands. She wrenched it out. She whirled and slammed it into the man's head, hard enough that she heard the crack of teeth and bone.

Panic, blood, her whole body pounding. She went down on her knees and scrabbled on top of him. Key, cold metal braced at his hip. The hilt of his sword. She pocketed the key and snatched up his saber. She held it in front of her, teeth bared.

"You thought I'd die so easily?" Priya demanded. She could hear footsteps pounding down the corridor. Yells.

"Your life for theirs," the remaining guard said hoarsely. Now that she was listening for it, she could hear the Saketan tinge to his voice. "Romesh spoke for you. He deserved better. You should have died willingly for your crimes, witch."

Priya couldn't step beyond the door. Her ankle ached when she wrenched at her chain. But in that moment, she realized two truths: She was not going to die right now, and she could not allow anyone to know that she had overcome the power of the heart's shell holding her.

Had the soldier seen what she'd done? There was a starburst fracture in the stone, but his eyes were hazy with blood. Perhaps. Perhaps not. But there was no time to kill him. The voices beyond the cell were closing in, almost here. There was time to inhale deep, and draw on her magic, and smooth the ground into wholeness again. So she did.

Then, and only then, she found her voice, the fullness of it, and yelled, "Don't hurt me! These men tried to kill *me*. Before you turn your swords on me, know that your empress will not forgive you if you take my life!"

Useless. They were all waiting for a chance to kill her. When they saw her standing over an unconscious guard, they would.

But there, at the head of them, was Sahar. Grim, brow furrowed—but Malini's personal guard, and acutely aware of Malini's orders. Sahar looked into the room. At the unconscious man on the ground, and the Saketan guard still in the cell, expression defiant.

At Priya, blood on her mouth and a saber in her hands.

"Lower the weapon," she said to Priya.

"Not while he carries his," Priya said, gesturing at the guard.

Sahar jerked her head at one of her soldiers, and the woman went in. The Saketan handed over his weapon without a fight. There was already a distance in his eyes. He knew he'd failed, and he knew what came next.

Finally, Priya let the saber drop. It landed with a clang.

Sahar nodded, her brow smoothing with relief.

"You," she said to another soldier. "Get the empress. Immediately."

58

MALINI

Malini was not running, but the torches were a liquid blur at the corners of her vision as she strode through the mahal's corridors. Her guards around her were making a riot of noise—a clanking of armored footsteps—that did nothing to drown out Lata's quick breaths, Lata's voice.

"It would be wise to leave their punishment to Lord Narayan," Lata said, hurrying to keep up with her, her footsteps a whisper against marble.

"I hear your advice, Lata," Malini said, striding forward. She wasn't running. No one could say she was running. "Be glad that I am not dragging Ashutosh in front of me for interrogation. That will have to be enough."

"They may not be Ashutosh's men," Lata protested.

"They're Saketan liegemen. They must serve a low prince." And it was Ashutosh, of all the low Saketan princes, who had a reason to desire Priya's death. His own liegemen had died because of her. Malini had seen the naked grief and anger in his eyes.

"Even if the low prince they serve knows what the guards attempted, or bade them to do it...this is no time to make enemies."

"Then they should not have tried to defy my will," Malini said. Her blood was aflame with anger.

The two Saketan soldiers were being held in a single circular room, with Sahar and a handful of guards on constant watch. The guards bowed their heads, gazes intent when Malini walked in.

"Sahar," she said.

"Empress."

"Summon Lord Narayan," she said. "He must be here."

She looked at the soldiers, bruised and bloodied, down on their knees and chained. They did not meet her eyes.

One had teeth marks on his face. Gouges where flesh had been torn free. She felt a current of emotion so intense it was as though she had left her body. If she'd been able to make her hands work, she would have slit his throat herself.

Finally, Narayan arrived, winded. He bowed.

"Has Sahar informed you of what occurred, Lord Narayan?"

"Yes, Empress. And I must beg for their lives to be spared."

She did not answer. She clasped her hands behind her back and looked down at the soldiers.

"Will you tell me, as you have refused to tell the head of my guard, whom you serve?"

Silence.

"You will refuse to answer your own empress," Malini pressed.

One of the men slowly—slowly—raised his head. The one with the teeth marks. He must have been in great pain. "We serve the empire," he said. "We serve Saketa."

Her clasped hands tightened, her nails cutting grooves into her own flesh.

"You must understand," Malini said, back to them, her voice tightly controlled. "The witch of Ahiranya is my hostage. I took her from the yaksa. I have chosen to keep her. It is not for you to question me. It is for you to have faith that everything I do is for Parijatdvipa, and Parijatdvipa alone. You risked Parijatdvipa out of a desire for vengeance." Her voice trembled with banked fire. "You defied the will of your empress. Of course there is a cost. Of course you will pay, and you will thank me." She turned to meet Lord Narayan's eyes.

"With their death, I will seek no further traitors," she said.

"No enemies. I will acknowledge all Saketa as my people, my allies, and these soldiers as traitors who turned their backs on their liegelords. Will you accept my judgment?"

A long pause. Then Narayan inclined his head.

"Cut their throats," she said crisply, and gestured at one of her own warriors. The woman drew her sword, and did as she was bidden.

Blood pooled across the floor.

"Lord Narayan," she said. "You will speak to Low Prince Ashutosh for me, and tell him that he remains beloved of me."

He read the warning in her words, and the frost of her tone. He inclined his head.

"I will, Empress."

"Good."

She swept out.

Finally, her anger began to calm. If her good sense was a boat being thrashed on stormy waters, then the calming allowed her to finally navigate her own thoughts with a steady hand.

"Leave me, Lata," she said. Lata was still behind her—a shadow dogging her footsteps.

"My lady…" She trailed off, then said, quietly, "Malini. I fear—"

"Leave me," Malini said again. "Sahar will stay with me." She should have been kinder, softer. But she had nothing but hard edges left in her—nothing but the cold blade of her anger with the heat leached from it.

Lata murmured her acknowledgment and drifted away.

Priya was no longer being held in a cell, but in a room set aside for caring for the sick. When Malini walked in, there were guards in the room. Priya had no ankle chain on her now, but the heart's shell was still at her wrists. Her arms were scored with lacerations. Her mouth was still faintly red.

When Malini ordered the guards out, it was Sahar who protested. She protested even more strenuously when Malini told her to wait outside too.

"She wears heart's shell, and I have my saber," Malini said flatly.

"Empress, she's a trained fighter."

"Sahar, I won't ask again."

Finally, Sahar left. When Malini turned back, Priya was watching her.

"Your health," Malini said abruptly, and found she had no more words. She wanted to strangle Priya with her bare hands, and wanted to weep, and wanted to gently cup her face and touch her own mouth softly to the wings of Priya's black hair. It froze her, those conflicting desires.

"I usually heal fast," Priya said. Her smile was thin-lipped, her eyes guarded. "But your cuffs are putting a stop to that."

Malini crossed the room. Someone had made a haphazard effort to care for her wounds. There was a bowl of pure liquor at Priya's side. Cloth. Malini dipped the cloth and took one of Priya's lacerated arms.

"What did you do to those soldiers?" Priya asked.

"I killed them," Malini said. "Stay still."

She cleaned the wounds. Priya didn't hiss or wince. Her arm was very still in Malini's grip, her skin a little cold, and abraded, and so familiar.

"Turning your guards away, killing soldiers, visiting me...I'm leading you astray, Malini," Priya said softly. "And I'm not even trying. You're turning into a monster over me."

"It is not monstrous to make the men who claim to serve me behave," Malini said tightly. "It is my right and my responsibility as an empress."

"If I didn't have these cuffs on," Priya said, her voice light, "I could draw one vine across the mahal. Just one. I could do it slowly and carefully...and I could slide it into your skull." She reached out and tapped a finger to the base of Malini's scalp. Malini's breath caught, fury snaring it in a quick net. She flinched back. Priya smiled, all teeth. "Just here."

"Do not touch me," Malini said. Priya's hand lowered.

"There isn't a single emperor who came before you who wouldn't have killed me or thanked one of their men for doing it," Priya said. "Your warriors call me a monster for a reason. Maybe you should heed them and think about what your duties really entail."

"Do you want to die?" Malini snapped, her grip tightening on Priya's arm. "Is that why you allowed yourself to fall into my hands, to absolve yourself of the responsibility of arranging your own death?"

Priya snorted, amused. But there was still no real mirth in her eyes. Just bone-deep exhaustion, reflected in the shadows smudged beneath them. "That isn't how I am. But it would be poetic, wouldn't it? To let you decide if I live or die one more time." Her voice lowered. "I put my life in your hands so many times, Malini. For faith, for duty, for pleasure. What's one more?"

"If you want to be poetic, you'll do me the kindness of shutting up," said Malini. "You have no head for poetry. You never have."

"You liked the letter I wrote you once well enough."

"I was a fool," Malini said. "Distracted by desires I can no longer indulge, and no longer wish to." She met Priya's eyes. "When I look at you I feel nothing but distaste," she said. "Nothing but revulsion."

Silence, as she took Priya's other arm and cleaned that too. As she finally brought a clean cloth, untouched by stinging liquor, and pressed it lightly to Priya's blood-red mouth.

She put the cloth down. Stepped back. She felt shaken, as if her hands had not obeyed her and were not her own. As if she had not chosen to touch Priya.

"You used to be a better liar, Malini," Priya said.

I am a good liar, Malini thought. *It is not my fault you see through me, as if every mask I wear is nothing but gauze, and my love for you a lamp.*

Without another word, she turned and left.

59

PRIYA

No one seemed to realize that she had stolen a key from a guard. She pulled it from where it had been tucked in the braid of her hair. She held the skin-warm metal in her palm.

It was impressive what you could get away with when you were wounded and stumbling, a small thing being carried between two men terrified that the empress was going to gut them. They'd said as much. *Did you see her face? I think she's going to kill those Saketans by slow inches until they're begging.* A shudder. *I wouldn't want that for me.*

Her path forward was no longer as clear as it had been. Leaving the others, leaving Ahiranya... it had felt like the only good choice she could make. Like Malini had appeared in her dreams, with those coaxing hands and gentle words, and offered her the only way to escape her fate as Mani Ara's carapace. Malini had been her only way to cobble together a third path.

The heart's shell had been placed around her wrists again, but there were no guards in the sickroom with her. The benefit of Malini terrifying everyone into submission, she supposed. She traced those cuffs with her fingertips, set the key in their lock, and watched them click open.

She'd broken their power. Her lacerations were already healing, fed by her magic. But it was pleasant to have her wrists free, to feel like her hands were her own.

And yet disappointment curdled in her heart.

The heart's shell had been a promise of hope. If Malini could hurt Ganam—could contain Priya—she could fight the yaksa. There was still power in the heart's shell, but not enough.

Priya stared down at her bare wrists, thoughtful.

She thought again of Malini's hands on her arms. The sharp, visceral sting of strong liquor against her cuts. The gentleness of Malini's grip, and then the harshness. She thought of their shared dreams, and the way it had felt seeing Malini again at the caravanserai—the yearning she'd felt for her, the tug under her breastbone that wasn't magic; that was nothing but desire.

I'm a better weapon than the heart's shell could ever be, Malini. I'll prove it to you.

Could her own yaksa-given power be used against the yaksa themselves? Could Priya fight them with the Parijatdvipan army behind her?

It was more than want or desperation that urged her to stay. It was a hope like a lamp she couldn't snuff out. It was the string and sinew of magic that bound her and Malini together.

She couldn't go yet.

And she had no interest in returning to her cell, either.

There were guards outside her sickroom, but they would be no trouble to deal with. There were so many green things in the imperial mahal—so many flowers, so many falling leaves. And if all else failed, Priya had the strength of her own hands.

She didn't need her magic to move quietly down corridors. To knock a guard unconscious, and grasp the knife at his belt. Those skills she'd learned as a child without a drop of water-blessed strength in her.

60

MALINI

Malini woke and for a long moment thought she was dreaming. Priya was there, after all—standing by the window, a knife held laxly in her hand. Priya was watching her, something soft in the shape of her mouth and her eyes. This had to be a dream.

A passing cloud shifted. Moonlight on Priya's face. Malini saw the shape of bruises on her limbs. The strange shadow of flowers, a tracery under Priya's skin.

Malini sat up.

"Where are my guards?" she asked.

"Not dead," Priya said, voice low. "I tied them up and gagged them." She lifted a hand in the air. The cuffs of heart's shell were gone. "They weren't expecting me to have any power."

There was a knife flecked with heart's shell under Malini's own pillow. She slid back and grasped it with a flick of her hand. For now she kept it concealed, and kept her eyes on Priya's.

"I could run," Priya said. "But nothing has changed. I let myself be caught. I don't want to leave until I've bargained with you."

"Then bargain with me," Malini said.

Priya moved away from the window and began to walk toward her. She'd always walked quietly. That hadn't changed. Her shoulders were squared, her gait confident. The mocking sharpness had left her, and she was just Priya again, strong and clear-eyed, and it made Malini's blood burn.

"If you want to negotiate with me," Malini said, "why do you carry a knife?"

"I have to be able to protect myself."

"You have your power again. You have no need for a weapon. There was only one moment when you needed a blade, and I paid the price." Malini kept her eyes on Priya's. "Put it down."

She saw Priya's hesitation. Saw Priya's body bend, as she moved to lower the blade.

Malini surged to her feet, heart's-shell knife in hand. Priya swore as Malini stabbed the blade toward her. She caught Malini's wrist, her grip iron, her thumb pressing the bones of her wrist so precisely that Malini dropped the blade with nerveless fingers. Malini tried to wrench her hand back, and when that failed, she drew a plain dagger from a band of cloth bound to her waist. It was unmarked by heart's shell, but it would do.

"You sleep with two knives?" Priya asked, incredulous.

"I sleep with three," Malini corrected, and slashed at the arm holding her own.

Priya released her, shoving her back. Malini stumbled, finding her feet, as Priya fled the bedchamber.

Malini had an empress's rooms—multi-chambered and vast, with so many shadows for Priya to dive into. But she did not need to see Priya to know where she was. She could suddenly feel her, that tug of magic binding them a guiding star. She ran after her as Priya crossed the room—as Priya grasped the movable lattice at a window, wrenched it open, and jumped. Malini went to the window and looked down.

Below were Malini's private gardens.

Malini didn't think.

She jumped out after her.

It should have hurt. But the ground met her softly, grasped her and held her steady. She straightened and kept on running, following Priya, who was quick, quicker than Malini could hope to be, who turned, her tangled hair whirling with her, and cried, "I'm not trying to fight you but I won't let you *carve* me—"

"Surely it's my turn," Malini snapped back. The ground rumbled under them. The knife was jolted from her hand and she was darting forward, reaching out hands to grasp at Priya.

Priya froze, stumbling. Going still. Malini had grasped her. But not with hands.

There were green stems rising out of the soil, tangling up Priya's arms, holding them together. And Malini's skin was thrumming—her chest ached, livid and sweet.

Priya's eyes were wide.

"Malini," she whispered.

61

PRIYA

The only thing holding her arms were flower stems—longer than they should have been but still fragile. Priya should have been able to break them easily, but somehow the magic—*Malini's* magic—had knotted them together in a frantic tangle, a web that ran from her fingers to above her elbows.

"Malini. Let me go."

Malini's hands were visibly shaking. "I . . ."

"Breathe," Priya said soothingly. "You can do it."

The panic was beginning to recede from Malini's eyes. But she didn't lower her hands, or release Priya from her power.

"Is this why you truly came?" Malini's voice shook. "Am I the yaksa's creature also—*changed* by you? Because I refuse that fate."

"No," Priya said immediately. "I don't know why you're like this. But the yaksa didn't do this to you." She could see the doubt in Malini's eyes, and the horror, so she pressed on. "Do you dream of a place where three rivers meet? Where stars live inside and outside the water?"

"I dream of you," Malini said. "Those are the only strange dreams I've had."

"Do you feel an outside presence in your mind? A thorn-mouthed god?"

"No."

"Then you're not like me. Whatever you are, you're not that."

Finally, Malini's hands lowered.

Her usual sharpness had returned to her eyes.

"A thorn-mouthed god in your mind," Malini said. "Explain."

"Every time I reached for my greatest magic...when I made the Veri river rise and fall, a yaksa spoke to me," Priya said. "Mani Ara. She had—flowering eyes, a mouth of thorns. She was the strongest. She still is. And she told me she would only give me the magic I needed if I took back my heart. From you. And when I tried to refuse, she told me...she would do it anyway if I didn't. That she would kill you. She'd kill everyone I cared for."

Malini's knuckles rose. Pressing to her chest.

"I'm her beloved," Priya said quietly, wretchedly. "I belong to her. I've fought so hard to protect my people, my family, *you*. But she told me I'm strong enough now to become part of her, to twine with her into one being so that she can finally walk the world and take the world, and once she does I won't be able to protect anyone. So I can't wait any longer. I hoped your heart's shell would be enough to fight her, that I could *help* you fight her."

Silence. Priya wanted to look away, but she couldn't. She forced herself to watch the slow unfolding horror and coldness in Malini's eyes as understanding came over her.

"She needs you," Malini said.

"Yes."

"Without you she can't come to our world."

Priya nodded, wordless.

Malini's hands clenched. The stems of the flowers flexed with her, like a human grasp.

"When you came for your heart, Priya." Malini's voice was a bright knife. "You could have spoken to me. You could have explained. You chose not to."

"I couldn't have," Priya said, defeated. "I could risk my own death, but not yours."

"I would have tried to help you."

"You couldn't help me," Priya said. "Don't you remember? You tried. But you couldn't give me what I needed. The yaksa wanted my heart, the heart I gave you, and not even a knife could carve that out. It was yours. It will always be yours."

"You stepped one unthinking foot in front of the other without even pondering what path you walk," Malini said, her voice furious and trembling. "You're a fool, Priya. An utter fool."

"What do you want from me, Malini? I can't change what's happened. I'm trying to fix it now."

"You *can't*." Malini walked to her and drew her close. She could feel Malini's breath against her hair, and trace the furrow of Malini's brow with her eyes as Malini grasped the roots and stems around Priya's arms with her fingers and began to unravel them. Her hands were deft and warm. In the coolness of the night, her fingertips were like soft points of fire on Priya's skin. Neither of them reached for magic, though Priya could have.

"If I kill you now, would it end?" Malini asked.

"You think I wouldn't have cut my own throat if it could?" Priya asked. "She'll try to shape others like me. Eventually, she'll make it into our world, and if she doesn't, it won't matter. The yaksa who are here have already changed the world. Besides..." Quiet. "You can't kill me. I know."

Malini's hands stilled on her arms. The stems fell away like a loosened knot, and Priya's arms were free of green—bare to Malini's palms.

"You truly want to fight them? Your yaksa?" Malini asked.

"I'll do what it takes to ensure that the world survives, and my people survive," said Priya. "I don't think your heart's shell is going to be enough. But I believe in you."

"Don't place that responsibility on me."

"I'm sorry. I'll use my power against them. And I think... around you, I'm stronger."

"Why do I have power like your own?"

Priya shook her head. "I don't know."

"I have my guesses, of course," said Malini. Her sureness was returning. "I gave you my heart, and the yaksa had me cut that heart from you. But I think the shape of what we were—the scar, the eroded stone where the waters of love washed over you again and again, reshaping you—those must still be there. The shape of love, even if the love is gone from it."

The love isn't gone, Priya thought. But she believed that Malini knew that. Maybe it was kinder to both of them to let the lie stand.

"If anyone learns about your secret..." Priya began.

"I am not sure if knowing I have something rotten and yaksa in me would be enough to destroy my reign now," said Malini.

"It might," Priya said. "But you've always known politics better than I do."

"I don't know if I am as clever as you believe," said Malini. "You're here, after all. I should never have brought you."

"I'm a valuable hostage. A weapon taken from the yaksa."

"Yes," said Malini, her voice even. "But that wasn't my reason. We both know it."

Their eyes met, and held. Malini was still holding her.

"I let you steal me," Priya said, not looking away from her.

"You fought me."

"I could have done so much more. You *were* foolish, Malini, to do what you did. I could have killed you so easily."

"You didn't kill me in my own court, when I was entirely vulnerable to you," said Malini. "You didn't kill me in my bed. I knew you wouldn't kill me by a lake in Alor, after all that.

"Do you know what the yaksa desires?" Malini asked. "The strongest of them—the one that calls you beloved?"

"Apart from me? She wants to live," Priya said, finally. "She wants to feel the ground beneath her feet. She wants the sun on her face. She wants her kin around her, whole and safe, with a world built to hold them. That's all she wants."

"It's a huge want," Malini murmured. "A want that breaks the world even now. Do you know more of her?"

A shiver ran through Priya.

"I know more than anyone," said Priya. And she could know more, if she was willing to pay the price. Skin, soul. "But none of it will allow you to destroy her."

"I won't let her have you," said Malini.

From Malini, it should have been a threat. But to Priya in that moment—it sounded like hope.

"I know you won't," Priya said. Her finger traced the edge of the last frayed vines at her wrists, raw as silk. "I know."

Malini's hands released her, slowly.

"No more heart's shell," Malini said finally, quietly. "No more prison cell. I do not know what to do with you, Priya. I need—I need *time*. But let us begin with this."

62

RAO

They made a strange group: a snaking line of priests on horseback or in carts, dressed in blue with the sun burning their skin red and then deep brown. Rao and his men—all of them armed—guarded Bhumika. Just one Ahiranyi woman, dressed in the Aloran style, with her lone guard chained beside her.

Rao kept turning to look at her. He couldn't help it. He kept expecting her to vanish at any moment—to slip away and escape.

He wouldn't have blamed her if she had. But she made no effort to run. She was nearly entirely silent, her gaze fixed on the distant horizon.

When they stopped to rest and make camp, three days from Parijat's border, Bhumika finally spoke.

"Prince Rao," she called out. He'd been helping to construct one of the tents, but he stopped when he heard her. She was still cuffed, seated on the ground by one wizened excuse for a tree, under its weak shade. "I must speak with you. Please."

Jeevan, cuffed and seated at a distance from her, watched hawkishly as Rao kneeled by her.

"I am here," Rao said. "What do you need from me?"

"I have given you and your empress the power to create a yaksa-killing fire, but I fear that you or your empress may use this power to destroy more than the yaksa. I fear for Ahiranya. I fear that even if you do not burn my people, your empire will turn blades upon Ahiranya. I cannot allow it."

"Are you asking me to speak for Ahiranya? For its people?" He shook his head. "I know you think I am—chosen. Special, in some way. But I do not have as much power over the empress or the empire as you believe. If the empress or any of the kings of the empire decide to turn on Ahiranya—"

"I have withheld something from you," she cut in. "I have given you the knowledge to kill individual yaksa. But the yaksa are more than individuals. They are the rot in the crops and soils. They are magic woven into our world. I have given you the key to killing yaksa, but I have not given you the knowledge of how to destroy them permanently, and ensure they never return. If your empress promises me the safety of Ahiranya's people, I will give it to you, and to her."

Rao swallowed.

"Would you believe any such promise, Lady Bhumika?"

A thin smile. "I have little choice," she said. "I have placed myself in a position where I can save the world, but my own people may perish. I must have done so knowingly. But I have regrets. I would fight for them if I can, even if it is futile."

"I thought your memories of your people were gone," said Rao. Carefully, he went on, treading strange ground. "Do you... do you remember enough to have regrets?"

She looked away from him.

"Reason with your empress," she said, voice a little more distant. "The yaksa must die. The Ahiranyi deserve to live. If she truly wants to free her empire, tell her to meet my demand, and I will give you the last of my knowledge."

It was a deep relief when they reached Harsinghar itself, crossing the marble streets, riding between peepul trees, until they reached the imperial mahal's great gates.

Their arrival had been noted by the city's guards and had clearly been carried to the mahal, because one of Malini's own personal retinue was waiting for them in her white-and-gold armor, squinting against the sun to track their approach.

"I need to speak with the empress," Rao announced. The guard looked beyond him and then back at him, curiosity in her eyes. But Rao was still a general of the Parijatdvipan army. Still the voice of Alor, even if he'd abandoned his duties time and time again. So she nodded, barked orders at the other soldiers, and then turned back to him and said, "Follow me. Someone will see to your horses in a moment."

They entered the corridors of the mahal together. The corridors were lined with more guards, the air heavy with tension. Rao, who'd been considering making a demand for refreshments for the priests and a chance to rest, decided to bite his tongue instead.

When he'd last left Malini, she'd grasped the heart's shell like water in a desert. He'd thought—hoped—it would make things better. Maybe because he'd clung to that hope all this time, he was surprised and disquieted by the tension in the corridors, the way the silence hung heavy in the air.

"Rao!"

A voice calling his name. And there was Lata practically running down the corridor toward him, her hair braided up into a corona, her eyes worried and her mouth shaping a wobbly smile. He felt an answering smile break across his own face.

They didn't embrace, but she did clasp his hands in her own. One brief grasp, and then she released him.

"I am glad you're here," she said.

"Although I'm glad to see you too, I thought we'd receive more of a welcome."

Lata was gesturing at one of the guards along the edge of the corridor. "Take the priests," she said. "See that they're cared for. My apologies for the abrupt welcome," she said to the priests. "The empress is glad to have you here. She will show her gladness to you once you've rested."

The priests, exhausted, obediently followed the guards who were ushering them away. Only Sunder remained, his gaze fixed on Rao.

"I will be there," Sunder said, "when you speak with the empress. She will trust my counsel."

Said with the absolute conviction of the head priest of one of the most powerful monasteries of Alor. Rao inclined his head in agreement, even though he was not sure that Malini would feel as the priest expected her to.

Only Bhumika and Jeevan remained. Bhumika looked calm. Her gaze was sweeping the hall around them, marking it with her careful, assessing gaze.

"I must warn you, Rao," Lata said, drawing back his attention. "Malini has... has not been herself."

"I had some inkling," he said.

She hesitated, then took a step forward, lowering her voice.

"She captured Priya," Lata said.

A sense of yawning inevitability, as vast as the voice of the nameless, filled him. Both temple elders were here. Two halves of Ahiranya's wholeness lay in imperial hands.

He wondered if the others—Sundar or Bhumika or her guard—had heard. There was a sharp look in Jeevan's eyes. Rao ushered Lata farther away, where they could speak in relative privacy.

"Is she still... alive?"

"Yes," she said. "Elder Priya is fine. And I think... as safe as she can be. But never mind that. Malini wants to meet you now."

"Is Sima well?" Rao asked. He kept his voice low.

Lata's nod was brief but emphatic.

"Come now," said Lata. "You can meet her later. First—Malini."

Malini was waiting in a private receiving room, with only her guards around her. Two of her guards ushered both Rao and the priest Sunder in, shutting the door securely behind him. In the corner, a scribe was writing, head tilted over their work.

He bowed low, as did Sunder beside him.

"I have another gift for you, Empress," he said. "Another answer."

"You have a rare gift for discovering truths, Prince Rao," said Malini. But she was listening, with light in her eyes.

He thought of Aditya's death, and the way the fire had bled into his own eyes, and followed him still; the ache in his skull was like a fissure in his mind, in the world. *This is where you must go.*

"I go," he said, "where the nameless wills it." *Where Aditya wills it.*

Then he told her what he'd learned from Bhumika.

When he had finished, Sunder stepped forward and spoke eloquently of what he had witnessed in the monastery—and of the sacrifice of one of his priests.

Malini's expression was unreadable.

"Your priest died at her hands, then," she said to Sunder. "I am sorry to hear it."

"Ishan died for faith," Sunder replied. His voice shook with feeling. "I am grateful to the Ahiranyi woman, Empress. It was no murder. It was a gift. In your service, we will see the yaksa destroyed and the empire saved."

"A death by faith. I see that we must honor this Ishan's memory, and revere him," Malini replied, compassion warming her voice. "Rest now, priest. I will speak with you privately later. We must ensure that your monastery is celebrated and thanked for your service."

After Sunder departed, Malini dismissed her scribe, then turned to her guards.

"Shri, Sanvi. Wait outside the door."

One of the guards frowned, but they both bowed obediently and left the room.

Now they were truly alone.

Malini exhaled, a rush of emotion flitting across her face.

"Faith powerful enough to kill the yaksa. *Faith.* Rao. You truly believe her? Can we trust her?"

"I saw a yaksa die with my own eyes," he said. He realized, his heart aching as he looked at her, what this meant. She did not have to burn after all.

"Tell me everything," Malini said, hope raw in her voice.

"Elder Bhumika doesn't know herself," he said. "Whatever she did to gain the knowledge she has—she believes it came at a price. Her memories. Maybe even her sense of self. She took a great risk to share this gift, and she may never be Elder Bhumika again." He hesitated, then said, "She claims she has a greater power. She could help us destroy more than individual yaksa."

"The rot?" Malini asked.

"The source of their strength, she said. She told me she can ensure they never return."

"And what does she want in return?"

Canny as always. "Safety for the people of Ahiranya," he said. "She won't share the last of her knowledge until we promise it."

Malini frowned thoughtfully, calculating, the rawness of her first emotions folding away.

"I am not convinced the yaksa can truly be destroyed forever," she said, after a pause. "I think all evils return. It would perhaps be enough to destroy them now. And my armies and lords want revenge against someone."

"If the yaksa can be permanently destroyed, surely it should be done," Rao urged. He thought of all those people in Ahiranya—faceless strangers to him—and felt a kernel of sickness in his stomach at the thought of so much needless death. "Malini, I promise you, with—with the same sureness that made me kneel in the dirt and give you the prophecy of my name—that this is an answer. A solution. The yaksa can be fought."

"The priests you brought with you are willing to die?"

"Yes," Rao said. "They are." A deep breath. Steeling himself. "As am I."

Her eyes widened. One small betrayal of how the words struck her—unexpected, unwanted, sharp.

"No," she said. "Absolutely not."

"Empress. Malini—"

"If faith is a requirement, then you cannot die," she said sharply. "My first faith is to the nameless god."

"Do not lie to me, Rao," she said, and there was a waver in her voice now—a furious edge, a sword whip in motion. "Your first faith was to my brother. It still is."

He sucked in a breath. Said nothing.

He didn't need to. Malini was pressing on.

"Aditya would never have asked this of you."

"No," he said. "He only asked it of himself."

Sima had new rooms. They were nearer to Malini's than her old ones, and under only the most discreet guard of Malini's own guardswomen. Malini had ensured her safety, just as promised.

Sima was waiting for him. On her balcony, elbows on the edge. Jaw set. His relief at seeing her safe and well turned quickly to unease.

"I've heard you've been busy," Sima said.

"News travels swifter than horses here," Rao muttered.

"The empress's guards talk to each other. Sahar told me." She turned to face him, stepping away from the balcony. "You should never have brought Lady Bhumika here," Sima said, and oh, he realized now how angry she was—her eyes were wet, her mouth a twist of fury. She slapped a hand against his chest, not enough to hurt, but enough to say *I would punch you in the jaw if I could.* "She helped you. You told the empress that she helped you, and you still trapped her and brought her here where you know she won't be safe, *how could you.*"

"Sima," he said. "Sima." He raised his hands to touch her arms, to stop her—then lowered them.

She had the right to be furious.

"I've come to care about you," he said, low. "But in the end—you've always known. My loyalty is to Parijatdvipa. As on some level you're loyal to Ahiranya."

"I'm not loyal to some—some concept of Ahiranya, some dream," she said scornfully. "I'm not loyal to Priya, though I care about her. I love her! All I want is to do what's right. Do you think you did the right thing, Prince Rao?"

"I did what was expected of me."

"Expected." Her scowl deepened. "Rao, *Rao*. Can't you make your own choices? Can't you be more than this? I know you better than you might like, and maybe I should be afraid of being honest with you, but I'm not. I'm not! What do I have to lose? You've refused to confront your own heart over and over again—what does your heart say?"

What he'd seen in Alor, and done in Alor—what he'd said to Malini, what he wanted to do, the fire waiting for him, *Aditya* waiting for him—

I want to die, he thought, with a terrible black panic. *Some part of me wants to die.*

"My heart is dead," he said, his voice hoarse. Sima flinched. He didn't stop. "Everyone I truly love is gone. I don't want your pity and I don't deserve it, but I can't listen to my own heart. There's nothing there. I..."

He bowed forward and Sima caught him: hands on his upper arms, her scowl melting into concern. But her voice was unyielding.

"Don't inflict the same fate on me, then," she said. "Don't make me lose everything I love."

"How can I stop it? We're hurtling toward disaster, Sima. Out of my control." He met her eyes. "What can I do?"

"You can do me one kindness," she said. And then she told him.

63

PRIYA

No more cell on her own, and no more heart's shell at her wrists. Ever since that strange, precious moment in a garden with Malini, they had not spoken of bargains or negotiation. Instead, Malini had carved her a little freedom. Priya had a room now, and Sahar to guard her.

Sahar had taken the orders with obvious unhappiness.

"Don't you find it odd that you've been told you have to watch me?" Priya had asked her. "Do you think you're being punished?"

"I trust whatever the empress wills," Sahar had said. "And I am still her head guard. I just have—additional priorities." Her nose had wrinkled.

Priya had refrained from saying anything to that.

Now Sahar entered Priya's bare, light-filled room at speed, face stormy. Priya was already standing, pacing.

"Something is happening," Priya said. She'd heard noise from the corridors, and clamor from the mahal's gardens and the city beyond its walls, echoing in through the window. "You can tell me. What's going on?"

"I'm not a courier," Sahar said, slamming the door shut. "It isn't my job to carry messages."

Priya leaned back against the wall and waited for Sahar to continue. She'd come here for a reason. Priya wasn't much for patience, but she could give Sahar a little today.

"Come with me," Sahar ordered finally.

"Does the empress want me?"

"No," Sahar said shortly. "Come."

Sahar didn't wait any longer. She grasped Priya's wrist and ushered her to the door. They went out in the corridor and walked swiftly along halls lined with guards.

"You killed a friend of mine," Sahar said abruptly, not looking at her. "I used to like you once. But now..." Sahar exhaled and shook her head. "Just don't give me a reason to hurt you. The empress wouldn't forgive me."

They were walking toward the prison cells. Priya considered resisting, but Sahar was so furious that Priya was half sure she would try to gut Priya, given the opportunity.

Sahar gave a sharp nod to the guards at the prison doors, and they moved to the side, inclining their heads. The door opened, and Sahar dragged Priya in.

Inside stood Prince Rao.

"I'm doing this as a favor to you and to Sima," Sahar replied, voice low. Her grip on Priya's arm was iron, and then suddenly— it wasn't. "Be quick. I won't give you long. Don't let Elder Priya in with her."

"Thank you," Prince Rao said. "Of course."

He turned his gaze to Priya, growing cooler, less friendly. He inclined his head.

"Elder Priya," he said. "I was asked to do a kindness. Please. I will take you to her, but first I must explain why she is—changed. And how she came to be here."

"Who is she?" Priya asked, a little exasperated.

"Bhumika," he said. "Your fellow elder."

She stared at him. She could not speak. Her mind was a roar of blood, her heart cracked open.

He spoke, and she listened.

Bhumika. Bhumika *alive*.

They walked. He gestured ahead of him to a cell with bars. A quiet cell, lit by a burning lamp. She was afraid, strangely afraid, that he'd lied to her. But there she was. A cell with a woman within—a woman who sat neatly with her hands clasped, who turned her head and met Priya's eyes.

Priya's heart splintered all over again.

"Bhumika," Priya breathed. She didn't give a shit what anyone said. She was going to break this prison into shards; she would turn every bar to roses. Bhumika was in front of her, alive and whole. Bhumika was here.

It took all her control just to slam herself against the bars, to clasp them and reach her fingers through for Bhumika to touch. To *not* rip the whole place apart. "Bhumika, Bhumika. You left me. You left Padma. You—where have you been? What did you do?"

It took her a second to realize that Bhumika was not reaching for her fingers in return, or speaking. There was a stillness about her that was familiar, but the look on her face wasn't. It made Priya's stomach drop and her voice die.

He hadn't been lying.

"You really don't remember me," she whispered.

"I'm sorry," Bhumika said, quiet in the absence that Priya's voice had left. "I have lost myself. I don't remember the woman I once was." Her hands gripped her skirt, creasing the cloth into half-moons. "We knew each other?"

Priya searched for her voice.

"You're my sister," Priya managed to say. "My family. You— you left. I didn't know if you were dead or just—gone. But it's okay, Bhumika. I...I'm just glad you're alive. You're here. It doesn't matter what you remember."

Bhumika rose to her feet and walked toward the bars.

"I am sorry for causing you pain," Bhumika said.

"I'm sorry I wasn't there for you," Priya said immediately.

Bhumika was looking at her face, taking in each of her features with care. There was no familiarity in her face, but there was tenderness. She reached out for the bars.

Finally, their hands met. Flesh. Bhumika was here. Bhumika was real. Priya could have wept, but she felt too much for tears. Her whole body was an unraveling knot. She leaned against the bars, her forehead against metal, their clasped hands.

Inside her, unfettered by heart's shell, her magic sang in recognition. Bhumika was not in the sangam, not in the shared waters their magic rose from, but dregs of the magic of the yaksa still moved in her—Priya could *feel* them. And Bhumika felt her in return. Bhumika's gaze was suddenly distant, fixed over Priya's shoulder—as if she saw something Priya could not see, and heard words Priya couldn't hear.

Bhumika closed her eyes. Opened them. She'd begun to weep, silent rolling tears.

"Bhumika, are you all right?" Priya asked, alarmed.

"I was told I would grieve," she said, which made no sense to Priya. Before she could question it, Bhumika grasped her hand tighter. "Leave us, Prince Rao," she said.

"I can't do that," he said.

"You owe me this at least," Bhumika said. Her voice was quiet but firm. "Please. We need only a moment."

He hesitated. But he looked at her teary face, and something in him visibly crumbled. "Be *quick*."

Priya heard his footsteps. A door shutting.

Then Bhumika blinked her tears away, her expression firm.

"I only cried to make him leave," Bhumika said. "He feels guilt for imprisoning me."

"As he should," Priya said sharply. Bhumika's grip tightened.

"Listen to me," she urged. "He told you the knowledge I shared, yes?"

"Yes. But what—"

"I did not share everything with Prince Rao, and he knows it," Bhumika said, speaking firmly and hurriedly. "I have given him the ability to kill yaksa but not destroy them in their entirety. I told him I would only provide it to him if he promised me the safety of the Ahiranyi people. But I will tell you."

"You can't trust me this easily," said Priya, hushed. Her skin felt like it was covered in sparks of lightning, alive. "You don't know me. What if I give this to the empress without asking for anything in return? I could have been sent here to trick you, I—"

"I feel what you are," said Bhumika. "It is not a matter of trust. You're needful. I am sorry for it. Listen to me: The place where the strength of the yaksa enters the world. Destroy that and the strength of the yaksa will die with it."

"The Hirana," Priya breathed. Of course.

To reach it, Malini would need her. Without Priya's thrice-born guidance, Malini's soldiers and priests would have to die in waves to break through Ahiranya's wall of trees. But Priya could lead them directly there.

That gave her leverage.

"I can save Ahiranya with this," Priya said, elated and relieved. "You had no reason to tell me this, no reason to put trust in me, but thank you for doing it. I'll negotiate with the empress. And I'll make sure she frees you, too."

Bhumika's grip tightened suddenly.

"There is another price," she said. "*She* was the one who opened the waters."

"Who?"

"The god who grows upon you like a strangling fig grows upon a hollow tree. I can see her in you. Feel her. The waters will survive, as long as a single cutting, a seed, a root of her remains," said Bhumika urgently, and Priya felt the realization rush through her body before it touched her thoughts.

Of course. Every part of Mani Ara had to be destroyed.

Even the parts that were Priya.

"I am sorry," Bhumika whispered. "I am so very sorry."

Priya shook her head, searching for words, wanting Bhumika to understand that there was nothing to be sorry for, that they both knew how cruel the world could be, that Bhumika had lost herself, and how could Priya do any less? But it was too late. The door clanged open, and Rao walked back in.

"Enough," said Prince Rao. "It's time to go."

"I'm not leaving Bhumika in this prison," Priya said immediately. "You must be a fool if you think I'm doing that. Someone tried to kill me when I was in a cell. The guards can't be trusted."

She saw him hesitate.

"Elder Priya," he said. "I promise Lady Bhumika will be given better accommodation, and I promise she'll be safe. Now please. Go, before Sahar gets angry?"

Malini came to Priya's room hours later. She left her guards at the door, sweeping in with the scent of flowers, gold glinting in the braid of her hair.

Time. Malini had asked her for that—begged for it with those dark eyes of hers, vulnerable despite all her power. But her gaze was steady now. She was glittering, untouchable, beyond Priya. She was the empress.

"You've been wandering," Malini said.

"I was taken to see Bhumika," said Priya. She took in a slow breath. Steeled herself. "She and I both want to bargain with you."

Malini looked at her, one elegant eyebrow raised.

"Do you?"

"She told me everything. Even the secrets she has kept from you."

"Everything? Remarkable trust from a woman with no memories," Malini murmured.

"We're still bound by magic," Priya said. "Still temple sisters. That was enough." Priya leaned forward. "Vow that Ahiranya's people will be safe and free, and I'll give you a way to destroy the yaksa forever. Fewer deaths of your soldiers *and* your priests. What do you say?"

"Yes," Malini said simply.

Priya blinked.

"What?"

"Yes," said Malini.

Priya stared at her silently. Malini stared back, calm and unsmiling.

"My scribes will arrange a contract," said Malini. "A true political pact between the Elders of Ahiranya and the Empress of Parijatdvipa in return for knowledge."

"You'll do it, then?" Priya asked, her voice small. "Spare Ahiranya?"

"I will. I don't fear killing," said Malini. "But if I have the opportunity to spare my own people and ensure that the yaksa never return, I'm going to take it."

She moved toward Priya. Hesitated, as if she feared to draw closer. Priya saw a flash of vulnerability in those dark eyes again.

"I wouldn't lie about this," Malini said softly.

Priya let out a shaky laugh.

"You hate me," Priya said. "You have good reason to lie to me. To hurt me. I thought I would have to fight you for this."

"Do you believe I still want to hurt you, or do you believe I *should* want to?"

Priya said nothing. From some reason, those words were more awful than any knife would have been.

"To destroy Ahiranya would destroy you," Malini said. "I don't want to destroy you. Not any longer."

Priya swallowed. The room suddenly felt too small, and she could think of nothing but reaching for Malini—of crossing the distance between them and grasping Malini's arms, drawing her close and tasting her again, the salt and flowers of her—

She clenched her hands tight. Her nails pressed grooves into her palms, grounding her. Did she deserve Malini's touch, her mouth, the tender promise that Malini did not want to destroy her? She knew she did not.

"Arrange the contract," Priya managed to say. "Then I'll tell you all you need to know. In return for saving Ahiranya, I promise, Malini—I'll win Parijatdvipa this war."

64

MALINI

Once the contract was drawn, she gathered her court around her.

"My lords and princes," she said. "My highborn women—my sage and my dearest advisors." She inclined her head to Lata, to Deepa, to the women that surrounded them. They no longer sat behind her but before her—the very head of her court. "We have a path forward."

She told them of the weapon of sacrifice. How Elder Priya would guide willing priests to the deathless waters where they would die, and burn the waters away. She spoke with confidence and calm, unsurprised by the panicked and skeptical looks of her men. She told them this was a vision of the nameless, confirmed to her by the mothers of flame. Sunder, the head priest of the sacred Nimisa Monastery, would stand with her on this matter. It was a story convincingly woven.

"Can the Elders of Ahiranya be trusted?" one asked.

"They fear that their people will perish," Malini said. "You can trust their desire for survival."

"And should Elder Priya show disloyalty," Lata said, "she will be surrounded by loyal priests willing to die for our empire, and soldiers with heart's shell to control her."

"Should she turn traitor, her land will burn," Malini said coldly, and the dissent in the room quelled.

One man stood.

"Forgive me, Empress," Ashutosh said. His eyes were cold, his chin upraised. "But you have been misled by the Ahiranyi before."

Malini smiled at him, a diamond-hard smile.

"I have her on my leash," she said simply.

"At the lacquer gardens in Srugna, you allowed priests to die," he went on. "Do you fear your own death so thoroughly that you will allow holy men to die for you again?" He did not speak of his dead liegemen—the ones who had tried to murder Priya—but she saw the feeling in his eyes.

She wanted to laugh.

"You remember wrongly, my lord," Malini said. "I did not kill the priests at the lacquer gardens. They died willingly for me, to save my life. You have heard the prophecy that named me heir to Parijatdvipa. Theirs was the fire that made my crown and placed it on my brow. I do not kill priests now, but I ask them to heed the will of the mothers and the nameless god alike: They *must* burn."

She leaned forward, ferocity in her voice. "The mothers and the nameless god have taught me this, through their visions and their guidance: I am not a mother of Parijatdvipa. I am not a son of flame as my brother Aditya is, forever beloved and eternal. I am an empress, and like the emperors before me it is my duty to hold the empire whole, and the duty of good men to die for me, and for Parijatdvipa. I am Divyanshi's scion, but I am also the scion of Emperor Sikander, and I will not betray my duties to the empire.

"The priesthood," she said finally, "will not dispute this. They know my purpose."

She rose to her feet, ready to depart.

She had said her piece. Hemanth, she knew, would come to her.

She was seated when he arrived upon her veranda. A peaceful position, overlooking Harsinghar, with the scent of flowers sweetly perfuming the air. Hemanth joined her, his face thunderous. He sat across from her.

"I and my priests speak for the mothers," he said, his voice controlled. "We were not involved in this. We know this will not save Parijatdvipa."

"You disagree with a scion of Divyanshi? The mothers spoke to me directly, High Priest."

He knew she was lying. His expression grew darker.

"I think you seek to save yourself, Empress. That you are reneging on the vow that won you your throne. You said you would burn willingly and save Parijatdvipa. You know in your heart you must."

The table was bare, and today she had no chaperones. No Deepa, no Lata. Just her personal guard beyond the door, each woman with her hand on her blade. That was enough.

"Lady Varsha was led astray by a priest," she said, and saw reflexive panic and shame flicker across his face. "He offered her power. A regency upon my death. He broke beneath torture, High Priest. He assured me strenuously that you supported his every move."

One beat. Another.

"Everything Mitul did, he did for Parijatdvipa," said Hemanth. "Just as everything I have done has been for our empire. Emperor Chandra's son must rule when you are gone. And you will soon be gone. You understand this."

"I understand that you betrayed your empress."

"It would mire Parijatdvipa in war if you called me a traitor," Hemanth said with utter confidence, his shame forgotten. "The priesthood answers to me."

"My brother gave you too much power. You have betrayed me, Hemanth," said Malini, forgoing his title to make sure the blow would without a doubt find its mark. "You conspired with my brother's widow. What did you hope to accomplish? To force me into a corner, to make me obey you?"

"You assured us you would only burn if you had your throne, Empress," Hemanth said, his eyes cold. "I would not take your throne and have you renege on your vow. But your death—if you spoke true—is imminent. It made sense to plan for your successor."

"Ah," she breathed. "You only sought to *hasten* my death. How much better that is. But now, of course, you see I need not burn at all."

"I know that an Ahiranyi man and woman arrived with Prince Rao," said Hemanth. His lip curled faintly. "This offer, this knowledge, is not a gift of the nameless god—which would still be lesser than the true will of the mothers, but acceptable to us—but a trick of the yaksa. How can you not see it? Does your desire to survive blind you so thoroughly? They seek to mislead you, Empress Malini. They lead you away from your true purpose. Your fate."

"You speak again and again of my fate, High Priest, because you look to the past through narrow eyes," said Malini. "You do not see what I see."

"Enlighten me, Empress," he said, his voice bitten off, sharp. "What do you see that I, High Priest of the mothers of flame, do not see?"

"Divyanshi was a woman of great faith," said Malini. "All the mothers were. They prayed and reached for a greater power—and the power served them and obliterated them. I have *no such faith.*" She leaned forward. "My blood would be far less worthy than the blood of priests who believe in their gods. Priests who have opened their souls to a greater power. I have never done such a thing. I am not even sure I love the mothers. Divyanshi gave me her blood, but she also condemned me to always be a sacrifice in waiting—no more than my organs, my bones. I do not thank her for that." She kept her eyes fixed on Hemanth, unblinking. "Does that fill you with revulsion, Hemanth? It should at least make you *pause.*"

He closed his eyes. A look of grief flickered over his face. "You are wrong," he whispered. "Wrong to turn your back on your fate."

"I know my fate," she said. "I know what will save us. You have choices now, High Priest. You can turn upon me and proclaim that I am misled, and the priests of the nameless with me, that

Prince Rao is wrong. And we will all die at the hands of the yaksa. Or you can yield to the truth and my will."

"Would you ask me to burn, Empress?" He leaned forward. "If it is dying alone you fear, then I promise you that my priests will die alongside you. You will not go alone. You will have the priesthood—you will have handmaidens at your side also, if you wish it."

"No." She thought of Narina and Alori and swallowed back rage. "You may plead ill health, if you wish," Malini said. "You're an old man, Hemanth, and I have no love for you. But you may fade now, with my permission. I have arranged guards for you, good Parijati men who will watch over you and see to your comfort until the day you die in your bed, forgotten."

He raised his head.

"You ask me to hand over the priesthood willingly," he said thinly. "To allow someone loyal to you to rise to my place. Someone who will allow you to destroy Parijatdvipa."

"To save it," Malini corrected.

"You think little of me, Empress, to believe I would save myself before Parijatdvipa."

"If you turn against my will," Malini said, looking down at him, as cold as he was cold, "I will ensure that everyone knows of your betrayal. I know it will cost me support of the priesthood. But I am no longer afraid as I once may have been. I have something greater than you. I have an answer to our war." The secret of sacrifice. The priests of the nameless who would follow Rao and Bhumika with light fervent in their eyes. "I have the *truth*."

She stood. "Mitul will be executed," she said. "Any priest of the mothers who wishes to join me may do so. But your journey is at an end, High Priest."

She stood before a court of priests. Priests of the mothers. Priests of the nameless.

Hemanth stood at the edge of the court, silent.

He could, she knew, have chosen to take the priesthood down

with him in disgrace. But she had made a catalog of his weaknesses. Weighed him up. He loved the priesthood and the mothers above all else. What made him a dangerous ally and a dangerous foe was that he believed utterly in his own righteousness.

But this he valued more than his own ideals: the order of priests, garbed in their simple robes, their foreheads ash-marked, who arrived as a group into her court. Who bowed as she looked down upon them, Divyanshi's scion on her throne.

As she told them what the nameless god had taught his followers in Alor. And what now they must do for all of Parijatdvipa.

Five willing deaths were enough to save the subcontinent in the Age of Flowers. Now they faced the yaksa reborn, greater, powerful. Would they face the threat? Would they die to defy it?

Slowly, surely, one by one men came forward and bowed and offered themselves. And Malini watched them, banked fire and hope growing in her heart.

Of course you saved yourself, she thought, looking at Hemanth, who stood at the edge of the court, his eyes fierce. Hemanth, who would give up his title at first light. Who would be High Priest no more.

We are alike, you and I. We've tasted true power.
There is nothing worthwhile for us after death.

65

SANVI

Sanvi walked down to the depths of the cells beneath the mahal. The air smelled fetid, of rain turned to damp, sour bodies and piss. One of the guards at the gate to the final corridor nodded to her as she approached the doors.

"Are you here for the priest?"

"She wants it finished," Sanvi said lightly.

He shrugged and let her by. He had no other questions. She was one of the empress's guards, and she was welcome and known here.

The farthest cell was locked tight, with only the smallest light within from a sickly clay lamp. She took the key from a chain at her own throat and unlocked it.

She stepped inside and shut the door behind her.

It smelled of blood, here. Sickness.

The guard at the end of the corridor was too far to hear noise from here. A torture cell needed thick walls. She kneeled down.

"Priest," she said in a low voice. "Mitul. I am here."

In the corner of the cell, a pile of rags shuddered and gave a low moan. He unfolded himself laboriously, painfully: bruised, broken limbs. A swollen face. One eye gazed at her, bloodshot.

"Sanvi," he rasped. "By the mothers. I am glad it is you."

She gave a choked sob and scrambled to him, lifting his upper body to her lap. He cried out in pain. She made a soothing noise.

"I volunteered," she said. "Does it hurt?"

"She wanted everything from me," he said.

"Did you say...?"

"A man will say anything when he is tortured," Mitul managed to reply. "Any truth, and any lie. I told her nearly everything. I betrayed the High Priest. But I did not tell her of you."

He was bleeding, her priest. His ring finger had been severed beyond the knuckle, and the digits surrounding it had been pulverized. His hands had been so elegant once. She wished she had held them even once in her own: traced their shape, kissed the knuckles. Not for love and not for desire, but so she would understand intimately what he had sacrificed here for the sake of Parijatdvipa and the mothers.

She wanted to hold every piece of his pain within her as she readied herself to face her own end.

"The High Priest will be safe," she promised. There were other guards who loved the mothers as she did—who moved through the ranks of the Parijati warriors who served the empress. They would protect the High Priest. She had faith.

"Sanvi," he said. "We who have no great destiny—our heroics may be forgotten, but the mothers will thank us when we lie in their arms." His voice shook. "The mothers will know what we gave to see the world saved, and they will cradle us kindly. I will meet you there, beyond. You and the empress both."

"I will lead her there," Sanvi promised, blinking tears from her eyes. "I will show her the way."

"Good." He smiled at her—a ruined smile, shining from his wounded face. "You have my faith, Sanvi."

"You've served the mothers well, priest," she said. She reached for her belt. "Now close your eyes. Rest."

He did as she had bidden him.

"Farewell," he said.

"Farewell," she echoed.

She held him against her chest, against her heart, and firmly, tenderly slit his throat.

*   *   *

She would have liked to return to her neighborhood shrine where she had first met him, where he had seen her faith and given her life a purpose. But the mahal was in tumult as the empress prepared her household to head for war.

She prayed in her room instead, by the bed she would never sleep in again. She clasped her hands and thought of his ruined hands, his ruined face. She thought of the empress with hatred and love and desperation that made her want to almost scream. *You must become what the empire needs*, she thought.

You must burn, you must, you must.

Later, dragged from her room by Shri, Sanvi mustered her strength. The priest had taught her so much in his time, and she would not grieve him any longer. The oil in her pack, the flint in her belt, would be her celebration of him.

She returned to work. Sahar was complaining, as she loaded a cart with weapons, about having even more people to guard and watch over.

"Some quiet lug of a man," she was saying. "What am I supposed to do with him?"

He was some Ahiranyi man—a guard or a soldier. He was not technically a prisoner any longer, but no one felt comfortable letting an Ahiranyi man ride freely toward his home country on a horse with a saber at his side.

"Who is he?" Shri asked, nonplussed. "Another elder?"

"I don't know," said Sahar, lifting another crate of weapons into the cart. "But Elder Bhumika seems very worried about him." A sigh. "More trouble."

She did not complain about protecting the other Ahiranyi woman, Sima. But that one had been returned to Prince Rao's care, so perhaps it was simply that she was no longer Sahar's concern.

Sanvi had never liked Sima. She'd been so angry and so quiet—except with Sahar, who'd always challenge her to an arm wrestle and then insist on sharing the best wine with her. As if some Ahiranyi fool, abandoned like dirt by one of her monstrous elders, deserved such kindness.

Sanvi had kept her silence.

She watched the city as they departed. The peepul trees. The white marble. Her heart ached for it all, as it ached for Mitul, and for all the precious things she had chosen to leave behind.

If all went to plan, she would never see the city of Harsinghar again.

66

PRIYA

They were all not quite allies to Parijatdvipa and not quite prisoners, so Priya willingly joined Bhumika and Sima in the same veil-walled chariot, with one of Malini's guards to steer their horse, and a retinue of soldiers in a perimeter on horseback to keep an eye on them.

Priya looked at her sister: at Bhumika's tangled hair, at her solemn face. At the distant way she stared through the curtain gauze, not seeing the world around them. Seeing something, instead, inside herself.

"Would it help if I told you who you used to be?" Priya asked once. "Bhumika, if I told you about Ahiranya, about—about our family. Would that help?"

The chariot jolted as it wheeled over a dip in the road.

"No," Bhumika said. "I asked Jeevan not to speak of it to me. I fear..." She shook her head.

"What?" Priya pressed.

"He told me I do not want to know what I left behind," Bhumika said finally. "And what I do know..." She paused, struggling. "I believe him."

Silence.

"He's doing well," Sima offered eventually. "He's, uh. More chained than we are. But Prince Rao and Sahar, they won't let him be hurt."

Bhumika nodded wordlessly and closed her eyes.

Priya watched her for a long time after that, her heart hurting. Sima leaned against her shoulder and tucked her own feet under her.

"I know," Sima said under her breath. "I know."

They clasped hands. The chariot kept on moving.

The sage Lata was the one who came to see them to their night's accommodation. The chariot had stopped—the army in its entirety had stopped—ready to make camp for the night.

"Come," she said to Priya when Sima and Bhumika were settled. Sima turned to look, a question on her face. But Priya couldn't answer it. She nodded at Lata, then followed her.

"I do not think the empress is acting wisely," Lata said, unprompted. She wasn't looking at Priya—only leading the way. "But she wants you with her."

Priya thought it would be wise to say nothing to that.

In Malini's tent, alone, she found herself restless. Found herself touching the silken bedding, feeling the softness of the rug between her toes. She touched the items spilling from Malini's trunk, left accessible by Swati: silk saris and boxes of jewels; books wrapped in cloth and boxes of attar.

She should not have looked at Malini's jewelry box, but she did.

Should not have found the gap at the base, where a little paper peeked out, but she did—and pried it out gently with her fingertips. And read.

And read.

"Priya."

Malini wore white, great chains of silver at her throat and moonstones at her ears, white jasmine a corona in her braided hair. She was every inch the empress, and she looked luminous in the darkness of the tent, bright as moonlight as she crossed the tent to where Priya sat on the bed.

"Every time I'm here, alone or with you, I find I can't stop searching. Looking, touching..." Priya's voice trailed off, a wisp of smoke, as she turned the letters over in her hands.

"Those are private," Malini said, after a beat.

"They're addressed to me."

"You tore the lining of my jewelry box to get them," Malini said, in a dry tone that did nothing to hide her feelings from Priya—her nervousness. The sharpness of her. "You know they weren't for you."

"You wrote me letters," Priya said softly. She couldn't defend herself, so she didn't try. Her fingers traced over them—the spidering ink was like dust under her hovering fingers, an imprint of lost time that could be destroyed with a brush of breath, a touch. "You wanted to reach for me. Over and over again, you thought of me."

"I did," Malini said. She sat beside Priya back on the bed. The silk of her sari rasped.

"You loved me," Priya said, voice thick.

A pause.

"I did," Malini said finally.

Priya nodded, slowly. Looked back down at the letters.

Malini's voice broke the silence.

"If you had written me letters..." Her fingertips touched Priya's on the paper. "Tell me," she said. "Tell me what you would have written."

" 'Dear Malini,' " Priya said after a beat. " 'I'm shit at writing letters.' "

A low laugh.

"A good start," said Malini. "But I know you have more poetry than that."

"You told me I'm no good at poetry."

"Did I?" Malini's tone was light; a leaf leaving a ripple on waters. "How well I lie."

Priya looked down at those words, her vision blurring a little. She closed her eyes.

"'Dear Malini,'" she began again. "'I'm afraid. I can't protect everyone. And serving gods, no matter how long you've worshipped them, is—cold, pitiless, ugly work. Whenever they ask me to change for them, to grow stranger and stronger, I think of how easy it was to become what you needed. You wanted to be saved, and even though I was angry I also...I said yes.'" She smoothed the paper down. It was that or crumple it. Her hands were restless. "You asked me to fight your war, and I said yes. You asked for *me*, and it was always yes. I wanted it to be yes." A breath. "And then I couldn't say yes any longer. I..."

A tear splattered on the page.

"Shit," said Priya with a laugh. "I'm an ugly crier."

Malini clasped her face then. Fingers gentle on her skin, wiping the tears away.

"Priya," she said gently.

"You shouldn't wipe my tears," Priya said, her voice wobbly. "You should hate me."

"You've said so before," Malini replied, following the shape of Priya's cheekbones tenderly with her thumbs. "I do hate you. As I hate myself. Perhaps I always will." Tender touches, fanning over Priya's skin. "Not because you left, Priya. But because I had so much faith in you that I did not *see* you, your pain, or the choice you faced—and you did not have enough faith to trust me." She spoke in a low voice. "I wasn't clever enough to keep you."

"Malini—"

"I won't be so foolish again." Malini's voice was determined. "I won't lose you."

"You put cuffs on me," Priya said, her tears turning into a smile.

"I did."

"Chained me. Insisted I was yours."

"I did," Malini said. Her hands were still holding Priya's face. "Will you hate me for that?"

"I've never been so sensible," said Priya. She turned her head, shifting from Malini's grip. Malini released her.

Carefully, Priya reached up to Malini's hair.

"I gave you a flower once," Priya said. "And then I took it from you. I took my heart from you, or tried."

She reached into Malini's crown of flowers. The flowers were strung on a thread wound through her curls. A few blossoms came away easily. They unspooled, growing tendrils in her hands. She lowered her hands, placing her own wrists together. Those tendrils curled in a tangle around her wrists, binding them together.

"This is my vow to you," Priya whispered. "Garland-strung. You can hold me here. I want you to."

Malini traced the line of flowers, the vulnerable skin of Priya's arms, above her joined wrists. Then she took Priya by the arms and dragged her in, and kissed her.

It was a firm kiss, a kiss that knew her; a kiss that *demanded*. It wasn't gentle, but Priya didn't want it to be. She thought of the way Malini had touched her in a water-swept dream and felt a hot ache in her belly, between her thighs.

Please, she mouthed, and Malini was pressing her down onto the bed, Priya's face to the blankets, her hands beneath her; Malini was sweeping Priya's hair aside and fastening her teeth to the nape of Priya's neck. Priya cried out soundlessly.

Hands under her blouse. Hands touching her, owning her.

"I'm not very human anymore," Priya said as Malini's hands mapped her skin: the vulnerable backs of her arms, the skin of her back, flushed with traceries of leaves and flower.

"You are life," Malini said, hushed. "There's nothing shameful in that."

She moved Priya, turned her until she was on her side with Malini behind her, looking at her and touching, cupping the curve of her hip, the softness of her stomach, the swell of her breasts. When Malini brushed her thumb over a nipple, as cruelly and tenderly as she'd brushed away Priya's tears, Priya felt a want so painful she thought it would drive her mad.

"You have always been life to me," Malini said quietly. "Always all things living and good."

"Even when you hated me? Even when we dreamt of each other?"

"And even then you were life," said Malini. Priya could feel the flowers at her arms winding tighter, drawing her elbows closer, raising her into Malini's hands. That wasn't her doing. It was all Malini's. She did not know if Malini was doing it on purpose. She didn't care.

Malini's fingers studied her, mapped their way down beneath the folds of her skirt, pushing them aside. She swept a hand over the tracery of vines and leaves at Priya's thighs, but her mouth was against Priya's ear, her body was hot at her back, all warm skin and the cold jewels still pinned to her throat, her wrists. "Even then, I needed you. How else could I have reached for you in sleep, in dreams?"

"Malini," Priya said.

She felt Malini's slender, knowing fingers slide into her and tipped back into her arms, surrendered, as Malini's mouth covered her.

Afterward, Malini used her own shivering magic to unwind the flowers. Used her mouth to soothe Priya's skin.

"Where will you go when the war ends?" Malini asked, in the dark, in the quiet.

"Nowhere," Priya said. It was the most honest she could be. She felt the sting of her wrists, the echo of teeth at her throat. "Nowhere," she whispered again.

Malini pressed a ghost of a kiss to Priya's hair.

"Sleep," she murmured. "I have you, Priya. I have you."

67

ARAHLI ARA

Ashok was dreaming.

He was drowning. The water was deep and blue, and then not blue at all. The waters were a darkness so vast it had no color. Stars raced through it, as keen and cold as thrown blades. He was trying to swim to the surface, but he did not know where the surface lay. His lungs were full of water. He was dying. He had, perhaps, been dead a long time.

He saw Riti and Sanjana and Nandi reaching for him, tangled in weeds like golden chains. Their eyes were empty. Their hands when they grasped him were cold. They were mottled blue, drowned, their clothes floating around them in white clouds.

Priya, he thought. *Bhumika. My foolish sisters. I'm sorry. I tried—*

Arahli Ara opened his eyes.

Yaksa did not dream like this.

He went to Taru Ara first. She was sleeping on the mahal's roof, curled in a bed of jasmine flowers. From her perch, the edges of the forest were visible. From here, he could hear and feel the Parijatdvipan army, bristling once again on the borders of Ahiranya. But this time, he could not simply laugh at them. The mortals had killed a newborn yaksa.

This time, he and his kin were . . . changed.

There was a strange pallor to Taru's skin: a brownness of mortal flesh, flushed with red mortal blood. Her torso, beneath the masking perfume of flowers that surrounded her, smelled of human decay.

She had wept when they had felt their kin in Alor perish. Wept like a mortal, fever in her veins and her wound rotting her from the inside.

He placed a hand against her brow. The skin of his hand was no different from her own.

No time, he thought. The panic clawed in his throat. He could not deny it any longer. Taru Ara's wound, their strange skin, the humanity stealing over him, the dreams...

They had sacrificed so much of their green to return and survive. They had donned faces of their dead worshippers. They had consumed mortality. And *this* was the cost. This awful fleshliness.

He had not known it would be like this.

When Mani Ara returned it would be better, he told himself. She was the most powerful of them. She would fix everything.

He pressed his forehead to Taru Ara's. *Sister*, he thought, in a voice that wasn't his own. She did not stir.

He thought of the temple children. He would take one—the oldest maybe, the boy Ashish—to the deathless waters. He would guide him in. Make a once-born of him. If they did not have Priya any longer, he could make more worthy vessels for the greatest of his kin. He left Taru Aru to seek the children out, his heart pounding, nausea a roiling sea in his belly.

The temple children were not in their beds.

His rage was heard all through the mahal—the trees shook and the birds took flight.

They were *gone*.

Cira Ara was the newest of them, and still the most green-veined in all the ways that mattered. She led Arahli Ara and his kin through the woods, following the subtle echo of their footsteps in soil, the whispers of trees. Arahli could not feel as she could. His senses were clumsy, dulled by the blood in him.

"Of course I feel them," she said merrily, flashing her sharp teeth in joyful malice. "Do you not, dear kin? Shall I kill the ones that are not temple children, flay them as an example?"

"No," he said. He could feel another presence. *Ganam.* Anger kindled in his breastbone. "Go to Ganam. Take Avan Ara with you. Keep him restrained. I'll find the children."

He and Bhisa Ara and Vata Ara sought the children who were on the seeker's path. Ashish saw them first—turned, and widened his eyes, and screamed, "Run!"

The children fled, but not swiftly enough. Arahli's kin turned the earth, bidding it to swallow them to the knees. Stuck fast, they sobbed. They were easy to collect—to tie with vines and guide back toward the edge of the forest.

Ganam was kneeling, lashed with vines, face set with rage. Next to him, Avan Ara was trembling. A blade lay on the ground beside him, violently cracked in two.

"He was carrying this," Avan Ara said. He jerked his chin at the blade.

Arahli Ara walked toward it and kneeled. He brushed only a fingertip against it and felt a repulsive emptiness—a negation of his own magic. He recoiled. He understood why Avan Ara had sought to shatter it.

He looked at Ganam. "Traitor," he whispered.

But Ganam was not looking at him. His eyes were on the children, his expression shattered, all grief.

"Rukh," he said. "Why are they all here? I told *you* to run."

"I'm sorry," Rukh said miserably, his fingers white where they gripped Bhumika's child. "I couldn't leave without them. When you told me to run, I told the others to come with me. I had to try." He swallowed. "I'm sorry."

Ganam closed his eyes in defeat.

"I should kill you," Arahli observed, "for what you've done."

"If you kill me you've got nothing left," Ganam said. "No temple elders. No Bhumika. No Priya. Just—weeping children. And you've got no time to test them, have you? The Parijati are coming. You've only got me."

"I should kill you anyway," Arahli Ara said.

"Do what you want," Ganam said. "I've got no regrets. Kill me, then. It makes no difference." His jaw was set. "I'll probably die when you throw me into the waters again anyway. So kill me now if you want. I don't care."

Viciousness curdled in Arahli's blood.

"I do not need the boy, Rukh," he said, low. "Perhaps I will kill him instead. That would serve to punish you."

One of the children behind began to sob.

"Hush, Pallavi," Ashish said, drawing her to his side. "It's okay. Hush."

Rukh did not make a sound. His expression was set, his chin raised.

A dizzying memory shot through Arahli Ara's skull. A child's weight in his arms. Fire in his throat, his eyes. Death at his heels.

Don't look, Pri. Don't look—

"Yaksa," a voice called.

Figures, standing among the trees. He had felt them approaching but thought little of it. They were his own people—worshippers, and outsiders who had sworn loyalty. They had heard his rage and followed his steps.

One stepped forward, a Parijatdvipan man. He bowed low to the ground.

"Yaksa," he said again. "Great ones, I beg you to give this honor of fighting the Parijatdvipans to us. We are fully grown and trained for war, and faithful to you. Let us drink deep of the waters. Let us fight for you."

"It will not make temple elders of you," Bhisa Ara observed.

"You are not worthy," Avan Ara said.

"We saw Ruchi drink waters broken from the source, and we saw her perish. We know what the cost of service is. But we would gladly take up this glorious burden," the man said, determined.

"Shyam," Ganam said roughly. "Don't do it."

"The children will grow strong and serve you in years to come," the man said, not looking at Ganam. His whole focus was on

Arahli and his kin, seeking them with his eyes, imploring them with every line of his body. "Let us drink and die for you now, so they may live." Finally, he looked at Ganam, then the children. "All of them," he said. "In return for our faithful service."

His words washed over Arahli Ara like relief, like a tide, and took the memory of a child Priya in his arms with them. Yes. Let the children live for now. Yes.

"Anything," he said indulgently, "for our loyal worshippers."

68

MALINI

Nowhere.

Priya's hazy, sleep-soft voice echoed through Malini's skull. In Malini's arms, Priya was a comforting weight. Her dark hair shone in the light of a single oil lamp by their bedside. Her gold-brown lashes were closed, a line like firelight against the dark skin of her face. Malini could have stared at that face for hours—that crooked nose, and that mouth that smiled so easily, and that stubborn chin. She stroked a hand through Priya's hair, feeling the weight of it, that pin-straight softness.

Malini had never understood Priya as she should have. She'd seen Priya's soft heart and her strength and never considered how Priya's strength and softness could lead her to lie to those she loved—for their safety, for their comfort. To defer grief.

But she understood Priya now.

Nowhere.

Priya was not planning to return from Ahiranya. She was planning to die.

Malini did not want to leave their bed. But her heart was a leaden weight in her chest. She pressed a kiss to Priya's forehead—simply for the pleasure of kissing her, of knowing Priya was hers to kiss—and then she slipped out of the bed. She dressed and left her tent.

Sahar was outside, head bowed, arms crossed. She raised her head, and Malini said, "Come."

Lady Bhumika had her own demesne, carefully protected by a handful of Malini's own guards. She recognized Sanvi, yawning into her hand—then suddenly straightening when she caught sight of Malini approaching.

"Wait here," Malini said to Sahar. "All of you: We are not to be disturbed." She entered the tent.

It did not surprise her that Bhumika was awake. She sat on her own pallet, with an oil lamp burning, as if she'd been waiting for company. She met Malini's eyes gravely.

"Empress," she said.

"I need to speak with you."

Bhumika inclined her head.

Malini had no room in her for artifice. Not when it came to this—to *Priya*.

"Tell me," Malini said. "When you spoke alone to your sister in my mahal, what did you speak of?"

"How to kill the yaksa." A mirthless smile curved her mouth. "It is all I speak of, Empress."

Malini walked to her and found she could not loom over Bhumika. She could not stand and tremble with rage and fear, and she could not sit as calmly as Bhumika did. So she walked, carefully measured steps, back and forth in the narrow tent. She did not care if it revealed her agitation.

"And Priya," she said. "Who shares her nature with a yaksa. Who must lead my priests into Ahiranya—why does she believe she will die?"

"It sounds as if you have all the pieces of your answer," Bhumika said quietly. "But it is simple. Mani Ara must be destroyed, and Priya *is* Mani Ara."

"She is not," Malini said sharply.

"She is not," Bhumika agreed. "And she is."

Malini forced herself not to falter or show weakness.

"So must Priya die," she said, "for the deathless waters to be destroyed? Is her life the price?"

"You can ask and ask again, Empress," Bhumika said. "It will not change the truth." A pause. "I am sorry."

That, more than anything, confirmed to her that Lady Bhumika had truly become a ghost of herself. The woman she had known would have grieved Priya. It made Malini suddenly furious. Strange, how the fury made her want more than anything to weep as if her heart were broken.

Unbidden, her mind conjured up images of her heart sisters. Alori, Narina. Gone. Aditya. Gone. She had loved them and lost them, and nothing could return them to her. And Priya—she *had* loved Priya. But now what she felt for Priya was something beyond love. It was the tether of magic between them. It was hatred, and it was the most joyous and sacred thing she'd ever felt. *You are life*, she'd told Priya, and it was true. Priya was her life.

She would not let Priya enter Ahiranya. She would keep her in the camp. She would bind her. She would not care what Priya said, she would—she would—

No. Those thoughts were foolish. She could not yield to them, no matter how much her heart wanted to.

There was no one else who could allow the priests safe passage, and no one else who could carve the way to the deathless waters. Priya had to go to Ahiranya, and Malini could not stop her.

"As long as Priya lives, the yaksa will never be truly gone from the world," Bhumika said, into Malini's silence. "But if you will let me go with her. If I can do anything to spare her pain..."

"No." She spoke before thinking. "*I* will go with her."

And I will bring her back alive.

The sacrifices made in this war would have to be enough. Malini was monstrous enough to seize a throne and murder a brother. She was monstrous enough to continue the glorious, bloody cruelty of empire. She had *made* herself so.

She would choose now to be monstrous enough to let an enemy live, for the sake of keeping what was hers. She would choose love over goodness.

Let future generations face the yaksa once more. Let the rot continue. Only, let me have her.

*   *   *

Rao and Lata were the first to hear her decision, and the first to beg her to change her mind.

They both met with Malini alone, without the interference of courtiers or administrators. In the predawn dark, in the privacy of Lata's own tent, Malini told them what she would do. Lata looked as if she wanted to weep, and Rao refused to look at her at all. He bowed his head as Lata kneeled down beside Malini. Lata's eyes were shadow-rimmed.

"You can't go into Ahiranya," she said, her voice hoarse. "My lady. Please. You *know* what will happen. If the yaksa or the Ahiranyi don't land a lucky blow—if the rot does not touch you—your own priests will turn on you eventually. There are still many who want you to burn, you know this!"

"Sahar will be with me, and she is trustworthy," Malini said. "Rao has vouched for the priests of the nameless. I won't be harmed."

"I vouched for their faith," Rao said roughly. "But I don't trust them with your life."

"Empress—Malini. You're far too clever to truly believe that. If you leave now, Empress, you will destroy your own legacy," Lata said slowly. Her voice was bleak. "The priests will make your brother's son into a puppet emperor. They will erase any memory of you—or make a mother of flame of you. You will not be remembered as Empress Malini, ruler of all Parijatdvipa. You will be forgotten."

That cut deeper than the rest. She had done what no daughter of Divyanshi had ever done. To imagine her legacy erased and discarded was infuriating.

But ah—what did she truly care about the tales that would be spun after her death? It was the tales told *now* that mattered. It was the life she lived inside them. And if her life, this life she had fought tooth and nail for, had to be empty of Priya, had to leave her with nothing but her grief, a knife scar—no. She could not bear it.

"Come now," said Malini lightly. "I will be a gold statue, at least. Perhaps the priests will place me next to Divyanshi, wouldn't that be nice?"

"Don't make a joke of this," Rao snapped. "You can't choose to die. Not now."

"I'm not choosing death. I promise you, I'll return."

"I'll come with you," said Rao.

"We both will," Lata said.

"No. You will remain beyond Ahiranya's borders. That is my command." Her tone brooked no argument.

Lata shook her head, affection and sorrow in the shape of her mouth.

Rao turned his face away.

"Don't be like him, Malini." His voice cracked. "Don't."

Her own heart ached.

"I'm not Aditya," she said. "And I will return."

"At least let me die with you," he said. "Don't leave me behind."

She shuddered out a breath. She would not weep over him, this fool who had loved her brother. This fool whom she loved.

"Aditya was looking for a reason to die, Rao," Malini said. "Perhaps he convinced himself that the nameless god and the mothers wanted his death from him. Perhaps they did. But he wanted to end in self-abnegation and sacrifice, and I know you do too. Your grief isn't a voice you can trust. Do you understand, Rao?"

He found his voice.

"I think you are the one acting from grief, Malini," he said. "You fear for Priya. You fear—"

She slammed her hand down on the table.

"No more," she said. "I am empress, Rao. Lata. And I will do what I know is right."

69

PRIYA

Priya woke in daylight with Malini beside her. It was still early in the morning, and the light creeping into the tent was pale. But Malini was dressed. Her hand was over Priya's heart. A gentle weight.

"You're ready," Priya whispered. "Is it time to go?"

Malini nodded.

"Our last journey," Malini murmured. "We'll see Ahiranya today."

Last journey. Malini had no idea how true that was. Priya drew her down for a single kiss.

Malini drew back. They met each other's eyes, and Malini laughed—a real, breathless little thing, her mouth shaping into a smile. There were tired shadows under her eyes, but those dark eyes were full of wonder.

"There you are," she said, cupping Priya's cheek. "My Priya. My love."

As they traveled, Priya held that moment in her mind's eye. *My Priya. My love.* If she was going to die, then she wanted to hold that image close—one taste of sweetness, one last treasure to carry her through to the end of her life. It made the burden of her fate easier to carry.

The Parijatdvipan army made its war camp far enough from Ahiranya that the trees of home were a smear of green on the horizon. But Priya could feel Ahiranya regardless.

Ahiranya was waiting for her.

There were bows being strung, and weapons being sharpened. The churn and noise of an army preparing for war. But Priya had no weapons to prepare. She found Sima preparing her own bow. When Priya approached, Sima looked up at her. Paused, her eyes narrowing.

"What's wrong?" Sima asked.

"Sima," she said. "I need you to come with me. Please?"

She'd already begged for Sahar's help, and the guardswoman was ready, waiting to escort them. They were led to a well-guarded tent.

The guards around the tent would not argue with the empress's personal guardswoman, so they drew back, allowing Priya to enter the dark tent with Sima beside her.

"Be quick," Sahar muttered as she went in. Priya nodded. She knew that Sahar—and everyone else, for that matter—had bigger things to worry about than Priya's farewells.

Jeevan stood in the center of the tent. He looked, despite his chains, as if he were ready for war, shoulders squared. His expression and his stance softened with relief when he saw them.

"Priya," he said, low. "Sima. Are you well? Have you seen Bhumika?"

"We're all fine," Priya said, feeling strangely teary. She forced the feeling away and went to him. She grasped his hand in her own. "It's good to see you. I thought I might not again."

"I believed the same." His gaze turned to Sima, questioning.

"Parijatdvipa's not been so bad for me," she said with a shrug. "I've been well protected."

Jeevan did not look like he entirely believed her, but he nodded.

"Jeevan," Priya said, drawing his attention back. "I need to speak swiftly."

She told him what Malini planned, and the deal she and Bhumika had made with the empress. He listened solemnly.

"What I want more than anything," she said, at the end, "is for Bhumika to be safe. Can I be sure of that with you?"

She pressed a key into his palm. Closed his fingers over it.

"These chains aren't so difficult to escape," she said. Low enough, she hoped, that the guards wouldn't hear her. "Take Bhumika somewhere good. Somewhere better."

"She wants to go home," he replied.

"She doesn't know what home is."

"You do not need memories to know the shape of home. I would not have believed so once, but I've seen it in her." His hand tightened on the key. "But I will take her away from here. I promise."

"Good," Priya whispered. She smiled at him and released him.

Priya and Sima exited the tent. Then she scrubbed her stinging eyes with the back of her hand.

"I'm going somewhere I probably won't come back from," Priya said quietly. "Am I a fool, Sima?"

Sima clutched her hands. Pressed their foreheads together.

"Yes," said Sima. "A huge fool. A madwoman."

"You can stop," Priya protested, laughing through tears.

"You're a fool for not taking me with you."

"Shut up," said Priya. "Do you think I'll be able to do anything if I'm worrying about you? Don't let Bhumika follow me, either. I know she wants to."

"And who is going to stop me from following you, huh?"

"Don't joke," Priya said, her voice wobbling. "I need to know you're both safe. I can't do this if I think you'll come to harm."

"The whole world's full of harm, Pri."

"Please."

"Fine. I promise." She clutched Priya tighter. As if she never wanted to let her go. "But you need to tell Bhumika yourself. You need to say goodbye."

"I know," Priya said. She was dreading it.

Sahar cleared her throat, and Priya finally let Sima go.

She went to Bhumika's tent, next. One step. Another. The sun was hot on her shoulders.

She couldn't do it. She couldn't look into Bhumika's eyes and see a stranger.

It was selfish of her. Selfish and cowardly.

She *had* to do it. Time was running short. Soon she would go into Ahiranya. She would take those priests to the Hirana and then she would die.

Even if Bhumika never remembered her, she deserved to know that her sister loved her. Priya owed her that.

She touched her fingertips to the curtain of Bhumika's tent. Drew a deep breath.

And stopped. And turned.

Lata was behind her. Lata had called her name.

"I'm sorry," Lata said. Her voice shook. "I need your help, Elder Priya. The empress is making a terrible decision. You must convince her not to."

Malini's guards and her maid were dressing her in armor.

It was armor built for movement—a fine and strong mesh over white cloth. She wore no jewelry now, no crown of flowers. But she was still empress—in bearing, in the fierceness of her eyes. In the way her people ringed round her, all those guards and soldiers she'd trained into loyalty.

But she was not meant to *need* armor. She was not meant to be going into Ahiranya. She was meant to be safe.

She shouldn't have noticed Priya—shouldn't have heard her— but somehow she did. Malini's gaze turned unerringly toward her. No smile shaped her mouth. There was no softness in her face. Her dark eyes were serious, almost furious. She knew exactly why Priya was here.

"Leave me," she said to the women around her. They left swiftly, some looking at Priya curiously as they departed.

"Who told you?" Malini asked.

"Lata," said Priya shortly.

Malini shrugged. "Well, I knew she'd meddle."

Priya took a controlled breath, then said, "If Mani Ara isn't destroyed, every part of her, then this doesn't end. Mani Ara's strength lies inside me. Her power, her memories." It was hard to say it, hard to face the reality of what lay ahead of her in the cold light of day, with Malini's dark eyes looking right through her to her fearful heart. "I...I don't want to die. But I know what I have to do."

"Tell me," said Malini. "Tell me exactly what you have to do."

"I have to lead your priests to the deathless waters. And when they destroy the waters, I have to. I." She stopped. Whispered, "Don't make me say it, Malini."

"You will allow the priests to kill you," said Malini. "You will let the power they draw upon consume you too. You will burn and you will perish. I understand. But I can't allow it."

Malini walked to her. In armor and white cloth, she grasped Priya's shoulders.

"You'll come back," she said. "With me."

"Coming with me won't save me," Priya said. "It will just— condemn you too. I can't bear that, Malini."

"Then live. I won't allow you to die," Malini said, her voice low. "I have no better leverage to use against you than my own life. If you die, then I die. So you will have to live."

"You're mad," Priya said, choked. "Malini. I have to do this. You understand what lies in me, don't you?"

"What lies in me, then? I share your magic. A piece of Mani Ara lives in me too." Malini arched an eyebrow, as if she'd made a worthwhile point instead of punching Priya in the stomach; as if she'd won. "If you must die, then I must die too."

"The whole point of this was so you'll live!"

"And I intend to. I intend for both of us to live."

"Malini."

"Priya. I have no faith in gods," Malini said. "I never turned to the guidance of the nameless god. I do not worship the mothers as I should. Every iota of faith I have professed, I used to my own ends. For my own survival, and my own power. So visions and prophecy say I must die. So your sister's visions dredged from the deathless waters say you must die. I reject it all.

"I will take this victory," she said softly. "I will accept the possibility that future generations will face the yaksa again. So be it. But we are going to destroy the deathless waters together, and then we are both going to walk away, alive and free."

Priya shook her head. Her head felt like it was full of fire. She couldn't listen to this. She couldn't *hope*. It was so cruel.

"We've paid enough, you and I," Malini said.

"Why should we live if those priests die?" Priya asked hotly. What worth did her life have, compared to anyone else's?

"Because they are willing and we are not." A hard smile curved Malini's mouth, reflecting the cold determination in her eyes. "Because I am selfish and hungry, and I make no apologies for it. I *want* us to live, Priya.

"I have won an empire, and we will kill your gods," she said. "If we want a future together—a *life* together—where we no longer need to wear masks, or shape ourselves into monsters, then we will have one."

Priya did not know if she walked to Malini, or if Malini walked to her, but Malini was drawing her close. Her head was against Malini's shoulder, against warm skin, cold metal.

"I still don't want you to do this," Priya said quietly. "I want you to be safe."

"I know," Malini replied. Her arms around Priya were gentle. "I know, my love."

They left Lata in the war camp. She exchanged quiet words with Malini, her eyes red, then watched them all go.

The army followed. Arrayed itself at the border. Malini and Priya—and their retinue of soldiers and priests—walked to the forest's edge.

Priya raised a hand. Before her, the thick wall of trees parted at her command.

70

MALINI

Malini walked through Ahiranya with Priya by her side. Above them, the trees threw vast shadows. When she looked at Priya she could only see her face in angles of darkness and light. The furrow of Priya's brow. Her closed eyes. Her steady feet, barefoot and confident on the soil.

But she could feel Priya: her magic, twining and twisting outward from her body, stretching tendrils of awareness out to the very edges of the retinue behind them. Priya was guarding every single warrior and priest, and Malini could feel her doing it.

Her chest ached at her scar, but it wasn't an ugly pain. It was an ache like hunger, an ache like desire. She was aware of every thrum of her own heartbeat and breath. There was magic in her, just as there was in Priya. She was going to see the deathless waters. She was going to witness the death of the yaksa.

Priya's eyes fluttered open.

"Malini," she whispered.

"Yes?" Malini whispered in return.

"Look behind you," said Priya. "And tell me what you see."

Malini did not stop walking as she craned her neck. Their entire procession was not visible to her—it couldn't be, with the thickness of the trees—but she could see her personal guard behind her, their heart's-shell weapons ready. Sahar, Shri, Sanvi. The first warriors from Parijat, helmed in white and gold. And priests behind them—priests of the nameless, garbed in blue, their eyes wide as they took in the forest around them. And priests, too, of the mothers—ash-marked, gray-faced with trepidation.

"Nothing unusual," Malini said.

"Look closer," said Priya. Her voice sounded strained. "I can feel them coming but there's something—something I can't see—"

Malini saw it. A flicker of shadow. Moving leaves. Her eyes saw what the magic within her could not.

"There is someone in the trees," Malini hissed.

Priya's hand whipped into the air, one sharp and cutting motion. The trees gave a crack and a groan, a rain of leaves falling as they splintered and opened a jagged path.

"Now," Sahar yelled at the people behind them. "Prepare to fight!"

Malini heard weapons unsheathe as her own guards drew closer to her, attempting to form a shield around her.

A figure leapt down from the trees, landing in front of Priya. It straightened. A man, no armor on him, holding a single small weapon. Priya gave a sharp inhale.

"Shyam," she said.

"You left this behind," the man said. He dropped an item to the ground. A heart's-shell blade, broken, hiltless. When he released it, a shudder went through him, and his shoulders straightened.

"The others are coming," he said. "You'll feel them soon. But I'm the first. I wanted to beg you to come back. To end this." His eyes were reflective in the semidark. "The yaksa are very angry, Elder Priya."

"Shyam," Priya said shakily. "You've drunk the waters broken from the source. You've poisoned yourself."

"For power, yes," he said, inclining his head. "The yaksa would have taken the children. I offered myself in their place."

"Ah, Shyam." Priya swallowed. "Thank you for protecting them."

"Someone had to," he said. "You would not. And I am protecting them still. Come with me, Elder Priya. Please."

"I'm not coming back to them. I can't. Let me pass, Shyam."

"I can't do that."

"I can stop you," she said. "I can stop all of you. Even Ganam. Even the yaksa."

"Can you?" He looked, then, at Malini. Bowed his head a little. "Empress. I served in your army once." A thin smile. "But I had the rot, you see. I had nowhere to go but here."

"Get out of my way, Shyam," Priya said. "Please."

"No," he said. "You may be able to fight us all, Elder Priya. But I have made my choice. You may have chosen to betray Ahiranya, but I have no choice but to die for it."

He raised his own hand in front of him, and thorns suddenly erupted from the ground beneath her and Priya. Malini leapt away as her own guards desperately scrabbled to move to safety. Priya stood firmly where she was. The thorns did not touch her, as if they didn't dare try.

They avoided Malini too. Priya looked at her sharply, the whites of her eyes wild.

"The others are here," Priya said, voice tense.

It was all the warning she could give. Malini saw them appear between the trees: Ahiranyi in wooden masks, magic flowing through them and scythes in their hands. They moved with brutal swiftness, hacking their way through Malini's soldiers with metal and green alike.

Malini whirled, taking in the gruesome sights around her. She saw bodies being speared between the trees and swallowed by the soil, saw blood spray and figures collapse to the ground. Only her soldiers with heart's-shell weapons were making an impact—hacking thorns, cutting through ropes of vines.

"Does it hurt you to betray Ahiranya?" Shyam was yelling, his voice ragged. "To betray us, the people you promise to protect?"

"Of course it does." There were tears in Priya's voice.

"Then we may stand a chance of surviving after all," he said. "Stop this, Elder Priya. Come home. Then we may live, we who came here for our families, for survival. We can stop fighting—"

Malini saw Priya pause, vulnerable to his words, and saw the man's hands rise. She felt the tug of his magic as he drew upon it.

She didn't wait to see what he would do. She drew her saber.

Sanvi, foolish girl, tried to grab her. "Empress, don't. You can't do this! This isn't your purpose. You're no warrior, please!"

Malini shrugged off her hands. Unfamiliar magic thrummed in her blood. She tasted metal, soil—the sap that made life.

"You do not know what I am," she said, and felt Priya's magic sing through her as she raised her saber again and stepped into the fray.

She was not as strong as a soldier, and she had only a shadow of Priya's power, and none of her control. But she had rage, honed all her life to a knife edge: rage and a cruelty in her, carefully leashed to her purposes. She unleashed it now.

The man was not looking at her. All his focus was on Priya. So he did not expect it when she lunged at his side and stabbed her saber through his abdomen—angled it upward, through flesh that resisted but parted with a sudden release, smooth as oil. She wrenched the saber out, then struck it deep again, then wrenched it free entirely. It happened in a breath, a moment. He was dead.

Priya's expression moved from incomprehension to devastation.

"You didn't have to kill him," Priya said, voice choked.

"He was going to hurt you."

"He wanted to bring me back! He wouldn't have hurt me."

"I had no reason to trust him. *Priya*, listen to me." Malini held her saber in one hand and cupped Priya's cheek with the other. "It will be over soon," Malini said urgently. "The blood, the killing, the dying. We must move to the Hirana swiftly. Can you get us there, Priya? Please."

Priya nodded, shaky. Then she released a breath, and with it her magic.

A seeker's path opened like a maw in front of them.

Malini began to move. Priya grasped her by the wrist, making her pause.

"Malini," said Priya. "There is a yaksa waiting for us. Ahead in the path."

Malini felt her heart thud in reflexive fear. She curled her fingers through Priya's.

"Can you fight the yaksa?" Malini asked. "Can you win?"

Priya's eyes were steady. Warm with determination. "Yes," she said.

"Then we continue," said Malini. "And I will be at your side when you do so."

71

BHUMIKA

The tent was growing warmer as daylight rose. She sat cross-legged and watched the play of shadows across the canvas as soldiers moved, all of them departing the camp for Ahiranya. Grief curdled in her heart.

Did she mourn her child? Ahiranya?

Was it Priya she would mourn? Her sister who moved like she owned the world, who grinned crookedly, who was far too strong and far too open? Surely if Bhumika had loved her once she'd feared for her. Surely she'd looked at that girl and thought, *That one will die laughing, die bravely, die young.*

When she had met Priya in the imperial mahal, looking at her had been exactly like gazing at one of her watchers—a creature bound to death, with waters flowing brightly through her. Bhumika's veiled ghosts had stood behind Priya—reached for Priya with mottled, yearning hands.

Bhumika did not know her well enough to mourn her. But the thought that Priya would soon be dead made her heart ache. Without her knowledge Bhumika should have been nothing and felt nothing—but she felt so much. She was aching with anger, aching to move. She wanted to enter Ahiranya. She wanted to save it.

She did not want Priya to die.

She had served her purpose as a vessel of knowledge, and

instead of emptiness, she had found in herself a well of determination that would not allow her to placidly rest.

There was a noise behind her. A blade, cutting smoothly through canvas. A figure stooped and entered.

"Jeevan," she said, relief coursing through her. She strode to him. "Are you safe?"

"We need to move swiftly," he said, which was no answer. "Sima waits for us. She stole two horses." His forehead creased in a frown. "I didn't ask how."

He was already turning to go.

"Jeevan," she said. He stopped, meeting her eyes. "I missed you," she said to him. "And I am glad to see you again."

"I am glad to see you too," he replied, after a beat.

"You'll take me to Ahiranya, then?"

He nodded.

"Why? You know what dangers face us there."

"You vowed you would go," he said. "And it's my desire too. Our people are there." Hesitation—a flicker of grief. "Your daughter."

She swallowed, the grief a knot in her throat.

"Jeevan," she said. "I need you to understand this now. For all that I have lost, I am glad I never lost you."

His eyes widened.

"Bhumika," he said. Only her name.

She took his hands. They were so much larger than her own, and scarred and callused, but they felt fragile all the same. They were a part of him, and that made them precious to her. She held them tenderly.

"You must trust that I mean it," she said.

"I trust you," he said. "I always have."

He raised their joined hands to his mouth and kissed them. It felt reverent, like a promise. When he raised his head he said, "My lady. Bhumika."

She did not tell him not to call her *my lady*. It felt different now. Precious.

They escaped the tent and met Sima with her two horses, standing near the edge of the camp.

"You took so long," she complained. "I'm not exactly able to hide, am I?"

"Apologies," said Jeevan.

"Thank you," Bhumika said to her. "Truly—thank you."

"I'm going for me, too," said Sima. "Even if you don't remember—neither of us wants to see Priya hurt. We'll make sure she's safe."

They wended their way to the border, dodging stray soldiers and warriors on horseback, until they reached the edge of the forest.

The trees were vast and forbidding. The ground treacherous with thorns. The horses were skittish, uncooperative, so Sima cursed and then slapped one of them on the rump, sending both running to safety.

"Can you carve us a safe path?" Jeevan asked, as the clatter of hooves faded.

Bhumika shook her head. "But I don't believe I will need to," she said. "The green knows me. It will let me in. And you with me." She held out her palm. "Take my hands," she said.

Sima took her left, as Jeevan took her right. Before them the forest rustled. She took a step forward, and another . . . and slowly, surely, the trees began to part.

The three of them walked into Ahiranya.

72

RAO

The remaining army waited in an arc around the border of Parijatdvipa.

The generals were arranged at the back of the army. Rao stood with Khalil, Prakash, and Narayan and watched the sway and bend of the trees. Beneath the usual noises of an army, there was an eerie hush—an absence of birdsong and wind that made his blood run cold.

He touched his fingertips to the heart's-shell dagger at his waist, then turned as Lord Khalil called his name. Khalil's eyes were narrowed against the sunlight. He gestured Rao over.

"No need to stay on guard," Khalil said, mild humor in his voice. "Everything rests in the hands of the brave soldiers and priests who walked into Ahiranya. We will live and die by their doing."

"How can I calm myself, knowing that? How can anyone?"

"Try," Khalil suggested. "Surely by now you know that war requires patience. The wait before victory or defeat would be interminable without it. Pray to the nameless if it will help."

It would not. It would only remind Rao that if he were following the bidding of the nameless, he would be in Ahiranya with Malini. He would be embracing his own death. But he nodded and said, "That's a good suggestion. Thank you."

"My wife," Khalil said, after a moment, "is wroth with you for bringing that Jagatay tribe into Dwarali. But I am not. I know you acted at the empress's bidding, and I can see the benefit of it."

"I am glad of that," Rao said, and found that he was.

"The heart's shell, of course, is useful," Khalil said, touching a light hand to his own brace of stone-tipped arrows. "But when I am sultan I will make allies of them. Marry together our lines."

"And then the heart's shell will belong to your family," Rao said slowly.

Khalil smiled.

"Perhaps it will have no worth in the new world the empress will carve," Khalil said. "But we will see. I would be a fool to reject any gift from the empress that empowers my family."

There was a thud of hooves as a rider approached them. Mahesh descended from horseback and removed his helm, giving Khalil a nod of respect. "No signs of fire yet," Mahesh said. "And no danger either. The trees move as they always do."

Mahesh, his loyal soldiers, and the warrior priests Malini had placed in his service had guarded the border diligently and knew it better than anyone. Rao nodded. He trusted him on this.

"Good, good," Prakash said. He was seated in his chariot. Exhausted. He had traveled directly from Srugna, which was suffering with a terrible devastation of rot. "Boy," he called out to a younger soldier, who startled and straightened up in response. "Bring Lord Mahesh water."

The soldier obeyed, and Mahesh drank deeply. There was, Rao noticed, a mark high at Mahesh's throat. A single line of lichen.

"Lord Mahesh," he said quietly.

Mahesh met his eyes and gave him a joyless smile.

"You cannot serve here long without rot finding you, Prince Rao," Mahesh said, grim acceptance in his voice. "I am glad you were spared that fate. But I have heard you have been following your own perilous destiny."

"I fulfilled my destiny when I named Malini as empress," Rao said. "Everything since then has been nothing but a series of disasters."

"They call you the voice of the nameless," Mahesh said. "Not the warrior priests the empress handed me, of course—those fanatical bastards only have time for the mothers—but the other soldiers speak about you. They say your sight is blessed."

"A series of disasters," Rao repeated. "But I am glad to hear that a grand tale follows me."

Mahesh gave him a look Rao couldn't read. Then he strode toward Rao and clapped a hand to his shoulder, drawing him away from the other generals.

"This work, this war...I do it for Prince Aditya," Mahesh said. "As you do, I believe." Mahesh shook his head. "For a while I thought we would lose you with him," he said. "You wept tears like fire for days after his death. My men were sure you'd slip into death with him. I am glad it was not your fate. We are all glad."

Visions played in licks of flame behind his eyelids. Snow beyond Dwarali. The lure of Alor. Fire, and Aditya's gentle smile, his beckoning hands. Rao looked away, toward the bristling wall of trees.

"As am I," Rao lied.

Mahesh's grip tightened. "Good." Released him. "That's good."

Mahesh had just mounted his horse and turned to supervise his men when cries of alarm rose up from the perimeter of guards around Rao and the other generals. Bows were nocked, arrows drawn, as they turned to a single rider racing toward them from the direction of the war camp. Rao's heart was in his throat.

"Is that—the empress's sage?" Narayan asked.

"Lower your bows!" Khalil barked.

Rao ran toward her. Lata slipped down from her horse into his arms, grasping his shoulders so tightly he thought she might rip through cloth.

"The High Priest," she gasped. "H-he and other priests and—soldiers from Harsinghar, only a small handful, probably faithful roped into his schemes—they're here, Rao. Riding to us now.

They came to the war camp, but I didn't wait to speak to them." She found her footing and he released her. "He should be in Harsinghar," she went on. "But someone betrayed us—set him free. So many priests with him. Rao, Generals, I—had to warn you all."

He turned to look behind him and saw that the other generals were watching. Listening. Their expressions were grave. They knew that Hemanth had tried to work against Malini and place her nephew on her throne. They knew that Hemanth's presence was an unnecessary complication.

"We cannot meet the High Priest with our weapons drawn," Narayan said. "Let us talk to him and see what can be done."

Hemanth approached with a crowd of priests behind him, all of them on horseback. He must have ridden swiftly from Harsinghar. His ash-mark was almost entirely erased by his own sweat. But his expression was entirely a priest's—tranquil despite the heat and the suspicion of the men around him.

"My lords," he said, his voice sonorous. "Where is the empress?"

"She is not able to speak with you, High Priest," Khalil said first, cordially.

"Ah." He looked to the forest. "Too late to face her directly, then," he said. His eyes were sorrowful. "So be it."

He gestured; a handful of priests rode toward the army at the border. Some of the soldiers around Rao reached for their weapons—Rao shook his head. He saw similar gestures from the other generals.

They could not simply attack unarmed priests. Rao knew that. And still, there was a bitter taste in his mouth as he watched them go.

"They are only passing on my words," Hemanth said. "There is no need to fear them."

"Your words," Narayan repeated.

"I told them what I would say to you," Hemanth replied. "They listened and drank my words like water." He held his palms open, vulnerable. "The empress has come to Ahiranya with men of faith," he said. "Men ready to burn. I prayed to the mothers, and in my dark grief, they spoke to me. They told me that those who love the mothers must help the empress face her glorious fate."

"There are already priests with her," said Rao, finding his voice. "High Priest, there's no need for this."

She has no need for you.

"She seeks to burn the temple of the Ahiranyi," Hemanth said calmly. "I know this. She believes the deaths of holy men will destroy the yaksa. But the mothers have shown me a different and deeper truth. The truth I have always known: Her death remains the answer. The temple of the Ahiranyi does not matter. The priests do not matter. Only she matters. She must die."

Lata jolted forward, rage on her face. Rao gripped her arm.

"If you attack the High Priest of the mothers of flame, what do you think will happen to you?" he muttered. Then he said, more loudly, "My men will hold you with respect and care, High Priest, until the empress's work is done."

Hemanth shook his head, smiling sadly.

"Soon the empress will burn," said Hemanth.

"The empress will *not*," Lata replied immediately.

"I have no doubt she will do her duty," said Hemanth. "Why else would she have entered Ahiranya? In her heart she has always known her purpose. When the yaksa are dead, and we are free of their presence, Prince Vijay will take the throne, and you men shall lead on his behalf. It will be a better world. You are lords and kings, and you will help him make the empire glorious once more."

How neat it would be. How tidy. No more empress. Another sacrificial statue carved in gold, a *Malini* to be worshipped by future generations. The priests would burn incense for her, and say she had been good and pure and righteous, and they would forget that the true Malini had ruled an empire for a heartbeat, a single moment in time, then died under the inexorable hand of her own priesthood.

He saw hesitation in some of the faces around him. Narayan. Prakash. It made anger roil in his stomach.

"No," he said roughly. "This was not what Aditya died for. I was there. I witnessed his death. Lord Mahesh and I—and our warriors—we made a *vow* to him. I will not betray my friend, my prince. I will not betray the son of flame. And that means I will not betray the empress. She has brought us here to see the yaksa finally destroyed, and our world free of their power. She has entered Ahiranya not to die but to show the priests the respect and reverence they deserve before they save us all.

"I was there when a priest of the nameless killed a yaksa," he said angrily. "I witnessed that, too. What have you done, High Priest? What will you do? Will you burn now, and die by your ideals?"

A shadow passed through Hemanth's eyes.

"To my regret, I must be there to rear Prince Vijay and teach him what it means to rule," Hemanth replied.

"Is that so?" Rao laughed. "You convinced Chandra—a rotten husk of a man even when he was a child, I remember *that* too, High Priest—that he was worthy of a throne. You made him worse." Rao's voice was trembling with anger. "You burned women and turned their remains into weapons. You may claim to act for the greater good, but I have seen the nameless and the void my god resides in, and I have seen the flames of holy fire, and I *see you*. You are not worthy of your title or the respect it brings you," he spat.

"Where are the soldiers who were left to watch you?" Khalil asked into the silence, his voice like stone.

"They are dead," Hemanth said simply.

"You killed the empress's soldiers," Khalil said flatly. "Left to guard you."

"I attempted to reason with them," said Hemanth. "And I grieve for them now. But their loss could not be helped."

Khalil gave a sharp nod to one of his riders. His soldiers surrounded Hemanth in an instant.

"Go with my men, High Priest," Khalil said. "They will treat you with respect, I promise you. The empress is following the will of the mothers and the nameless in this, and we will not turn against her. Not even for you."

Hemanth's exhale was soft. His eyes closed, then opened. He lowered his arms.

"I hoped you would listen, my lords," he said. "I hoped you would see trust. But if it is not to be—well. So be it. It begins regardless."

Lata made a shocked noise. She'd turned, looking away from Hemanth. Looking to the army.

Rao turned, slowly, to look with her. Behind him Hemanth's voice was heavy. Prophetic. "Ahiranya will burn," he said simply. "Everything will burn, until the empress chooses a willing death. That is what my priests pray for. That is the only gift that will quench their fire."

And as Rao watched, the distant priests turned from flesh to beings of light, and then beings of pure fire—and the Parijat-dvipan army, surrounding them, was hit with a deluge of flame like a tidal wave.

73

PRIYA

Shyam, dead. She'd felt it when Malini's saber had gone through him. She'd felt it when some of her mask-keepers had died, broken on heart's shell.

Shyam had told her the yaksa had let him drink; let them *all* drink. She felt dizzy with grief and with rage, and guilt for her own failures.

This had to end. The sooner the better. She needed the yaksa to be gone.

She and Malini walked together, side by side through the path Priya had carved. Malini's surviving guards and soldiers and priests followed behind them in a narrow line. The path—and Ahiranya itself—were not built to welcome the broad swathe of an army. At least within the path they could move more swiftly than they would have beyond its tree-lined borders.

Priya looked through those trees. The world beyond was blurred, soft and strange. She could see no one. Not the Ahiranyi warriors she'd left behind, and no new enemies. That was some good luck.

The only enemy they needed to face lay ahead of them on the path.

She was conscious of all the people behind her. Some wounded, some limping forward, using one another for support. Cira Ara was ahead of them, waiting on the path, crouched patiently in the green and soil.

"I'll go first," said Priya. "I have to." She turned to look at Malini. "I'm not leaving you behind," Priya vowed. "But a yaksa is…different. I should face her."

"I'm not arguing," Malini said. Her gray eyes looked deep into Priya. It was as if she saw and felt what Priya did: the vibrant, green life of a yaksa ahead of them. That call in the sangam.

"Go," Malini urged, and Priya straightened her shoulders and walked ahead of her.

Cira Ara was crouched in a ring of leaves. Cira Ara wore her long-dead temple sister Riti's face, carved into a new shape by soil and stone. She straightened when she saw Priya, and held one hand out to her.

"Little one," Cira Ara rasped, her voice a rough-hewn stone. "Mani Ara is waiting for you."

"Why have you come for me, Cira?" Priya asked. "I'm here, aren't I? I've come back for Mani Ara. You didn't need to seek me out."

A creak of her neck, a low noise from her throat, a grating laugh.

"Lie," said Cira Ara. "Arahli told me you lie. Look at your army of mortals. Shall I make the soil swallow them?"

"No," Priya said sharply. She stretched her magic, touching all of the people behind her that she could. Holding them, in case Cira turned on them. Oh, if only she could have escorted those priests here without a wall of guards. The soldiers were more a hindrance than a help. "I need them. Leave them be."

The yaksa began to walk toward her. Still unsteady on her legs, coltish and new—or as if she lacked an understanding of the joints she needed for seamless movement. There was too much stone in her, and too much deep ore.

"The others should come and collect you," Cira Ara said. "But they could not."

"Why?" Priya asked. She could feel Malini not far behind her, more strongly than all the rest. "Were they too busy?"

Bared teeth—pearling gray and sharp. "They grow more

mortal," said the yaksa. "They fear it. Terror runs in them. But I am still freshly born to this world—still green and strong. You drew me from the ground and I can feel my power running through me, no blood at all." Her eyes flashed, malevolent. "Come with me, Priya."

"No."

Cira Ara lurched toward her. Roots erupted from the ground and caught her arm before it could touch Priya. Behind her, Priya could hear a sword being unsheathed once more.

"Don't make me fight you," Priya said, voice hard. "I will if you stand in my way."

"As you fought the mortals we sent to find you?" Another movement of her head. Her eyes, the most human part of her, fixed on Priya. They were Riti's eyes—brown, wide, soft-lashed. "Poor poisoned soldiers. They tried. But I am not like them. You cannot kill me, little Elder."

Priya gave an ugly laugh. "Are you sure?" Another step closer. "Do you understand how you've changed? Mani Ara dragged you into this world long ago. Made you one with the trees, the soil, the flowers. The earth was yours. But you *died*, Cira Ara. And now you grow more and more like humans were—are—before they're touched by rot. You'll soon be meat, gristle, bone." Priya took a step closer. "Your kin are right to fear it. Meat can die so easily, after all."

A hunted look flickered over the yaksa's face.

She opened her mouth to speak—and looked, suddenly, beyond Priya's shoulder.

That was when Priya heard the screaming begin. A panicked tumult of noise from within the seeker's path, all howling and begging—and behind it, the crackle of fire.

No.

The people behind them surged forward, panicked. Priya was forced to grab them with her power to stop them from crushing one another.

"Priya." Malini was striding toward her, blade drawn, the

guardswomen ringed around her. Her gaze darted from the yaksa to Priya, her face taut with tension. "We need to run."

"Did the priests…?" Priya shook her head, shock holding her fast. "Did they choose to die? Did they make this?"

"It doesn't matter where the fire comes from," Malini said tightly. "What matters is that it is coming *here*."

Malini grasped Priya's arm fiercely. "Take us to the Hirana, Priya. Take the priests and me now, before—"

Too late. Malini's words were swallowed by a roar of fire. The fire was quick, too quick. There was no *time*. Flame raced through the trees lining the path, setting them alight. With horror, Priya felt the people she was holding with her magic turn to kindling in the blaze. She released them, but it was too late for some. The smell of burning bodies filled her nose.

The rest surged forward, moving toward Priya and Malini and the guardswomen in a wave. Sahar grabbed Malini, shielding her, even as Malini's grip on Priya tightened and she tried to draw Priya close to her.

They should have been crushed by the press of bodies, but Priya was using all her focus to carve a defense around them—a wall of stone and soil and raised roots to force the wave of soldiers and priests to part around them. The trees were golden, as good as bars on a cage, pinning them onto the path. Her head pounded. The fire hurt. It felt her yaksa magic, the green in her blood, and it *hungered*.

"I don't need to be protected," Priya protested, struggling to breathe. "Let me go, I need to carve a way out—another path, a way free of this—"

Malini's hand spasmed. She released Priya with obvious reluctance, teeth bared, terror in her eyes. "Do it," she commanded.

She tried. Oh, she tried. But her magic was like tangled thread between her fingers, impossible to unknot. *Run*, she thought wildly. *We should just run.* But they could not run between the trees, slipping from the seeker's path to the embrace of the forest. The trees of the path were burning, burning, and they would not part at her command.

There was nowhere to go. The fire was everywhere.

Cira Ara stepped back from the flames, wind and motes of ash brushing her hair into a dark flag that streamed behind her. The flames were moving intently—rippling through the air in a scythe aimed squarely at her. Holy fire seeking out a yaksa. Marking her for death.

Cira Ara flinched. Her human eyes were wide in her face as she met Priya's gaze.

"They were right to fear," Cira Ara said tremulously. The fire consumed her.

Priya felt her die. The pounding of her skull intensified, and something in her chest began to pulse. A foreign heartbeat. Malini's magic tangling with her own, panicked and powerful. She drew upon it. Too late for Cira, the trees tore open into a crooked arch before them, cutting through the path. Providing an exit.

"With me," she yelled, and grasped Malini's arm and dragged her through.

Bodies followed her. Malini, and the guardswomen, and a handful of priests. The gate was not enough. The fire was following them. So Priya ran, and ran, carving paths and exits with speed and finesse only fear could give her. She tore through the green, struggling to outpace the fire, as heat and pain nipped at her heels. She drew on every part of her strength, every green and water-drenched part of her—until finally she could go no farther.

One last archway. They tumbled together to the ground. The fire was coming for them, but Priya had strength enough left to shut the path brutally behind them.

One last gout of flame spiraled through the door as it vanished. Exhausted, she watched the fire turn, rippling toward them.

Toward *Malini*.

Priya did not think. She was breathless from the feel of the yaksa's death—from a god's agony stretching hands inside her rib cage. The sangam was wild and churning, a blackness between her eyes. But even if she had not been shocked to numbness, if magic hadn't been rising in her like a mist, she would have done what she did then. It was in her nature, written into her like ink on paper, or stars upon the sky.

She leapt in front of Malini.

The fire hit her square between the shoulders. Heat, so much heat. And then it stretched, arcing like vast wings, and she felt her pain stretch with it. She was burned skin, flayed open—she was in agony so black and vast and formless that it was like tumbling through the sangam, through its rivers and stars, and drowning, drowning. She felt her hair singe and her legs give way.

She saw Malini's mouth move, through the halo of flame surrounding her own body. *Priya. Priya. Priya—*

Please, no, no—

Something knocked against her. There was a thump and a sizzle of flesh.

Priya stared, uncomprehending through her agony. Sahar was in front of her, panting. Sahar's arm was burnt from the fingers to shoulder. She was still holding her heart's-shell blade in front of her in that burned hand, wielding it like a shield. Her grip trembled. Priya's ears were ringing, and there was blood in her mouth, and as if from a great distance she looked at her own body. Burnt, blistering. Wounded beyond her comprehension.

I will not survive this, she thought. And that, too, seemed distant. Strange. Was this how death felt, all lightness and horror?

Someone reached for her. She screamed, or thought she did, as she was raised from the ground. Her face against a shoulder; hands on her, holding her still.

Malini's palms, cool against her unburnt face.

"I was always destined for the fire," Malini was saying, her voice wild and trembling and broken. "N-not you."

"That's a lie," Priya whispered. "A lie you were told. You don't—believe. There's no magic in that. The fire never wanted you," she managed to say. And then her vision wavered and went, in one breath, dark.

74

ARAHLI ARA

Ahiranya was burning, and Taru Ara could not climb the Hirana alone.

She had revealed her wound to their kin when they had felt their newborn sibling die in Alor. She had screamed and wept, bared to them. *I am broken, ruined. I am not what I should be.*

None of us are, are we? None of us are!

Since then disquiet had spread between them. The Parijati had a weapon once more that could kill them. Mani Ara had no vessel. And they were changing, he and his kin—growing flesh and feelings, growing *human*.

Their last hope was extinguished. Cira Ara had promised to find Priya. But Cira was dead. He had felt her go, as he'd felt their poor newborn kin in Alor perish. He watched Taru now and wondered if he would soon feel the unraveling of her life. The part of him that was Ashok and always would be could not believe she still lived, rotten through as she was.

"I am weak," Taru said, furious, as Sendhil—*Vata Ara*—reached for her. "I am not the creature Mani Ara made me to be. I fight the pain and yet it grows and grows. Brother, my kin, you should leave me."

"Weak you may be," Vata Ara murmured. "But you are ours."

He lifted her and walked to the Hirana. He would rise to its highest zenith, as far from the flames as possible. Avan Ara followed, light on his childish feet. There were pilgrims trying to scramble up the Hirana's surface in a panic, seeking shelter and the kindness of the yaksa. Some had already fallen. Arahli saw a handful of broken bodies upon the ground, arms splayed, necks broken. A dozen living pilgrims, fearful of the climb, reached for Avan Ara as he crossed their path. He shook them off with a bristle of thorns.

Bhisa Ara watched them go.

"I slept last night," Bhisa Ara said into the silence, "as humans sleep. At last light, I walked into a deep lake and submerged myself, and I could not breathe. I should not have needed breath. When I rose, my body grew mottled like it wore mortal flesh.

"I am trapped in this monstrous body. And I see the same monstrousness on you. I even dream," she told him, with a bitter laugh. "I dream Chandni's dreams, and her life, and I wake with salt on this face." She touched a fingertip to her cheek. "Do you think we will forget what it means to be green, Arahli?"

"Climb the Hirana, Bhisa," he urged her. He could hear the growing roar of fire. "I will follow."

She smiled. Sorrow in her eyes.

"I know this is your fault, dear heart," she said. "You let Elder Bhumika go. Filled her up with secrets. She is our death, and you are our death."

"Ashok acted," he said roughly. "Not me."

"Are you not Ashok? Am I not Chandni? Oh, sweet one, we are sickened with their mortal longings and mortal acts. You destroyed us. We should have feared little Bhumika, but we did not understand what mortals can do with nothing but their bodies and their dreams, did we?" She lowered her hand. "Now we know."

"Priya is in Ahiranya once more," he said, and thought he might scream. His throat hurt. He felt too much, far too much. Humanity's curse lay heavy on him. "I will go to her—save her—"

"She is surrounded by fire," said Bhisa. "She is dead. As Cira is dead, poor little one." She said it without emotion. She began to walk to the Hirana. "Come," she said. "Let us wait for the fire together."

He watched her for a moment, then turned and walked away.

Bhumika was here, in Ahiranya. Bhumika had come home. The others of his kin could not feel it. But he was the one who had ripped her from the waters, and he knew the shape of her magic. He marked where she stood.

He walked calmly into the mahal, where people were screaming and running for their lives, and walked down a corridor. Another.

There was a room with a door encased by roots so thick and rot-riven that no mortal man could cut through them. He parted them with a glance and walked through the door. Inside sat Ganam. Rukh, and Bhumika's child, fastened close against his side. Ganam looked up at him, tired and defiant, and said, "Yaksa. Please."

Perhaps Ganam begged for forgiveness, or mercy. Arahli did not know or care. "Take your people to the Hirana," he said. "Climb it. Take the temple children too." He turned away. "If you try to walk the paths you carved to escape, I will make them close over you and pierce you to death with thorns. Or I will break your necks with vines. I haven't yet decided."

Ganam scrambled to his feet. "Yaksa—why?"

"Fire is coming," Arahli said, already walking away from them. They would obey or they would not. It no longer mattered to him. "Go to the Hirana, and you may survive. Walk into the forest and you will burn."

He heard Ganam's shaky swear, and the boy Rukh's high-voiced question. But then they were running—Ganam yelling at people to follow him now. Farther into the mahal he found the broken hilt of the blade Avan Ara had taken from Ganam.

He steeled himself and picked up the hilt—and with the hilt, the black shards of stone still upon it.

Emptiness, cold and painful, swallowed him.

The stone was a negation of magic. Magic green or magic flame, it was all the same. It would hurt him, but perhaps it would also protect him.

Arahli left the mahal. He walked into the woods. In the distance, the trees smoldered an awful gold.

He walked to Bhumika. The flames were coming from the border of the forest, and had not quite reached him yet, though he felt them. But Bhumika had clearly run from fire. Ash stained her face. She stood in front of the two mortals with her, shielding them with her body. Her eyes met his own.

"Bhumika," he said. The leaves above them moved with his voice, spearing her face with shadows. "Why did you come back?"

Her look assessed him slowly. There was no fear of him in her eyes.

"I promised myself I would keep the Ahiranyi people safe," she said. "I came for them, and my child, and my sister. You know me, yaksa?"

"Yes," said Arahli. "Of course I know you."

"I knew you once," she said slowly. "I feel it."

"I was the one who broke you from the waters," he told her. "I was the one who gave you the knowledge of how to end our lives." A step closer. "The fire will burn Ahiranya entirely," he said. "It burns everything in its path. We have killed Ahiranya, you and I."

"We can lead our people out of the forest," said Bhumika. "Seeker's paths could lead them to safety." Her gaze was unflinching. "I won't easily give up on hope."

Strange, to have her brother's memories, fresh and bleeding within him, and not be her brother. Strange, that she could be so entirely Bhumika, and yet empty of her old memories. Perhaps it was this strange kinship, this twisted mirroring, that made Arahli extend a hand to her.

"Come," he said. "Your child waits for you on the Hirana. Take my hand, and you can see her once more."

The man behind her stiffened. But Bhumika stepped forward and took Arahli's hand with utter trust.

"Yaksa," she said. "Show me the way."

75

MALINI

Priya lay in her arms.

I should not have picked her up, thought Malini. But Priya was no longer screaming. She was silent and unconscious. Her face was unmarked, apart from the glow of leaves under her skin. But the rest of her...

Malini swallowed, raising her head. Sahar's teeth were gritted. Her bare arm looked awful. Two priests of the nameless who had tumbled out of the path with them came to kneel beside Sahar, and one carefully examined her arm, not quite touching it.

"How did you stop the fire?" Malini asked Sahar. "It burned the yaksa to nothing. How did you save Priya and yourself?"

"I don't know, my lady," Sahar said helplessly. Her face was gray with pain.

"You were holding a knife."

"Heart's shell. But I thought it only had use against the yaksa and their power."

Heart's shell clearly had power against fire, too.

Light and shadow flickered over all their faces. "If you can run, we must," one priest said. "E-Empress. If you can carry the uh, the Ahiranyi..."

There was a thud. Sahar jerked at her side and fell to her knees.

An arrow protruded from her shoulder. Malini stared at her, uncomprehending for a moment before horror dawned. Then her voice returned to her, as her heart gave a painful thud.

"*Sahar*," Malini gasped out.

Sahar's mouth moved soundlessly.

The priests scrambled away, but Malini did not move. She could not. She was holding Priya. Instead, she could only watch as Sanvi lowered her bow and met her eyes. Shri lay on the ground dead, throat slit, beside her.

"Empress," Sanvi said, her voice steady. She looked calm—calmer than she should have in a maelstrom of fire. "Priests of the mothers have chosen to die alongside you. Their fire is here. Did you not see, Empress? The fire followed you. It sought you out so sweetly. The priests will burn this land and our empire, Empress, until you burn willingly and take the yaksa with you. It's time."

Malini stared at her. If she'd had any emotion left in her, she would have felt betrayed—and worse, foolish. She should have seen the viper in her own personal guard.

Too late, now.

"If I burn here, the yaksa will survive," Malini said.

"An Ahiranyi falsehood," Sanvi said swiftly. She looked so *sure*. Malini had only ever seen such certainty in the faces of priests. Sanvi lowered her bow and took a bottle from her belt. Opened it and raised it above her head, letting it pour like water over her hair, her skull.

Oil.

"It will make it easier," said Sanvi. "Oil, flint, a spark. It's better than drawing on faith alone. Priest Mitul told me what to do. You don't need to be afraid, Empress. I'll be with you."

Sanvi held her arms open.

"You were always meant to enter this forest," Sanvi said, smiling. "You are here because you're ready to die willingly, Empress, whether you admit it to yourself or not. But the time for falsehood is over."

Ash and motes of fire were being carried on the air. It would not be difficult to go aflame.

"My lady," Sahar said raggedly. "Don't."

"Sanvi," Malini said. Her voice shook. "I'm afraid."

"You don't need to be, Empress!" Sanvi walked to her. "I'll go with you," she said, hushed. "Together."

Malini swallowed. Nodded.

"Come here," she said. "Please."

Sanvi kneeled down. She held the flask of oil out, radiant with belief. Malini reached out a hand.

She didn't take the oil. She curled her fingers into a fist.

The magic inside her responded to her movement—to the demand she infused into it. The green shook, and the soil splintered. Sanvi shrieked, dropping her oil to reach for a weapon, but it was too late. The soil had opened and swallowed her up to her waist. She flailed her arms and Malini smoothly drew a short blade—one concealed at her own waist—and pinned Sanvi's right hand to the ground.

"I considered suffocating you in the ground," Malini said, with utter calm. "But this is slower. Better. You may burn as you wished to."

In response to her magic, the fire arced toward her again. She flinched and felt Priya stir. An exhale from Priya, and the earth rose up in a wall, holding the fire at bay. For now.

She heard a noise. One of the priests was still there. Crouched and terrified, only feet from her. She saw resolve filter into his eyes. His hands clenched, and he raised himself up.

"Let me come with you, Empress," he said hoarsely. "Let me fulfill our purpose."

"No," she said numbly.

Fire-hot wind caught her hair, making it fly around her.

She looked back at Sahar, who was alive but grievously wounded.

"Let the sacrifices that have already been made be enough. Take my guard to safety. You need to stop her bleeding. Her weapon—the one made of stone—may protect you from the fire."

"I won't leave you," Sahar said.

"You've served me well, Sahar," Malini said. "But I won't allow you to die here." She looked again at the priest. "Take her. *Go.*"

Despite Sahar's protests, he managed to get her to her feet. She watched them limp into the forest. She could not do more for them.

She picked Priya up in her arms and made hushed apologies as Priya cried out.

How far were they from the Hirana? Too far, surely. Malini could not outrun the fire. The fire was seeking her out.

But she needed to take Priya to the deathless waters. Those waters could heal Priya. That feverish thought caught her and held her. If anything could save Priya, it was the waters that had made her strong.

Malini tried to stand. The movement jolted Priya awake. She made an awful noise. Her eyes, unfocused at first, fixed on Malini's face. Malini froze in the process of lifting her, and lay her carefully back down.

"M-Malini?"

"I'm here, my love."

"I...need to—get to the Hirana." She was panting hard, her breath breaking her words into shards. The whites of her eyes were vast—the wild whiteness of a spooked horse. "Need to..."

"Shh," Malini soothed. "I know."

She knew now that she had made a terrible mistake coming here, and believing that what she had put into place would be enough to leash the priesthood. She had used their faith against them over and over, but faith was a flame that could not be grasped forever. Eventually it would turn on its wielder. It had.

No turning back. The priests would have what they wished. Her death, one way or another.

She felt oddly calm. It was one thing to be dragged to a pyre. To be afraid, and used. But it was different to kneel on burnt soil with your love dying in your arms, pondering a choice.

"I will take you into the Hirana myself," she said.

Priya made a groan of protest.

"I'll go—*myself.*"

"You cannot go on your own. Surely you recognize it," Malini said softly. "You and your yaksa are bound. And you and I are bound. Your magic..." She breathed, and exhaled, a deliberate parting of her mouth—and knew Priya felt it all through the green, a susurration, a song. "I'll take you."

"You shouldn't have come with me," Priya said, voice small. "You were meant to—to rule. To hold on to power first."

"What does it matter," Malini said, her voice splintering. "If I don't have you? If you are gone where I cannot see you or feel you or dream you again, then what is any of it worth to me?"

She cupped Priya's face tenderly between her hands. Tilted Priya's face up.

"I have escaped death so many times," Malini said, in a voice that trembled but was fierce, fierce. "I am done. Priya." A kiss to each closed eyelid. "Show me the way to Mani Ara."

Priya exhaled a rattling breath.

No seeker's path opened before them. Instead, a line of flowers— jasmine and ashoka, needle-flower and oleander—bloomed in a line before them, marking the way to the Hirana. A wall of rock shuddered out of the ground behind them.

A way forward and a shield at her back. Priya was so good to her.

"Thank you," she whispered, and heaved Priya up into her arms. Priya made one sound of agony then went silent.

Malini did not know how she would carry her all the way. Her arms already ached. Her lungs burned from smoke. But she clenched her jaw and began to walk.

It went on forever, hot and awful, the fire screaming at her back. She felt the green magic shiver around them. Priya's magic.

"I cannot carry her alone," she said to it, and felt the green respond to her. Vines crawled their way up her body, twining over her arms, until they cradled Priya with her, carrying her along with Malini. It was easier after that.

She landed heavily on her knees on the ground at the base of the Hirana. It was her hand that she placed against the Hirana's stone, and her borrowed magic that somehow opened a tunnel into the Hirana. Blue light glowed at the end of it, beckoning.

She lifted Priya up once more and walked in. She closed the stone behind her.

There were no more vines to help her. She carried Priya's weight alone.

She walked until she was deep into the heart of the Hirana. Until there was blue light around her, and blue water before her.

She waded in to her knees.

Behind her, beyond stone, a fire was pulsing, roaring. It would follow her down into the depths beneath the Hirana eventually. It would find her at the deathless waters, and it would kill her. But not yet.

"The waters can heal you?" Malini asked. She felt as if she were begging.

A rasping breath from Priya. Then, "No. I don't know."

"They're your yaksa's waters. Mani Ara's. They made you strong before."

"Yes."

"Then she will save you," said Malini decisively. She had to believe it. If she didn't, then Priya was as good as dead. "And you'll come back to me. Promise it, Priya."

"Promise," Priya echoed. Then her heavy eyes snapped open. "The priests. Where are they?"

Malini shook her head.

"You didn't bring a priest," Priya said. "Not one? Malini. We need them. The deathless waters—they need to be destroyed." Priya's grip was painful on her arm. "They need to be, or the yaksa will continue changing the world, their magic will..."

"I will make sure the waters die," Malini promised. "When you return, when you're safe, I will open the Hirana to the fire and let the waters burn."

"You—you'll die—"

"I won't," Malini lied. "I won't, Priya."

"If Mani Ara comes out of the water wearing my face— Malini, you won't even know."

"If Mani Ara comes from the waters wearing your face, I will know," said Malini. "Because I know you." She brushed back Priya's hair softly from her forehead. "And if she does I will burn us both. I will destroy her with my faith. I promise."

"No."

"We leave together, or not at all," Malini said quietly. "I've chosen."

A rattling breath.

"But you have—no faith. To burn."

"I have no faith in the mothers," whispered Malini. "But I have faith in you."

Malini lowered her into the water. And let go.

76

BHUMIKA

They climbed the Hirana with the yaksa.

It was a high, unnatural mountain—covered in carvings, serpents and fanged teeth. Bhumika's body knew it, though, knew how to climb. And absurdly, she felt as if the Hirana knew her in return. It welcomed her as easily as the forest had.

She watched the yaksa as she climbed. The long fronds of his hair. His pale, inhuman eyes.

He wore the face of one of her watchers, though her watcher was just a boy. He wore that face older and harder, wrought strange by wood and leaves. Or perhaps her ghost wore his.

They are both false, she thought. *Both echoes of someone I lost.*

There were people huddled everywhere, on the Hirana's zenith. And also four who were not people, but something else entirely.

"Nandi," the yaksa murmured, gesturing. "Sanjana. Sendhil. Chandni. That is what you called them."

"Not their true names, then," Bhumika said in return.

"No," he said. "You may call me Arahli Ara."

That was a true name. Strange, that he denied her the false one.

"Kneel," said the one he had called Chandni. "Show respect."

In their faces she saw pain of the living. She saw it in the exhausted look in Sanjana's eyes, and the smell of sickness rising from her skin. In the way Sendhil stood over Sanjana, protective, aware of the illness upon her. In the inwardness of the yaksa child Nandi, his head bowed, all the pointed bones of his upper spine curved. The more they sacrificed, and the more the world changed, the more human they grew. It had to terrify them.

"Bhumika," Nandi said. "Do you come to fight for us? Or to fight us?"

"I come," she said, "to see these people to safety. To ask you to open a path for them out of Ahiranya."

"You want us to burn alone," Sanjana said. She sounded petulant. "Well, we do not want to burn at all."

Then you should never have come to this world, Bhumika thought. She did not say it. There was animal terror working its way up her spine. Sima was steel-eyed beside her. Jeevan was calm, visibly calm. She held on to his calm and Sima's steel like an anchor.

A boy, gangling, growing into his strength, walked determinedly toward her. His face was full of light.

"Lady Bhumika," he said. "Is it—is it really you?"

She did not know him, but she knew what to say.

"Yes," she said.

"Her daughter," Sima said abruptly. "Rukh, where is she?"

"Sima!" The boy's mouth gaped and suddenly shaped a shaky smile. "Sima, you—"

"*Rukh.* Is Padma all right? Is she here?"

"Yes," he said. "Yes, yes she is. She's with Khalida. Khalida?" He turned, craning his neck.

A woman—Khalida—stood and walked toward them. She was carrying something—someone—in her arms, swaddled in cloth, hidden carefully by her shawl. The small figure moved, the shawl and blanket alike sliding back.

And after that, she could not think of anything but the child before her.

I know you, she thought. It struck her like lightning. She hadn't expected it—had expected grief and alienness, and had braced herself for it. But she saw that small face, those wide eyes, and something in her heart flowered—something that had hurt in her, constantly, abruptly eased.

I know you.

There was wonder in those large eyes—a forgetting and a knowing in the child's gaze, as there surely was in hers. And yet Bhumika's hands twitched at her sides, and then her arms reached out, and she did not know if she would flinch if the child, her child, recoiled, but she had to try anyway.

Her daughter fit easily into her arms. Squirming and heavy, too large to be held like this. It was perfect.

"Elder Bhumika." A quiet voice. She turned.

Arahli Ara stood before her.

"Bhumika," Sendhil said, his voice determined. "Dear one. Will you remember?"

Arahli Ara's gaze was steady. "I can give you yourself back, now you are here," he said.

"And what would be the price?" Bhumika asked. "Loyalty?"

"When you are one with us again, and know yourself," he said, "you serve us. Your sister will soon be one with Mani Ara. We will need people like you when our mother is among us again."

"No," said Bhumika. "I'm afraid I'll do no such thing. You're dying, yaksa," she said. "Dying here, with fire beneath us, and still refusing to do what is right for Ahiranya."

"We are not dying," Sendhil snapped. Chandni looked away.

"We fight for Ahiranya still. Our loyal worshippers walk the forest, empowered by our waters," Nandi said. "The forest will always be ours."

"Fighting is not what Ahiranya needs from you," said Bhumika. "It needs your death."

Sendhil strode toward her. He reached for her, a grasping hand, sharp-taloned. She did not know if he wanted to hurt her, but her heart thumped, her blood ran cold. Bhumika clutched her daughter tighter, turning to shield her with her back. The air thickened. Jeevan's saber was drawn.

Sima got there first.

A heart's-shell knife slid through the yaksa's chest. He staggered.

Red blood poured from his wound. The sound he made was wet, guttural with horror.

"You're dying already," Bhumika repeated, with a great calm she did not feel. "At least make it a death worthy of you." She met Arahli Ara's eyes. "Leave the Hirana. Go, and face your fate. You know you must."

77

RAO

In the chaos—the fire and screaming, the tumult of bodies—
Hemanth managed to get on a horse and ride away.

"Someone stop him!" Rao demanded.

"I'll go," Narayan said. "With me!" He ordered his men, and
Rao saw them move into formation, unsteady with terror as
flames arced overhead, sinuous as serpents.

Someone was riding toward them. Mahesh, again.

"You must leave! They've turned on each other," Mahesh said
savagely. He was wounded, blood pouring from his side. He listed
unsteadily on his horse, then keeled over. A handful of soldiers
grabbed him before he could crack his skull and helped him
carefully to the ground. "Those warrior priests. Those *bastards.*"
He winced. "Fucking Hemanth has warrior turning on warrior.
What a time for fighting over faith."

Rao raised his head. The whole army was fighting itself, and
those who weren't fighting were burning. He swore. He could
have been sick.

"My most loyal soldiers know what to do," Mahesh was saying grimly. "They'll slit the throats of any priestly warrior they
see. Those fucking fanatics won't make it beyond the perimeter
of my own men. You know the strangest thing, Prince Rao?" He
coughed, blood on his lips. "Not all of them fight against us," he
said. "Some fight for us. The empress truly swayed them."

A soldier was racing toward them, tumbling over his own feet.

"The fire is targeting people with rot first!" he yelled. There were leaves in his hair. He ran without stopping.

Rao looked down at Mahesh, eyes drawn to the lichen at his throat. He felt his heart thud.

There was a crash. A horse felled. The ground ahead of them began to burn, as a horse and rider were engulfed. The fire began to roll toward them, a wave of golden heat.

Mahesh met Rao's eyes. His smile was joyless, knowing.

"Tell my daughter," Mahesh said, his voice a rasp. "Tell her..."

The fire swallowed him like a fist. Rao leapt back, landing on his back, narrowly avoiding the burst of fire. His face felt painfully hot, his lips singed, eyes stinging. He scrambled to his feet, reaching—but Mahesh was writhing in agony, rolling on the ground. Mahesh was going still. Mahesh was gone.

"Rao!" Lata called, terrified.

"Take a horse," Rao heard Lord Khalil bark at her.

"No, I—"

"You're no warrior," he told her brusquely. Rao could barely hear him over the crackle of flames, the screaming. "And the empress will need your guidance when this war is done. *Ride*, Sage Lata. Go to the war camp and wait there."

"A horse will not ride through flames," she said, her voice choked.

"You think I didn't train my horses to face fire, after our war with Chandra?" Khalil's grin was all teeth—fierce and wild. "Go now, or Prince Rao will be too worried to face battle."

Khalil helped her onto one of the horses. It raced away, Lata on its back, and Rao felt some terrible fear unknot in him.

Good. At least she'd live.

Khalil offered Rao a hand.

"With me," he said. "We have long been the empress's allies. Let us remove this thorn from her side together."

They could not stop the flames. But they could stop the maker.

Rao took his hands and leapt onto horseback without fear.

The Dwarali horse was a powerful steed—despite their combined weight she raced across the field of fire, her mane streaming and her muscles rippling powerfully.

Hemanth was ahead of them, surrounded by a handful of soldiers. He must have brought them from Parijat with him, or perhaps they had defected from the army. Rao did not care. In front of him, Khalil nocked his bow and, without pausing, shot one man, then another, and another. They were felled. He and Khalil kept on racing forward.

Lord Narayan lay dead on the ground, throat open and eyes sightless. His chariot had fallen.

Hemanth has something. Some weapon we don't see, Rao realized. He opened his mouth to say it—and felt an awful weight hit them.

The horse went down with a crash. Khalil tumbled. There was a sickening crack and he was still.

"Lord Khalil," Rao called, coughing, finding his feet. His left leg was agony. "*Khalil.*" It was broken, perhaps. He ran to Khalil anyway. He collapsed next to him and felt for the man's breath, pulse. Khalil groaned.

Alive, Rao thought with relief. Injured, but alive. He looked at the horse.

They'd been hit with a thrown spear tipped with fire.

Hemanth's soldiers were dead, arrow-struck. But a black box lay by one of their bodies. And Hemanth held a spear that glowed with flame.

False fire. Chandra's fire.

Hemanth followed his gaze.

"It is imperfect," Hemanth said. "But we kept it from the empress. It is not a fit weapon for the yaksa, but it serves to punish men like you."

"You have no skill with weapons, Hemanth," Rao said.

"And yet I will stand against you and those like you, Prince Rao," he said, with sorrow and righteousness in his eyes. "And my priests, even the greenest boys among them, will stand against you."

Rao drew his heart's-shell dagger and strode forward.

He lunged first. Hemanth swung, and the fire arced through the air. Rao should have had the benefit of speed, but Hemanth had the greater reach, and Rao had a broken leg. Rao leapt out of the way. Stumbled, pain shooting up to his hip. His blade fell—

Hemanth struck him again. A blade of fire almost hit the armor at his shoulder. He lurched away. Not enough.

A spear-butt cracked against his skull.

Blackness.

78

ARAHLI ARA

"I won't die for them," Vata Ara said raggedly.

"The Parijatdvipans have a weapon once more that can destroy us," Arahli said. "Priya is in the flames. We have nothing."

Vata Ara shook his head, blood pouring from his wound. His face was pale. "We will find a way to survive. If we wait here, when the forest is all burned, we may walk free."

"The fire seeks us," he said. His gaze swept over them. "Not them. You remember how it was last time."

"Better than you do," Taru Ara said thinly. "I didn't stumble about believing I was mortal. I remember clearly what we were. The fire…" Her hand trembled in his own. "The fire felt like emptiness," she whispered. "And the emptiness was long, and our sleep was dark. I did not dream or think for so long. Maybe not until you freed me from the tree where my bones grew."

"Sleep isn't so terrible," said Arahli.

"Brother, you will not turn to wood and soil and earth," Taru said to him, grasping him by the arms. Her eyes were wrong, terribly wrong—leaking salt water, red-veined, her cheeks flushed with mortal blood. "You are more flesh than green now. Do you understand what may become of you? A permanent death. Something we can never rise from again."

The fires were rising below.

He knew what Mani Ara would do in his place.

She was not a creature of gentleness or sacrifice. She was pitiless and strong and she did what was necessary to survive. She would fight to the bitter end. In the sangam, she was fighting. She *loved* them. He knew it.

In his place, she would let Ahiranya burn to cinders before she accepted her own death, or theirs.

He should not have cared if the Ahiranyi lived or died. But Ashok was a sickness in him. As long as Arahli lived, Ashok would live in him too, and he would grieve for this rotten land.

"I won't die," Vata Ara said roughly. "I won't do it. I won't."

Vata Ara was still bleeding from his chest, sluggish red blood. Taru was holding her clothed stomach, holding in her wounded innards—flower, intestine, vine.

"The fire will kill us," Arahli rasped. "But we can spare the mortals. They are all that remains of us. My kin. My family. Please. If anything can survive us, our death will have worth."

"They do not even care for us," Taru Ara whispered, and now she wept. Sap trickled from her eyes. "If they did, they would die for *us*."

He clasped her face. Her face that had once belonged to a thrice-born temple elder: a girl who had laughed, and grown leaves on her sister's skirt, who had been sweet and cruel and mourned by her brother Ashok all his short and unjust life.

"Some of them did," he said gently. He looked at his other surviving kin.

"I know you dream as humans dream," he said quietly. "I know how it hurts you. I know how your bodies ache and twist around you. I know the agony of being mortal." A breath. "I miss the stars. I yearn for the great void. But I will accept the quiet of death, if it will spare me the pain of living. Will you join me?" His voice broke. "I do not wish to die alone."

Silence.

It was Bhisa Ara who finally stepped forward, placing a hand against his cheek.

"Yes," she said gently. "We will go together."

Avan Ara hid his face against her skirts, as overwhelmed as a real child. Vata Ara closed his eyes.

"Together," he echoed. "Yes."

He went to Bhumika. Kneeled down beside her.

He placed a hand against her throat.

She held very still under his hand. Waiting for death with grim, fierce calm.

"I do not envy you," he murmured. "I know what it means to be mortal now. It is grief and pain and love that destroys you. I will be glad to be free of it. But you—you may have it. For Ashok's sake. My last gift to him." He tightened his grip upon her throat. "Remember," he said. "And grieve, sister. Grieve us all."

He dragged her into the waters.

He felt the sangam around them, her spirit and his. He felt her become whole again. Then he dragged them free once more.

He heard her gasp, and spasm, and fall. Someone yelled and ran for her, grasping her before her skull touched stone and splintered.

A simple thing. It was done.

He turned his head.

"Taru," he said. "Can you walk?"

She shook her head. She was weeping, furious and miserable. But she allowed him to lift her. She gasped with pain, then went quiet.

The echo of Ashok was in him still, and with it the animal terror of running for his life. Of holding another child and running from fire. Now he ran toward it.

They made their way down the Hirana, where the flames waited, gold and furious. He held Taru tighter, even though Taru Ara was not a child. "Don't look," he whispered against the fronds of Taru's hair. "Don't look, don't look—"

And even though Taru Ara was not a child, she let out a hitched and human breath. She closed her eyes. He exhaled and closed his own.

At least they would be spared humanity.

At least there would be peace.

79

PRIYA

She sank for a long time.

Deep. Deep under the deathless waters.

Closed her eyes...

She woke in the sangam. She was living, breathing, not yet killed. But she was also in Mani Ara's grasp. She sat up in the water. Moved to her knees. Then, trembling, she stood and turned, to the place where three rivers met, where Mani Ara waited for her.

The waters were wild and churning around her, salt-rich with grief. And there was Mani Ara, standing as Priya stood. She wore Priya's own face, Priya's own tears on her cheeks.

"My kin," Mani Ara whispered, "have burned and died. What use are you to me now?" The distance between them peeled away, and Mani Ara's cold-thorned hand cupped her face. "You are the only kin I have left," she said. "That last of my own."

"Kin," Priya whispered. Maybe fire had burned her words away. Maybe the grief pounding in her head had done it.

"We have died before," whispered Mani Ara, dark tears streaming from her eyes. "We were starlight once. Beings of the void. We ran from our enemies when they turned on us. Swam like fish to the shores of your world."

Now that she had shed green and flesh and the hollow ghosts of the people Priya loved, Mani Ara was all starlight. If she was a fish, she was the kind that could swim the cosmos, the great sangam that cradled the world. The hands that cupped Priya's face were brilliant with stars. The eyes that met her own were multitudinous, lidless. Their pupils were entire worlds, burning and collapsing into darkness.

"Why did they turn on you?" Priya asked softly, entranced despite herself. "Why did you have to run to survive?"

"Why do mortals fight one another, sapling? For the same reasons, small and terrible, vast and deep. We sacrificed our own strength. We left the void. We became part of this world: its soil, its trees. But they followed. They learned what we had learned." Her hand moved to press over Priya's heart, cold and sharp-fingered. "Human faith is a door that we may walk through," said Mani Ara. "They followed us. Those creatures of fire and prophecy. Through their mortals, who prayed to them for knowledge and visions, they killed us again."

"And then you sacrificed once more," whispered Priya.

"Flesh is awful," said Mani Ara. "Humanity worse. Your dreams, your emotions...I hunger for peace. But I watched my kin die and I thought: *anything* to live."

Priya looked away from the burning darkness of her, at the waters beneath them and the cosmos above them; the waters where her kin had drowned, and yaksa had emerged wearing their faces.

"The sangam," Priya murmured. "It's...it's your door, isn't it? Made from the faith of so many temple elders and temple children." Now that she'd said it, she *knew*. "You used my kin, those temple dead, to bring yourselves back again, didn't you?"

"Yes," Mani Ara said. Simple, and awful.

Yes. It was like the words had come from Priya's own mouth. She saw memories like they were her own: crawling from the sweetness of the void into the mortal world. A human's faith, an open door. Her kin, her *children*, changing from light and stars to green and soil. Temple children, dead by faith, their sacrifices holding open the door of the sangam, a constant flow of magic.

And then fire, and fire, and death.

Priya closed her eyes.

"I remember," she said, "what it was like to sleep. Endless, under the earth. You may hunger to live, but now that your kin are dead, you hunger just as much for death. Peace. You cannot lie to me, Mani Ara. I'm your heart."

She turned and Mani Ara turned—the two of them looking together at the waters.

"You were never meant to be here," Priya said. "Not for so long. Your gifts are meant to touch this world briefly, reaching mortals through fire or water, dreams or silence. Not reshape it." She tasted the wrongness of it now—like rot. "Staying won't save you, or bring back your kin. It has destroyed you, and it is destroying us.

"Let go, yaksa. We can die together. One heart, one life. We can close the doorway. These rivers can carry what remains of us back to the great sea beyond."

"I think," Mani Ara said, "that you speak from human weakness." Her grasp was tight, sharp, and her gaze sharpened with it. "I did all for my kin, sapling, and I will live for them too—if I must walk the world alone, I will do it."

Horror, sudden, crept down Priya's spine.

She had failed.

"I wanted a glorious world, sapling," Mani Ara said. "Rotten with green and with flesh. We would have made it together. And now I will have it alone." Her mouth of stars and thorns pressed to Priya's own and then—

And then—

80

MALINI

The fire was growing closer. A gust of burning wind brushed her hand as she reached out to the water and grasped—nothing.

She kneeled on the edge of the water. Shivering. The absolute blistering heat followed by the shock of cold water up to her knees had left her shaking. Her arms felt too light, too empty.

There was gleaming—blue, bright. When she'd lowered Priya into the water she'd seen the shape of Priya vanishing. Blistered skin, closed eyes. The shadow of her hair fanning out around her face. The shadow of her body.

Now there was nothing. Priya had sunk deep, deep.

Had Malini condemned them all? Would Priya rise from the water with a stranger behind her eyes? Malini had told herself she had followed Priya here to stop that. What a lie. She was, perhaps, the instrument of the yaksa's successful rise into the world.

She could not find it in herself to care, not as she should have. Panic and grief were metal between her teeth, on her tongue. She could smell fire, and the scorching smell of fat and skin and hair burning.

If Priya rose out of the water, light pearling her skin, her face wood-whorled and strange—if she smiled a stranger's smile, and looked at Malini all cold and unfeeling, too inhuman to love in the ugly and desperate way Priya and Malini had loved each other—

I will burn myself, and burn her with me, Malini told herself.

Another outcome occurred to Malini, worse than all the rest: that Priya would not return at all.

She blinked, her own breathing overly harsh in her ears. Blinked again, and realized why her vision was fading.

The light in the water was dimming. Growing dark.

The light of the water went out.

The darkness was absolute.

She couldn't laugh, or cry. Only close her eyes. Only feel something—the green in her blood, in her ribs, her heart—waver as if it were a candle flame, and die.

Her own voice, a bitter voice, coiled in her skull:

Burn, so at least you may have some bitter remains of glory.

Burn, so all of this at least has some meager worth to the world.

A drumbeat behind her eyes, in her ears.

She was not meant to burn. She had told herself so, so many times. She'd wrestled a future and a crown for herself and yet...

She'd brought herself here to this place and this darkness, and lowered Priya into water that could kill her or make a god of her. And the only fire left that could kill a god—that could destroy it here in darkness, in a carapace, far from the fragile human lives that lived beyond the Hirana—lay in Malini.

There were dreams, or nightmares that lived in her skull. Not visions from the nameless, but paths she'd charted in the dark night on the road to war.

A dream of an old, embittered queen. Alone on her throne. Famed and powerful and utterly empty. A hollow monster, no different from the emperors who came before her.

Another of a golden statue, her own face carved and still, a means to an end. An infant crowned in her place.

A world of nothing but rot and green, where what it meant to be human was forgotten.

A world burned and scarred, where Ahiranya would be nothing. History's dust and ash.

She wanted none of those paths. None of the tales that had

been written for her. Both the great empress and the dead mother of flame were *not her*.

What she wanted, more than anything, was to be the woman who lay beneath all the masks. And that woman did not believe in the mothers, or empire, or the nameless god.

That woman had placed her faith—her fractured, ruinous faith—in a person who'd given Malini her heart, then stolen it back, and then returned it to her once more. A woman who was gone.

"I believe in you, Priya." Her voice was a rasp. Thin in the dark, the absolute quiet. With her eyes closed, she could pretend that Priya could hear her. "I have faith in your humanity. In all of you that is broken and hurtful. I have faith in all of you that is mortal. You have many faces, Priya. The mortal one, the flawed one, and the one with power, this *immortal* one—they're all mine. If you will allow it. They're all mine."

She opened her eyes. Gold light, the very edge of fire, gleamed like a river in the veins of her wrists. Her arms. There were flowers growing beneath her knees.

Around her, shadows flared. In the flicker and hugeness of the flames she saw figures form. She knew them even without the color and texture of flesh or cloth.

Alori. Narina.

Aditya.

She realized her face was wet with tears.

Sacrifice was terrible. Monstrous, when it was bred into you, inflicted. But it could be an act of love too. It could destroy one part of you and set the rest free. For a priest, a priestess, a worshipper kneeling lonely on soil by deep waters—

It did not have to be death, even when it was.

"Priya," she whispered. "Find your way back to me."

Then she stood and stepped into the water. The fire was at her back. It glowed on the walls of the cavern.

The waters were poison. She remembered that. The waters were a trial, and not one meant for her. To enter them would be a willing death.

But there was green in her too, and Priya's soft dreams—and Malini could not let her go. Could not, without reaching out, one last time.

What was a little more poison, willingly imbibed? Malini slipped into the water without fear. The fire followed her path as the water swallowed and clasped her life in its palm. The gold in her skin was a fire from another world, and water could not blot it out.

81

BHUMIKA

She lay gasping on the ground. The waters were overtaking her. She could not breathe through them. Her ghosts were drawing in. Jeevan was holding her steady, his hand over her own. Khalida was leaning over her, calling her name. Crying.

She saw her ghosts, and suddenly she knew them.

They were all her temple siblings. All children like her, who had served on the Hirana and passed through the waters—and drowned, or burned. She knew their names, their dreams. She mourned them.

They were *knowledge* from the deathless waters. They were the scraps of themselves—face, voice, memory—that the waters had saved long after they died. They were corpses given brief life.

She knew now. The waters left in her were returning to the sangam—and all that she had left in the sangam, her own voice and memory and spirit—were flowing into her in turn.

She turned horrified eyes on the ghost kneeling closest to her. His bowl was empty. His veil was gone. He was smiling.

"Ashok," she said, voice splintering.

"I told you that you'd mourn," he said.

He vanished. She reached a hand for him, trying to grab him. Trying to hold him.

She followed him into the sangam. Left her flesh behind.

She fell.

*   *   *

He'd been right. She grieved. He was gone.

She kneeled in star-flecked water. The three rivers of the sangam churned, storm-driven, breaking their banks. She could see the shadow of Ganam, a distant light. But there before her was Priya.

She knew her sister now. Knew all the terror and love that Priya induced in her, just by being her brave, bright, awful self. It rushed through her.

Priya wasn't just shadow. She stood in the rising, rough waves untouched by them. Her body was immovable. Her body was at war with itself. Flowers and flesh—brown eyes and marigold irises. She was a yaksa and she was not. She was more than any yaksa Bhumika had seen before, and she was also Priya, always Priya.

"Priya," she called out, the sangam rippling, twisting. "Priya, please, can you hear me? You idiot, you fool, what have you done?" She crawled through the water and held a hand out.

Priya's eyes met her own. Gold flowers. Brown eyes.

"Bhumika?" she whispered. "You remember? You remember me?"

Bhumika could have wept.

"Even when I didn't know you, I never forgot you," she said, her voice trembling. "Come on, Priya. Wherever you are—come home."

Slowly, shakily—as if she didn't know how her flesh worked—Priya reached out a hand.

For a moment they touched across the sangam. Two sisters. And Bhumika remembered herself, utterly remembered herself. She saw Priya through the waters and remembered Priya as an angry child; Priya as a sullen adult; Priya smiling at her when she left to fight the empress's war, that last time Bhumika had seen her and known her.

The water grew wilder and wilder. The sangam was churning into an endless sea, and Priya was at the heart of it. Priya was bound to a yaksa, and Priya was being swallowed whole.

"I have to destroy the waters," Priya said. "Bhumika. I have to make them nothing. Or Mani Ara—or I, or we—will never be gone. The world will be twisted by magic that shouldn't be here. I'm so sorry. I have to fight her. I have to win." Flowers turned to starlight on her face. Turned, inexorably again, to flesh.

"Priya," she called. "Priya, don't. Priya, Priya—"

Her sister smiled. Her sister mouthed a word.

Goodbye.

Back into her body. She coughed and coughed, lungs aching. Found her voice. "I'm fine," she said. "Don't worry. I remember. Jeevan, I remember." She was herself. And she did grieve then, as her memories rushed over her, as she realized what price she had paid. Her family.

She reached out her arms. "Padma," she said. "Please."

Rukh came to her. Padma in his arms. Her daughter tucked herself tighter against Rukh, and Bhumika wept, joyous and grieving, because her daughter was alive, and because her daughter did not know her.

But knowing didn't matter. The love and relief Bhumika felt were enough.

The ground of the Hirana was trembling, the triveni's stone cracking.

"The Hirana is going to fall," Bhumika said. She could feel the magic fading in the stone around her. Somehow, Priya's battle in the sangam was weakening it. "We need to go."

"If we go down, we're going to die by fire," said the boy Ashish tightly. "It swallowed the yaksa, but it hasn't stopped burning. I know. I watched."

"I don't want to die," a little girl wailed.

"Hush, Pallavi," Rukh said. He drew her against his side. "You're not going to. We're going to be okay. The fire's just taking time to die away, that's all."

The ground shook again, more violently.

"We need to climb," Ganam said firmly. "All of us. Can you do it?"

"We can climb," the boy Ashish said. His expression was grim. "Priya told us to learn. She started teaching us—and we kept on going."

Bhumika looked between the children and adults gathered together. She remembered, distantly, her own childhood—the temple siblings who'd died, falling to their deaths, on their first climb down the Hirana. How Bhumika had cried herself sick after her first climb, muffling her tears with a pillow so Sanjana would not judge her. How Priya had laughed all through her own climb, jumping down on light feet, delighted with her own strength and with the Hirana's love for her.

"Come," she said, and watched a dozen eyes fix on her trustingly. "We need to move swiftly." She looked at Ganam's arm, bound close to his chest. "Can you do this one-handed?" she asked.

"I'm going to have to."

It was a terrifying journey down. The children were moving slowly, carefully, with the eyes of the adults on them. Bhumika had quietly ordered a number of the strongest people who'd been trapped on the Hirana to move down directly beneath the children. If one lost their footing and fell, those people had a chance of catching them—and not toppling down to their own deaths in the process.

Climbing was hard. Perhaps it was because she had only just returned to her body. But she didn't think so. Something had changed in the sangam, and her magic shuddered and broke along with it. Even maintaining her own footing—a task she had never struggled with on the Hirana—was difficult. She was glad that Jeevan carried Padma, safely wrapped against his chest.

The sound of a storm roared in her ears. But the air around her only smelled of smoke, and sang with fire.

"Ganam," she called out, letting the smoke-filled air carry her voice to him. She craned her neck. He was below the children, but she saw him look up. "Can you feel it?"

He winced, a ripple of pain crossing his face. "I can," he said grimly.

Rukh, near him, yelled, "The stone's cracking!"

There was an ominous groan of stone, so deep it was like the bellowing of a beast. Fire-flecked wind brushed Bhumika's cheek.

"Keep moving steadily," she said, not letting her panic show in her voice. Panic would make them careless. Panic would make them fall.

There was another roar—this time of water in her skull. She swayed, and so did Ganam.

"Bhumika," Jeevan called.

"I'm fine. Someone hold Ganam steady," she ordered. Khalida clutched him obediently, pinning him to the wall. "Don't let him fall." She hooked her own feet into crevices, and looped her arm around a carving. They had precious little time; they needed to keep moving. But if she moved now, she wouldn't make it. She was dizzy.

She felt a firm hand on her arm.

"I'm not letting you fall," Jeevan gritted out. His arm trembled where he held her. "I would never let you fall."

Hold me, she begged the Hirana, shaping the words silently on her lips. She was thrice-born. The Hirana knew her. It had always welcomed her, always shaped itself to her body. But now the stone fractured and shook, dust under her fingers.

Jeevan knew her better.

"I will," said Jeevan, as Bhumika's daughter cried. "I will."

"We need to keep going," she said, her body shivering as if she'd risen from cold water. There was no time left to worry about inducing panic; panic was now reasonable. She blinked awful tears from her eyes, locked the searing arrow to her heart away, away.

They made it to the ground. Bhumika braced herself for fire. Her feet met soil—

And the fire faded.

Whatever the flames had come for, they had it now. Ahiranya was burned and splintered, the forest shorn to ash, but the Ahiranyi—at least some of them, at least this crowd of people who surrounded her, shaking and weeping with relief—had survived.

82

RAO

"Wake up," said Aditya. "Rao."

Rao groaned and opened his eyes. It was dark around him. Formless darkness. He rolled onto his side and saw Aditya sitting cross-legged on the ground, watching him.

"Do you remember what stars are, Rao?"

"Am I dead?" Rao asked.

"Sunata, then," Aditya said patiently. "You remember his teachings. The kai spoke to you of him."

Rao stared at him.

"I am dead," he whispered. Aditya was here, at last. Serene, dark-eyed Aditya. They were together again.

"The tale he told you was wrong," Aditya said. "No great king died to make that stone. It was born from the earth's own strength, which is no magic. It is the strength of time and heat and cold; the strength of lifetimes upon lifetimes. The *not* magic that makes mountains." His mouth shaped a smile. "I've had time to learn, you see.

"Heart's shell is empty, Rao," he said. Rao reached for him, and Aditya came. He held Rao in arms of light, his hands, callused and beloved, cradling Rao's face. "It is a promise that there is more strength in our world than in anything from the void."

Firelight shone on Aditya's skin. He shifted like candlelight.

"Do you understand what emptiness is, Rao? It's a gift. It is a promise. You need no god. Only your own fate, carved by your own hand." He kneeled over Rao. His gaze was gentle, and vast—a world of soft starlight. "I am nothing," the wavering image of Aditya said, smiling at him. "What you see here is nothing. Forget me."

"Don't leave me again," Rao said. He was weeping.

A hand closing over his own. "*Live.*"

He returned to his own skin. His hand was closed into the fist Aditya had made of it. Inside that fist lay the hilt of his heart's-shell dagger. Even unconscious, he must have reached for it.

Hemanth was raising his spear of fire for a killing blow. Rao raised his heart's-shell dagger to meet it.

The fire broke around the blade, spreading wild tendrils in every direction but Rao's own body. Hemanth's eyes widened. It was distraction enough.

Rao surged to his feet, ignoring the pain in his leg. He roughly pushed Hemanth to the ground, pinned him, and raised his blade.

"Your death will not save the empress," he said. "But your death will save Malini's heir. It will save Parijatdvipa from your influence."

"There will be other priests who fight for our faith, who speak truth," Hemanth said raggedly, fighting him still. "You will never be forgiven for killing me."

"There will always be men like you," Rao agreed, pinning him harder. It was easy. "But they will not be *you*. That's enough for me."

He held the knife to Hemanth's chest.

"I don't kill you because it is right or good, or because any great sense of justice compels me to," Rao told him. "I am killing you because you deserve to die, and the world will be better with you gone. I am killing you because you do not *deserve* to choose the shape of your own death."

"Rao, Prince Rao, do not—"

He stabbed Hemanth in the heart. Hemanth seized under him, his face a rictus of agony. His hands scrabbled uselessly against the blade. Rao did not move.

In a matter of moments, the High Priest's eyes dulled, and he was gone.

83

PRIYA/MANI ARA

Once, she had been starlight. Once, she was a fish in a great river. Now she was flesh. Ugly, and heavy, with death written into its very nature.

Her heart was beating. The weight of it hurt. Her lungs were a fragile weft. Blood and breathing were a compulsion. Her fleshiness was monstrous. The world was changed, rot-riven, green and sweet, and yet it made her retch. It did not want her. She did not want it.

Mani Ara had wanted to take the world for her kin. That part of her keened in horror for what she had lost, for the kin she had carried over cosmic waters who were dead and lost to her. She had felt them die—the pain, the fire, and the utter nothingness that followed.

If they could not live in the world, then she would tear the world apart. Rend it to shreds. For so long, she'd shaped it tenderly for them, and now. Now, now—

Now the part of her that was Priya was being overwhelmed. A human life was so small. No more than a flicker—swiftly born and swiftly lost.

Stars raced over her. She dreamt, in a blink of an eye, of her temple siblings. She dreamt of Bhumika and Ashok and Sima and Rukh and Padma and Malini, Malini, always her, always all of them.

She could not overcome Mani Ara. She had been a fool to hope. Even if Mani Ara did not want to continue. Even her *not* wanting was a tide, as strong as her hate.

She tried to speak their names. Tried to suck in a breath. The waters filled her lungs. She had no room left in her, nothing left to hollow, and nothing left to give.

She drowned.

A voice was calling her. A light.

Priya.

Golden light. Fire and starlight. The fierceness of the sun.

Tender hands, reaching for her own.

The sangam was not truly a river, and yet—she saw her. Malini, on the shore, with a light in her hands. Malini, with her tangled hair and her eyes like wells of gravity, like the darkness that light could be stitched upon.

A part of Priya remained human. A part of her remained in the world. She had left it there, even though she had been told to cut it away, to hollow it.

Sometimes a hollowing was a space where the echo of you remained. It was a place where a new thing could grow, take root. A vine, tying Malini to her, and her to Malini.

Priya reached for it.

Sleep, she said to the rest of herself. That great, endless, grieving strength that roiled inside her. *Sleep until the world crumbles, until the stars welcome you home.*

Sleep. All you love is gone, and there is nothing in the world for you here.

The part of her that was ancient clawed at the waters. The part of her that was ancient bared its teeth and wept—because it no longer remembered how to be only stars, and had lost too much.

But Priya knew who she was.

She had one last task to do.

She crumbled the sangam around herself. Broke the banks of its rivers. Reduced its churning waters. Destroyed the way, until only the smallest flickering sliver of water was left. Just enough to keep alive what the sangam—and the yaksa—had already made.

People with rot. Once-born. Temple elders. Ganam. *Bhumika.*

Her Malini. Malini should have been dead, drowned and burned, but Priya's immortal magic was shot through her like gold. She was a yaksa's beloved now, because she was Priya's beloved. They were wound together like two halves of a whole. As long as Priya lived, so would she.

It was just enough.

She woke in her own body. Flowering, and no longer strange. A weight filled her arms, as Malini settled in her grasp, wreathed in light.

She kicked her feet and rose to the surface of the water. Walked, with the weight of Malini in her arms, across the ground. Around her the soil flowered. It knew them both.

My beloved, Priya thought with all the wildness and tenderness of a mortal woman over the woman she loved. And with the abstract vastness, the emptiness, of a yaksa loving a mortal who was part of her. A mortal with a piece of a yaksa forever in her heart.

My Malini.

I'll come back to you. I promise.

The Hirana opened, a dizzying kaleidoscope of light—and Malini slipped from her arms, onto the safety of the earth, onto the welcome of new blooming flowers. And Priya...

Priya closed her eyes and let the Hirana—the falling Hirana— close over her.

84

RAO

He staggered through woods on makeshift crutches, through throngs of screaming people, wounded soldiers. But he found Sahar near the Hirana, as he'd half feared, half hoped. He hobbled to her, sweating with the effort. Kneeled down beside her with a hiss.

She was bleeding. Her clothes were sodden with the blood. His stomach lurched at the sight. But she was awake, conscious, alive. There was still hope.

"Tried to staunch it," Sahar gasped. "I grabbed...a cloth..."

"You need more than a cloth wadded against your side," he said grimly. "At least tell me it was clean."

"I can't promise that."

He tried to help her up, and her hand clasped his arm, her grip like iron.

"I waited for her," Sahar said. Pain had made her vision hazy, but she was clearly trying to focus. "Went back. Waited and—went to look for her. In the end. She'd gotten out somehow from that fucking temple."

"Did she go to burn?"

"I don't know—what she went to do," Sahar said slowly, painfully. "Only that—she did it. They're gone, aren't they? The yaksa."

He breathed carefully, slowly. Nodded.

"Was Elder Priya with her?"

Sahar's gaze darkened.

"No," she said. "No. She's gone."

He tried to assist Sahar up again. She gave an awful, wrenching cry.

"I'm getting help for you," Rao said. She grasped him tighter.

"The empress first," she said.

"You deserve to live," he snapped. "Sahar, I—I'll protect her myself. I'll make sure she's well."

"You don't understand," Sahar said. "She's—behind the rocks. Go. Look at her."

It was clear Sahar wouldn't be dissuaded. So he released her. Went to look.

He understood immediately.

Malini was alive. Unburned. Lying unconscious, soaked to the bone, on a bed of black flowers. When she breathed, they moved with her. A heartbeat of life.

He took a step back. Another.

"She burned," said Rao.

Sahar stared at him. "What?"

"She burned," Rao said again. "That's what you saw. And she stepped out of the flames unharmed. She saved us all. That's what we'll say. When you survive this—and you *will*—that's what you'll say. She's a living mother of flame. A living goddess. You understand?"

Through the pain, Sahar's expression cleared. She nodded.

"Yes," she said, more firmly. "That's what I saw."

No one would have power over Malini again.

85

MALINI

She woke alone.

The temple was in rubble, Lata was telling her in a low voice. A careful voice. The Hirana had crumbled. Elder Bhumika had allowed a few chosen members of Malini's council to see what remained of it—to examine the dirt and the stone and find nothing in it, no yaksa, no Priya. No life at all.

She is not dead, Malini thought. She grasped the thought like dust, like sand, ash trying to drift through her fingers.

She is not dead.

Priya.

Priya.

"I will meet with Elder Bhumika," said Malini. "I offered her the safety of Ahiranya if she and Elder Priya helped us, and she kept her part of the bargain. Parijatdvipa will keep its vows."

No one argued with her, even though she spoke from her sickbed, surrounded by court officials and scribes and highborn—a scene so like her father's own death that it would have made her laugh, if she'd had the strength for laughter.

She saw her life stretch out before her. She would be a great empress. A living mother of flame. She would be alone, friendless and powerful, as Raziya had warned her she would be. She would die alone, mourned but truly loved by few. She would never hear Priya's laughter again.

She felt no pain at the thought yet. She knew now from experience that a grave wound was often painless when fresh because the hurt of it was too great for the mind to grasp. The agony would come later.

It was weeks before she dreamt of darkness, and fingertips against her lips.

The yaksa are gone, she said—or tried to say. Reached out, and felt Priya's smiling mouth beneath her palm.

The yaksa are gone, agreed Priya.

But I'm not simply a yaksa.

She woke and allowed Swati to brush her hair, and looked at her own face in the silvery glass of her mirror. She was not golden carved, or a living mother of flame. She looked mortal and tired.

But in the night, a flower had grown at her chest. A black bloom.

A promise.

86

BHUMIKA

Her magic was gone.

She reached for the sangam again and again

Her magic was gone, and Priya was dead.

She could still feel the trees, the sway and motion of them. The song of water, of roots uncurling. But she could move nothing, shape nothing. Perhaps this knowing was what all people who'd never tasted the deathless waters felt.

If they dug away the rubble of the Hirana they would find nothing, she knew. No deathless waters, gleaming with blue inner light. No Priya. Everything was gone.

But Malini wanted to bargain with her.

"I believe she wants to truly negotiate. But for the sake of caution, take them to safety," she said to Jeevan. She lifted Padma from her hip and placed her in Jeevan's arms. He took her tenderly. Their fingertips brushed. "Use the paths Ganam carved. Lead the children away, at least. Keep them safe until I bring news."

Jeevan nodded.

He did not tell her how much he did not want to leave her; did not tell her that he loved her, and how much he'd feared losing her in the horrors of the temple, and all the horrors that came before it. The sickness on their journey to Alor. The bandits, the hunger. The roiling waters around the village. The yaksa who awakened beneath the monastery, and the fire. But he said, "Bhumika." And she knew.

*   *   *

An opulent tent. An empress, gray and tired, unadorned, dressed in unrelenting white.

"The yaksa are dead," Malini said. "You have held up your part of our bargain. Sit."

Bhumika sat.

"There are many who say I should ask a vow from you," said Malini. "A vow of loyalty, as nations of the empire make. But I do not think you will make that."

"I won't bargain away the soul of Ahiranya," Bhumika said. Once, perhaps she would have. She had sacrificed many ideals for safety and survival. "Ahiranya has given up enough."

Malini met her eyes, her gaze searching. Then she nodded.

"There is a wheel turning," Malini said. "A wheel where flowers bloom and die and bloom again. If I bind you to Parijatdvipa, will Ahiranya one day ensure something like the Age of Flowers returns? Will we crush you in turn, until time ends? No. I am tired of the cruelty of the wheel. Have Ahiranya's freedom, Elder Bhumika. Rule your home well. We will ink contracts, and I will tell my people that if they defy me, they defy a mother of flame made flesh. They won't gainsay me."

87

RAO

He watched Malini speak in front of a roaring crowd of Harsinghar's citizens. Jasmine flowers were thrown. The air was filled with exultation. And Malini, a thin figure in white, stood above it all, and proclaimed the future with as much authority as the nameless god.

This war was won with the help of the Ahiranyi, who turned on their gods for their own sakes, and ours.

They showed courage.

We will bargain with them. We will move forward in peace.

Peace. He wondered what it would look like.

In the midst of the celebrations he found Sima—sitting alone, on the roof where he'd once sat and drunk himself stupid. She had no liquor with her. She was staring up at the sky, but when he called her name, she slid down to join him. His leg wasn't fit for roof climbs quite yet.

They sat together, listening to the sounds of the city in celebration.

"I think Priya's dead," Sima said, eventually. Her hands brushed her cheeks. They came away wet.

"I'm sorry," Rao said quietly. He couldn't refute it. He'd seen the devastation in Malini's eyes. The hollowing weight of it.

"She changed my life, or maybe I changed my own," Sima said, looking at the horizon—the gold of it moving over her face, liquid, making her eyes blaze.

"I can't stay in Ahiranya," Sima said finally, her voice small. "I can't go back. And I—I don't want to stay in Parijat. I need an escape."

Perhaps there was a possibility there—something he'd felt in the drumbeat of quiet when he'd stood beside Kai Ehsan, and the lord had placed heart's shell against his palm, his fingers warm, his grip an offer and a shelter.

Or perhaps not.

He thought of the kai. He thought of Dwarali's snow, and how vast the world beyond the Lal Qila had looked and felt. He wanted that for himself. Whether he went to Alor or not, he knew where he would end up: walking into a blue-white horizon.

Ehsan had given up the dangers of the world beyond the Lal Qila for the safety of Parijatdvipa. But Parijatdvipa had almost destroyed Rao. He would have died for it, and he no longer wanted to live in it. He wanted to see stars under a new sky.

It would be like walking straight into a fire that couldn't burn or break you. A light of possibility.

"As a start, someone needs to watch Kai Ehsan," said Rao. "He's a stranger to us, still, for all the good he's done. And some- one will need to keep the peace between him and the ladies of Dwarali and the Lal Qila."

"You think the empress will let you be the one to watch him when you're the one who brought him to her?" Sima asked.

"Yes," said Rao. "I think she will."

Sima was watching him. Thoughtful.

"And what after that?" Sima asked. Like she was hoping. Waiting.

"There is a world beyond Dwarali," Rao said quietly. "Beyond the Lal Qila. Beyond even Kai Ehsan and his Jagatay. I know nothing of that world. I've never dreamt of it. The nameless god won't reveal it to me. I know no one there, and no one there will respect me for being a prince of Alor, or a general of the Empress of Parijatdvipa. No one will judge me for murdering the High Priest of mothers, monster though he was. I want to go to it," he said. "I want to see it. I want to see what I might become out there. But, Sima, what do you want?"

"There are people I don't want to leave," she said finally. "But... I don't want to be a maidservant, or an advisor, or a prisoner. I want to go with you." A pause. "When I've said goodbye— when things are more stable. If you can wait... I'd like to go too."

He smiled.

"I can wait for you," he said.

"You spun a fine tale around me, Rao," Malini said to him. She was still thin, still exhausted—but her smile was real, a light on her face. "Even my own courtiers think I am some kind of god now."

"It was Lata who did it," he said.

"Oh, don't lie," Malini replied. "She told me where it began. Lata has a great respect for the provenance of knowledge. Rao..."

"Yes?"

"You are free of the burden of having your fate tied to mine," said Malini. "When you are ready to leave, you may go. I can offer you that."

He swallowed. He should have refused her. He should have told her he would stay at her side.

"Thank you," he said instead.

Later, Lata hugged him.

"I thought one day I would be a sage again, traveling the world," Lata said, muffled against his shoulder. "But how can I leave her? And how can I ask you to stay? I can't, Rao. I can't."

He embraced her in return.

"You are going to be one of the most important people in the empire," he said against her hair. "And me? I'm going to go out into the world and learn what it is. Like a true sage."

"Write it all down," Lata said, tears in her eyes. "And send it to me."

88

VIJAY

There were many stories about Empress Malini.

People did not tell stories about Vijay, but that was because he was a boy of fifteen. He was crown prince, but he was a *green boy*, as his sage would scoff, smiling with affection in her eyes. *But I've trained green boys before, Prince Vijay. Never fear.*

On his fifteenth birthday he sought out the empress in her gardens. He told her about his training, not with the measured grandeur he'd been advised to, but straightforwardly. Swords were fine. He didn't want to discuss swords. He liked ships, he said. He had studied the mechanisms required in shipwright work. He would like to travel the seas and see what lay in the world beyond. What, he asked, did the empress think of that?

"Did your mother not tell you to fear me?" The empress sounded amused.

In truth, his mother told him that spies watched her constantly, and watched him also. It had frightened him when he was a boy, but now he was a man, or near enough to being one.

Besides, he had also been told other stories. By Dwarali's sultana, an older woman with a proud bearing and a graceful mien, and her husband the sultan, who was gruff and humorous and traveled everywhere by horse because of an injury he'd gained in the war. Their stories had been of the empress's grand adventures and heroism, but he'd heard smaller, more revealing stories from the empress's advisors. Some of those advisors were utterly unapproachable, but Lady Deepa always had a ready smile and a tale of the empress's kindness. When he had been younger, she'd always let him drink sherbet or eat sugarcane sweets in her office when he wanted to hide from saber practice. His sage Lata had disapproved and scolded Deepa constantly for it.

"I am not a child anymore," he said now to the empress. His days of sugarcane and sherbet were long gone.

"You are still a boy," she said softly, looking into his eyes. Her eyes were dark and cold. He had wished, often, that he had inherited the imperial look, but everyone said he was his mother's boy, and his Saketan blood shone through strong: brown eyes and a short stature. If he had anything from the imperial line, it was his curling hair and that alone. "You won't have the privilege of being a young boy for long."

"I won't?"

"No," said the empress. "But you have wise and able advisors. Trust them and all will be well."

The empress was not . . . not *young*, exactly. She looked young, of course, but everyone said that was because she was a living mother of flame, and her light made her appear eternal. But she wasn't old, either. It was strange for her to speak so, as if she would die.

The jasmine flowers fluttered in the breeze around them. The empress's eyes crinkled into a smile.

"You do not have the heart to rule," she said kindly.

"I do," he protested.

She shook her head.

"Let me offer you advice I know you will not take, Vijay: When I am dead and gone, learn to lie. You will need many masks to survive."

89

MALINI

Priya,

Think of my delay as my love letter to you. My final love letter. If I find nothing of you and cannot seek you out—I have none-theless done what you would have wanted from me. I have made sure Ahiranya is safe, and it will survive. I have made an ally of your sister.

I have counted each year. I remember your arms around me in the Hirana. The smell of you—water and lotus flowers, the things that reach through the darkness and survive.

I know you live.

You will never see this, or you will. I wrote you letters once that you were never meant to see, and still you did. So I must trust that you will find a way. You were always stubborn enough, my love.

Priya, the world is vast and strange, and it is mine. I have the kind of power men die for, and yet I tire of it. I remember a dream of garlanding you and I think—

—I think it is more powerful and strange than any crown. To live without masks. To swim through rage and grief and rise, alive, on the other side.

Priya.

I am coming.

*   *   *

In the night, she woke and found flowers growing through the walls of her chambers. She lifted a lamp and saw them—the black of them, the way they bloomed joyously at the sight of her. She lowered the lamp and laughed and wept, smiling.

She knew it was time.

She had ruled as well as she could. She had built her court around her, and filled it with clever, cunning women. They would give Vijay wise counsel if he was willing to accept it.

She met Lata now, once again, on a veranda as the sun rose. Lata watched the light thoughtfully. Then she turned her eyes onto Malini.

"When will you go?" Lata asked. Lata had always known her too well.

"This year," Malini said. "Before the monsoon."

"You could stay," Lata said. "Rule until a grand old age. Become a legend. Change the empire entirely."

"I will not become a grand old empress," Malini said softly. That she was sure of. She wasn't entirely human anymore. She had thought herself mortal after the Hirana fell. But in the years since she had not aged, and flowers still turned easily to her grasp, seeking her light. Whatever had happened to her in the waters—deep in Priya's power—had changed her forever.

In the aftermath of the yaksa and the second Age of Flowers, there were many who still had rot—who lived with the mark of it. Forests of flesh still stretched across Parijatdvipa. Though the rot grew no worse, it grew no better, and strangeness had become commonplace. But Malini was still stranger than the rest.

There had been magic, for Priya, in being Mani Ara's beloved. Terrible, cursed magic. But perhaps being Priya's beloved would be a kinder fate.

"The prince is very young," Lata said with a sigh. "And yet too old for a regent. The throne will be a hard trial for him."

"He will grow," said Malini. "All children do."

And if he was too weak for the throne—if he could not hold

Parijatdvipa—then let it crumble. Perhaps the time had come to release them all from old vows, from the ever-turning wheel.

She traveled to Srugna first. This time there was pomp and ceremony. A banquet, and awed eyes upon her. She smiled through it all, impervious. All of it would be done with soon.

That night she slipped away from her guards and walked alone into Srugna's countryside. Then its woods. Then, without pause, into Ahiranya's own forest.

People claimed there was no magic in Ahiranya's woods any longer, but she felt it. She could have followed it with her eyes closed. It was a beckoning. A tug beneath her breastbone. A calling.

Come home.

She found her way to a waterfall. Beneath it, a pool rich with lilies. She unbound her own hair.

Maybe there was no Priya to be found here. But it was a tenderness and blessing that the forest knew her at all. It was enough. It would have to be. She had done everything she intended to do, and now she could sit quietly here in this water, until she was ready to move again. To start anew. To die, all forgotten bones as she'd threatened, or to start again as Rao had—striding over the horizon, gold-eyed, never to be seen on Parijatdvipan soil again.

Even if she was wrong, the world was vast and strange, and she would welcome it.

Rao had written to her at times over the years—thick letters, faded from sunlight, or touched with mold from the ruinous mingling of heat and rain. He'd written to her of golden mountains, and seas the color of emeralds.

The same griefs and joys live everywhere, Malini, he'd told her. *But I find peace in seeing that we all rise and fall on the same waves. Maybe you would, too.*

She slid into the water. Waded into it, the coolness of it rising to her waist. Closed her eyes, feeling the light on her skin.

"There is a story I once told a girl," a voice said. It was a familiar voice and also—not. "Of a man who garlanded a tree until it came alive and married him."

One deep breath. Another. She could not turn. Her heart would break if she turned and found nothing behind her.

"I know that story," Malini whispered.

A faint sound. Half a laugh, half a sob, so *human*, and it made tears come to Malini's own eyes.

"It's hard, you know? Wrestling a god into sleep. You helped me to do it. I saw the light of you and I followed it and it saved me. It helped me fight her. But even then, I couldn't remember how to *be* anymore. I had to learn again." A sound. The swish of leaves. Of water. Maybe breath. Maybe a body, deep in the water behind her. "I left you for so long. I'm sorry."

Malini closed her eyes and listened to that voice. Drank it like wine.

"It's all right," Malini said. "I gather trees grow very slow."

Another laugh. This one had no tears in it.

"If I garland you?" Malini asked. "Will that make you human enough to stay with me?"

"If I send you flowers through the soil and through your skin, will that make you magical enough to stay at my side?"

"You know the answer," Malini said shakily. "I'm here. I had the world in my palm, and I found it wanting. I'm a greedy creature, Priya. I came here for you. There is a flower in my heart, and it grew for you."

A heartbeat passed, and she was sure now that she could hear a body in the water. A hesitant breath.

"Look at me," the voice said. It was very close. An entreaty behind her.

"I am afraid," Malini admitted.

"If you garland me," Priya said quietly, tenderly, "I will love you and marry you. I will stay with you until time ends, and the green is no more, and there's nothing but cold stars left." A pause. A gentle hand grasping her pallu. "Look at me, Malini."

Malini turned and met Priya's eyes.

EPILOGUE

BHUMIKA

It was Padma who told her about the new river cutting through the forest.

Her daughter was still small. She was almost grown now—whip-clever with a mind like steel—but she would always be small. *A knife of a girl*, Khalida muttered once, and Bhumika could not dispute it. But Padma had never let her small stature stop her from seeking trouble. She often wandered alone into the forest, or in Hiranaprastha itself. Bhumika did not have the heart to stop her, and had never tried.

Besides, her daughter was uniquely blessed with friends. Lord Ashish, new to his title but wise with his wealth, and Pallavi, one of the youngest and canniest warriors Ganam had chosen to mentor now that he was in charge of staffing and training Bhumika's personal guard. And Rukh, of course—Padma's brother in all but blood, who ran the mahal like he owned it, argued with Ahiranya's ruling council for hours on end, and still climbed trees with Padma when she demanded it.

She watched Padma slink out of the trees and run toward Bhumika. Her long braid whipped about in the air behind her.

"Mama," she said. "The river runs through the bower."

"Does it?"

Padma nodded sharply. "And there was someone there—a woman," she said. "She asked me to get you."

There were often people seeking her out. She was only one of

Ahiranya's ruling council, but there were people who still valued the old ways of temple elders and called her High Elder still.

The crown mask lay in a chest by her bedside, and sometimes she would unwrap it and remember those days, seeking magic on its surface. Nothing ever answered her.

So she expected nothing unusual when she nodded, and told Padma to find herself something to eat, and made her own way toward the bower of bones.

In the time since the yaksa, Ahiranya had settled into its bones—sometimes literally.

Graves had been dug here for the mask-keepers, and the souls who'd drunk waters broken from the source, for the sake of Ahiranya. There were wishes written now on the ribbons in the bower of bones. Wishes for a peaceful future. For good harvest. The yaksa were gone, but the Ahiranyi knew themselves and worshipped the earth still.

Bhumika stood beneath the bower's leaves and looked. There, at the edge of the bower, lay a silver stream, water rippling over rock. And in the water stood a woman who was all flowers.

Bhumika's heart froze.

She had seen yaksa. She had seen the skin of her loved ones worn by monsters. She feared—a deep and terrible fear—that she was seeing the same curse again.

But then the woman made of leaves and flowers was gone, and the woman who stood before her was Priya. Just Priya, with her dark skin and easy smile, her pin-straight hair and squared shoulders. Priya, who'd always loved too much and too tenderly, who'd died and still found a way to say goodbye.

"Bhumika," she said. Her smile was shaky. Her eyes familiar brown. She hadn't aged at all. "I'm sorry if I scared you. I know—I've been gone a long time."

Bhumika could not speak. A trick, a yaksa trick.

"I don't know how long I can be here, standing in front of you," said Priya. "I'm...not like they were. The yaksa." She held her arms wide. "Didn't you wonder why the trees stayed so strange in Ahiranya? Why they seem to hear you? Maybe you don't know, but the world isn't like that for people who aren't at least once-born. There's still a little power left, and it moves through me." She lowered her head. Raised her chin. "The rot isn't fading on its own, you know. It's tiring work."

Bhumika stepped forward. One stumbling step. Another.

She threw her arms around her sister.

"Priya," she said brokenly, tears in her eyes. "Priya, how could you have left me for so long?"

Priya's arms surrounded her.

"I didn't have a choice."

"You're a monster for leaving."

"I'm a monster generally." Her grip tightened. "I love you too, Bhumika."

Slowly, they untangled, and Priya looked at her smiling, her eyes just as teary as Bhumika's.

"I'm not alone," said Priya. "And neither are you."

"I'm not alone," Bhumika agreed, voice thick. "And you...?"

Priya's smile deepened.

"I never thought I could have her," Priya said. "But I have her. She has me. We're going to see the world. It may take lifetimes." She touched a hand to Bhumika's and took a step back. The sunlight, dappled by leaves, shone through her.

"I'll see you again," Priya said. "Tell Padma to eat more, will you? Our little grandma's too small by half. And tell Rukh—tell Rukh I'm proud of him. I always will be."

"I will," Bhumika said weakly. And when Priya vanished, she slowly sank to her knees.

Kneeling in the grass. Dappled light on her shoulders. She heard footsteps behind her. Her daughter's silvery, light tread. Her husband's heavier footsteps.

"Bhumika," Jeevan said, his voice low and concerned. "Are you well?"

She exhaled, a smile on her mouth. Tears in her eyes. She'd wipe them away soon enough, but not yet. Not yet.

"Yes," she said. "I am."

ACKNOWLEDGMENTS

Oh wow. Well, here we are. We made it.

We made it!!

There are so many people I need to thank for the support they've given me.

My lovely and insightful editors old and new, Tiana Coven, Priyanka Krishnan, Jenni Hill, and Hillary Sames. My constant champion and agent, Laura Crockett. Publicity, including Nazia Khatun, Angela Man, and Ellen Wright. My fantastic cover artist Micah Epstein, and Lauren Panepinto, for her stellar art direction. Shiromi Arserio, for bringing my books to life with her audio narration. My foreign publishers and translators, for all they have done for these books.

My family. Carly, always. My mother, Anita Suri. Rajesh and Ritu Suri; Ritika, Nishant, and Arjun Mendiratta. Thank you for all your support.

I have so many friends to thank, too! The wondrous Bunker. Daphne, Tori, and Kat, for those early days of sanity you gave me during lockdowns (and everything since). Harveen, Hannah, Cherae, and Alice for your kindness and friendship. Karin, Samantha, and Saara—you're family to me. Thanks for all the naan rolls and for being the best people I know.

Kate, Sophie, Ellie, and Paul—you may notice that this book is dedicated to you all. It's because you've changed my life for the better. I wish you nothing but nat 20s forevermore.

I'm going to thank my pets now because no one can stop me. Merlin, Galahad, Lan Zhan, and Wei Ying—thanks for being no help. Also thank you to Asami, who wasn't here for this book, but saw me through the first in the trilogy, so deserves a final thanks and a goodbye.

And finally, thank you to my readers. What a ride it's been, and what a privilege it is for me to have shared it with you. Thank you for going on this journey with me. Thank you for reading this trilogy. I couldn't be more grateful to you. This series is yours now, and always will be.

CAST OF CHARACTERS

Ahiranyi

Arahli Ara—Yaksa, wearing the guise of Ashok
Ashish—Temple son
Ashok—Temple son, deceased
Avan Ara—Yaksa, wearing the guise of Nandi
Bhisa Ara—Yaksa, wearing the guise of Chandni
Bhumika—Temple elder, carrier of knowledge
Billu—Cook in the ruling household of Ahiranya
Chandni—Temple elder, deceased
Chetan—Highborn lord
Cira Ara—Yaksa, wearing the guise of Riti
Ganam—Mask-keeper, twice-born, ex-rebel against Parijatdvipan rule
Jeevan—Guard to Bhumika, ex-captain of the guard to the elders of Ahiranya
Khalida—Maidservant to Lady Bhumika
Kritika—Mask-keeper, ex-rebel against Parijatdvipan rule
Mani Ara—Yaksa
Nandi—Temple son, deceased
Padma—Daughter of Bhumika
Pallavi—Temple child
Priya—Temple elder, ruler of Ahiranya
Riti—Temple daughter, deceased
Ruchi—Refugee from Parijatdvipa, rot sufferer
Rukh—Servant in the household of the rulers of Ahiranya, rot sufferer
Sanjana—Temple daughter, deceased
Sendhil—Temple elder, deceased
Shyam—Refugee from Parijatdvipa, rot sufferer
Sima—Priya's friend, prisoner of war in Parijatdvipa
Vata Ara—Yaksa, wearing the guise of Sendhil

Aloran

Alori—Princess of Alor, attendant of Princess Malini, deceased
Bidisha—Villager, rot sufferer
Gulnar—Villager
Ishan—Priest of the nameless, Nimisa Monastery
Manjeet—Headwoman of a village
Rao—Prince of Alor, general of the Parijatdvipan army
Sunder—Head priest of Nimisa Monastery
Viraj—King of Alor

Dwarali

Asma—Daughter of the lord and lady of the Lal Qila
Khalil—Lord of the Lal Qila
Raziya—Highborn lady, wife of Lord Khalil
Sahar—Head of Empress Malini's personal guard, previously guards-woman to Raziya

Beyond Dwarali

Bahar—Sister of the kai of the Jagatay
Ehsan—Kai of the Jagatay
Qutlugh—Sister of the kai of the Jagatay

Parijati

Aditya—Ex–crown prince of Parijatdvipa, priest of the nameless, deceased
Chandra—Previous emperor of Parijatdvipa, deceased
Deepa—Advisor to the empress, daughter of Mahesh
Divyanshi—First mother of flame, founder of Parijatdvipa, deceased
Hemanth—High Priest of the mothers of flame
Kartik—Priest of the mothers of flame; faceless son; deceased
Lata—Sage, advisor to the empress
Mahesh—Highborn lord
Malini—Empress of Parijatdvipa
Mitul—Priest of the mothers of flame
Narina—Noble attendant of Malini, deceased
Sanvi—Guardswoman to empress Malini
Shri—Guardswoman to empress Malini

Sikander—Father of Malini, deceased
Vijay—Crown prince of Parijatdvipa

Saketan

Ashutosh—Low prince of Saketa
Narayan—Highborn lord, general of the Parijatdvipan army
Prem—Low prince of Saketa, deceased
Romesh—Liegeman to Low Prince Ashutosh
Varsha—Daughter of the deceased High Prince of Srugna, widow of
    Emperor Chandra, mother of the crown prince of Parijatdvipa

Srugni

Aravind—Srugani soldier
Lakshan—King of Srugna
Prakash—Highborn lord, general of the Parijatdvipan army
Rohit—Highborn lord

extras

orbit

meet the author

Shekhar Bhatia

TASHA SURI is the World Fantasy Award–winning author of the Burning Kingdoms trilogy, the Books of Ambha duology, *What Souls Are Made Of*, and *Doctor Who: The Cradle*. Once a librarian, she is now a part-time writing tutor and a full-time cat and rabbit wrangler. She lives with her family in a mildly haunted house in London.

Find out more about Tasha Suri and other Orbit authors by registering for the free monthly newsletter at orbitbooks.net.

if you enjoyed
THE LOTUS EMPIRE

look out for

THE SCARLET THRONE
False Goddess Trilogy: Book One

by

Amy Leow

A dark, heart-thumping political epic fantasy by debut author Amy Leow—full of scheming demons, morally gray heroines, talking cats, and cutthroat priests, this delicious tale of power and corruption will captivate from beginning to end.

Binsa is a "living goddess," chosen by the gods to dispense both mercy and punishment from her place on the Scarlet Throne. But her reign hides a deadly secret. Rather than channeling the wisdom of an immortal deity, she harbors a demon.

But one cannot remain a living goddess forever. When her temple's priests decide that Binsa's time in power has come to an end, a new girl, Medha, is selected to take over her position as goddess. Binsa refuses to be discarded into a life of uncertainty as a young woman, and she strikes a deal with her demon: She will sacrifice her

*people's lives in order to magnify his power, and in return, he will
help her seize control from the priests once and for all.*

*How much of her humanity is she willing to trade for the sake of
ambition? Deals with demons are rarely so simple.*

1

The False Devotee

A woman had been crushed by a goat that fell from the sky.

Her husband, Uruvin Vashmaralim, humble spice merchant,
now kneels before me, haggard bags underlining his eyes and tear
stains slashing down his cheeks. He laments the loss of his wife
and the suspicious circumstances hanging over her death. She was
a pious woman, he claims, who always set the mangoes and wine
before the family shrine and prayed to them three times a day. One
day, however, a terrible illness befell her. She didn't place her offerings before the family shrine. She died the next week, not from
illness, but from a goat falling on her while she was drawing water
from the well.

Lies, a childlike voice hisses in my head.

The man bursts into sobs at the end of his tale. I observe him
with my back straight and hands folded demurely on my lap. My
lips are pressed into a thin line, but my brows are soft and relaxed.
My brother has told me that this is my best regal pose, assuring
everyone that the spirit of the goddess Rashmatun lives in me, with
every muscle, every limb perfectly poised.

Even if Rashmatun never possessed me. Even if Rashmatun
doesn't exist.

"My goddess!" the man wails. "Please, have mercy. I know not what my wife has done wrong, save for the one day she forgot to placate our ancestors' spirits. Her death has grieved me so. Rashmatun, what can I do to rectify the calamity that has fallen upon me?"

I stay silent, contemplating the situation. A goat dropped on an unsuspecting woman. It would have sounded ridiculous if not for Uruvin's solemnity as he delivered the tale. In fact, I am still in disbelief, even though I allow him to continue wailing.

Meanwhile, Ilam, the demon inside me, trails slow, taunting circles in my mind. His presence is as unnerving as a monster lying beneath still waters.

"Uruvin, how long has it been since your wife's demise?" I say, my reedy voice amplified with deeper, overlapping echoes. The acoustics of the concave niche carved into the wall behind my throne creates an incandescent quality to my tone. My brother did it himself, claiming that the sculpture of Anas, the ten-headed snake god, would protect the living goddess from any harm. What the temple dwellers do not know about is the hollow that lies beyond the niche, large enough for a grown man to squeeze into and eavesdrop on my daily audiences.

"Two weeks already, Your Grace," Uruvin replies. He wipes a tear away from the corner of his eye. "I miss her terribly."

Two weeks. Snivelling Sartas. They'd have cremated the body by now. "Pray tell," I resume smoothly, "was she a good woman?"

"Why, of course, Rashmatun! She was everything a man could ask for." He waves his arms in a vigorous manner, as if it can convince me of his sincerity. "A wonderful cook, a meticulous cleaner, a patient listener. Oh, my dear Dirka!"

He falls into another round of incoherent sobbing, forehead planted onto the fiery red carpet beneath him.

I narrow my eyes at Uruvin, studying him intently. The hems of his suruwal are suspiciously clean, neither a trace of ash nor dust on them. He probably never visited his wife's remains after the funeral. The Holy Mound is where we keep the ashes of our dead, open to the public and frequently flooded with visitors. If he were truly mourning her, he'd have spent plenty of time there.

Or perhaps he is so overwhelmed with grief that he cannot bear to step into the Mound.

Lies, lies, lies, Ilam chants with sadistic glee.

Where is the lie? I ask.

Open your eyes, girl. Open your eyes and see.

I draw in a breath, and Ilam gets to work. He worms his way to the front of my mind, shoving me aside and suffocating my thoughts. After nearly ten years of communing with a demon, you'd think I'd have become accustomed to the constant crawling up my spine.

But I endure it to have this power.

The demon burrows straight into Uruvin's mind; the man himself is unaware of the intrusion. A rush of resounding *truths* pours into me, and a brief flash of pain splits my skull before fading into a dull pulse. My senses sharpen, so sensitive that I can hear Uruvin's erratic heartbeat and catch the faint scent of perfume on his smooth, creaseless clothes. Ilam's magic amplifies the truths such details carry. Each of them pierces through my mind like a fire-tipped arrow streaking across a moonless night.

Throughout this, I maintain my tall, unflappable posture.

Then Ilam is done. He slowly retreats, and the world fades into its usual palette, the saturation of sounds and scents ebbing into the background. I inhale deeply. Using blood magic always leaves me with a discomfort that carves deep into my bones. After all these years, I still cannot tell if it's an inherent side effect of blood magic, or if it's my own revulsion towards the practice.

Meanwhile, Uruvin is still choking on melodramatic sobs.

I wait for him to swallow his tears. Now I see where the lie reveals itself. If not for Ilam, I would not have caught the subtle yet alluring fragrance of frangipani on him, commonly used as a perfume by Aritsyan women to usher good luck in love and life. I would not have seen the shrewd gleam in his eyes.

The part about the falling goat must be true—as absurd as it is—since Ilam did not say it was a lie. A mystery to be dealt with later. But Uruvin is no honest, grieving husband.

He hopes to earn some sort of compensation for his unprecedented losses. Just like many of the insufferable fools who walk in here. Some devotees are genuine, but plenty are out to take a bite out of the goddess Rashmatun's bursting coffers.

Fortunately, I'm not as gullible as these people would like me to be.

"You live by the banks of the Nurleni, Uruvin?" I ask after the man wrests his sobs under control.

"Yes, my goddess. I'm sure that the chief priest would have told you all you needed to know." He sniffs loudly. Perhaps he's wondering why the great Rashmatun is asking such menial questions.

"Is it Harun who will relieve you of your plight?" I say, allowing an edge of irritation to coat my tone. "No. It is I. So answer my questions without hesitation nor falsehood."

Uruvin's fingers drum against his thigh. "Yes, Your Grace. My humblest apologies, Rashmatun."

"Excellent." I tilt my head. "Is your business doing well, Uruvin?"

"Why, of course! The demand for spices is always there, no matter how poor the economy. And the river always brings good business." His fingers continue to *tap, tap, tap.*

Interesting. It hasn't been raining for the past few months; the waters of the river have receded so much that large boats can barely sail down without their bottoms scraping against rocks. Does the merchant think that I am ignorant to the workings of the world at large because I don't step foot outside temple grounds?

I stay silent for a while, tempering my anger.

"Do you think me a fool, my child?" I finally say, voice dangerously soft.

His eyes spark with alarm. "Your Grace?"

"I have given you a chance to speak the truth, and yet you have lied to me." I lean forward ever so slightly, careful to not let the weight of my headdress topple me forward. My shadow, cast by the braziers above my head and distorted by Anas's ten snake heads, stretches towards Uruvin. "You call yourself a follower of

Rashmatun, yet you dare to let falsehoods fall from your tongue in my presence? Why must you use your wife, even in her death, to compensate for your failing business?"

Ilam cackles in delight. He loves it when I truly *become* a goddess, when none can defy me and all must bow to me.

Even I have to admit I enjoy the feeling.

The rhythm the merchant taps out grows even more erratic. "Your Grace. I assure you that I have been speaking nothing but the truth. My wife—"

"Is dead. That much is certain." I pitch my voice low; the echoes induce trembles in the man's limbs. "But for all her wifely qualities, you never did love her, did you?"

Uruvin's lips part dumbly. "I—I—Rashmatun, no," he stammers. "I loved her, with all my heart!"

"You are lying *again*." I slowly adjust my arm so that my elbow is propped atop the armrest encrusted with yellow sapphires, my temple resting against my fingers. "If you did love your wife so, why have you found yourself another lover already?"

His eyes widen in shock and guilt; his expression is stripped bare of pretence.

I cannot tell if the satisfaction welling in me is mine or Ilam's.

Uruvin sinks into a panicked bow. "Oh, Rashmatun!" he cries. "Your eyes see all. It was foolish of me to even think of deceiving you. Please, my goddess, I beg for your forgiveness! Please grant your servant mercy!"

I close my eyes, exasperated. Sweat trickles down my neck; the back of my jama is uncomfortably soaked. I am eager to peel off the four gold chains weighing down my neck, and my rump is sore from sitting the entire morning. I've given this man more than enough time to redeem himself.

"For your transgressions, you shall be prohibited from entering the temple for the next five years," I declare, opening my eyes languidly. "And you will pay a twenty percent increment of yearly taxes, since according to you, your business is bustling. My priests will ensure that the necessary paperwork is filled out."

His face takes on a sickly pallor. "My Rashmatun has been merciful," he murmurs.

"Get out," I say, quiet.

Uruvin ducks his head and rises to his feet. He scuttles backwards until he is out of the worship hall. Ilam's amused laughter continues ringing somewhere at the back of my mind.

With a tired sigh, I sink into my throne. "Harun." A portly man whose eyes resemble a bulging frog's steps into my direct line of sight. I've grown somewhat accustomed to the chief priest's permanent expression of gross surprise. "Anyone else?"

"No, my goddess," Harun replies. He adjusts the orange sash thrown over his left shoulder. "That was the last worshipper for today."

"The maximum number of devotees is twelve." I pinch the bridge of my nose. "That was the twentieth."

"The land is in a dire state now, Rashmatun. We did transport a sizeable portion of our grain stores to the armies' supply centres before the drought hit us." He stares at me with his frog eyes. "Your people are growing desperate. Many are flooding your temples, and more still wish to have an audience with you."

"I see."

Clever, clever goddess, Ilam laughs. *How your people love you so.*

I try not to bristle in reflex. No use getting furious at a demon you cannot control.

Harun clutches the length of prayer beads around his neck; his eyes slide towards the priests lining up behind him, their mouths shut in an eerie, complete silence. "My goddess, perhaps if you actually do something about the drought—"

"The Forebears bide their time, Harun," I say, waving a dismissive hand. "Is Hyrlvat thriving? Are the cornfields of Vintya lush and abundant? The gods are staying our hands for reasons that will be clear in a time to come."

Harun presses his lips into a thin line. I've been using that same vague reason for the past two months now. Even as most of our supplies are being given to the Aritsyan army, which has been battling the Dennarese Empire for decades, leaving precious little in our silos. Even as our crops wither and the prospects of a hungry winter grow exponentially with every passing day.

Do I have a choice? No. The only reason why the people of the city of Bakhtin have not rioted against me is because the rest of the country is suffering as well. Anyway, this is not the first time such a drought has occurred, and certainly not the first time Bakhtin's goddess abstained from bringing food to her people.

The chief priest still doesn't look convinced, though.

"Why do you not use your own magic to enchant the clouds, then?" I suggest scathingly. "If you're so worried about the drought?"

"My goddess, you know that our power has greatly weakened over the years. Besides, we can only cast enchantments—"

"When I'm around. Yes, I am well aware," I cut him off. *Excuses,* I think, but don't say out loud. The priests have no problem coaxing trees to bear fruit and casting needles to mend their elaborate garments when they think I'm out of sight. Minor spells, but ones that speak volumes about the temple's priorities. "Enough," I continue, vexation growing in me the longer this topic drags out. "I will only admit twelve devotees per day. At most. Am I clear?"

He dips his head in deference. "Yes, Your Grace."

"Good. And see to it that the necessary compensations and punishments are dispensed."

"Of course, Your Grace."

I dip my head. "Till tomorrow, Harun."

"Till tomorrow."

I stand up and step off the elevated dais. My bare foot touches the carpeted floor. Immediately my posture is not as straight, my head not held as high. I let my knees buckle, as if they were not accustomed to the weight of the ornaments I wear. Harun reaches forward to steady me, a fatherly smile on his face.

In a split second, I am no longer Rashmatun. I am Binsa, vessel of the goddess of wisdom, an ordinary girl whose life was touched by the extraordinary.

"What did she do today?" I ask Harun. My routine question after I've broken out of my "trance."

"Many things. Many great things." His routine answer.

"Will she bring rain soon?"

"She..." His grip on my shoulders tightens ever so slightly. He shakes his head and presses a hand against my back, guiding me out of the Paruvatar, the worship hall. "Come, child. You should rest."

I follow his lead without another word. We exit into a courtyard shadowed by long, straggling branches and lush emerald leaves. The rhododendron bushes planted all around the space are at full bloom, the vibrant red of the flowers resembling cloaks woven out of fresh blood. The sun overhead blazes bright, yet its full heat is lost on me with the mountain winds cocooning the temple, which lies high atop blustering cliffs. All enchantments by the hands of the priests; while the rest of the city withers, the sanctity of the temple must be maintained, which includes tending to its environment.

Harun claps his hands. Muscular palanquin bearers materialize before us. I step into the litter; the chief priest walks alongside.

The palanquin sways with a rhythmic lull as the bearers walk in perfect synchrony, marching through the various temples in Ghanatukh's complex at a languorous pace. They let me down before a two-tiered building, its red walls basking in the glow of the sun. I enter the Bakhal, the goddess's place of residence. A tall, imposing woman appears from behind one of the pillars, her generous girth clad in white. Jirtash claps her palms together and bows her head. Harun nods, leaving me to her care.

We wind our way through the sprawling maze of the pillars and shrines in the Bakhal's lowest floor, the scent of sandalwood drifting lazily through the air. We cut through another courtyard—a dry fountain in the middle, a luxury the priests didn't bother with—before arriving at my chambers. The furnishings hardly match the grandiosity of Rashmatun's power; while they are not falling into decay, they are as plain as a commoner's taste in fashion. The size of the room makes up for the lackluster decorations, though.

Any room is better than where I used to live, back when I was a child.

Jirtash tugs me towards a full-length mirror. I follow her like the obedient girl I'm supposed to be. She's the chief of the hand-maidens and the oldest, having attended to four other vessels of Rashmatun before me. She carefully lifts the headdress away and places it on a finely embroidered cushion; the absence of its weight is liberating.

Meanwhile, Ilam has curled into a comfortable ball at the back of my mind. The demon rarely emerges during my day-to-day activities, only coming to life when something catches his interest or offends him, or when he wants to taunt me. Typical of a demon, only giving attention to matters that involve them, and remaining apathetic towards everything else.

More handmaidens scuttle towards me, peeling away the layers of my uniform with reverent efficiency. The four gold chains, each with a different design, representing the four cardinal directions. The bhota and jama, both fiery red and embroidered with golden flowers, catch the brilliant rays of sunlight streaming in through tall, narrow windows. My earrings and bangles are removed. Jirtash wipes my forehead with a cloth soaked in coconut oil, removing the seven-pronged star painted onto it. She whispers a quick prayer, a plea for forgiveness, as she temporarily breaks Rashmatun's con-nection to her chosen vessel. With the star gone, she moves on to the rest of my face—the thick lines of kohl around my eyes, my bloodred lips.

Soon I am left naked, save for a pendant of yellow sapphire hung from a crude length of woven threads. Its uneven surface rests comfortingly against my chest, where my ribs protrude beneath my skin. My arms and legs are as thin as sticks, and my breasts are pitifully small. Not that it matters, since no one dares to comment much about my appearance.

The handmaidens unwind the thick coils of hair piled atop my head. It falls almost to my knees, thick and luxuriant, a soft sheen running down its trails. The only physical trait I am proud of.

Jirtash takes my hand and leads me towards the bathtub. I sink into its waters, contentedly allowing the handmaidens to lift my arms and legs and scrub them clean. A layer of grime gathers and floats on the water.

When I'm done, Jirtash towels me down and outfits me in a red kurta—I must always wear a hint of red somewhere—and a loose-fitting suruwal. I sit before the vanity table, and she braids my hair as her helpers tidy up the place.

"Oh child, what a woman wouldn't give to have hair as gorgeous as yours." Jirtash sighs in admiration.

Ice seems to gather at the nape of my neck. The ghost of a rough hand yanks the ends of my hair and sets it aflame.

I play with a near-empty bottle of perfume on the table, pushing the memory away. Jirtash has combed my hair almost the past ten years. This is just another day, another routine. She has no ill intentions. She has nothing to do with my past, I remind myself.

A past that she can never learn about.

I hope she doesn't notice the tremor in my fingers as I run them over the perfume bottle. "Thank you," I murmur.

She doesn't say anything else. I know what is on her mind: If only the rest of me were as gorgeous as my hair. I am close to sixteen now. Other girls my age have developed bosoms and swelling hips already. Me? I might as well be a withering tree trunk.

It's unusual for a girl to not have menstruated already, she told me two weeks ago, and what is even more unusual is that I have not shown signs of puberty. She once suspected that I was malnourished, but quickly dismissed the notion when I pointed out that I ate three full meals a day.

I did not tell her that I always dispose of two of those meals.

She finishes braiding my hair and claps her hands over my shoulders. "All done," she says. "There now, don't you look pretty?"

I don't agree with the sentiment. My nose is too large for my pointed chin and thin lips, my cheeks are as hollow as empty bowls of alms, and my eyes are too large, too fierce. But she is trying to be kind, so I muster a smile. "Thank you."

She nods, then releases me from her grip. A platter of food has been served, placed on a table by the window. I polish off the meal thoroughly; it's my only one every day. When no one is watching, I retrieve a vial from under my table and pour a drop of its contents into the clay cup of water, turning it into a murky solution. I drain the cup, trying not to wince at the foul taste. This is forbidden medicine that poisons my ovaries—another one of my methods to delay my bleeding for as long as possible. A small price to remain a goddess for a little while longer.

But my medicine is running dangerously low.

I haven't heard from my supplier in weeks. I grit my teeth, suppressing the anxiety rising up my throat.

When I'm done, I head towards the exit. I sense a hint of grim disapproval from Jirtash. "Off to your lessons, now?" she asks, more out of courtesy than genuine interest. She does not think that I should be paying so much attention to books and education. I should be more concerned about growing into a woman and finding a good husband, like the many girls who came before me. The latter won't be too hard, considering that everyone wants to receive some form of blessing from a former living goddess. Assuming that I choose to marry.

However, that means that I have to give up my status as the vessel of Rashmatun. The thought hollows out my stomach, as if someone carved my skin open and emptied my insides.

Who am I, if I am Rashmatun no longer? A scrawny girl with no inherent title or wealth to her name. A nothing, someone whose face will fade from the memories of all who have seen her.

I shake the notion out of my mind. I am still a living goddess, I remind myself. "Of course, Jirtash!" I chirp innocently. "Lessons won't wait!"

I traipse out of the room.

Follow us:

/orbitbooksUS

/orbitbooks

/orbitbooks

Join our mailing list
to receive alerts on our
latest releases and deals.

orbitbooks.net

Enter our monthly
giveaway for the chance
to win some epic prizes.

orbitloot.com